SPI
EGE
L&G
RAU

The Local News

a Novel

MIRIAM GERSHOW

Spiegel & Grau

New York

2009

This book is a work of fiction. Names, characters, businesses, organizations, places, events, and incidents either are the product of the author's imagination or are used fictitiously. Any resemblance to actual persons, living or dead, events, or locales is entirely coincidental.

Published in the United States by Spiegel & Grau, an imprint of The Doubleday Publishing Group, a division of Random House, Inc., New York.
www.spiegelandgrau.com

SPIEGEL & GRAU is a trademark of Random House, Inc.

Library of Congress Cataloging-in-Publication Data
Gershow, Miriam.
The local news: a novel / Miriam Gershow. — 1st ed.
p. cm.
1. Young women—Fiction. 2. Brothers—Death—Fiction. 3. Grief—Fiction. 4. Loss (Psychology)—Fiction. 5. Domestic fiction. 6. Psychological fiction. I. Title.
PS3607.E785L63 2009
813'.6—dc22
2008033391

ISBN 978-0-385-52761-3

PRINTED IN THE UNITED STATES OF AMERICA

10 9 8 7 6 5 4 3 2 1

First Edition

To Rebecca

&

To Jordan

Drifters

1.

After my brother went missing, my parents let me use their car whenever I wanted, even though I only had a learner's permit. They didn't enforce my curfew. I didn't have to ask to be excused from the dinner table. The dinner table, in fact, had all but disappeared, covered with posters of Danny, a box of the yellow ribbons that our whole neighborhood had tied around trees and mailboxes and car antennas, and piles of the letters we'd gotten from people praying for Danny's safe return or who thought they saw him hitchhiking along a highway a couple states away. I didn't have to do any more chores.

Years later, I joined a support group for siblings of missing or exploited kids. It was amazing how a group of like-minded individuals could make the most singular and self-defining of circumstances feel simply mundane. I suppose for some, such a thing would be normalizing, since everyone in the circle of couches and folding chairs had experienced equivalent tragedy. For me, it was deeply disconcerting. I had no idea how to compete with other people's misery. It was in that group that I heard about the two types of parents: clingers and drifters. The clingers became micromanagers and wildly overprotective, tightening the reins, imposing new rules, smothering their kids with unwanted attention, buying gifts like a canopy bed or a new stereo system. The drifters, on the other hand, lost themselves to some mysterious netherworld, existing on coffee and crackers and minutes of sleep per night. They forgot to take the garbage out. They let the kitchen floor grow sticky. They looked like they were listening when you spoke (they became expert at empathetic nodding), but really they were staring just past you, glassy-eyed. The concerns of the corporeal world became inconsequential to them, except for the fine, red-hot point of finding their child (not you; their other child). Aside from that, they, well, drifted.

My parents were drifters.

We couldn't keep the refrigerator stocked; its contents dwindled to bread heels and condiments in a matter of days. My mom started smoking again, years after having quit. Her energy was both frenetic and focused: she designed posters, concocted overly elaborate phone trees to recruit people for the area sweep searches, and added to her steadily growing stack of index cards, each one scribbled with a "clue" to help the police. *Allergic to penicillin*, she scrawled on one. *Capricorn*, she wrote on another. *Born on night of a full moon.* My father became quietly obsessed with the TV news—local, national, international, as if he couldn't rule out any possibility. Maybe Danny was part of the throngs of Bosnian Serb refugees; maybe he'd been victim to the floods in the Philippines. Dad could go days without speaking. He could sit for hours (six and a quarter, I counted one day) in his sunken chair without once getting up. And we kept running out of toilet paper. Over and over again we had to use tissues instead, until those ran out too and we moved to paper towels, which quickly clogged the pipes. I'd never before had to think about the supply of toilet paper in our household. It had always simply been there. I was fifteen. Up to that point, I'd believed that the world more or less worked—toilet paper sat on its roll, dinner was served hot at the table, everyone came home at the end of a day—simply because it was supposed to and it always had.

"There's no proper or improper way to grieve," the woman who ran the support group would say. I did not return after that first visit; the impulse, it quickly became clear, had been a mistake. The woman's face was chalky with powder, her cheeks too bright with rouge, her eyelashes clumped with mascara. The collar of her blouse rose up around her neck, tied into an improbably flouncy bow. The look of her offended me. She was all wrong; how was I supposed to take her as an authority? Other participants hunkered down low in their chairs, weeping appropriately into soggy tissues. Or nodding appreciatively. Or wringing their hands. They had the raccoon-eyed, red-veined look of the haunted.

Finding myself backed into the overly familiar terrain of heartache and desperation brought out the worst in me. I was cornered, wanting to scream or kick my chair over or run my nails along the chalkboard where the woman had made us brainstorm a list of feeling words about our siblings (*love, confusion, fear, sadness*, the list began, predictably). I wanted to reel off my own list of shitty things Danny had done to me when we were teenagers (calling me *the titless wonder*, mashing my face in a pillow once until I couldn't breathe, ignoring me in front of his friends). I wanted to be irreverent and inappropriate. I wanted to shake up the righteous anguish. Going missing, I wanted to yell from some deep, dark pit in the middle of me, was the only interesting thing my brother had ever done.

2.

In the first weeks after Danny's disappearance, I drove. I would spend long minutes in the garage before starting the car, adjusting the rearview and side mirrors, moving my dad's seat up and down and backward and forward until I had just the perfect view of the world behind me. I'd practice looking over my left shoulder to see past my blind spot, imagining that the bushy maple in our yard was a semi trying to barrel past me. Finally I'd back down our long driveway, my head out the window, the warm summer air making my cheeks feel blushed.

The whole act was fraught with a particular anxiety. Aside from being not strictly legal, I could never forget the smallness of me compared to the bigness of the car and the gaping margin for error created by the contrast. One wrong move and I could easily swerve into the oncoming lane or plow through a red light into a bustling intersection. The very act of driving—the successful negotiation of feet on pedals and hands on steering wheel and eyes in mirror—felt death-defying.

But I kept going back to it, night after night, and not just because it was a way to get out of the house and away from my parents and whichever well-meaning, wet-eyed neighbors or family friends were visiting. Even with the nervous thrum in my belly, driving managed to calm me down, focusing my attention on palatable, bite-sized fragments of data—two yellow lines, a green arrow, a bright red taillight. I had just finished the summer-school offering of driver's ed the month before and my stops were still jerky; I often overestimated how much gas I needed and regularly peeled out from stops; I scraped the curb on the few occasions I tried to parallel park. I was drawn to it in the same nagging way I was drawn to anything I wasn't yet good at, like when I'd spent the summer before eighth-grade algebra learning polynomial and quadratic equations, or when I'd spent weeks memorizing every strait in the world after losing the middle-school geography bee (Joshua Belson had beaten me, knowing that the Naruto Strait connected Awaji Island and Shikoku in Japan).

So each night, after my parents absently nodded in my direction and the raspy-voiced neighbor or family friend leaned in to hug me or place a sympathetic hand on my shoulder, I slipped out to the garage and into Dad's car. But I didn't have anyplace to go. I'd spent the bulk of my life up to that point either in school or in my room studying or in my best friend David Nelson's den paging through books and listening to music and generally lolling around. Most nights now, I'd deliver stacks of Missing Person posters to the ring of businesses surrounding our city. In the beginning, the sympathetic attention of strangers was still intoxicating.

The lady in the Kroger made an *ohhh* noise as she promised to hang it on the community bulletin board at the front of the store. The manager at the Blockbuster called me *sweetheart* and offered me a coupon: rent two, get one free. The kid who scooped ice cream at Baskin-Robbins said he'd take two because he worked another shift at the store in Belvedere. He looked, honestly, like he could cry. It was months—sixty-three days, actually—before anyone told me no. The guy behind the counter at the Texaco Mini-Mart just shook his head and said, "Sorry, ma'am." He couldn't post it in the window. Company policy.

"What company policy?" I asked, pointing to the poster for *Once Upon a Mattress* at Jefferson Middle School and one for the Red Cross: *Give Blood. Save a Life.* He repeated his line about manager approval in his thick, mumbling accent. His dark face was drawn, with wiry bits of hair growing in uneven patches across his chin. He was yellow around the eyes, which made him look sick.

His name tag said *Kito.* East Asian? African? Middle Eastern? I couldn't tell from his bland, bored features. It seemed like he could be anything. I assumed his bad attitude came from all the Franklin High jerkoffs who'd come in here before me, making *What up, Apu?* jokes or calling him Mohammed. But I was capable of talking to Kito like a normal person. I was capable of discussing the Oslo Accords or the Indian-Pakistani conflict over Kashmir, and not just because I could regurgitate facts from Mr. Hollingham's AP history class—which I could—but because I took a particular pride in actually reading newspapers and listening to the radio.

The fluorescent lights buzzed loudly above me. "Can't you take this now and get manager approval later?" I asked, sliding the poster across the rubbery mat on the counter. Danny was posed in his football uniform, down on one knee, a football socked in one armpit, his face broad and unobjectionable as a meatloaf, smiling as if Santa Claus himself had snapped the picture.

Beneath the photograph in bold, blocky letters it said, *LAST SEEN 8/2/1995*. There were other details scattered in a bunch of contrasting, discordant fonts and sizes and colors, because my mom, its designer, was a leaky container for panic. In italicized blue Courier, it listed what Danny had been wearing (Reebok gym shoes, shorts, gray T-shirt, Tigers ball cap); in huge red Times New Roman, how much my parents would reward someone for information leading to his whereabouts ($25,000; up another $10,000 from the last poster); in bolded Arial, where he was last seen (two miles from our house, leaving the basketball courts at the Larkgrove Elementary School playground, where he'd just finished a game with his musclehead friends, Tip and Kent). It didn't say *musclehead* on the poster, didn't even mention Tip and Kent.

Kito (*Kite-o*, I wondered, or *Kee-toh*?) told me no. No manager tonight, he said.

"Can't you hold it somewhere in the back until a manager arrives? Leave it on the manager's desk? Maybe put a note on it?" I was trying to stay reasonable, but I could hear my voice getting loud. A couple of guys had come into the Mini-Mart, one opening and closing the cooler doors, the other standing right behind me. I could smell the faint odor of gasoline coming off him, but I didn't turn around. "Please," I said.

Kito looked at me, yellow and expressionless. I was sure he had not the highest opinion of Americans, as most probably came in here for a six-pack of Bud or Marlboro menthols or a whole strip of lottery tickets with their Slurpee. Still, I wasn't used to strangers unmoved by tragedy.

"Listen," I said, speaking slowly and evenly. "I am not asking you to hang this poster immediately. I will leave it here to get whatever approval you need."

He called me *ma'am* again, even though he was old enough to be my father, and told me *Sorry*. "Sir, I can help you?" he said to the person behind me.

I curled my fingers around the rickety wire rack that held local maps, not quite sure what to do with myself. I wanted to tell Kito to go screw himself, but adults, even adults manning a gas station counter, still held relatively unassailable sway with me, so I chickened out and instead flicked my hand in his general direction, an insane motion, as if I were sprinkling fairy dust on him. For a second he opened his sick eyes a bit wider and I thought maybe I was starting to get through, but then, still, nothing. I left the poster on the counter, just to make a point, though I pictured Kito almost immediately throwing it into the metal wastebasket beside him, already overfilled with Snickers wrappers and Doritos bags.

The man behind me called over my head, "Pump eight." Kito started pressing the keys of his cash register. I opened the door hard on my way out, the bells on top clinking loudly and also, I hoped, angrily and indignantly and ultimately pityingly, for Kito and his sad little life there inside the Mini-Mart.

I dropped off posters at Wendy's, Arby's, Valu-Rite, and the Chevron. The car wash, the dry cleaners, and the Comerica branch were all already closed—it was nearly nine on a Tuesday. I scanned the radio for news. An AM host talked fuzzily about fallout from the O. J. Simpson verdict with a lady who yelled about how it was open season on battered women. On another station there was a story about riots in Lyons that broke out after the police killed a local bombing suspect. Bad news was soothing, as if at least it was the whole world that was screwed.

The lights of the A&W were still bright, the booths half full. Inside, there was a flash of purple-and-yellow letter jackets, which gave me a quick, instinctual stutter, a chill up the back of my neck. My new therapist, Chuck, would've told me the feeling was a grief response. Chuck thought everything was a grief response. And sure, you could have interpreted the jackets as a reminder of Danny, who likely would've been in there with the rest of them, eating burgers and slurping root beers and burping words. He'd be play-punching his friends on the arms, except his play punches would be hard, and soon two or three of the guys would end up in a dramatic little scuffle, Danny in a headlock, Tip or Kent with an arm around Danny's neck, tousling Danny's hair and saying, "What you want, pretty boy? You want to throw down?" and everyone would be laughing, even Danny, and maybe he'd spit burger out of his mouth or root beer would come flying through his nose. The whole crowd of them would make a huge racket, disturbing all the other A&W customers without even noticing or, if they noticed, without giving a crap.

But the queasy feeling I had now as I slowed past the bright windows was no different from the feelings I'd had before Danny disappeared. The noisy, forceful presence of Franklin athletes had always made me feel small, always elicited an instinctual response to run and hide. I pulled into the parking lot anyway, thinking briefly about going in. Because things were different now. Kirk Donovan, the reporter at Channel 7, knew me on a first-name basis; when he came to our house for interviews, as he had again just that afternoon, he'd wave and say, "Hey, Lydia," like he'd come over just to hang out. And I'd accumulated new friends, all kinds of new friends (except for the sincere kind, or the actually-liked-me-or-cared-about-me kind), who'd materialized suddenly out of the dank, sweaty hallways of Franklin High in the first weeks of my sophomore year. Mrs. Rabinowitz, the school librarian, had arranged it so that everyone in study hall had to sign a wall-sized card wishing me well, and they all did, except for the few boys who scrawled nearly undetectable messages in the corners about my small boobs and beaver teeth. *Get braces,* one wrote, *for your beaver teeth.*

I watched through the windshield now as Michael Chemanski and Lyle Walker—both seniors, both on the football team—sat perched on a booth back, laughing so hard it looked like maybe they were sobbing, their eyes screwed shut, their mouths huge as caves. Four others were crammed into the opposite side, their backs to me, their bodies swaying and jostling as if sitting on the deck of a boat, riding out a storm. They had such an air of careless happiness—they always did, it was their specialty—it gave me a numb, worn-out feeling. Even then, even only sixty-three days into it, I was acutely aware of the weightlessness of other people's lives, of the willowy way everyone else moved through the world. If I'd ever had such ease (maybe in flashes, in particularly unguarded moments just after waking), certainly it was lost to me now.

I hated them anew.

I didn't go in. I turned back onto the main four-lane road and then made a left onto one of Fairfield's residential streets. Away from the strip malls and gas stations, the roads were mostly empty, parents socked away in dens or living rooms, kids studying or messing around. We'd moved to Fairfield three years before, from another suburb that had done a better job at faking being a real town. At least in Abernathy they'd had some local shops: a little diner with corned beef sandwiches and eggs over easy, a used bookstore that smelled wormy and moist, a market run by an old guy named Ed who'd swat kids playfully on the wrist if they opened the beef jerky container that sat on the counter. Abernathy had black people. Abernathy had parks where kids actually played. And block parties with traffic cones lining the ends of the streets, picnic tables piled with food in the middle of the road. Fairfield, on the other hand, was just one big square, three miles deep in each direction, houses inside of it, crappy businesses lining the perimeter on all four sides, as if the city planners had hoped to build a fortress against outside evils through a few well-placed Jiffy Lubes and Radio Shacks.

I wasn't really driving in any direction, just drifting past aluminum-sided houses and buzz-cut grass, signs for DEEVEY FOR MAYOR and VOTE NO ON 38. Porch lights made lawns look pale and shadowy. Yellow ribbons hung limply in the night air, glowing in my headlights. I slowed for two squirrels who stood in the street, fat and unafraid of cars. I wasn't ready to go back home. Being on the eleven o'clock news would unite and distract us for a few minutes, but until then there were nearly two hours and Mom would ask desperate questions (*Anyone recognize him? Any new information?*) and Dad would sit in his chair, clicking between channels, acting as if he wasn't listening or maybe really not hearing.

On the radio they talked about three hundred dead or injured in an earthquake in Turkey. I thought about how Turkey had my favorite-named strait: Bosporus. When I'd first learned the word, it sounded like a swear. David Nelson and I went through a phase where when we stubbed our toe or got a bad grade, we'd say, "Oh, Bosporus!"

That was what I was thinking about—Bosporus—when my rearview mirror lit up in a flash of reds and blues. For a second I thought dumbly, *Pretty.* The colors had a fireworks quality to them—sudden, startling—which disarmed me for the first beat or two. Then my brain pieced it together: cop car, cop car behind me, cop car behind me with its lights flashing at me. I grew suddenly aware of my flesh, my skin hot then cold. I pulled to the curb behind a double-cab pickup.

When the officer leaned into my window, his face was smooth and pale, his eyebrows so blond they nearly blended into his skin. It gave him a plastic, alien appearance. "License and registration," he said.

"I'm only fifteen," I blurted.

He blinked slowly a couple of times, staring at me. "Then what are you doing operating a motor vehicle by yourself?" he said.

"I—I . . . errands." I thought of *The Trial*, Joseph K. being interrogated by the Magistrate.

"Fifteen-year-olds aren't allowed to do errands in motor vehicles by themselves," he said.

"No, I know," I said. "I'm sorry."

The officer called me *young lady* and asked to see my permit (*I'm hoping you at least have a permit,* he said, to which I nodded like a lapdog) and registration. I pawed through everything crammed in the glove compartment: a pen light, a mini-screwdriver, contact lens solution, a tall stack of mismatched fast-food napkins.

"I try to be careful," I said stupidly as I handed him the slips of paper. "I had Mr. Grenwich for driver's ed." He nodded at me, not in a way that signaled empathy or understanding but in a clipped, expressionless way that meant *shut up*, and then walked wordlessly back to his car, where he stayed for a long time. I couldn't right my internal thermostat. My body continued to cool, then heat, then cool, then heat; my armpits grew wet, the hollow of my back sticky against my shirt.

Whenever I tried to see what the officer was doing, I couldn't make out anything beyond a silhouette in the driver's seat. The overhead lights were still flashing. I screwed my eyes shut, holding tight to the steering wheel, fighting the urge to scream. It was an awful feeling, being found out. Not just for being an underaged driver. I was held together in those days by the scattershot reassurances of random grown-ups—the piteous cooing of the shift clerk at the Farmer Jack's, the *Very good job* from Mrs. Bardazian as she handed back my paper on the use of surrealism in *Oliver Twist*, the wave from a balding driver as I slowed to let him veer into my lane. In the absence of that, I felt split open, revealed: a shitty sister, a vacant hole of a daughter, a terrible person deficient in even the most basic emotions like sorrow or grief.

Someone peeked out from behind the front curtains of the house next to us, an oval-shaped man or lady who stood very still. The porch light showed off a fall garland made of pinecones and spiny branches and red-orange leaves. I couldn't stop staring at the meticulous arrangement of foliage. I wanted to live in a house with a fall garland at its door, with an oval-shaped sentry who had nothing more to worry about than a fifteen-year-old being pulled over out front.

When the officer finally came back, he said, "Lydia Pasternak?" and flashed the permit at me.

"Yes?" I said, his two words leaving me feeling vulnerable and exposed. It seemed like a terrible thing for him to say.

He sighed and handed me back my permit and registration. His fingers smelled like my mom's, ashy from cigarettes. "I'm sorry about your brother. Tough break."

"Huhr," I said, more a noise than a word. It still surprised me, the spread of our local renown. "Okay," I said, my voice throaty and hoarse. He turned on his flashlight and shined it on the posters in the passenger seat. It was a dramatic gesture, a floodlight passing over and back across Danny's meaty face, highlighting over and over the thick hair gelled up around his head like a crown, the cheeks ruddy and speckled. Defensive end Danny. All-State swimmer Danny. Homecoming court Danny. *Don't fucking touch my PlayStation* Danny.

"That's what I was out doing," I said. It was impossible to look at him without getting blinded. I shaded my eyes with my hand.

He clicked off the flashlight. "You need not to be driving at your age."

I nodded, struck by the strange syntax of his sentence.

"You see that stop sign back on Branson?" he said.

"Yes," I said, though I wasn't sure which street was Branson. All the streets in Fairfield blended together.

"Then maybe you can explain why you rolled right through it." He had a congenial voice now, as if he were my helpful uncle.

"Sorry," I said. "No, I guess I didn't see it."

"I'm going to let you off with a warning this time. But you need to promise me you won't get in this car by yourself again." I promised. "Why don't you give me some of those for the station?" I handed him a bunch of posters, ten or so, more than he'd ever really use, but it was good to get rid of them. He patted the top of the car as he left—it made a loud noise—and I jumped a little in my seat. "Drive safe back home, Ms. Pasternak," he said.

I sat for a while after he turned off his flashing lights and drove away. The street was quiet and dark without him. My body buzzed with something different now—adrenaline maybe, the heady kick of having gotten away with something. My hands felt strong on the steering wheel, my smile momentarily cute in the rearview mirror. That feeling of power and rightness, of the world being on my side—this was what it was like, I thought, to be Danny.

3.

I looked like a sickly bird on the news, pale, my chin coming to a weird point as if the bones had been broken and reset. My hair stuck up in a cowlicky loop in the back. It was always demoralizing, having whatever tenuous notion that I looked halfway decent shattered by the image of myself on the television.

They always arranged us the same way, me sitting between my parents on the couch. Kirk Donovan would sit in Dad's chair, leaning toward the three of us sympathetically. Before we'd start filming, he'd ask Dad to put his arm around me, and Dad wouldn't quite touch me but would wrap his arm around the back of the couch instead. I could smell his Ban Roll-On, spicy and dense. The camera crew would cram themselves in by the fireplace, and our beagles would get locked in my bedroom for being too yippy and unable to sit still. My mom adopted all our beagles from a rescue, and they always tended toward high-strung or unruly, making you wonder what strange or awful things may have preceded their lives with us.

On TV now, Dad was saying that there hadn't been any new news in the past week but that the police were working hard with little to go on. He thanked everyone for the donation drive, especially his colleagues at the Fidelity Bank and all the kind folks at Ford Hospital. He said everything loudly, flatly, like he was reporting baseball scores, but with a slight edge beneath it, as if he could at any minute start bawling someone out. On TV, Mom had a quivering lip. The camera panned to her, tears silently rolling down her face as she sorted through her index cards, while my dad talked about the new reward money. Always now she carried around her index cards. Kirk Donovan had tried to coax them from her, saying she'd look more natural if she just "spoke from her heart," but she'd told him flatly no, as if he'd suggested she drop her baby in the gutter or kick one of the rescue beagles in the snout. She read from them that we'd hired a private investigator. "Howard," she looked up and told Kirk Donovan, as if the reporter might know him. She read that we were thinking of renting a billboard along the highway. Her delivery reminded me of the stilted student presentations on "How to Pitch a Tent" and "Why the Constitution Is Important" we had to sit through during speech class.

In real life she was crying again, making a soft clucking noise that made me want to rip my ears from my head. She was the only one on the couch now. Poppy, one of the rescue beagles, lay draped on Mom's lap, half asleep. My mom stroked Poppy's head with such an intense neediness it made me feel bad for the dog, who just lay there and took it. I was on the floor, close enough to the TV that in other circumstances my parents might have told me to move back so as not to ruin my eyes. Dad sat in his chair, doing an imitation of a tired statue. Oliver and Olivia, the other two rescue beagles, pulled on opposite ends of a braided rope toy, dragging each other around the family room and making loud snorfling noises. It was like someone laughing during a funeral, and I found it a relief.

Our house had an uncomfortable stillness now, without Danny barking into the phone to friends or bounding up the stairs with such force it seemed as if he could bring the house down around him or dribbling a basketball against the vestibule tiles as Dad told him halfheartedly to knock it off. And a smell. There was a smell now. It lingered, seemingly carried only on select air currents. For days it would appear to be gone, and then suddenly, when I sat down in the breakfast nook or stepped into the shower or wiped my feet on the doormat inside the sliding back doors, it would hit me just as strong, and I'd wonder if it'd been there all along and I'd just gotten used to it, like people who lived downwind of paper mills. It was not easily identifiable. It reminded me a little bit of my fishbowl, the murky tang of the algae if I waited too long to clean it. But there was a more pungent quality to it, one that went right to the back of your throat. I'd sniff around, trying to find the source, but it seemed to move as I moved, to suddenly permeate everything—couch pillows, coats in the front closet, tablecloths. Years later, when I was reminded of it while unearthing a Tupperware of forgotten food in the recesses of my fridge, I decided it was the impermeable smell of neglect.

On TV, Kirk Donovan talked about some of the new leads the police had been following, like Danny sightings downriver in River Rouge. Then Kirk said to me, "Lydia, what is it you miss most about your brother?"

I smiled like an imbecile, my teeth looking colossal. There was—and still is—a pervading ordinariness to my looks. But at certain angles I glimpsed a hint of grotesquerie, an asymmetrical freakishness to my features: one eye sat slightly higher than the other; a hump jutted from the bridge of my nose. It would be years before I could even vaguely appreciate the surprises of my face, when a college boyfriend admiringly called me androgynous, when a punky, mohawked friend said she'd give an eyetooth for my profile. On the news I squinted into the lights—even after all these times, I still wasn't used to the lights—and said, "I don't know. Just him." Then I paused. Then I said, "How he'd sit at the table and eat his cereal in the morning."

They panned to Kirk Donovan nodding morosely, as if I'd said something that had actually meant something. Then the camera panned to my mom again, still crying, while Kirk said, "A Fairfield family, coping with uncertainty and loss, one day at a time."

A commercial came on for cold medicine.

My mom pushed herself up from the couch. "We did good," she said unconvincingly. The tears still streamed down her cheeks, her nostrils and upper lip shiny with snot. When she left the room, Poppy trailed after her, the dog's tongue hanging partway out of her mouth.

The phone rang. It always rang after we'd been on the news. We never answered it: too draining for my parents, too humiliating for me. It was David Nelson. He called to say I did a great job. He liked my orange shirt, he said into the answering machine. He'd left similar messages every time we were on the news. "Sayonara," he said at the end. David Nelson's parents had taken him to Japan the summer between seventh and eighth grade, and he'd been saying that ever since. Some people found it annoying.

"Bash," Dad said softly as he got up too. It was the nickname he'd had for me forever, long severed from its original meaning, if it'd ever had one. I nodded at him, and his unshaven face was so drawn and hollow, I felt compelled to add, "Sweet dreams." He blinked wordlessly, as if I'd spoken Farsi.

Soon I was alone in the living room except for Oliver and Olivia, still at it with the rope toy. Back from commercial, the next news story was about a kid two towns away who needed treatment for a rare bone cancer; he was bald and eyebrowless and nine. Next, a family's section-eight housing had burned halfway down because of faulty electrical work; they were suing the city. It was a parade of local heartbreak, me with the front-row seat.

Later I couldn't sleep. This was something my new therapist, Chuck, wanted me to talk about. He'd lean forward in his chair, interested in a Kirk Donovan sort of way in my insomnia, but I never had anything to tell him. I couldn't sleep now. That was it. I lay in bed, awake as noon, my eyes wide and wandering across the ceiling as I tried to come up with a foreign language for every letter of the alphabet (Arabic, Bengali, Croatian) or a backwards list of vice presidents (I always forgot Alben Barkley and then, later, George Dallas). The house creaked and moaned around me and trees rustled outside my window. Strangely enough, it was the time Danny seemed most absent. A long, flat silence came from the room beside mine. No bass thumping of his stereo or tinny resonance of his Discman turned up too high or raspy whispers into the phone well past when he was allowed to be on—all such maddening sounds at the time, so illustrative of the enormous amount of space he'd taken up. But in the middle of the night it was unsettling, the utter absence of them. It rattled me in some cavernous, wide-awake place.

Out of so many memories, already he'd been distilled to an oft-repeated few, like a cheap card trick of the mind, the eight of clubs or the king of diamonds turning up with each uncanny shuffle. In one, Danny and I ran around the basement of our old house, back in the days when we still played together. He was building a bridge across the span of the floor. This was one of his favorite games, lining up all of our toys and furniture so we could walk from end to end without once touching the floor. He'd shout about crocodiles and poison eels in the carpet below. I was maybe six or seven, Danny nine or ten.

"Hurry!" he'd yell as I dragged over one of our folding chairs, then his long-unused Big Wheels. "The dump truck! The dump truck!" he yelled and directed me to push it against the stack of books he'd laid on the carpet. We'd spanned nearly half the room, and Danny dragged over the beanbag chair and an old, crushed Tinker-Toys box. He nodded wildly at his design, clapping his hands together. It was a silly game, really. I never believed in the crocodiles or the eels; that wasn't the way my imagination worked, even when I was little. It was always hard to suspend my disbelief. Already I was the sort of child who preferred thinking about parallelograms to princesses, fractals to fairy tales. Already I preferred reading the books to piling them on the floor.

But still. There was something about playing with Danny—maybe his enveloping enthusiasm or his bossiness, which held none of his later cruelty, or his ardent belief in his venture—that made it so easy, so natural to fall into step beside him. Even then, when he'd been bony and slight, not all that much bigger than me, he had a charisma that pulled me along, he the bumbling boy dictator, I his servile assistant.

It'd been years since I'd thought about the bridge game. Danny would later become such a force, such a brutish sort of fool really, his very presence eclipsed any thoughts of that boy—it was impossible to believe he had ever existed. But now he emerged from some banished place in my memory, meeting me at night and leaving a metallic taste in my mouth, a clamminess in my palms. I stared and stared into the dark. When I finally drifted off—after my body had gone rigid from hours of effort and my mind had twisted in on itself like a Möbius strip—it was while listening stupidly for sounds of bedsprings or footfalls on the other side of our thin wall.

4.

The day after the news broadcast, school was particularly frenzied, the new friends buzzing around like mosquitoes who'd been swarming too long in a fleshless jungle. Lola Pepper was on me before I'd even made it to the front entrance. She was in my grade and on the flag team, one significant and humiliating step down in the Franklin High hierarchy from the actual cheerleaders. The flag-team girls usually had a little too much fat or unmanageable hair or shiny braces. Lola Pepper, to her credit, was probably the most attractive of them. She was skinny, green-eyed, and short enough to seem cute without being dwarfish. Her only deficit seemed to be her nearly translucent skin, which was covered with freckles, and not the neatly speckled kind but fat dollops coloring her face with distracting ellipses and Rorschach blotches.

She'd been one of the girls who'd followed Danny around

incessantly, offering to walk his dog or do his homework or have his kids. Me, I don't even think she'd known my name. We'd never had much opportunity to cross paths in Mr. Stark's World History Club or the National Junior Honor Society dinners. Now, though, she grabbed my arm—Lola had an annoying habit of needing to hang on to you while she talked—her words coming out in a rush.

"You guys did really great," she said. "I was crying and my mom was crying too. My mom says Kirk Donovan is gay. She heard it from one of the ladies at her health club who knows one of his ex-boyfriends. She asked me to ask you what he was like in person." She told a long story about the dream she'd had of Danny walking along a beach, throwing a baseball. "I don't think he ever really played baseball that much, did he? That psychic lady was on *Montel* yesterday. If we could get on there, we could ask her questions. She seems nice."

Lola chomped on pungent strawberry gum, giving the air around us the smell of plug-in air freshener. She had a way of talking that didn't leave room for the other person to say anything, which seemed to work out best for both of us.

Inside, we were quickly accosted by Min Mathers, senior class secretary, and Cindy Kahlen, varsity cheerleader. Both had a bad habit of unnecessarily elongating their words. "Ohhh my goddd," said Min when she saw me. "How saaad is your mom. Pooor thiiing."

"I knooow," added Cindy. She wore a yellow ribbon around her wrist like a bracelet. Min had one in her hair, fashioned as a ponytail holder. "Are you okaaay?" she asked.

They both stared at me as if I were a specimen. I stared back. Min had a birthmark that was so well placed (due northeast of the corner of her lip) and so perfectly round it could have been applied meticulously with eyebrow pencil daily. Cindy tipped her head in just the right way to make her layered hair fall dramatically against her cheek. Lola Pepper stood quietly beside me; she, I had quickly discovered, was constantly attuned to rank, easily cowed by anyone from the higher rungs. Min Mathers and Cindy Kahlen, whose faces dotted the yearbook candids, who had the power to single-handedly bring back strange styles like leg warmers or blue eye shadow, who leaned in close to apply grease pencil to the faces of Franklin athletes before their games, easily qualified.

"I'm fine," I said.

"Hi, you guys," Lola Pepper said, and I almost felt bad for her when neither even looked her way.

"You'd look really good with a bob," Cindy said, touching the ends of my hair. I hadn't even showered that morning. My hair sat greasily in Cindy's manicured fingers. Despite myself, I felt ashamed. Cindy didn't act like she even noticed.

"Yeah," said Min. "A bahhhb."

They both smiled at me, nodding. One of them smelled like peppermint.

"A bob," I repeated pointlessly. And I thought, not for the first time, how easy it would be to be seduced by them. Standing right next to them, smelling them, I could see the pull of pretty, the mesmeric power of the shiny teeth and huge smiles and evenly powdered skin and evenly separated eyelashes. Even if you knew better, you could start to think what they said was true. You could start to *hope* it was true.

They told me a few more times how cute I'd look. Cindy told me the name of her stylist; that's what she called her haircutter. Lola Pepper chewed softly, dejectedly, on her gum. Min said, "Look what I found last night in my old French book" and handed me a folded-up piece of paper. "It's from Danny. I think he wrote it like sometime last year. Weird, huh?"

It didn't seem weird at all. That was how I imagined Danny

spent his time in French class, passing notes to girls like Min Mathers. It was his chopstick-sloppy writing on the front of the note. *Min*, it said, underlined a bunch of times. All three of them stared at me, ostensibly waiting for something dramatic, for me to unfold it right there and read it tearfully. Or maybe jam it tearfully into my back pocket and say, *I can't handle this right now.* Or maybe tearfully thank Min.

I thought of the beagles, how in the first days after we rescued them they were sick with gratitude, following us around the house, lapping at our faces until we pushed them away (otherwise they'd keep going and going until they left a scratchy-tongued welt), answering to any name you gave them. "Horace!" Danny and I would yell. "Beauregard!" "Tootsie Roll!" Anything, just to see if they'd come. And they would.

Lola, Min, and Cindy stared. I knew I was supposed to be their rescue beagle. We stood there wordlessly for so long it started to get strange. The note sat like a wafer in my palm. For a second I had an irrational fear that it would blow away. I shoved it in my pocket, shook Lola Pepper's hand from my arm, mumbled "See ya," and left. When they called my name, I pretended not to hear.

I passed the shrine on the way to Mr. Dooler's social studies class between second and third period. I always passed the shrine between second and third period. The only way to avoid it was to take the long loop around the science halls, which would make me late, giving Dooler occasion to peer over the rim of his glasses and scratch some angry notation into his attendance book. The shrine had formed spontaneously, starting with the Missing poster during the first week of school and growing steadily ever since, spanning a larger and larger patch of cinder block between the gym and the library. There were his yearbook shots from all three years, sports photos from the school paper, the article from the *Free Press* about the best swimmers in the state, a bunch of handwritten notes: *Love ya, man; Come back soon, come back strong; Go, Apaches!* Each time I walked past, I tried not to look closely, but the side of my face would grow warm, and I would feel almost bad for the people coming down the hall in the opposite direction, the ones who saw the shrine and then saw me and hardly knew what to do with their faces. Look at me? Look away? Smile? Frown? Scowl with concern? Cough into their hand? Pretend none of this was happening? Not that it really mattered; after one, two, three steps, they were safely past me and back to the sure footing of their lives, left only with the slight thrill of being, for one awkward moment, part of some dark and awful thing.

For lunch, David Nelson and I sat outside on the concrete dividers in the student parking lot. Only juniors and seniors were allowed off-campus for lunch. Technically, sophomores weren't even supposed to wander this far, but the parking lot was the best alternative to the jangling noise and sweaty competition of the cafeteria, and David Nelson had long ago discovered that if you were smart and quiet and not a troublemaker, the hall monitors would cut you some slack. It was chilly out and we ate with our coats on. I watched the white air come out of David Nelson's mouth as he talked about Uganda.

"I'm not sure of the good of a new constitution," he said, "if there are still limits on political parties. Are we creating a more democratic system or dressing up a dictatorship?"

"Is the new constitution going to lead to reforms?" I said. "I read somewhere that most Ugandans die before they're fifty."

"Museveni's no monster," he said. The tips of his ears and nose were red from the cold. "He's probably doing more good than bad. You can't even compare the economic development of other countries in the region to Uganda's. He blows them out of the water. But what's going to stop him from being in power forever?"

"Don't make him out like he's perfect," I said. "He's not managing that little civil war so well."

We loved these conversations, both of us just as busy admiring ourselves as participating. This was the closest we came to team sport.

"Sure, sure," David Nelson said, pausing to eat his turkey sandwich. He took such a big bite, mustard stained both corners of his mouth. I told him to wipe his face. He asked me to name a rebel army nastier than the LRA. I couldn't think of one. My butt was freezing against the concrete.

"Calling oneself the Lord's Resistance Army does not bode well," he said. "That's not the name of the good guys, I'll tell you that much."

"I don't think the Lord is all that into kidnapping and enslaving children," I said.

David laughed. He laughed easily, especially when we were getting worked up. I'd known David since seventh grade, when we were taken out of our regular classes three afternoons a week and put in the talented-and-gifted room, where we solved basic trig problems with colored beads and wrote government charters for invented utopias. My utopia had been called Plutune, a combination of the two planets farthest from Earth, and David Nelson's was Adnarranda, because he'd been obsessed with palindromes.

One of the hall monitors stalked past us in the lot. It was the old apple-faced lady who every so often showed up with her hair out of its bun, a thick white mane falling surprisingly down her back.

David Nelson called out, "Cold afternoon, Mrs. Sholack."

"Sure is," she said, making a dramatic display of cupping her collar around her neck. David Nelson thought it was politically expedient to know all of the hall monitors by name. I tended to agree.

"Way to shmooze, Museveni," I said once the hall monitor was out of earshot.

"That's *President* Museveni to you, plebe." David Nelson elbowed me gently in the side. Then: "You did good on the news last night," as if that was what we'd just been talking about.

I didn't want to talk about it. David Nelson was the only person I didn't have to talk about it with. When I sat there quietly, he knew to change the subject, asking me what I was doing after school. I told him I had Chuck.

"Upchuck," David Nelson said, which was the same stupid joke he made every time I mentioned my therapist, but it made me giggle anyway. For a while we leaned against each other for warmth, our jackets making slithery, rustling noises.

My mom always used to mistake David Nelson for my boyfriend. When I'd refuse to go to school dances, she'd say "Didn't David ask you?" and I'd explain that David was two inches shorter than me and weighed about seventy-four pounds. "But you love David," she'd say, and I'd tell her, "You don't get it," and she'd ask me what there was to get. If we spent all our time together, wasn't it fair for her to assume we were a couple? David and I, I tried to explain to her, were too up close and on top of each other for that kind of love. He'd once given me head lice. I'd seen the pox of his chicken pox. My mother and I ended those conversations like we ended most, with her thinking I was utterly incomprehensible and me feeling sorry for her small little understanding of the world. Danny, with his apelike attitude toward girls—he sought out only the hot, doting ones and then dated them for weeks before dumping them—seemed much more understandable to my parents.

Upperclassmen started to come back from lunch, trickling through the parking lot in pairs or larger groups, carrying Taco Bell or McDonald's bags and slurping pop loudly through straws. The spaces that had cleared out forty minutes ago started to fill again with shiny SUVs and tricked-out Japanese imports. The parking lot at the end of lunch was always a bit of a defeat, the aliens returning to claim the planet that had been briefly, barrenly ours.

Tip Reynolds and a couple other football players spilled out of the cab of a pickup truck, their bodies bulky and almost unmanageable-looking. I suddenly busied myself with a crack in the pavement, hunching forward to examine it closely, but Tip saw me anyway and came stumbling over, followed by two of his loyal minions.

"Lyd!" he called, putting his hand to his forehead in a strange salute. I could feel David Nelson tensing next to me. Before Danny went missing, it hadn't been uncommon for David Nelson to be thrown against a locker or get his books slapped out of his hands, if not by Tip, by someone just like him. Being Danny Pasternak's little sister's best friend had held no cachet back then. More often than not, it made things worse. "Hey, faggot," Danny used to say each time David Nelson appeared at our front door.

But Tip and friends came today in peace. Tip stood right in front of me, hands on his hips, his crotch essentially in my face. How's your mom, he wanted to know. What happened with that thing about Danny being seen in River Rouge? How's your dad holding up? *Fine, nothing, fine*, I told him. One of the other football players, Gregory Baron, said, "I'm sure Danny just took off. Dude's just chilling, smoking a doob somewhere, high and stupid as shit."

Tip told him to shut the fuck up. Gregory said he was just trying to stay positive. Tip said not to call Danny stupid. Gregory said he didn't mean it like that, he just meant Danny'd be so high he'd forget to come home. Tip told him to shut the fuck up again, and then said, "It's his *sister*," emphasizing *sister* like it meant "holy one."

"Sorry," Tip said to me. "He's an asshole." He said this as if Gregory Baron weren't standing one foot from us.

"It's fine," I said. David Nelson scowled skeptically at Tip, like he couldn't believe apes had learned to speak.

Tip had been one of the last guys to see Danny. The police questioned him for hours and hours over a number of days. Nothing; Tip had nothing for them. He and Kent Newman and Danny had met up at the Larkgrove playground at around four on a Tuesday, played a couple hours of basketball, and left for their separate homes well before dark. They'd walked together as far as the parking lot, where Tip had offered Danny a ride and Danny had turned him down. It was a nice night, Danny told Tip, and he could jog the two miles home in fifteen minutes. It was 6:30 then. Tip's mom and two neighbors confirmed that Tip was home by 6:45. Witnesses from the second basketball court at Larkgrove confirmed Tip's version—the three boys were there for a while, messing around on the court, playing some one-on-one, a couple games of horse. Tip passed a polygraph. So did Kent. No one ever really thought they'd had anything to do with anything.

But being the last to see Danny had seemed to change Tip, who used to come over and snatch books from my hands and read them aloud in a girlish, mocking voice or hide my backpack behind our garbage cans, seeming primarily to exist as a magnifying glass for Danny's sluggish stupidity. Nowadays he acted like he owed me something.

"You want?" he said, waving a half-eaten carton of fries in front of David Nelson and me. They had the pallid shine of being cold already, the cardboard carton spotted with grease along the bottom.

"No, thank you," David Nelson said in a staccato, *fuck you very much* tone.

"Sure," I said, grabbing them. "Thanks."

Tip then pulled ketchup packets from his pocket and held them out to me, which seemed a little laughable. Tip kept ketchup packets in his pocket, probably warm and slightly gross from the friction of his jeans and his massive thighs. Still, I reached my arm out, as if it weren't even my body that it was attached to. "Thanks," I heard myself repeating. Tip had what Cindy and Min did, that inexplicable gravitational pull that made it hard to say no.

"Later," Tip said, holding up two fingers in a peace sign. Gregory Baron mumbled an apology as they left. The fries tasted pretty good. David Nelson sat next to me quietly, telling me no one time, then again, when I offered him some.

5.

Chuck wanted to talk about my dreams. I told him I didn't remember my dreams, which was a lie. I often found myself lying to Chuck, which was not a habit of mine in general. Back in August, I'd been excited when my parents, at the urging of the huddle of cops who'd been camped out at our house for weeks, told me about the arrangements they'd made for me to talk to a counselor. I imagined a pillowy room filled with deep couches and soft light where I would reveal my every everything and be rewarded with warm embraces or at least the same sort of suckers my pediatrician used to give out after shots. I imagined my new therapist saying things to me like "That was a great insight" or "I've been waiting anxiously through my other patients to get to my time with you."

But there were no pillows in Chuck's office, no deep couches. He sat in a swiveling desk chair, sometimes spinning himself just slightly back and forth as if staving off boredom, and I sat in a wooden-armed, tightly upholstered chair that reminded me of a waiting room. There was only one window, and its venetian blinds were always down, open just slightly, so I could make out only thin stripes of pale sky. Chuck rarely smiled, talked in a low monotone, stared directly at my face, and habitually slid his thin, wire-framed glasses up the bridge of his nose. I wanted to like Chuck—or, more accurately, I wanted Chuck to like me—but it was slow going.

Even with his early speeches about this being a safe space and no one else being privy to these conversations, not even my parents, and this whole process being free of judgment, I had the sense of being on the precipice of unwittingly implicating myself in some terrible thing. With his methodical questioning, his expressionless reactions, and his irregular and distracting habit of jotting something down on his pad while I spoke, I had free-floating guilt, as if all I had ever done wrong was soon to be revealed (yes, I cheated off Lisa Barney's social studies exam when I fell asleep the night before without getting to the Geneva Protocol; yes, I was the one who made both of Oliver's paws bleed after trimming his toenails too closely). A single poster hung in the office, behind Chuck's desk. It was a reproduction of a Hockney-like painting, a front door of a house opening onto a sudden, serene ocean instead of a front lawn. I'm sure it was meant to be soothing—an ocean of opportunities awaits you just outside your front door—but it struck me more as a warning: take one wrong step and you're sunk.

"I don't sleep enough to dream," I said. I could remember part of one from the night before where I was getting married in a glittery purple dress and I had to clutch the dress to my chest because it was strapless and the elastic was old, so the whole thing felt like it was going to slip off.

"Dreams can be just minutes long. Do you remember even part of one?"

"Sorry," I said.

Chuck sat quietly looking at me. He was particularly skilled at this. Sometimes I looked away. Sometimes I catalogued his face: the brown soul patch, the unusually full lips that made him look slightly feminine and pouty. Sometimes I thought things like *Does he have a girlfriend?* or *How often does he have sex?*

"Okay," he finally said. "How's school?"

"Fine."

"Are you still getting a lot of new attention?"

The question embarrassed me, making me wish I'd never revealed the fact to begin with, as I had grown quickly to act as if it were unremarkable. I shrugged and briefly considered telling him about Tip at lunch, but I wasn't sure what I'd say about it.

"We can just sit here," Chuck said. He said that a lot. "I'm not here to do the work for you."

"What work?"

"What work do you think we have to do?" He nudged his glasses up his nose.

It was disconcerting, really, the way he had of looking at my face. It made me want to blow my nose or check for sleep in the corners of my eyes.

"I have something," I said after a while, reaching into my pocket, figuring he'd like this. "I have a note from Danny. Well, from a friend of Danny's, originally written by Danny. She gave it to me today."

"What's it say?"

"Haven't read it yet."

Chuck looked surprised—only for a second, but I saw it, his face flexing, then relaxing back to neutral. He leaned slightly forward. "Maybe you want to talk about why you haven't read it yet."

I sighed. "Can I just read it?" I said. "I thought you'd be excited."

"Are *you* excited?"

I rubbed my eyes with the palms of my hands. "No," I said, the word drawn out and plaintive. Chuck's questions brought out an achy weariness that, once elicited, felt ever-present, as if it'd been trailing me all along.

"Okay, why don't you just read it?" he said, sounding a little resigned. I was, I knew, a source of ongoing or at least regular disappointment to Chuck.

I unfolded the paper, already regretting this, trying to tamp down a nervous feeling that rose in me. " 'Min,' " I began, and then stopped to clear my throat. " 'This is so boring. Madame Guignan looks like a penguin. What are you doing this weekend? We're going to Haber's after the game. You should come with us. Bring Penny. Chemanski thinks she's hot. Write me back. I'm bored as shit.' "

That was it.

Chuck watched me, waiting for a reaction. I watched him, doing the same.

"There you go," I said, "my deep and introspective brother." But that wasn't what I was really thinking. I didn't tell Chuck that *Mme.* was abbreviated incorrectly to *Mdm.* and *penguin* was spelled *paingwim* and that Danny had dropped the apostrophes from *Haber's* and *I'm*, and that he'd used a homonym for *write me back* so it came out *right me back.* And that there was barely a period in the whole thing, most of the words running one right into the next. I didn't tell Chuck that all of that gave me a bad feeling, the way Danny came across as little and stupid.

Chuck didn't know anything about Abernathy, about how before we moved to Fairfield, Danny had been scrawnier than David Nelson. He used to get teased all the time, and not just because of his size, but because he was dumb. All through middle school he'd been terrible at reading out loud, his words coming in a slow, unintelligible sputter. He brought home papers scrawled in red, with notes from teachers about needing to talk to my parents. He had to go get a bunch of tests and was given a constellation of diagnoses from dyslexia to dysgraphia to ADD. By ninth grade he spent parts of his days in what they called a resource room, which was basically special ed. He came home one time with a crusty shine at the back of his head, leftovers from an egg someone had thrown at him.

Throughout, he had a joking sort of vulnerability, a self-deprecating humor that made him the magnet of our household. At the dinner table he would go on long riffs about how they made kids do math with colored felt squares in the resource room (*like they're going to hurt themselves with a regular multiplication table*), or about how Jerry who sat next to him had a hole in the back of his skull that he would let people stick a finger into for a quarter, or how it wasn't Danny's fault that he got confused about prepositions when he was writing (*If those words are so important, why are they so little and annoying?*). "Mississippi," he'd say, "that's an important word." He'd sing: "M-I-S-S, I-S-S, I-P-P-I." My parents were quick to laugh at his silliness, even when it wasn't particularly witty or clever, which it often wasn't.

He shared an easy rapport with them that I could never quite muster. My parents, I knew, were mostly befuddled by my studied seriousness. How, I wanted to know, did anyone ever come up with the big bang theory to begin with? Where exactly was East Timor, and why were people there so angry? "Was the milkman a Nobel laureate?" my father often joked to my mother. My mother tried to turn every conversation back to things like why didn't I grow my hair out or get my ears pierced. "Madame Librarian," Danny often said when I tried to start dinner table conversation, making my parents chuckle. And I would chuckle too. There was something soft in such jibes, as if he were poking me only as hard as he poked himself.

But then the summer after his ninth grade we moved to Fairfield and he grew three inches and his voice dropped and he spent every day in his room lifting weights and panting through a series of ever-increasing sets of sit-ups and push-ups. The boxes weren't even unpacked, and an unending stench of warm sweat wafted from his room. He drank powdery energy shakes for breakfast. He had three servings of whatever we ate for dinner. Dad was proud, talking to him about what to bench safely, when to use the help of a spotter. Mom was nervous but relieved; you could see it in her face, the searching way she would stare at him across the table, trying to figure out who this man-boy was. I would catch her smiling at him when he wasn't looking. Danny started running a mile, then two, then three a day. He swam laps at the community pool.

Mom and Dad set him up with a tutor, who came over three nights a week and Saturdays too, sitting at our kitchen table and trying to make Danny's tongue wrap around words like *intriguing* and *thoroughfare* and *physiology.* Danny would press his fist to his temples and stomp his feet against the floor. Afterward he would stand in the doorway of my bedroom and tell me how lucky I was not to need a tutor. "The dude's mouth smells like dog crap," he'd say, "and he sits like one inch from me." He would come up to me then, imitating his tutor, sticking his face right in my face and breathing heavily onto my nose, and I would laugh. "You so *smaht*," he'd say in a fake Chinese accent, pulling the corners of his eyes back. "You so *rucky* cuz you so *smaht*, Rydia." I would laugh and laugh, more than the comments merited. Those were long, lonely months. I was twelve and scared, in a new town, friendless. My parents were even further away and fuzzier than usual, preoccupied by the wallpaper that had to come down from the bathroom and the ivy to be pulled from the yard. Danny was what I had.

By the end of summer, he'd made a deal with my parents: he'd do ninth grade over if they'd take him out of special ed. My parents agreed. So by the time he started Franklin, he was big and new and full of the pent-up, vengeful charisma of someone who'd had to fight his way to it. The football coach took him as a late walk-on even though he'd missed summer practices, and his first girlfriend, the catlike and breathy Hindy Newman, followed shortly after. His dumbness hardly mattered anymore; it was muted by his repetition of ninth grade and, more important, almost expected of a standout athlete, which he quickly became, attacking opponents with praiseworthy viciousness.

My entrance into the seventh grade made barely a blip, save for the girl in science who complained to the teacher that she wanted to be lab partners with one of her friends instead of "that new girl" and the three boys in PE who took to imitating the way I ran, their legs splaying out at their sides as if in need of stabilizing braces. Each night Danny would come home late after practice, sweeping past me up into his sweaty, dank room as if I were a museum piece, a relic of a forgotten era. One night after a particularly bruising day—no one would sit with me at lunch, my haggish new English teacher said I had "misapprehended" the themes of *The Old Man and the Sea* in my first assignment—I went into his room as I had many nights before, slumped against the wall, and waited to begin one of our lazy, aimless conversations. I wanted to be distracted. Danny was good for distraction, but this night he lay on his bed, perched on his elbows, flipping through a notebook. I couldn't see what he was looking at. I knew he knew I was standing there.

"What are you studying?" I finally asked.

"None of your business," he said.

"No, seriously," I said, and flopped on the end of his bed.

"Go the fuck away, Lydia," he said, scowling at me. His face was so wide and squarish now, barely even his face anymore. I stared at the strange blue veins of his biceps. It was a stunning moment, one that lingered in my mind for years, not because it was particularly dramatic. Likely it was a moment he soon forgot. But it marked for me the first stinging rebuke, the first appearance of the casual cruelty that had come from apparently nowhere but would stick, would become simply who Danny was, or at least who he was to me.

My parents, as they cleaned his uniforms and bandaged his injuries and listened raptly to stories of scrimmages, win/loss records, and tackles, fell easily into the role of devoted fans. I, on the other hand, didn't know what to do with myself. Now when he made fun of me at the kitchen table with a screeching imitation of my voice, a pointed *Enough already* in the middle of one of my stories, it did not strike me as jocular, it did not seem like I was in on the joke. The shift felt seismic to me, the pitch of sudden anger directed my way, as though I were somehow responsible for all those years of teasing, as if retaliation upon me were the thing that would right those past wrongs.

And even though his neck grew thick as a stump and he was trailed by a dusty cloud of new friends, I was onto him. Even then, I was onto him. I had some sense of the particular combination of chance, timing, and circumstance that had rescued Danny from himself. Had we not moved from Abernathy exactly when we had, had he not grown exactly when he did, had he not been given long summer months to prepare, he never would have completed his transformation so fully and dramatically. It wasn't the diet or the exercise or even the determination that had changed Danny. It was the precise alignment of events falling exactly in his lap at exactly the right time that had turned his life into a fairy tale.

Dumb luck, I used to sing to myself, over and over again, as he breezed past me or as he said smirkingly, "New hairdo?" *Dumb luck. Dumb luck. Dumb luck.* It soothed me.

But now here was this note, full of *paingwim* and *Im*. He was still that stupid little kid, and as I sat in Chuck's stifling office, it brought me no solace. Danny had spelled *Chemanski* wrong, one of his best friends, who'd played football alongside him for three years. *Shemanskee*, Danny had written. And it made me wonder where he was now. Not in the daydreamy way I usually wondered, picturing him stretched out on some nice lady's lawn chair in a warm-weather state or on a surfboard along a coastline. I wondered now if his luck had changed back, if midnight had come and gone, if someone or something had come to prey on this dumb, pretty jock and set terrible things loose upon him.

6.

When I got home, Dad was sitting at the kitchen table, his face clenched and red, his fist balled around a dirty envelope and an equally dirty scrap of paper. It looked like a page torn from a phonebook. Melissa Anne. Melissa Anne wrote us every few weeks, sometimes more, sometimes less, always on random pages—a corner torn from a newspaper, the back of an advertising circular—though the block-print penmanship was so neat, so precise and perfectly proportioned, it may as well have been sent on the triple-lined paper of grade school. There was never a return address, aside from the two words of her name. The postmark sometimes read Fairfield, sometimes a neighboring suburb.

Dad was still in his suit, his tie tightened around his neck. He had his coat on. His briefcase sat at his feet. When he saw me, he just shook his head. His eyes glittered. Melissa Anne's letters were always the same, her words printed neatly in the margins of the page or on top of existing text, spaced like a couplet:

I had a vision of your son.

He is buried in the ground.

The first line never varied. The second did: *His mouth is filled with dirt. He is encircled by worms. He is smothered by silt.*

That was it. Every letter, only two lines long.

My father's eyes searched the table now, his chest rising and falling. Melissa Anne had become a flashpoint for my parents, getting under their skin in a particularly powerful way. Other letters, inappropriately evangelical ones about what Jesus could do for us in times of crisis if only we'd accept him into our hearts or long, rambling ones about the importance of strict discipline in the home to prevent this sort of tragedy, left them unmoved. But Melissa Anne got to them. Maybe it was the childlike writing or the simplicity of the message or my parents' impotence in the face of it or the way it pointed clearly to a larger, systemic impotence. The police had been unable to identify the sender and eventually told my parents her letters were meaningless—if they were a legit lead, they'd contain more information, and if they were threats, they'd contain a demand of some sort, ransom or otherwise. There are a lot of kooks out there, the police reminded my parents, which was supposed to be reassuring.

"Can't you dust for prints or something?" my father had yelled at one squinty-eyed officer who'd stood in our kitchen the day we'd received Melissa Anne's seventh or eighth letter. The officer just looked at my father with a pitying smile, my dad another poor schmuck who'd watched too many cop shows. "You can't," he said with the stern sympathy police seemed so well trained in, "get worked up about every nut job out there. Ignore it. Throw them out as soon as they arrive. Don't even open them."

But my parents were incapable. My father seemed to tear into Melissa Anne's grimy but meticulously addressed envelopes with a vigor rarely seen otherwise. He shook the torn page now. "What are we paying Howard for?"

Our private investigator hadn't been able to find the sender either, or do much of anything else. Aside from coming over and rapping his knuckles on our countertop while wearing a suit a size too small, and reciting obvious facts everyone already knew, Howard seemed largely to specialize in sending my parents expensive invoices for amorphous things like "casework" and "background analysis."

My dad was staring past me with a steely, tight-jawed look, as if he could punch something. I'd never seen my dad punch anything, never even really seen him yell before all of this started. He'd once been the sort of guy who just flopped easily into his chair at the end of the day, amusing himself with corny jokes. *What do you get when you cross a parrot and a shark?* A bird that talks your ear off. *A hula dancer and a boxer?* Hawaiian Punch. He grasped the phonebook page so hard now his arm was shaking, as if by will alone he could discern or destroy it.

David Nelson came over later and sat at my desk while I sat propped against my headboard with a bunch of pillows. We were trying to finish *Richard III* for Mrs. Bardazian's English class. David loved crazy Queen Margaret and he kept reading her lines out loud: "Hie thee to hell for shame, and leave this world, thou cacodemon!"

"*Cacodemon*'s a good one," I said, but my heart wasn't in it. Oliver sat at the foot of my bed, licking his front paws incessantly, the sound wet and distracting. I told him to knock it off, but the dog eyeballed me sideways and kept going.

"Is it better than . . . hang on," David said, paging through the play. "Better than *elvish-marked, abortive, rooting hog*?"

"*Cacodemon*'s better."

"Even though it's redundant? *Caco* means bad. Cacophony." He said the last word slowly, as if I were being an idiot. "So she's calling him a bad demon. What other kind is there?" He looked smirky and very proud of himself. Twisting himself around in my desk chair, he cracked his back.

"Well, what's an abortive hog?" I said. "A premature pig? It's a more powerful insult to call someone a terrible demon than a piglet."

"*Abortive* also means deformed," David Nelson said. "And *elvish-marked* means possessed by elves. Who are supposed to be spiteful little creatures. That's far more creative than just calling someone demonic." He had a zit the size of a mosquito bite on the side of his nose.

"Whatever," I said. "Margaret's insane anyway."

"Not as insane as Richard," he said.

"Richard's not insane," I said, just to fight. At times things went off-kilter between David Nelson and me, our normal interactions becoming suddenly grating. It could be exhausting, always trying to prove who was smarter. "He's just a megalomaniac."

"He kills his brother and his nephews and tries to marry his niece. That's not insane?"

"Knock it off," I yelled at Oliver, who quit the licking for a second. I patted his head with my foot to make up for yelling. "It's too simple to just call him insane," I said, not even believing what I was saying. "He's got a clear political agenda. All his actions are in service to that."

"His madness is inextricably linked to his megalomania. He used his madness to become king and then being king only turned him into more of a lunatic. You're being intentionally obtuse if you're just reading this as the story of a political schemer."

"Jesus. Stop lecturing me." It came out more harshly than I'd intended.

David Nelson's face went slack, his mouth pulling down at the corners. "Sorry."

"You don't have to apologize," I said, but not convincingly. Oliver had already gone back to the licking.

We read for a while, David hunched over his book at my desk. I could see the gray-striped elastic of his underpants coming out the back of his pants. *"Hell-hound,"* he said, but tentatively now. "That's a pretty good one."

I ignored him.

There was a knock at my door, and my mom came in holding a mug in each hand. Oliver stood on the bed, wagging his tail like crazy.

"I made you floats," she said, practically shouting, though her voice was frayed, as if she were at the tail end of a bout of laryngitis. There was something both familiar and creepy in this, the sort of oddly placed and invasive gesture she used to be more temperamentally prone to but that had disappeared entirely of late. She was smiling now, though she looked like she'd been crying recently, her eyes red-rimmed and mongoloidal, the tiny veins around her nose bluer and more spidery than usual. Her hair was unbrushed, the back matted down and clumpy.

"Thank you very much, Mrs. Pasternak," David said in the kiss-ass voice he always used with my parents. "Delightful," he said as we both took our mugs. I wondered where she'd gotten the ice cream and the pop. These were not items we kept around these days. Had she made a trip to the store? Unlikely. The whole thing made me uneasy.

"How are you kids doing?" she said. She was still practically shouting, though staring at something on my bookshelf, my old *Encyclopedia Britannica*, it looked like.

David Nelson slurped his float, nodding.

"Fine," I said. "Trying to read." I held up my book.

"How are you doing, Mrs. Pasternak?" David Nelson said. I wanted to tell him she wasn't a hall monitor; he didn't need to use her name in every single sentence.

"Melissa Anne wrote again," Mom said, patting the back of her head, like maybe she'd just realized it was tangled back there. She recited the couplet, talked about wanting to call the police but knowing they would do nothing. Her words came out quickly. She was wearing the same sweatsuit that she'd worn the day before. David Nelson had a smile pasted on his face that was starting to look painful. My mom was on leave from her vet tech job. In the first days she'd said it was because she was needed by the police and the search-and-rescue teams and reporters camped out on our street, which was more or less true. Now, though, she filled her days scribbling notes, calling the Red Cross and Goodwill for food donations for the searchers, calling the police for updates, organizing and reorganizing the impromptu filing system that was taking over our kitchen, a tall rusting filing cabinet dragged from the garage and placed next to the table. It was filled with letters and area maps and newspaper coverage and less explicable items too: pictures of other missing kids ripped from milk cartons or junk mail flyers, handwritten lists of Danny's favorite foods, a whole page of his nicknames—Nack, Danny-O, D-Man. I'd never heard anyone call him Danny-O or D-Man. Those, it seemed, my mother made up in some fanciful, self-soothing abandon.

"Dad told me," I said, reminding her of all the things that the police told us: harmless, nut case, best to just ignore it. She nodded at me, in a way that did not mean yes as much as *Go on, go on.*

I didn't know what to say. I never knew what she wanted, really. I held up my book again, reminding her of her interruption. This sort of dropping in and chatting, this wasn't something she and I had ever done particularly well. It always seemed a strange, pale imitation of the way she stood in Danny's doorway as he curled his free weights, the two of them talking lightly about nothing. How was his practice? What was that bruise on the back of his thigh? Was he getting enough sleep? Had she told him the story of the three-legged dog who came in for shots and nearly licked her to death? I would half listen to them through my door, derisive, curious, jealous, relieved.

"I still need to call the Kiwanis for Saturday," she said with a nervous laugh. "I've left two messages already and nobody has called back." We were on to the searches. This is how conversations worked with my mom now. "And I don't think the phone tree worked this week. I know there are still a whole lot of people who don't know where we're starting from."

"I'll be there," David said quickly. "Near Shore Acres Mall, yeah?" Mom nodded at David. It looked like she was going to say something, but Oliver started barking at her. She picked him up and cooed at him about being a good boy. He nuzzled his wet nose into her chin. "Good boy, good boy," she kept repeating.

"Okay, thanks." I lifted my mug in a salute. "Thanks for this. We have to get back to work."

"Sure, sure, sure," Mom said. She kissed Oliver on his dog lips. David Nelson and I exchanged disgusted glances.

After she left, David brought his mug to the bed and sat Indian-style where Oliver had just been. I curled my legs under my butt, making myself smaller. I had the feeling of a cactus or a porcupine.

"Your poor mom," he said.

"You sound like Min Mathers," I said.

"I'm just saying . . ." He paused, as if he were trying to figure out what he was saying. "It's got to be tough."

"Duh." I leafed through *Richard III.* Queen Elizabeth's noblemen were begging for their lives; Richard, about to kill them anyway, didn't give a crap.

"Do you think about it a lot?" he said.

"What do you think?"

"I don't know. You act like you don't, but how could you not?"

My float sat untouched on my nightstand, the ice cream melting into the pop. *Today shalt thou behold a subject die for truth, for duty, and for loyalty,* one of the noblemen told Richard.

David scooted himself closer to me. A thin mustache of ice cream shadowed his upper lip. "It's okay to be sad," he said, sounding like he'd been practicing the line for a while.

I started laughing, which I felt almost bad about when I saw his mouth pucker in surprise. But this type of heartfelt earnestness, especially from David Nelson, had a tendency to make me itchy and restless, as if the last flimsy barricade protecting my life from a completely maudlin wasteland were giving way.

"I'm trying to read," I said.

"You're so tough." I couldn't tell if he meant it as an insult or a compliment. He sat funny, balanced strangely on his knees, hunching forward, his mug in one hand, the other grasping my comforter. He looked right at me. "Can you imagine how some other girls would be handling this? I mean, remember Gina LeShawn?"

Gina LeShawn had been a passenger in a drunk-driving

accident our freshman year. The driver, a junior from another school, wrapped the car around a tree and ended up with a broken collarbone and a jail sentence. Gina broke her ankle and ended up a local celebrity, regularly gathering swarms of people around her in the hallways to retell the story of the accident and the emergency room and, months later, the sentencing hearing for the driver. For a good portion of the year she could be found sobbing in the cafeteria, as girls in ponytails and polo shirts squeezed her shoulders in concern.

"Well, I'm not Gina LeShawn," I said.

"And thank god for that." He looked at me like Chuck looked at me, straight on and steady. His zit was huge.

"Come on," I said.

"Come on, what?"

"Go away. Go back to your chair."

He didn't go back to his chair. He kept staring, as if I had something on my face. "What?" I said to him. "What?" And then he sprang forward, far more agile and quick than I knew David Nelson to be, crushing my book, spilling some of his float into my lap, jamming his mouth to mine. His lips were sticky and sweet, his teeth clicking loudly against mine.

There was one long, slow moment (really, it must have been just a nanosecond) during which I felt nothing at all, a weightless, limbless remove. And then, in a dizzying rush, I was back—in my room, in my bed, with the full weight of David Nelson upon me, a weight far more substantial than I would have guessed. He had me pinned, his nose buried in my cheek, a knee digging painfully into my thigh, an elbow poking my hip.

He was a jack-in-the-box newly sprung, breathing hard, trying to shove his tongue in my mouth. His breath was sugary but sour.

"Cut it out," I managed to say, but he kept at it, lapping me with his tongue, one hand pawing at my hair, but hard, so it was more like hitting me in the head. For a few more seconds I just sat there and took it, stunned, a bug speared to the corkboard, wings splayed. The faces of all the boys I'd ever thought of kissing—Barry from World History Club, whose hair was the almost outlandish gold of fairy-tale princes'; bookish Mr. Jarris, who sometimes subbed for Hollingham and nervously twiddled his hands in his pockets as he talked of the Byzantine Empire; Joey Jeremiah, from that silly high school show that used to run on PBS—flashed through my head. David Nelson's ceramic mug pressed coldly against my rib cage, giving me a feeling like I might cry.

Finally I dislodged my arms from the tangle of him and shoved my palms against his chest. He bounced backward on the mattress almost comically, losing hold of his float entirely, the mug bouncing on the bed, pop spilling darkly along my comforter. He lay sprawled at the foot of the bed, panting, staring at me wide-eyed, like a cornered animal.

"What. The. Hell?" I said, and his cheeks turned a bright, cartoonish red.

"I'm sorry," David said in the voice of a little girl. He wiped me off his lips with the back of his hand. "I'm really sorry."

"You should be," I said, and I could feel my eyes stinging stupidly. I watched his chest as it flittered like a jackrabbit's, his terribly cut, uneven bangs, his eyes that bulged from his skinny face. "What the hell?" I repeated, louder now.

"Shhh!" he told me, as if it were his parents downstairs. He pumped his hands toward the ground, like he was tamping a fire. "Calm down," he said.

My blood coursed hotly through me, behind my cheeks, down

my neck, through my cramped-up legs, as if it had turned to lava. "You calm the fuck down," I said, "you rapist." Some dark, crushed, nameless thing was propelling the words.

He was so red and flustered-looking, it seemed like he was the one who was going to cry. I'd never talked like that to anyone, certainly not David Nelson, and I felt a quick pang of regret. I had to clench my teeth not to suddenly scream, my jaw trembling with the effort. Chuck would say later that it was because what David had done was assault. That I was a sexual assault victim reacting with perfectly normal and understandable shock. I believed Chuck for a while, relieved to have so easy an answer (and wasn't that what therapy was for—providing self-satisfying and palatable answers to inexplicable questions?). But it wasn't that. All David Nelson had done was kiss me. He hadn't even tried to grab my boobs.

It was that he'd crossed a line, a line which I knew—instantaneously—we couldn't just cross back from with the hopes that everything would revert to its rightful place. He'd changed things, created a moment after which nothing would be the same. I already had one of those, recently acquired. One was too much. I couldn't have another. Not now. Not from David Nelson.

I started shaking.

"I didn't mean it," he said in a low voice. Then, more shrilly, "I don't mean I didn't mean it. I meant it. I didn't mean it like that." And finally, terribly, "I've been waiting so long."

I felt my chest sinking into itself like he was sucking the air right out of me. *Dupe,* I thought, suddenly and quickly. *Dupedupedupedupedupe.* He stared at me as if he expected something. I could not imagine what. David Nelson was my only friend.

"Shut. Up," I said, but what I wanted to say was, *You're making it worse.*

"I should go," he said, scrambling quickly off the bed, grabbing his books from the desk, his coat and backpack from the floor. He was a blur of motion, nodding fast, picking up his mug, rubbing his hand uselessly over the pop and ice cream that had already seeped through my comforter and sheets, already spread into a brownish stain in my mattress, one that would never wash fully clean, a blob I would spy for years whenever I changed the sheets, the sight of it reminding me of the scooped-out feeling of that night. The meaning would slowly fade, though, and I would eventually come to eye it dispassionately as I snapped clean linens between two fists and spread new sheets over the mattress. From one angle it looked a bit like the storm system on a weather map, from another a mangled butterfly.

"I can clean this up," David said, crackly-voiced.

I jammed my palms against my eyes. "Just go," I said. My chest filled back up with air, too fast now, my heart thumping like it could burst. I listened to him stumbling to get his shoes on. To him saying my name. To unintelligible mumbling, a swallowed sentence about *didn't want to* and *never mind.* To the wriggling of my doorknob. To quick footsteps down the stairs. To my mom saying something and David Nelson saying something back. To the front door opening and closing. To the sound of this house without him—the low buzz of a television barely on, the creak of a couch spring, the hum of a cavernous fridge—noisy with quiet, teeming with it, like a breath held too long, painfully paused and waiting.

7.

He didn't show up at the Saturday search. I knew he wouldn't. We'd quickly and instinctively winnowed separate channels for ourselves through the school hallways. There was only one run-in, on Wednesday, between fifth and sixth periods, near the chem labs, corrected by Thursday. I chose the longer route to Ms. Villara's Spanish class via the second-floor history and psych rooms. In Bardazian's English class and Fontana's trig we perfected the art of staring intently and unwaveringly past each other. He commented incessantly about Queen Margaret during the *Richard III* discussion, and I felt hotly satisfied when Mrs. Bardazian did her usual "Why don't we give a chance to some of our quieter classmates?" as David raised his hand for the millionth time.

I spent three days of lunches in the cafeteria, hounded by Lola Pepper and girls who ended every sentence with a question mark

("This tuna loaf is like a brick?" "We're hanging out at Devon's after school?") and modified every verb with *so* ("I so failed that history quiz," "I so wouldn't wear those pants with those saddlebags"). They had predictable questions about Danny—*What was he like at home? What did he have in his room? Do you have any idea where he is?* Sometimes I pretended I didn't hear. Sometimes I gave them a word or two, like "Just normal" or "Stuff" or "No." Lola had a habit of looking at me a lot while the other girls talked among themselves, as if she were trying to gauge my response to their conversation about a CD from a band I'd never heard or how one of them could get Lyle Walker to notice her in world civ class. I didn't really know what to do with myself as Lola stared. Pretend I didn't see her? Act like I was absorbed in the conversation? Smiling seemed the most effective—a closed-mouth, noncommittal smile—placating her enough to turn her attention, at least for a little while, back to the rest of the table.

By Saturday morning I was tired, more tired than usual. It was a lite version of those first days after Danny was gone, when it seemed like there was so much effort to every step, every word, every eye blink, not because of grief so much as disorientation. The reference points had gone awry: cop cars parked regularly in our driveway, strangers brought casseroles, our name was flashed over and over again on the local news as if a recent hurricane or tornado had been named for us. I found myself doing things like opening the medicine cabinet and, upon seeing the Listerine bottle, thinking, *Listerine? What is Listerine?* even though that same green bottle, or one just like it, had been sitting in that same spot for years. Everything was suddenly being relearned—Did I have a brother? Did I not have a brother?—causing my brain to stutter and buckle.

This time it wasn't so bad, not nearly as dramatic; now I just longed for sleep more than usual. I was gritty-eyed and exhausted by the time we got to the field where this week's search would begin. People milled about, standing in weeds and grass still wet from the rain that had just fallen and was sure to return soon. They all had their hands pocketed in raincoats, heads tucked under hoods. A few grown-ups held bullhorns at their sides. Several ladies in bright plastic ponchos passed out the orange safety vests and whistle necklaces. People always brought their dogs; today, a German shepherd pulled at its leash and a pit bull barked at a patchy mutt. Some off-duty cops spoke into walkie-talkies. The on-duty cops had been pulled the week before, after we'd passed the two-month mark. "Can't justify the overtime anymore," a lieutenant with a walrus mustache had told my dad. "We still have to entertain the very real possibility of a runaway." The vein in my dad's temple pulsed so quickly and so visibly I thought he would pass out or punch the guy instead of just walking away like he did. No other idea was as quick to incite rage in my dad or hysteria in my mom as the runaway one. Whenever police or even Howard the PI mentioned it, my parents heard an accusation, one meant to squarely shift responsibility—*This is* your *problem, not* ours.

Lacking a ransom note or direct witness of abduction, my parents had spent the first weeks after the disappearance yelping to anyone who would listen, *Starting defensive ends* does not *run away. Popular kids about to begin their senior year* do not *run away. Someone just finishing a neighborhood basketball game with friends* does not *suddenly run away.* If the runaway idea should have held some comfort in its relative quaintness or normalcy, this seemed lost on my parents. They loved Danny slavishly; he loved them back, if not quite slavishly, then with his own brand of brutish devotion. So there was never any doubt for them that he'd been gotten. And the idea of *gotten* mobilized people. It evoked panic, contagion, a need to march through wet, marshy fields or across vast cement lots for the wild-card possibility of finding who had done this getting, or where, or why, or how. And my parents needed this. They needed everyone to step up and help, to be squawky and persistent and hysterical on our behalf.

A quick scan of today's crowd revealed the swelling ranks of kids from Franklin—Tip and all his athlete buddies, the kid who sat behind me in Hollingham's history class, a freshman girl who was already famous for bleeding through her pants on the second day of school and then again on the fourth. The Saturday searches had quickly become the official time for the student body to display their collective, vicarious grief. A knot of girls from the student council stood crying loudly in the center of the field now. They seemed to have an endless reserve of tears, truly an amazing, regenerative supply.

A ripple of attention moved through the crowd as we arrived. My mom had her hand on my shoulder in a distracted grip. We'd gotten another letter from Melissa Anne the day before, written on the back of a soup label (*He is suffocated by soil*), which made them extra-jittery. My mother passed out the laminated cards she always prepared for the searches: *Things to Look For*, they read across the top, with a list beneath, starting with *Tigers cap, blue nylon wallet, Reebok shoes.* People stopped their conversations; one girl gulped down a laugh in a quick hiccup as we passed. Several women stopped us, holding on to my mom's forearm and saying low, consoling things about faith and mysterious ways. *Bernice,* they kept repeating, *Bernice, Bernice, Bernice,* and it still surprised me how many people knew her name. Men nodded at my dad, a wordless parade of bobbleheads. Soon they were both sucked into the crowd. My mom used a megaphone to thank everyone for coming, and my dad talked to the off-duty cops huddled around him like a football team around its coach.

I stood in the grass, trying to think of what to do with my arms. A lady handed me one of the orange vests and a whistle. David Nelson was actually fairly annoying at the Saturday searches, reciting probability statistics and complaining about his loafers getting soaked and not really leaving a moment of quiet. But still, this was the time he and I would normally huddle together, making low jokes about everyone around us, him telling me distracting stories.

The first drops of rain began to fall. One of the off-duty cops took the megaphone from Mom and started in on the standard announcements—not to travel in groups under four, to hold hands with arms outstretched to form the most comprehensive sweep, to look for anything notable or suspicious, to stay out of the abandoned factory a half-mile west of here. Blow your whistle if you find something and a search organizer will find you.

People began moving more purposefully, forming their groups. I drifted away from my parents, not wanting to hold outstretched hands with them. My dad would ploddingly stop at every shrub, dirt pile, or garbage can to paw through its innards, while my mom would take sharp breaths whenever we happened upon something shiny—a gum wrapper, a soda can, the one hypodermic needle we found weeks earlier in the tall grasses next to the Wal-Mart.

I soon found myself among a group of well-coiffed, middle-aged synagogue women who acted as if we all shared a close friendship from B'nai Israel. The synagogue ladies were much like everyone else in this sense, naturally eager and upon me, having in recent months embellished the most paltry of shared histories until it became something of significance. Now they touched my arm and spoke my name, even though I barely knew them. I couldn't remember the last time we'd been to B'nai Israel. We were not a religious family. My mother hadn't even been Jewish until she'd married my dad; before that she'd been Episcopalian. The conversion, though they never talked about it, seemed a decision that had little to do with any conviction aside from appeasing Dad's parents. Some years they forgot entirely about the High Holidays. My mom still faked the words to the seder songs. In December we had both a Christmas tree and a menorah. All of our religious practices seemed to come from some patchwork of ambivalence and obligation. I sometimes called us Episcajews and Jewapalians, but really, we were nothing.

Now, though, the synagogue ladies acted as if I were the messiah, arrived. They cooed at me and called me *sweetheart* and said the things strangers said now with surprising uniformity, *Poor thing* and *I can't imagine*, which, instead of having their normal gratifying effect, gave me the feeling of being a few steps away from myself, impassively watching the whole scene play itself out. I imagined a lifetime of these scenes, where the only expression I encountered was a tearful one and all physical contact was limited to either the sympathetic arm squeeze or, if the person was bolder, one of my hands grasped in both of hers.

The rain continued to fall more steadily, and a low wind moved easily through my coat and shirt. One of the ladies asked me about school, if I was doing okay in school. I nodded past her. Today we were searching in the abandoned stretch of land behind the Shore Acres Mall, several miles south of the basketball courts. We'd been here a couple times already; it was the spot where the police dogs had sniffed out scents of Danny forty-eight hours after he went missing. This was my least favorite search, with its deep alleyways and burned-out storefronts, dark corners and bottomless-seeming dumpsters.

Another synagogue lady was telling me a long and awful story about her child who had died of lymphoma and how that had been almost more than she could bear, only to find that she *could* bear it.

There was lipstick on one of her front teeth. When she finished, she stared expectantly, as if now it were my turn, though I could not think of a single thing to say. Quickly the day was growing tinged with the sense of things being odd, the waypoints askew. So when someone ran up behind me and grabbed my hand and I turned to see Lola Pepper's familiar, smiling face nearly on top of me, what I felt was sudden, unabashed relief.

I told the synagogue ladies good luck with their search and thanked them while Lola pulled me across the field toward her friends, words flowing from her as easily as they always did—*How are you? Doesn't the rain suck? What did you do last night?* She'd gone over to Rochelle's (I didn't know who Rochelle was) and they watched *Pulp Fiction.* Had I seen it? It was good but so weird. Really violent. I should maybe see it if I like that kind of thing. How was I? Searches were strange. Did I feel okay about searches or did I think they're strange too?

"No, they're strange," I said. For a second Lola looked surprised that I'd actually said something back, staring at me for a long beat.

"Why do you think they're strange?" she said. The freckles on her left cheek resembled a sailboat.

"I don't know. I mean, you really want to find something but also you hope you don't find anything at all."

"Yeah, right, exactly. You only want to find something like a note from Danny saying, *Hey guys, everything's cool. I'm fine.*"

I laughed a little. "That's pretty much it."

The officer made his last few announcements—stay warm, stay with your group, watch out for cars—as Lola marched me up to her friends, her fingers still laced through mine. It was all the girls from the lunch table plus the only guy from flag team, an exchange student from France who brushed his curly hair into a lightly greased wave and had cheeks so bright he appeared to be wearing blush. He introduced himself to me formally, shaking my hand and doing a slight dip. His name was Bayard, which I already knew since there were only three exchange students at Franklin: Bayard, a Swedish junior named Maja, who all the guys wanted to date because of her blond hair and tiny waist, and a Brazilian freshman named Eduardo, who buoyed the entire JV soccer team. Usually being an exchange student meant easy popularity, but Bayard, with his proclivity for flag routines and shoes that appeared to have slight heels, was largely understood to be gay and friends mainly with Lola Pepper.

"Nice to meet you, Lydia," he said, his accent making it come out *Nize tuh mitchu, LEED-yah.*

Lola took my hand on one side, Bayard on the other, the lunch-table girls forming the ends of our chain on either side. There were seven of us altogether, walking over the already trampled weeds, heading toward a vacant strip mall. The sense of low-level disorientation lingered; strange hands held mine, Lola's grip tight and nearly crushing, Bayard's loose and damp and fishlike. Lola was uncharacteristically hushed as we walked. Searches always did that to people. Even the lunch-table girls held their impenetrable, giggly conversations at a far lower volume than usual, barely a whisper. As we marched, my arms were pulled taut at my sides, as if we were little kids playing a game—ring-around-the-rosy, Red Rover, Red Rover. I needed almost no momentum of my own, the snaky line pulling me along. For that I felt a quiet, grateful surrender.

Moving onto pavement, people hunched forward to examine bits of leaves and debris. I scanned the ground quickly. It was easy to let my attention drift to the chains of people around us, moving purposefully and slowly, speaking in hushed voices or not at all, giving the whole scene a choreographed yet alien feel. What, I wondered, would Danny think if he were watching this? I often imagined Danny lingering just above, somewhere in the tree line, not because I thought he was dead, but more because I thought he was somehow omniscient, in on some big joke that none of the rest of us understood. He'd be amused by this, I guessed, tickled by the spectacle. *Look,* he'd say, *Tip's holding hands with Dave Macaw.* That would crack him up. *Fudgepackers,* he'd say.

One of the lunch-table girls stopped to pick up a wet piece of paper. She turned it over meaningfully, even though from three people away I could see it was just an old movie ticket stub.

"Nothing." She looked at me apologetically. She wore a rain hat with two cat ears fashioned playfully on the top. I shrugged. She dropped the stub, but one of the other lunch-table girls with a hint of a double chin told her not to litter. The cat-eared girl said the stub was already there. The double-chinned girl said that doesn't make littering right. "Pick it back up," she said. "Are you on the rag?" the cat-eared girl said.

"Is strange," Bayard said to me as we began walking again. *Eez strinj*, it came out, and I wasn't sure if he was referring to the interaction between the girls or the whole idea of this search. Either way, I agreed.

"What do you think of Chirac's election?" I said a little too loudly as we all slipped into the alley behind the mall. The rain pooled in low puddles beside the buildings.

Bayard shrugged. "Nothing, really." *Nuzzing, reelee.*

"You like him better than Mitterrand?"

"I don't follow politics," he told me. I didn't know what to say. Pas-de-Calais was the strait separating France from Great Britain, connecting the English Channel to the North Sea.

"I bet Paris is beautiful," Lola Pepper said.

"Is beautiful for tourists," Bayard said. "Like Las Vegas. Like Disneyland."

"I love Disneyland," Lola Pepper said agreeably.

"Then you love Paris," he said.

"I *know*," Lola Pepper said, oblivious to the derision in Bayard's voice. "I can't wait to go there one day. There and Venice. Gondolas."

A chain of older men was stopped ahead of us, already fishing through the alley's one dumpster. We scooted quickly past them before they could ask for help. Lola Pepper picked up a fingerless glove, dense and waterlogged. One of the other girls found what appeared to be an antenna broken off a radio. Neither, of course, meant anything. Sometimes during searches I suspected people just picked things up so as not to feel as useless as we surely were. By the time we came out the other side of the alley, the abandoned factory stood in the distance. Some of the girls were already complaining of being cold. One bitched about how wet her socks were. We'd been out twenty minutes, maybe a half-hour.

Lola was getting frustrated with her friends. Each time one complained during our slow march toward the factory, she sighed or shook her head. Finally, after one girl nearly started crying because her shoe had been sucked half off her foot by the mud, Lola said, "*Listen*, you guys. Would you be complaining about a dirty sock if it was *your* brother we were looking for?"

I made a weird sound then, a kind of coughing laugh, and looked at my shoes. It was sweet of her—at least now I can see that it was sweet of her, the way she naturally came to champion me, the way she wanted so badly, so determinedly, to right things. It was humane and kindhearted in a way I could scarcely comprehend at the time, when it just felt humiliating. I remember wanting to tell her to shut up, wanting to tell the grousing girls that it was okay, I wanted to turn around too. I was cold and my feet were soggy and one shoulder of my raincoat was coming loose at the seam, the rain seeping all the way to my skin.

"Sorry," the girl with the sucked-off shoe mumbled in my general direction, momentarily chastened. We continued toward the factory, where orange-vested groups already circled the perimeter. I had no idea what the factory used to manufacture. It was five stories tall, spanning most of a block, the whole building a dingy gray, a good number of its windows knocked out. The feeling of futility only increased as we neared. What could we possibly find, traipsing around in the same circle that all these groups were already traipsing in? I thought I saw my mom on the end of one of the human chains, her back curving, her neck stretched forward, long strands of hair escaping her hood and hanging down wet in front of her.

When we finally reached the sidewalk in front of the building, Bayard said, "Let's go in," so simply, as if that were our obvious next step. *Lez guh een.*

The police had searched the factory more than once. They'd found nothing. Civilian searchers weren't allowed inside. The double-chinned girl said quickly, "We can't," and a girl with bubblegum pink nails said, "No way I'm going in *there.*" Cat Ears said, "That place is nasty," drawing out the final word.

Bayard smiled at us. Not exactly a boastful smile, but closed-mouthed and sly, like he knew something the rest of us had no inkling of. He seemed briefly arrogant, in spite of being bright-cheeked and spindly and wearing high-heeled shoes. His hand sat in mine still, loose and impassive. I stared at the dirty brick of the building; this close, random patches looked blackened, as if they'd been charred by fire. Yellow caution tape fluttered in one doorway, flapping in the air like a party streamer.

The longer we stood there, the more feverish the lunch-table girls grew in their objections ("We're not allowed to separate," "You're going to be *trespassing*"). The rain was fully upon us now, sure and constant. A few groups of searchers passed by on the sidewalk, nodding wordlessly. One man looked at the ground near our feet and asked, "Did you find something?" and shook his head sadly when we told him no. Bayard still had that smile, and the feeling of surrender rose again within me. I would let him lead me inside. This awful building seemed suddenly to fit perfectly with the general strangeness of the morning.

"I'll go," I said, and Lola looked between me and her friends, her freckles brightening on her face. I thought she might burst into tears. Inside meant respite from this rain and this search, from these squirrelly girls, from my mother and the inevitable circle she was making back toward us now.

I squeezed Lola's hand. "Come with us," I said, the first generous thing I ever said to her, really. And she did.

8.

There was a musty, charred smell to the place, not smoky, more like the bitter sharpness of crossed wires. It reminded me of the smell that wafted from the voc hall at school as students patched together busted radios in electronics. Glass and debris littered the floor; our steps were noisy and crunching. It was hard to see, as the inside was cavernous and most windows were clouded over with a dirty film. The broken ones let in jagged streams of light and a steady patter of rain. You could hear a few voices from outside, but just barely. Lola kept making mewling noises behind me, gasping as she walked into cobwebs. There was a constant film of them, shocking at first, the intimate way they clung to your face.

"You guys," Lola kept saying. "You guys, is this a good idea?"

Bayard marched ahead of us like a drum major. "Don't be scared," he called. *Dun be skeered.*

We moved past hulking, unidentifiable machines. In the dark, one looked like a loom, another a gross imitation of a grand piano.

"What'd they used to do in here?" I called, my voice loud and echoy. Neither answered, but Lola let out an unusually high-pitched squeal followed by a loud, skittering noise. When I turned around, she was down on all fours, splayed like an animal.

"I tripped!" she said, her tone as if she were accusing us of something. "I tripped!"

When I got to her, she was breathing heavily, examining her wrists for scrapes. I helped her up by the elbow. She had an expression I hadn't seen before, far more intent and fiery than normal. She looked like she was working hard to bite back something. The sight of it made me like her more than usual. It made me give her more credit. I helped brush the dirt off her pants.

"I'm cut," she said. She held her palm to my face. There was a thin trail of blood on the fleshy pad beneath her thumb. "I think there's some glass in there."

I felt around her hand impotently, imitating something my mother must have done a long time ago. I couldn't feel anything.

When Bayard got to us, he proclaimed, "Come on. This will be fun." The hood of his rain jacket was pulled back now; several curls had broken free of his gel and popped from his head like loose bedsprings. His ears were huge. I felt like laughing.

"Zis weel be fan," I said to Lola. That made her smile a little.

Bayard found a dark stairwell that smelled rancid, as if someone had long ago left meat to defrost there. Lola cupped both hands over her nose and mouth as Bayard bounded up the stairs ahead of us. The darkness was so dense I held my arms out in front of me protectively. The smell was potent; it went right to my throat and I started coughing. For a quick moment I thought, *Danny*. I felt, briefly, a fleshy, sweaty sureness. An image popped into my head—some long-ago Halloween, him swaddled in toilet paper, his face paled with white powder, red grease-pencil blood dripping from the side of his mouth.

Soon Lola's hand was on my back. "You okay?" she said.

I'd stopped on the stairs, was hanging on to the railing now. "Sure," I said. I cleared my throat. "Sure."

"Just don't look," she said, and as my eyes adjusted to the darkness, I made out a faint, feathery carcass in the corner of the stairwell. It was huge, certainly bigger than a pigeon, and dark, with its wings splayed at strange angles. A dense shadow fanned out beneath it. Blood.

"Poor crow," Lola said.

"Crow," I said, as if I'd never heard the word before. Lola was patting my back.

I couldn't stop staring. There was a bit of movement near the beak, and for a second I thought it might still be alive until I realized maggots were slithering around in the eye sockets. I tried not to gag and hurried up the rest of the steps two at a time, listening to Lola's footsteps behind me.

As I came out of the stairwell, my blood pounded in my ears, my face felt weighty with a rush of blood. The second floor looked just like the first except even darker, with fewer broken windows. Bayard sat waiting for us, cross-legged beside a huge machine with a conveyer belt. His jacket was spread out beneath him, as if he were on a picnic.

"What took you so long?" he said. I wondered if the smug unflappability was a French thing. It was starting to bug me. "Have a seat," he called, fanning his arm in front of him.

I tried to slow my breathing. Lola performed a long, meticulous ritual of sweeping away the debris with the sides of her shoes before laying her coat down. She made worried, chirpy noises at what she thought were spiders but were only dusty clots of dirt carried along by the low wind currents. I sat too, feeling uncomfortably small in the shadow of the machine. The air was cool and musky. There was a steady patter of rain against the windows. My one shoulder was freezing.

"What do we do now?" Lola said.

"I don't know," Bayard said. "Tell ghost stories?" *Gust sturries.*

"Eh," I said. I was unenthused about ghost stories. Lola examined the cut on her hand, pressing a finger along the line of blood. Bayard sat with a placid expression, seeming utterly at home. I wondered what my parents were doing, which field they were marching through, what sort of soggy receipt or abandoned shoe they were picking up and fingering. I wondered when they would head back to the starting field, and what they would do when I failed to arrive, if their hands would fly around their faces, if they would shriek, run in circles, fall to their knees.

"I really loved your brother," Lola said. Her face was drawn again, serious as when she fell.

"I know you did," I said, nodding, though I could feel the tiredness at the base of my neck like a weight.

She ran her finger along the dirty floor. Bayard stared between us. It was strange and comforting, the fact that he'd never known Danny, that Bayard had been an ocean away the last time Danny's whereabouts were known, that all Danny was to him was an idea.

"Why did you love him?" I asked, trying not to sound defensive, trying to sound curious instead. Which I was.

"I don't know," she said. "*You* know." She looked at me as if of course I knew. What did I need *her* telling *me*?

Years later I would sit in a child development class during my short and ill-conceived phase of wanting to be a teacher (I was not nearly patient enough and lacked the necessary empathy by about half). I listened to my professor explain a set of rat studies that tested Pavlovian theories about intermittent stimuli. Rats had had to press their nose against a button to get food. For one set of rats, they pushed the button, they got food. For another, they pushed the button and they got an electric shock along with their food. For the third, sometimes they got a shock with their food, sometimes not. "Which group," the professor asked from behind his podium, "do you think fared the worst?" and then looked pleased when the majority of hands rose for the rats with the constant shocks. *Wrong.* A good number of those rats developed compensatory skills, he told us, such as pressing the button for shorter durations or with less frequency. They survived, hungrier than the shock-free rats but relatively intact. The rats with the intermittent shocks, though, those were the ones who chewed their tails to a nub and rubbed so hard against the wire of their cages that they sheared away first their fur, then their skin. Those were the ones who ate their own feces. "Inconsistency," the professor declared excitedly, "is the single most destructive force on a being's psyche."

Had Danny administered his shocks daily, I could've grown inured to him. I could have built up my defenses. But between the long weeks of his dismissive silences, he'd slouch every so often in my doorway and say simply, "How's it going, Lyd?" After a campaign of ripping pages from the books on my bookshelves (only a few here and there at first, so I thought it was just a strange anomaly, page 212 jumping to 215, until slowly the last page of every book on my bookshelf was gone, the remnants jagged and fluttery along the spine), he'd hand me, unbidden, an old Eric Clapton album, saying he didn't want it anymore. In the same week he could tell me, "That coat is cool" and "You better start wearing makeup if you don't want to look so unappealing." Peabody, he'd call me sometimes, in a giggling, congenial way, the name of the genius with the Wayback Machine from the cartoon we used to watch together Saturday mornings. Duckling, he'd call me on other days, always with a snarl and often in front of his friends, which to my knowledge was the only literary allusion he'd made in his life.

I was stuck always between wanting him and hating him, between hoping he'd come sit on the edge of my bed and hoping he'd have some gruesome accident that would scar him or paralyze him or both. I was—long before he went missing—the crazy rat.

"Tell me," I said now to Lola, drawn against my better judgment to her simple, rose-colored version.

"He was really funny," she began, looking at Bayard, not me. "And he made people feel good. You know?" Bayard shrugged. "And he didn't treat you like crap just because you weren't an upperclassman. There was this one time last year when we were out on the field practicing before the Thompson-Perkins game and Beth kept tangling up her flag." Bayard rolled his eyes knowingly. I didn't know which one Beth was or what her tendencies toward flag tangling were.

"And it was pouring out and we were all really starting to get frustrated and we just wanted to get it right. And Danny comes out from the lockers, all suited up for practice. When he sees us on the other side of the field, he runs over and he can see we're all unhappy, and he just says, 'Ladies, may I?' and hands me his helmet and holds out his hand for my flag, which I give him. And he takes over. I'm not kidding. He's shouting *one, two, three, four*, and waving my flag around and kicking up his feet like a Rockette, and everyone's laughing. He starts marching around and everyone follows him. I mean, he's got his shoulder pads and cleats on and everything." She giggled at this memory, then looked almost embarrassed by her noise.

"It doesn't sound that funny now, but it was. When he hands me back my flag, he says, 'You guys are doing a good job.' " She looked meaningfully between me and Bayard. Bayard shrugged again. "You know how many football players tell us that?" Lola said. "Not many. Not any, really. They don't bother with us. I know what the rest of them call us. *Cowgirls. Heifer Brigade.*"

There was a breathless look about her, as if the story had really taken her for a ride. She stared at me like now it was my turn. The longer I remained quiet, the more her features changed, as if she were remembering where she was. Her eyes grew wide and watery, her lips drooped. One tear slid down her cheek, and Bayard made a weird, soft, *awww* noise, which I found so disappointing. Her tears—there were more—created a bitter, pulsing knot in the base of my throat, one that held back all the terrible things I longed to tell her about how she'd been fooled, about how Danny had never so much as mentioned her, about how he had always juggled a handful of girls, all of whom were lither and leggier and prettier than she.

His—I was so tired of everyone being his. In the absence of David Nelson, in the grime of this factory, in the midst of the cold, rainy patter of this day, I needed someone—okay, anyone—to be mine.

We stayed there for a long time. Bayard told stories about France, mostly to do with how frustrating it was not to be able to find particular foods here. He mused lovingly about boursault cheese and congolais cookies and Mirinda soda. I found it a waste that out of all the exchange students from France, we ended up with one who could speak of his culture in only the most minute and palate-driven terms.

From outside we still heard occasional voices of searchers, sometimes one rising more loudly than the rest, a peaked word or phrase (. . . *head north . . . Ready?*), but mostly it was quiet. Sporadic creaking or a slithery noise would come from within the factory, but beyond exchanging startled glances, we didn't do anything.

For once I found Lola's airy, tangential stories soothing. Her grandmother's shih tzu had no depth perception and walked into walls. She had heard a rumor about Mr. Feldkamp, the band teacher, who supposedly had an affair with a first-chair clarinet player several years ago. The stories struck me now like the occasional Popsicle or celebrity magazine, surprisingly satisfying because of their substancelessness.

"What do you do for fun?" she asked me at one point, and it struck me as a funny question, like we were on a date.

"Um . . ." I tried to think. It was a harder question than I thought. "I don't know. I liked driving for a while." I told the story about getting pulled over. They both seemed impressed. Lola had gotten her license six weeks earlier and "had like a total spastic meltdown" whenever she saw a cop car.

"What else do you like?" she asked, so naturally eager it was both disconcerting and endearing. I wondered what Danny had really thought of her, if he liked this or was put off.

"Reading," I said. "I like to read quite a bit."

"What are you reading?" Lola said.

"A couple things. One's called *The Perfect Failure.* It's about the Bay of Pigs."

"I don't really get the Bay of Pigs," she said.

I laughed a little—I hoped not meanly—and said, "Do you want to know?" and she nodded, though I suspected she would nod at anything. I explained some about Cuba and Castro and our fear of his allegiance to the Soviet Union. She listened smilingly. Bayard sat with his head tipped against the conveyer belt machine, his eyes closed, appearing to be napping.

"We lost the Bay of Pigs," she said, the words coming out somewhere between a question and a statement.

"Right. It was a failed attempt. We were underprepared. Kennedy inherited the mission from Eisenhower, but Kennedy was ambivalent, so he didn't put enough resources toward it."

"I like Kennedy," she said. Then: "Marilyn Monroe, you know?"

I laughed again. Lola was a silly girl, but I appreciated her attempt to have this conversation with me. She talked about how handsome John F. Kennedy Jr. was and didn't I think he was cute (*Sure*) and remember how he saluted his dad at his funeral, can you even imagine that (*Not really*), and I let her words wash over me, steady as the rain outside, until she tired of talking, which was not for a long time.

Finally, after our butts had grown numb and our legs had started cramping in every new position we shifted to, we collected our coats, ran past the dead bird in the stairwell, and marched knowingly back through the first floor. The rain was lighter now, barely a drizzle. We didn't hold hands on the way back, since it no longer was a mandate. The quiet had returned between us, and I was struck with sudden melancholy, wanting to say something before the day slipped away from us, but not sure what. I wondered how long my parents had been forced to wait. I wondered if we would soon hear shouts of my name. By the time we'd crossed back through the mall parking lot, the melancholy had taken hold, settling into my chest.

"Thanks," I said. "For taking me with you."

Lola told me, "Of course." She told me, "This was so much fun," and then stammered apologies about not meaning to say searches were fun, and I told her it was okay. She said, "Do you want to go to Lucien Daws's party tonight?"

Lucien Daws was a senior, a lanky tennis player who had run in the same general circle as Danny, though not really a friend. He had a reputation for throwing crazy parties. Stories circulated for days afterward about holes kicked in walls or glass coffee tables upended. I'd never been to one. I'd never been to any Franklin party.

"I don't do that kind of thing," I said.

Lola squinted at me. Then she started to laugh. "What does *that* mean?"

I felt embarrassed and a little exposed. I made a noise like a laugh, which wasn't a laugh. We were nearing the starting field by then, and I caught sight of the few straggling groups—some of the cops, a few of the Kiwanis breaking down their table. My father was leaning over, tying his shoe maybe. My mother stood with her hands deep in her pockets, looking at something, possibly scanning the horizon. But as we got closer, it was clear she was just staring off.

I had the sense of marching straight back into nothing. I was not ready to separate. From Lola Pepper, of all people. Which was how I came to tell her yes, okay, I would go with her to Lucien Daws's party, an answer that at once sent my stomach alight and filled me with dread. She squeezed my hand then and hopped like a bunny.

"Goody," she told me. "Oh, goody, goody, good."

When the three of us neared my parents, my mom nodded and stretched out a hand. My dad said simply, "Ready?"

I introduced them to Lola and Bayard and they nodded without recognition. Lola kissed me quickly on the cheek as she said goodbye. She held her pinkie and thumb to her mouth and ear. *I'll call you,* she mouthed.

"How long have you been waiting?" I asked my parents.

They told me twenty minutes, maybe a half-hour. I looked at their faces when they said this. Nothing. This was how it always had been between us, me the responsible one, requiring little thought and even less worry. Which worked, in the sense that they'd never been right up on top of me and I was left to do whatever I wanted. But still.

"We got really lost," I lied.

My dad's face blinked awake, if only for a second. "Where?" he said.

"I don't know. If I knew, we wouldn't have been lost."

My mother made a squeaky sound. I felt bad for my tone; this, a crappy time to pick a fight. They looked wrung out—damp hair, chapped red hands, faces droopy as bloodhounds'—the way they always did after searches.

"Somewhere by the factory," I said. My dad put a hand on my head, nodding. He said he was glad I made it back before dark. "Where's David?" he said, just now noticing his absence, as if maybe I'd lost him by the factory too.

I shrugged, then told them, "He wasn't feeling well. I'm going to his place tonight." The lie came without forethought, from an instinct not to reveal anything that might tip them toward needless poking and probing. I mostly liked the expanses between us, the imbalanced balance. It seemed easiest just to keep everything as much the same as possible.

Had we found anything, my mother wanted to know. I told her no.

"That's okay," my dad said unconvincingly.

When I took my mother's hand it was cold and stiff, and I squeezed, trying to thaw it while we walked toward the car, but by some trick of thermodynamics, the opposite occurred, and instead my hand chilled in hers.

9.

The main precept of chaos theory is that any system which may appear random and free-willed from one perspective, when viewed more closely, actually falls within a completely deterministic and predictable pattern. Lucien Daws's party *was* chaos theory. As we walked through the front door, assaulted by the smell of sweat and beer and cigarette and pot smoke, the droning bass of a stereo system turned up so loud it made the walls pulse, the crush of bodies (a literal crush—people had to hold their plastic beer cups above their heads to get through the front hallway), I felt an almost swooning regret. I was convinced I might pass out right there, so forceful was the realization of my mistake. Lola was already pressing her way through the crowd, pulling me along as I strategized the best way to get her to take me home. Offer to let her paw through Danny's room? Make myself cry? Both?

All social convention was off. People elbowed each other out of the way, toes got stepped on, girls were dressed as if it were summertime, in short skirts with tight tube tops or halters. A boy I'd never seen before pushed against me from behind. When I turned around, his shiny face was inches from mine and I felt myself heating inside my pea coat. I was simultaneously totally overdressed and underdressed in my jacket, T-shirt, and heavy jeans. Within seconds someone had spilled beer on me and then roughly, drunkenly apologized. It was a girl I recognized from PE, her bleary eyes scanning my face for a long time.

The kitchen was even more crowded, if possible, than the hallway. The keg sat in one corner, and there wasn't so much a line of people waiting to get to it as a throbbing, impatient amoeba. Someone stepped on the back of my shoe, giving me a flat tire. I teetered in the crowd as I stood on one foot, trying to slip it back on. "You okay?" Lola said, putting a steady hand on my shoulder. Lola too wore a strappy tank top that highlighted her small but nipply boobs and her collarbone full of additional freckles.

"Who *are* all these people?" I had to shout to be heard over the music.

"I *know*," Lola said, but her voice was filled with the wrong emotion. Excitement rather than bewilderment.

As we neared the keg, which sat in a long, shallow pool of spilled beer, Lola yelled "Two! Two!" and held her fingers in a peace sign to the zitty boy who was filling red and yellow cups. When we finally got ours, she nudged her cup against mine and yelled "Cheers" before taking a long, deep gulp. We fought our way back through the crowd, which collectively scowled at us—for going against the flow of traffic or for having achieved the goal that still eluded them, it wasn't entirely clear—and only reluctantly stepped out of our way.

Lola seemed to have the schematic map of Lucien Daws's house memorized, as she swiftly navigated through a new hallway and more ribbons of people, and then through a back den where a huddle of guys watched a wall-sized television displaying huge, pixelated dirt-bike racers going round a dusty track, and finally out the back sliding doors to a concrete patio and a nearly endless expanse of dark lawn. There were plenty of people milling around out there, but the cold had kept most inside. And even though there was a JV football player shouting from one of the swings of the old metal swing set, and a couple making out loudly on one of the patio lawn chairs, and a group of guys standing around a woodpile talking about setting fire to it, compared to inside, it was nearly relaxing.

"Drink up," Lola said before taking another long guzzle of her beer. A foam mustache sat on her lip. Her cup was almost empty already. I stared into mine. I'd drunk beer twice, both times when Danny had snuck Dad's bottles from the fridge and brought them upstairs, both times just a few sips because it'd tasted bitter like a stomachache. Since I'd started high school, our parents had taken to letting us drink wine on vacations. The last time had been the winter before, when we'd stayed in a condo in Florida, my mom making pizzas in the gritty-floored kitchenette as my dad poured each of us a glass of white wine. It tasted fermented but sweet, and I remember feeling mostly tired and saying "Beezle" when a black-shelled beetle skittered across the condo floor. "You're drunk," my mother said, laughing, and for the rest of the trip someone would say *Beezle* and everyone would laugh, because we were like that on vacation—easily prone to amusement, lighthearted, inclined toward in jokes.

I drank some of my beer. It tasted horrible, like something you'd swallow on a dare. Lola laughed at the face I made. She told me it was an acquired taste.

"Lydia. Flippin'. Pasternak," someone shouted from the dark of the lawn. Drunk people, I realized, took readily to shouting. It was Dawnelle Ryan, one of Danny's old, fleeting girlfriends, bounding across the lawn toward us, pushing her long brown hair out of her face over and over again as if she were trying unsuccessfully to get a strand of it out of her mouth. "Holy shit. What are you doing here?"

Dawnelle had spent last Thanksgiving with us, since her parents let her stay home while they visited a sick aunt. "Lymphatic cancer," Dawnelle announced matter-of-factly at our table. "She had a tumor on the side of her neck the size of a damn fist." She held her own fist to her neck. Her father was in sanitation, and she peppered dinner with stories of weird things people threw away. Complete dinette sets. Full refrigerators. Framed and matted art. Her father once thought he'd found an original Giacometti. He hadn't, "but it was a damn good copy." My parents kept exchanging glances at the swearing. Danny didn't even seem to be listening. I found Dawnelle fascinating, mostly because she was louder than any of his other girlfriends and her boobs were so big that they rested on the table while she ate.

Now she was right up on top of me, her breath sour and hoppy from the beer. "How *are* you?" she said, and then suddenly touched my face. It was very strange to have her touch my face. Her hand was damp, and I wasn't sure what to do.

"Fine," I said.

"What's a nice girl like you doing in a place like this?" She laughed at her own joke and then paused, and I was unsure if I was supposed to really answer. I drank more of my beer. It was slightly easier if I tried not to breathe through my nose while doing it. Dawnelle stared at me smilingly. She asked the standard questions about how my parents were doing, if we had any news.

"Okay, this is going to sound completely silly," she said, and then told a story about one of Danny's hooded sweatshirts she still had—he let her keep it, she clarified; she's not some crazy stalker—and how she'd done this "like Buddhist" ritual to it with sage and a smudge stick that she'd read about in a book, and it was meant to protect Danny, and she'd gotten a really good vibe from it so she thought we were going to get some good news soon. "I really, really think so," she said, her face so close to mine it seemed like we were going to kiss.

"Thank you," I said dumbly. "That's nice." And it was, in a sense. Better than her coming up to me and crying.

She and Lola talked about Peter Cohagen, who was dating Dawnelle's best friend and who Lola heard had mono. I wasn't sure I could identify Peter Cohagen in a lineup. I drank. Soon Dawnelle told us she'd see us later and bounded back onto the lawn. Lola offered to get us more beer. I had nearly my whole cup left and Lola said I couldn't just sip all night. "You ever do shots?" she asked, and I told her no. "Well, it's like shots," she said. "You just have to open your throat and let it go down. You can't think about it."

I tried drinking it in bigger and bigger gulps, which I found wretched, but Lola stood next to me saying silly things like "Atta girl," and "There you go," and I felt an almost laughable pressure not to disappoint her. I thought of those mindless chumps in the movies they made us watch in health class, the kid who let his friends talk him into PCP, only then to jump off a roof thinking he could fly, the girl who smoked pot and accidentally shot her sister. And already, even before my first cup was empty, I could feel the first hints of drunkenness with its hazy remove, as if a soggy netting had been laid over my skull. It was not a bad feeling.

When Lola headed back to the kitchen for refills, I found an empty patio chair, the braided plastic cold and taut through my pants. Positioned along the clear path between the backyard and the keg, I could see how the disorder that had so panicked me was slowly giving way now to clearer patterns: people were going either to or from the keg, looking for a place to sit, or searching for a familiar face and giving loud shouts of discovery: *HABER! What up? . . . Brenda! BREN!* There was an almost ritualistic moment of exclamation when someone stepped outside: *Damn* or *Shit*, followed by a variation on *It's cold out here.* Nearly every guy wore a baseball cap. Nearly every girl had goose bumps along her bare arms. In almost any given moment, you could hear someone proclaiming how fucking drunk they were.

A near-constant stream of Danny's friends stumbled upon me and voiced their surprise or delight or confusion at my appearance here. Gregory Baron kept calling me Linda. Kent Newman offered to get me a beer and didn't seem to understand when I tried to explain about Lola. "I can get her one too," he told me. Melanie St. John told a long story through half-closed eyes about the compass she found on the search today and how she really thought it meant something. "Danny wouldn't even know how to work a compass," I said with rare frankness, and to my surprise, Melanie laughed. Everyone was drunk, which grew more and more endearing, since it seemed to steer people away from sentimental and more toward slightly careless and friendly instead.

"Look who I found," Lola said upon her return, her arm laced through Tip Reynolds's. She was grinning so broadly it was as if Tip were the Queen of England.

"Holy shit," he said. "I had to see it to believe it." He held two cups of beer, and he did a strange curtsy-type thing as he handed me one. "What's up, Bluebird?" he asked.

The nickname threw me, in both its overfamiliarity and its nonsensicality. I was no bluebird. I didn't even have blue eyes. The consumption of alcohol, I was beginning to realize, meant that all bets were off. In the final, waning moments of my own sobriety, I remember thinking there was something both exhilarating and awful about that. From a purely sociological perspective, I was curious about what might be discovered in this sudden funhouse of human behavior. But also I had one last urge to run away and seek shelter beneath the sheets of my bed or on the nappy carpet of David Nelson's den or even on the couch as my dad flipped mindlessly through the full array of channels.

There were no more empty chairs, so Tip and Lola sat on the concrete in front of me. Lola sidled up so close to him, she was practically in his lap. Tip looked funny trying to sit Indian-style, given his bulk; his knees bent barely at all. He reminded me of a beanbag chair. Lola told a loud, rambling story about the undercover report they did on the news about how dirty the bedspreads were in local hotels. I drank my beer more assuredly now. Out of necessity, I fashioned a system of holding my breath and counting down as I swallowed, making it a test. If I could drink for three counts, the next time I would try five.

"Semen," Lola was saying. "Vomit. Blood."

Tip asked how I was doing, if the search had turned up anything. He said that all things considered, you know, my folks looked pretty good that morning. "We found a dead bird," I said, and let Lola tell the story of the factory. Tip referred to Bayard as "the French fag" and Lola scolded him, but in a joking voice. She was draped against him, her shoulder pressed against one of his beefy arms, one of her legs hooked around one of his, her hands dangling in his lap, as if she were trying to weave herself, pretzel-like, into him. I felt a wave of contempt for Lola right then, the mindless, unapologetic way she seemed to devote herself to the attention of boys. She and Tip were chuckling about something, I wasn't sure what. The disgust morphed loosely into: envy, annoyance, fascination, and a hopeless certainty that I would never be capable of whatever guilelessness or wiles or bravery made Lola Pepper Lola Pepper.

By the end of my second beer, I could swallow for a count of seven. My throat grew thick and gummy. My fingers started to feel far away. I was tingly.

The group around the woodpile passed a joint, the smell wafting onto the patio. One of the guys was coughing so hard he was doubled over as his friends either ignored him or laughed. People made out in dark corners of the lawn. A particularly bold couple was pressed against a tree trunk just north of me, the girl's shirt practically up around her neck, one of her hands slipping down into the back of the boy's pants.

"Look at them." I pointed. Lola acted aghast. Tip said Tracy Weller was a slut. I laughed. I wasn't sure why I was laughing, but I was laughing. Already the beer was making me feel unbound, loosened from the harness of self. I had the urge to shout "Bleh!" or "Hah!" I wanted to wave my hands in the air. I wanted to be tickled so hard I might pee. Almost instantly, I loved being drunk. I still do. The prospect of it is dangerously seductive, much more so than the pot or acid all my roommates grew so enamored of in college. Those drugs, the ones that steered you more deeply into yourself, held no appeal to me. Drinking, though, in the way it made me foggy and loose-limbed and slightly dim, was a revelation. A blessed relief.

We sat out there for a long time, Tip going inside to refill our cups every so often, coming back with all three clasped together in his huge hands, as if he were our waiter. "Your brother," he said at one point, "tried walking across that last year." He pointed to the top bar of the swing set. "Climbed up there from the slide and tried balancing for a long time, finally made it a few steps before falling on his fucking head. Could've broke his neck, the bastard. But then he jumped right up, like one of those gymnasts, his arms up over his head, like it didn't even hurt him, except his face was all bloody and muddy."

"You're a poet," I said. "And you don't even know it."

On the swing set now, three girls sat spread-legged, butt to crotch at the top of the slide, trying unsuccessfully to come down together; they were too wide and stuck. They did a lot of squealing. It was so easy to picture Danny here, I could almost taste him—salty, tough, sinewy. I could feel him in the back of my jaw. I remembered the night Tip was talking about, or the next morning at least—Danny sitting at the kitchen table, his forehead and cheek scraped a rashy red, spots of pus leaking from barely formed scabs. He fell down, he told my parents bluntly. They'd looked worried but somehow knowing and conspiratorial too, in the way they always were with him, nothing ever really condemned.

"That's what made him such a good defensive end," Tip said. "Un-fucking-breakable."

I didn't want to talk about Danny. I was feeling good. "You know what I think about football?" I said loudly. "You know?"

"No, what?" Tip said. Lola was watching me with her regular bright-eyed expression, ever hopeful.

"One word," I said. "Homoeroticism."

Tip squinted at me. Lola put her hand to her mouth.

"An excuse for boys to touch boys. An all-male environment that condones a level of physical contact that borders on the erotic." I laughed. Lola laughed too, but in a nervous way. I could tell that this wasn't necessarily the best idea, but the drunkenness propelled me forward. Even that first time, I could see how it made for a good excuse. "Like a fraternity. Like a monastery," I said.

"Monks?" Tip said. "You're saying monks are homos?"

"No, not necessarily. But maybe some men are drawn to monkhood because of a need to repress and fulfill unspeakable urges."

I went on for a while about a monk's vow of chastity. I compared that to football's bullying heterosexuality. I think I said something about fraternity gang rape. I talked and talked. I was warm-cheeked and emboldened. I could feel my eyeballs.

"So now we're rapists?" Tip said, two deep lines creasing his brow. Lola was still at it with the nervous laugh.

"No, no, you don't get it." I tried explaining it more, though I started losing my train of thought. I was on something about the movie I'd seen in social studies the year before about the African clan whose men would take monthlong retreats together when Tip broke in with, "You're crazy, Pasternak. You're one of those people who knows so much stuff, it makes them crazy."

He was smiling at me, but his brow was still tightly knit and I saw something of a glare in his eyes. It was a shade of the old Tip, the one who held my fridge door closed with one broad hand when I tried to get a pop out. I glimpsed quickly how I may have gotten careless and overly familiar, saw the way things could go wrong between us. It gave me that same uneasy feeling I used to get in conversations with Danny, when he would turn red-faced, sure that some comment or offhand remark was intended to make fun of him. It was still early enough in the night—I was still more or less in control of my faculties—that I was able to right things, socking Tip lightly in the arm, saying simply, distractingly, "I've come to like beer."

This made him laugh. Lola stroked his shoulder like he was her pet. He was shaking his head, looking openmouthed at me like *Where did I find this one?*

Later, in the bathroom, I peed longer than I'd ever peed before. My breathing was loud and strange, almost panting. I was sweaty, hot from the contrast between outside and in. There was no toilet paper. In the bathtub there was one red shoe. "One red shoe," I said out loud, which seemed funny. There was no hand soap. The hand towel lay crumpled and dirty on the floor. I wiped my hands along my jeans. I stared for a long time in the mirror at my pores—how had I never noticed before they were so huge?—and at my red splotchy face.

I let the crowd bandy me about in the hallway. They were an ocean of people, elbows, earrings, fingernails, and I tried to make myself rubbery and soft for when they knocked into me. Someone said my name; I couldn't tell who. The carpet felt spongy beneath me. A girl said, "Are you okay?" and I told her I was fine. She put a hand on the small of my back, which seemed nice, and I leaned a little back into it. "Whoa, girl," she said.

The rest of the party passed in a blur. We kept drinking. Aside from the brief hiccup, Tip seemed to have anointed himself, alongside Lola, as my steward and protector. He led me at some point into the kitchen, where I witnessed my first beer bong, Tip guzzling an endless amount of beer through a giant-sized funnel, most of it frothing out of his mouth like a rabid dog. Lola lay across the den coffee table late in the night and let a freshman drink tequila out of her belly button. The freshman followed her around for what seemed like hours after that. A war movie played on the huge TV and everyone cheered whenever someone got blown up. And it all made sense to me in the sloppy, hazy way alcohol made sense of things. I could see why Danny loved this life, why this or a rough equivalent of this in some other parentless house was where Franklin students flocked every weekend. It was so absent, so free of weight or heft—it was life as meringue pie, life as whipping cream.

We tried to play some euchre, but the rules made little sense to me, even after they were explained a few times. "You're smart," Tip kept saying. "You'll catch on." He and I were a team, and he had to keep reminding me which suit was trump and how jack was higher than queen. All the people waiting to play huddled behind us, some looking at my cards and giving me advice during my turn, since I kept holding up the game, staring foggily at my hand, unsure what to put down. Tip took to leaning across the table to peek at my hand and advise. I was too swimmy and cotton-headed to care how poorly I was doing. It was nice being stupid, the way it made people take care of me.

For a while Lola fell asleep on one of the couches, her tank top riding up and exposing the pale, blotched skin (she literally had freckles *everywhere*) of her belly. Some of her eye makeup had started to run, black smudges dotting the crescents beneath her eyes, making her look interesting, like she had a story to tell. When she woke up, she was cranky and disoriented, blinking and blinking like a child. She wanted to go.

It was not until those very last moments, as we were heading out the door and down the front steps, that the beer began churning in my stomach and an acidic gas rose up my throat and dizzied me. Within seconds of our departure, I was bent over in the grass, sick on my coat and the tips of my shoes and all over some sort of shrubbery that the Daws family had pruned so severely it looked to have been left for dead.

Tip held me up in the backseat as Lola drove us home. My throat burned and the car smelled of vomit. The front windows were rolled all the way down, the air freezing. Lola stomped hard on the gas and the brake, making our bodies shudder regularly, but Tip braced me against him. It reminded me of the roller coasters that locked you in by a harness around your shoulders.

Lola was saying sorry for letting me drink so much. Tip was saying, "Easy, easy," about her driving. "Red light!" he had to yell once. We pulled over once for me to throw up out the side door. My ears rang from the music still.

"Are your parents going to kill you?" Lola said, and I knew they would be long asleep, having assumed David and I were up late reading about Namibia or quizzing each other on the physics of Arctic ice floes.

"I don't know," I said. "Are *your* parents going to kill *you*?" I felt like I was very funny. In spite of my sick, I felt proud of myself; for what, I didn't exactly know. Surviving without David Nelson? Going to a party? Escaping myself for some number of hours? It was no matter. I was filled with a drunken satisfaction. The night had offered me possibility that there could maybe be a life here in the *after*, something beyond just waiting for Danny to come home. What that something was exactly, I had no clear inkling. But that was no matter. The possibility of possibility—it was enough.

Tip and Lola walked me up the stairs of my front porch, but I kept telling them I was okay now, okay, okay, okay. Tip let go only after I, with considerable effort, fit my key in the lock and pushed open the door. Lola patted my head. We all said our goodbyes in loud stage whispers.

My head was buzzing as I fell into bed, still in my clothes. I had managed to rummage a bowl from the kitchen cabinets and rest it next to the bed, though it would come to no use. Yes, the room spun, and yes, my stomach lurched, but only for brief moments, because for once sleep came like an anvil, heavy and sudden and relievedly free of thought.

It was the desk drawers that woke me, slamming open and closed. I opened my eyes to thick darkness, the middle of the night still, though it felt like I'd been sleeping for days. My head pounded like a drum; swallowing felt impossible, my mouth dry and pasty, tasting like garbage. My ribs hurt. It took a moment to place the noise, the heavy footsteps and slamming drawers, the grunting. From nearby.

From Danny's room.

I jumped out of bed, far more quickly than I thought possible, and ran into the hall, nearly tripping over Olivia, who was sniffing the air in Danny's doorway. The furious motion, the stooped figure—it was not Danny. It was my father, moving through the room like a pre–*Homo sapiens*, his back bent, his head and arms dangling intently as he pawed through the desk drawers, throwing pens and blank pads of paper and crumpled receipts on the floor, banging impotently on the keyboard of the computer. The trash had been strewn from the plastic can, the trophies knocked from the bookshelf, the mattress pulled off its axis, now drooping crookedly on the floor, large sections of box spring exposed.

I throbbed. My whole body was throbbing.

"Daddy?" I said, and he looked at me wildly, his chest heaving. For a moment he said nothing, his face doing a bizarre curdle, and

I feared he could smell my drunkenness or he was seeing the alcohol rising off me in misty, vaporous plumes. I wondered if he would chastise me, an idea that both horrified and thrilled me. But the sound out of his mouth was like nothing I'd heard from him before, not even after that first night Danny did not return and the next morning and then the night again, when it was clear something had gone terribly wrong. It was a throaty hum of a noise, high-pitched and childish-sounding. No, dog-sounding. He was whimpering. He looked around the room as if he'd just arrived to find it this way, staring disbelievingly at the posters that now hung askew, the blankets torn from the bed, the garbage littering the floor. His eyes pooled with moisture.

I steadied myself against the doorframe. I felt like I could fall over.

For a long time we stayed frozen like that, my father staring at me, me clutching the doorway to stabilize myself. For years I would replay the moment in my mind, one of my father's cheeks still bearing the red imprint of his pillowcase, his hair mussed into a sparse crown, an undone button of his pajamas exposing his curly white stomach hair. He blinked at me, as if he would never look away. It had been so long since he'd looked at me. It seemed like years since he'd softly pinched my ear and called me Chicken for my skinny legs. Since he'd asked what you got when you crossed a cheetah and a hamburger.

"What is this?" my father said, the words crackling, his expression naked and pleading, as if I were someone who knew the answer and, *dear god*, could I please just stop holding out on him. I opened my mouth to speak. The pull cord on Danny's blinds swung back and forth. The other dogs made their way up the stairs, the cockroach-like skittering of their nails on the wood growing louder and louder. My mother had to be awake now too, maybe lying in her bed, studying the dark ceiling.

I made a noise, a dizzy, drunken, wordless sound. It was all I had, a low sort of growl. And that was the moment I really knew—the sick, sudden, ugly moment—how incapable we were, how impotent and inconsolable, how limited our reach. Grief had already, in a few short months, mined an impassable trench between us. We were—like a boy buried in a ditch or bloated in salty ocean water or starved in some sadist's basement—beyond rescue.

A New Language

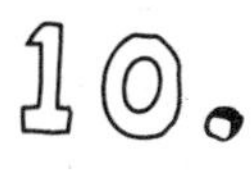

Winter came early. The first big snow fell in the second week of October, then a huge storm hit days before Thanksgiving, three and a half feet covering the town with an eerie blankness and adding an extra two snow days to vacation, which seemed to make everyone giddy to the point of feverish, though the effect on our household more resembled a quarantine. Drifts blockaded our front door for days, until I finally chiseled away at the hard-packed, icy barricade. The search was canceled that Saturday and never really started up again in earnest. By December only the hardiest volunteers still showed up, and even those petered out over the holidays and the freezing January rains. Kirk Donovan stopped coming over. The librarian took down the wall-sized card from the school library; the administration dismantled the shrine in the hallway. I expected at least a brief outrage, cheerleaders tearing at their clothing or orchestrating a few well-positioned bawling fits; there was nothing.

David Nelson and I halfway reconciled by the time winter semester started, our interactions characterized by his refusal to use a contraction—"I could have called you earlier but I did not want to bother you." "I do not think that it is a good idea to study together in your room anymore." "I am glad that we are talking again. It is nice to be talking with you"—which made him seem even more bookish and robotic than usual. There was something both comforting and homesicky about being with him, a same-but-different quality that made me sometimes miss him even when he was right in front of me. He'd taken up with one of the Dungeons and Dragons freaks, Adam Deselets, and his speech was now peppered with references to feats and spells and foes. He was a first-level paladin. I nodded when he told me such things, asking, "Is that good or bad?" to which he'd answer that he was base class but with XPs he would be able to get to prestige. It was like listening to a small child who had made-up words for everything.

There were times I caught him staring at me and I would wonder, is this different from before? Was the look in his eyes—a look that seemed altogether more wistful and more probing—new, or was I just imagining things? We'd be in the middle of a discussion about whether or not Mr. Hollingham had false teeth or about the presidential election in Haiti, and I would see him, cloudy-eyed but intent, his Adam's apple bobbing earnestly, staring as if he were seeing me for the first time—or maybe the last—and things between us would tilt uncomfortably. I'd find myself going cold inside, brittle and impatient and wanting to say, "You're an idiot." I was unforgiving in the way I would later be unforgiving of boyfriends who talked to me in baby voices or seemed too easy with their gifts or praise. Starting with David Nelson, any visible display of longing stopped me cold. Such displays always felt deceptively insistent, cloaking a desire to split me open and see inside. I didn't want to be split open. I didn't want my insides seen.

And so it was that Lola Pepper became my closest approximation to a best friend, though it was a relationship predicated on a mutual agreement to pretend our differences didn't exist or at least didn't bother us. Never did we have the sort of relationship where things could be taken for granted or sentences could be finished for each other or we could entirely relax. To her credit, she was unfailingly persistent (it was hard to be lonely with Lola Pepper around) and largely good company, as she was almost always in a light, fluffy mood. Her house had an otherworldly quality to it, mainly due to her walk-in closet full of toys she'd never relinquished from childhood: Cabbage Patch dolls, Chutes and Ladders, Candyland. She would ask, "Have you ever played Hungry Hungry Hippos? It's hilarious" as she unearthed the box from the bottom of a stack. She didn't much seem to care about winning or losing, happy to bash the lever that controlled the mouth of her purple hippo as the marbles spun around the board. I would do the same with my green hippo, and such was the way we'd let minutes slide easily between us.

When she first started coming over, I was irritated by the reverent way she insisted on tiptoeing through Danny's room (*Please, can I just peek in there for a minute?*), gingerly touching old swim goggles or his pillowcase. She'd never been in there when Danny was still around; now she treated it like the end of a long pilgrimage. "Come on," I'd say, standing in the doorway. "Let's see if there's ice cream downstairs." Or "I have something to show you" (I didn't). Or "Let's watch something stupid on TV." It was always easy to find something stupid on TV. Lola was as beguiled by talk shows where hosts harangued lovesick guests as she was by infomercials selling get-rich real estate schemes as by cartoons where buildings morphed into cars, cars into superheroes.

It was mostly nice having her around, for the sake of the noise and the way she obliviously shook things up, especially with my parents. Noticing my dad watching golf, she fired off a whole round of inquiries about Greg Norman versus Steve Elkington and if John Daly was ever going to be consistent. Which did he think had been a more competitive course this year, the Ryder or the U.S. Open? With my mom, Lola acted as if a vet tech were akin to a rare form of celebrity. *Did you ever treat a gecko? Have you ever seen a tumor removed from a guinea pig? How do you get a gerbil unstuck from its Habitrail?*

Sometimes my father just stared sleepily as she rat-a-tatted away, as if she were a human alarm clock he did not know how to silence. Often her conversations with my mother were frenetic and garbled, each of them interrupting the other, nobody listening. But other times I'd be surprised. My mother, it turned out, had in fact used a makeshift concoction of tongue depressors and Vaseline to loosen a gerbil from its Habitrail. My father favored Greg Norman over nearly everyone else.

One night my mom came into my room after Lola had left, coming behind my desk chair and grabbing both of my shoulders. The unexpectedness of the contact made me flinch a little beneath her. She didn't seem to notice. "Such a nice girl," she said. "That's really something, the flag team. A flag girl."

I had no idea how to respond. I didn't find it something at all, Lola's flag-girl status. I found it one of the many *in spite of*s of our friendship. But I knew what my mom meant. She meant I'd finally arrived, finally friends with someone involved in an extracurricular not centrally concerned with world history or geopolitics. And her enthusiasm was so irritating, it was almost enough for me to stop inviting Lola over. Except watching Lola flitting around my parents, undaunted—not even seeming to realize she should be daunted—and creating such easy, effortless access points with them felt very familiar to me, very much like Danny was back, or at least a part of him was, the part that softened things between everyone and made it, for all his failings, that much more livable here.

But of course he wasn't back. Danny stayed gone. Through the freeze and the snow and the whitewashed weeks of winter, there was still no sign of him. In the first days after my dad tore his room apart, I went in and tried to put everything back together, though the room took on a strange, artificial quality after that. The bed was made too neatly, the papers and pencils centered too squarely on the desk. When I tried to mess them up, setting magazines and notepads at odd angles on top of each other, that too felt wrong. Even the garbage, placed piece by piece back into the receptacle next to his desk, seemed somehow showy and fake now.

His toothbrush still sat in the holder in the upstairs bathroom. Sometimes I pressed my fingers to the hardened bristles, sometimes my whole palm; one time I brushed with it, out of curiosity and antsiness, though it quickly felt like a betrayal and I stood whispering *Sorry, sorry* to no one as I rinsed out the paste and hurried it back to its metal rung. One of his tube socks ended up in a dryer full of my clothing. When I found it in my basket, the toes a dingy gray, the stripes along the cuff a faded green, I took it to be some sort of sign and spent the next couple days in high-alert mode, anxious each time the phone rang, hotly anticipating the arrival of the mail. It turned out not to be a sign, of course, just a stray sock that had been wedged in the deep recesses of the washing machine, pulled free finally by a zipper of my jeans or a collar of my shirt.

A new set of unspoken rules solidified around our household, like eating solitary dinners over our laps on the couch; or choosing silence over the stilted chitchat about *how was your day, some weather we're having, that's quite a sandwich*; or building stack after stack of magazines in the front hall, the ones that kept coming in his name—*Sports Illustrated*, *Maxim*, *Hot Rod*—as if preparing the bounty that would greet him when he finally came back through the front door.

I still lay awake for hours most nights. I fell asleep and woke with the same dull stomachache. There were days I easily mixed up the republics of Malawi and Burundi, or forgot the name of the South African president before Mandela, or grew convinced that *Uruguay* was spelled with one less *u* and an additional *a*. There were other days, though, when the empty room next to mine felt just that, empty, rather than lacking someone, or when the ashtrays got dumped out and the air would smell of something temporary and new like the bananas on the kitchen counter or the pulpy pages of the newspaper, or when an offhand moment on television—a home video clip of a cat with its head inside a yogurt container, a newscaster flubbing the name of a nearby town (he twice called Farmington Heights Harmington Fights)—caused more than one of us to chuckle aloud together.

And those days were okay. Just fine, really.

I still saw Chuck. Our sessions had taken on the tinge of White House press briefings, his goal to goad me with questions, my goal to reveal as little as possible while giving the appearance I was saying something. We talked ploddingly about school, my parents, David Nelson, Danny.

"So you went to a basketball game?" he said during one session, an eyebrow raised. He liked to turn everything into something. "That doesn't seem like something you would have done a few months ago. Do you see your interest in sports now as a way to stay connected to Danny?"

"I was never connected to Danny," I said, which was an exaggeration, the sort I was prone to in here. Talking in absolutes seemed the best way to subvert the conversation into nothingness.

"Did you go with Lola?" Chuck had a way of elongating the *o* in Lola's name, as if deriving sensual pleasure from the word. It was creepy.

"Lola's on the flag team. She can't go to games. She's *performing.*" I thought of their elaborate turquoise-sequined costumes, which, without exception, clung to all of them in the least flattering of places, the girls looking wide-hipped and pregnant, Bayard's pantsuit version making him look like an iridescent string bean. I pictured the way they all tried to manipulate the unwieldy flags, and the horselike dance steps that one or more were always stomping slightly offbeat. Lola looked so proud when she was performing, her smile huge and toothy, her freckles glowing. And it made me love/hate her, the way she had no clue of what idiots they were making of themselves, her natural capacity for oblivious happiness.

"Then who did you go with?" Chuck said. The half-open venetian blinds showed white stripes of sky, the snow having long bleached out all the blue.

"Whom?" I said.

Chuck gave a little laugh. He always did that when I corrected him.

"Okay, with *whom* did you go?" he said, making a production out of the word.

"Tip and those guys," I said, trying to sound casual.

"You don't say?" Again with the raised eyebrow. "So Danny's friends." Chuck swiveled in his chair. It made a low, squealing sound like it needed to be oiled. *Wickee, wickee, wickee.*

"They're just guys," I said.

"Do you see any significance to your association with these *particular* guys?"

Association made it sound like we were some sort of crime syndicate. For someone who talked all day, Chuck often seemed careless with his words.

I told him no. I told him it was nice to get out of the house but didn't mention that these *particular* guys had an ingenious system of smuggling in Pepsi bottles half filled with rum, which they passed around during the first half. Or that they talked of ridiculous things, like shoot-'em-up video games or hockey teams or race car drivers—topics that I had no entrée into, and therefore nothing was expected of me. I could just watch the monotony on the court that had everyone else so worked up, which I found almost meditatively lulling, the ball bouncing down the court and back, and down the court and back again, with the predictability of a metronome. These *particular* guys were so big, so physically big, sometimes I found them comical and clownish, like a completely different species. Tip's arms were thicker than my thighs, Lyle Walker's neck was like a fire hydrant, and I had a sense of such smallness, sitting amid them in the bleachers, especially after the rum started to seep in, a sense that was soothing rather than intimidating.

And yes, I saw significance in the fact that these were friends of my brother's. But not in the nostalgic way Chuck hoped; I didn't have a tender, soft-bellied story to tell about any remembrance or connection that these boys offered me. These were the same boys who six months earlier had snorted loudly when Danny said *Hot* as I walked past them in my kitchen, who might add, *Is that a stylish new pair of jeans?* for the easiest of laughs from my brother. Now these boys were apt to nod when I walked through the doors of the gym, to scoot aside to make a space for me as I climbed up the bleachers toward them, to pat me on the shoulder as I sat, calling me Pasternak, the same name they used to—and still did, in absentia—call Danny. How quick they'd been to accept me after just a couple more parties with Lola and a feigned interest in winter varsity sports.

"I used to think you were boring," Dale Myerson told me. It was a typical comment, delivered entirely without irony as I wordlessly drank from the spiked pop bottle and stared glassily at the sweaty, grunting basketball players, whose shoes squeaked loudly against the gym floor like a series of alarms.

It was not particularly edifying being with them. It was numbing and hazy and more than a little tedious. But still, I felt like wagging my finger at the Danny of my imagination, the Danny who hovered above these scenes, vaporous and smirky. *See there,* I wanted to say to him. *See me now?* It was as if I were suddenly ahead in the game, the one that'd been playing out between us for years, whose rules I'd never really understood, whose in-bounds and out-of-bounds had constantly shifted and blurred, the one that my brother had always been so handily, so effortlessly winning.

11.

It seemed we could go on like that all winter, in more or less a holding pattern, until one day the doorbell rang and Melissa Anne appeared on our doorstep. I didn't realize it was Melissa Anne immediately. In fact, she never formally introduced herself. But as soon as I opened the door—my father still at work, my mother asleep or otherwise spaced out in their room—I knew something was not right. The woman didn't have a hat, and her jacket looked like a slicker you'd wear in the more mundane months of April or September. Now the late January snow swirled behind her in white mini-tornados. Her ears were such a bright red, they looked as if they might snap off the sides of her head, and her lips were deeply chapped. She had a bad dye job, her hair a strange bluish black hue. It was hard to tell how old she was; she had a round face, so round, in fact, it gave her a babylike appearance, except for the deep lines beside her eyes and from her nose to her mouth.

"Oh!" she said when I opened the door, bringing her hand up to her chest as if I'd surprised her. Then: "The girl." Her eyes, jumpy in their sockets, darted quickly past me to the rest of the house.

"Can I help you?" I said. The cold air whooshed in.

"Hell-o," she said formally. "I've been meaning to see you for a while now. By you, I mean your family." She had a slow, breathy way of talking, as if she'd recently been let off a respirator. Her eyes scanned the outside of the house, the hallway behind me, the book in my hand: *The Virgin Queen*, an Elizabeth I biography.

"Yes?" I said, without particular patience. She'd interrupted my reading.

"Did you get my letters?" she said. My skin prickled at the nape of my neck. I was wearing only a sweatshirt and pajama pants. I wanted to call for my mother.

"What letters?" I feigned ignorance.

"Your brother is buried," she said, clasping her thin coat shut. Her hands were as red as her ears, the tips of her nails torn off unevenly, the edges ragged and violent-looking.

"Go away," I said. My voice sounded silly and girlish. I was whining.

"There are horizons of soil," Melissa Anne said. "Humus first and then topsoil and eluviation and subsoil and then, and then . . ." She stopped to think, chewing on her lip. She was staring at something at her feet, then something at mine, then something behind me. A flurry of ideas ran through my head—slam the door, slap her across the face, tell her she's insane—but I just stood there, listening. "Regolith," she finally said. "It is regolith before the bedrock." She was nodding.

"I'm closing the door," I said, even though I wasn't.

"He's in the topsoil. The good news is that he's only as deep as the topsoil. You need to find him. He's scared."

"Fuck you."

"Oh!" she said again, with the same surprised look that had greeted me. My words surprised us both. Tears sprang to my eyes from the cold. Her eyes settled fully on my face, as if just now seeing me. Something in her expression changed; it mellowed, as if the spark that had been igniting her were suddenly cooling.

"You thing," she said, "you poor thing." She held out a raggedy hand like she was going to touch me. I scooted back, my slippers shushing against the tiles, seeming suddenly very loud. She smiled at me then. Her front teeth were badly yellowed, her bottom ones overlapping, crowding messily on top of each other. Coupled with her round face, it gave her an ominous jack-o'-lantern look. "Such sadness," she said. "It is not even to do with your brother, is it?" Then: "It's just to do with you, isn't it?"

"What?" I said, though I'd heard her. She was beaming now, as if she'd just been crowned Miss Fairfield 1996. Her body buckled forward, not so much a fluid movement as a hiccup, as if she were trying to lurch into the house. I pictured her hands on me, her rancid breath in my nose. With just inches of space between us, she said, "You will always be like this." She said it simply, as if she were saying, "Winters will always be cold" or "Birds will always fly south."

She still smiled her Halloweeny smile. Then she pursed her lips, like she could kiss me. "Find him," she said, and I pushed the door into its jamb and screamed like a child: "Mom! Mommy!"

• • •

The police station workroom was numbingly antiseptic, a line of identical desks sitting in a neat row, large pale tiles lining the floor; the one chalkboard scribbled with *Perp* and *DWI* and *Drive-by* offered the only hint that this might be something other than a tax attorney's or actuary's office. The Fairfield cops didn't have a whole lot to do. Aside from missing kids, the most action Fairfield saw was teenagers with open containers and false burglar alarms. Two of the Danny posters hung on a bulletin board, between an announcement about the annual police auction and a reward poster for a lost German shepherd. Bessie was the dog's name, and it had watery brown eyes.

The chair I sat in reminded me of the chair in Chuck's office, unforgiving and hard. An officer I didn't recognize—*Reyes*, the coppery name tag over his badge said—hunted and pecked into his computer as I talked. My mom stood next to me, and I was embarrassed for the untucked back of her shirt, the funky smell of her breath.

"She said he was buried," I told Reyes.

"Did she give any specifics? Indicate that she had any part in the burying?"

"She said he was in the topsoil. She knew about all the layers of the soil. I don't really think she had any part in anything. She just seemed nuts." I told about the dyed hair and the teeth and the fingernails and the ears and the jacket. I didn't mention what she said about me.

"Was she in any way threatening?"

"No," I said. "She said he was scared."

My mom made a gulping noise then, like choking on her own saliva. Reyes looked at her. I didn't. She put her hand on my shoulder, and then, as I was repeating Melissa Anne's physical description, ran it roughly through the top of my hair, as if she were having a hard time controlling herself.

Eventually Reyes told us, "Thanks for coming in, you never know what will turn into a real lead, we'll certainly keep alert about this."

"That's it?" my mother said.

"There's not a lot else we can do now, Mrs. Pasternak," Reyes said. His eyes were brown and apologetic, like Bessie's.

"She came to our *home*!" my mother said, and Reyes went into a spiel about how the alleged Melissa Anne seemed neither a direct threat nor in violation of any law. We didn't even, he pointed out, have verification that this was in fact Melissa Anne.

"There's no law against knocking on people's doors and saying something upsetting." He added quickly, "Unfortunately." Then he looked at me. "I'm sorry this happened to you." It seemed wooden out of his mouth, something he'd been taught to say at a mandatory in-service about talking nicely to people who came into the station with inconsequential complaints.

During the car ride home, my mom kept patting my knee, asking if I was all right. All of a sudden, it seemed, she couldn't stop touching me. I made sounds, like *mmm*, to show I was okay, not wanting either to worry or to encourage her. It was a little suffocating, being in such an enclosed space and so much in her focus all of a sudden. I cracked my window even though it was frigid out. When my dad came home from work, he and my mom had a quiet conference in the living room, and I heard my mother stage-whispering her version of events: *crazy* and *woman* and *nothing*.

That night I lay in bed listening to the sounds of the house. Nighttime activated my senses. From only the slightest change in pitch, I could anticipate when the refrigerator was about to rev its motor into full hum or the furnace about to cycle a short blast of warm air. I could, from a floor away, hear the wheezy breathing of one of the sleeping dogs, or from several blocks, the rush of car tires against slick roads. Soon creaky footsteps came from my parents' room. I was used to their occasional trips to the bathroom, the low squeaks of faucets turned on, the sustained, airy gasp of a toilet flushing and refilling. But tonight someone walked the halls. From the weight of the footfalls, the pronounced thud of each step, I guessed my father. The sound grew louder and louder, as if heading this way. My parents never paced the house at night. When the noise finally stopped, I could sense someone right outside my door—not that I could hear breathing, just the electricity of another body nearby—and it put me on edge beneath my blankets, my toes tensing, a low whir in my ears.

When the door finally eased open, my dad's broad outline came clear. I watched him drooping against the doorframe, one hand and then the other moving through his hair, and I wondered if he was sleepwalking. Wondered too if he could see the whites of my eyes watching him. The very idea made me feel caught, made me quickly close them.

The footsteps continued toward my bed until I felt the weight of him at the foot of it. My mattress bowed easily beneath him—it was not a very good mattress—and my body listed slightly toward him. He made a strange, slobbery noise, something like the razzing sounds he used to make when we were little and he'd press his lips to our bellies and blow, he the tickle monster, Danny and I his howling victims.

He said my name now. At least I thought he said it. His voice was thready and whispering, just above a hush. I opened my eyes again. There he sat, slumped in on himself, his hair an unkempt plume from where his fingers had just been. He put a hand on my foot and lightly squeezed my ankle.

"Hi," I said quietly.

"Oof." It was a sudden noise, of alarm or maybe embarrassment, I couldn't tell. "Did I wake you?" he said.

"Mmm," I said noncommittally. It seemed shameful to admit I'd been up.

"We'll get her," he said.

It seemed odd and needlessly vengeful, the idea that we'd get Melissa Anne. I didn't really think she needed getting. I just wanted her not ever to come back. I recognized, though, he was just trying to be reassuring.

"I know," I said.

For a while he just sat there and I didn't know what to do, what to say. The birch tree in our backyard made soft cracking sounds from the weight of the snow on its branches. One of the dogs was awake downstairs, walking along the kitchen linoleum.

When he spoke, his voice was already different. "Okay," he said, more composed and Dad-like. More daytime. He patted my foot officiously, two quick taps. When he stood, his joints cracked, a low imitation of the birch branches. "Sleep tight, bed bugs bite," he said, a phrase he hadn't spoken in years. As he moved back toward the door—how long had he been in here? One minute? Ninety seconds?—I filled quickly with a sad, fretful version of nighttime, alone in the dark, creatures lurking under bed frames and behind closet doors. I felt suddenly years younger, and not in a good way.

Already he was in the hallway.

"Thanks," I said, wondering how long he would've stayed, how long he would have sat and held my foot, had I kept quiet.

Within days of Melissa Anne's appearance, my parents fired Howard and tracked down Denis Jimenez, a private investigator referred by one of my mom's old vet tech coworkers. The coworker had hired Denis to investigate her husband during their divorce, and by the time Denis was done, he'd uncovered tax fraud, a sometime girlfriend, and several marijuana plants growing in the soon-to-be-ex's new apartment. *Tenacious as a bulldog*, my mom's old coworker said of Denis Jimenez.

By Saturday he was at our kitchen table. My mother paged through her fat manila folder of notes and recited stories about everything from Danny's brief and early aptitude for painting to his love for Diet Pepsi to that girlfriend of his she found to be snobby (*You know,* she said, turning to Dad and me for help, *the one with the Polish name*). She flipped through Danny's baby books and his later photo albums. "Here," she told Denis. "Fifth-grade graduation." "His first swim meet." "After his driver's license exam."

At first Denis listened to her with the intent stare you'd expect from a private investigator, complete with notepad in hand, young assistant by his side. He and my mother took turns vying for the ashtray in the middle of the table. But as my mother drifted to the noncancerous mole Danny had had removed from the back of his neck two years earlier and the sprain in his ankle during sixth-grade gym and the funny way he dropped the *s* from *specific*, Denis began to sense, it seemed, that there easily could be no end to this. He started subtly, and then not so subtly, slapping his pad against his hand, clearing his throat, trying to ask questions. At one point as he began to speak, she held a hand in the air. Denis looked to my father for help, but my father had the glazed, faraway look that came so naturally to him when my mother was like this. None of this behavior was new, though in front of an audience of watchful strangers, I felt fresh shame.

"Mrs. Pasternak!" Denis finally said, almost yelling. "Can you show me the boy's room?"

We all trailed upstairs together, my mother in the lead, followed by Denis, his assistant, Dad, and me. As we crowded into Danny's room, my mother continued to talk (*Danny didn't have the arm to be quarterback, though that's what he always wanted. What boy doesn't want to be quarterback?*). Denis nosed through Danny's stuff with the tenderness and care of a bulldozer, pulling comic books off shelves and saying things like "Not much of a reader," pointing to the St. Pauli Girl poster on the wall and asking, "Big drinker, your son?" and even pawing through the dirty laundry basket still sitting in the back of the closet and commenting on the funk.

"You can wash this, you know," he said to my mother, the statement that finally quieted her. "If he'd been snatched out of this room, that'd be another issue. There might be evidence in here. But given the circumstances, no reason you can't clean these. Might help with the smell in here." My mother blanched. It wasn't clear if Denis was scolding or trying to be helpful; his tone seemed to fluctuate only between impatient and strident.

The assistant, Kimberly, smiled in our general direction. With her honeyed skin and blond-brown hair pinned back with several well-placed barrettes, she looked like the effortlessly pretty girls who appeared in the college catalogues that had already started coming in the mail for me. She wore a neatly collared short-sleeved shirt, her collarbone showing through the V neck. It was such a poised collarbone, so sharp and symmetrical, with a thin pearl necklace resting above it. I would never be a girl with such a nice collarbone. I couldn't even picture mine.

"I can meet you downstairs when I'm done," Denis said to my parents. An offer or an order, it was unclear, though none of us moved. I watched as he roughly fingered the contents of Danny's dresser, pawing through sweat socks and unfurling sweaters. He was not particularly attractive. He had deep-cocoa-colored skin rutted with the faintest hint of pockmarks at the cheeks and temples. His black mustache was spotty and looked to be a product of neglect rather than choice. His fingertips were yellowed, probably from the chain-smoking. A faded brown stain ran down the front of his shirt. But I already liked him for his unsentimental zeal. He was a one-man windstorm whipping through our stale little house.

Back at the kitchen table, Denis peppered us with questions—what kind of kid had Danny been, what did my parents fight with him about, what did I fight with him about, who were his friends, who did he confide in, was he a partier, did he display common sense, where were his favorite hangouts, what rules did he most commonly break, was he a virgin, what were his secrets? (Denis said he knew that was an oxymoronic question. I didn't point out that he was misusing *oxymoron.*)

My mother shuffled through her index cards. She answered the most basic questions with long, tangential monologues. My father maintained his dazed expression. Kimberly continued to smile at us, which seemed to be a key part of her job. Another part seemed to be jotting down notes. Her most important duty, though, appeared to be exchanging meaningful glances with Denis whenever one of us said anything apparently noteworthy, such as the mention of Danny's growth spurt or his dyslexia. They were constantly looking at each other, Kimberly and Denis, like a couple showily suppressing a secret.

My mother lit new cigarettes with the still-burning ember of her previous one. She fiddled with the pack, sliding it back and forth across the table. My father kept swallowing, the only noise he made; I could hear the saliva going down the back of his throat. It was not until Denis asked if Danny was into any hard drugs that my dad spoke: "This is my *son* you're talking about."

"Listen," Denis said, "I can understand the desire for someone in your situation to be protective. But that's not going to do any of us any good, and it's certainly not going to help me do my job." My father shook his head. Denis went on. "You know more than thirty percent of kids in suburban high schools admit to at least one occasion of cocaine use before graduation?"

My mom blew smoke out of her nose. She looked like she could cry, though she always looked like that now.

"He smoked pot," I said. "I don't think he did other stuff. All the jocks are paranoid about getting caught."

Both of my parents stared as if I'd just spun my head around or presented the Shroud of Turin. "I don't know for sure," I said. Then: "No, I pretty much do."

Denis nodded at me with a look that I would grow more used to in the coming months, but that first time it took me by surprise. I felt girlish and giggly, like I might have to jam a palm into my thigh to suppress escaping laughter. In general, Denis had a suspicious watchfulness about him, which could quickly leave you feeling exposed. Already, barely an hour into our first meeting, my parents bristled in their chairs, my mother worrying bits of paper to pulp, my father's face having morphed into a brow-heavy glare. But as Denis nodded at me, tipping his chin forward and curling his lip into a cagey smile, he made it seem that he was bringing me into the fold, conferring a certain undeniable power on me. For just a beat, his eyes brightened and things between us grew intimate and conspiratorial. I felt a warm heat rising through my chest.

As quickly as it had come, though, the expression disappeared. But the warmth lingered. I found myself clenching my teeth against a smile. Denis, in the meantime, moved on to more questions: was Danny more passive or aggressive, more stubborn or flexible, more of a thinker or an actor, more contemplative or impulsive? These were easy ones. I left them to my parents.

"Who are his enemies?" Denis asked.

"He didn't have enemies," my mother said quickly.

"Bernice," Denis said. "Do you mind if I call you Bernice? I don't think you're bullshitting me intentionally, but I sense some BS in that answer."

My mother made an *eek*ing noise. It seemed to come from her nose. The paper she was kneading was an old, yellowing copy of Danny's immunization record. *TB*, I could read upside down. *Measles, mumps, rubella.*

"Now you listen," my father said in a voice so quiet it drew us all forward in our seats. "Do not come into our house and make insinuations about our boy. I don't care how good you are—"

"Harris," Denis said, "I understand the difficulty—"

"That's Mr. Pasternak," my father said, and I felt so embarrassed for us.

"Mr. Pasternak," Denis said, his first attempt at a more cordial tone. "Believe me when I say I can imagine how difficult this is." He was talking slowly now. "But the only way I can help you find your boy is to take an utterly unflinching look at the situation. In some very preliminary poking around, I've heard your son could be a bit of a bully at times. Any truth to that?"

"Not that I know of," my father said.

"He was very popular," my mother said.

Denis looked at me, a flash again of that sly knowing.

"He pushed kids around sometimes," I said. "The nerds. He used to pick on my best friend. Well, the kid that used to be my best friend. He's not really my best friend anymore." I was stammering. "Danny shoved kids around sometimes. Gave them swirlies. Called them names. You know?"

My mother puffed on her cigarette as if it were an oxygen machine. My father shifted in his chair, the rubber bottoms of the legs braying against the floor.

"He wasn't the worst of them," I said. "There are meaner jocks. And I don't really think anyone he picked on was capable of revenge. It was mostly like the wimps."

Kimberly jotted down notes. Denis nodded at me. "Thank you, Lydia," he said, with heavy emphasis on the first word, an unmistakable *see there* tenor to his voice, as if he were just shy of holding a thumb to his nose, twiddling his fingers, and spitting a raspberry at my parents.

"You're welcome," I said, and already I was a little in love.

12.

Denis was there all the time in the beginning, asking additional questions, searching the files of Danny's computer, examining the meager contents of his bookshelves, mining the depths of my mother's disordered file cabinet. Of Melissa Anne's dirty scraps of letters, he said simply, "Nutter. One. Hundred. Percent."

Most of the time Kimberly came too, taking notes as Denis talked in shorthand. *Sublit*, he said after paging through one of Danny's school notebooks; *Agro*, he said after examining the football trophies. He and Kimberly could often be found standing in a corner, their heads tipped together, their faces inches apart, murmuring low murmurs. Even though he was probably twenty years older than she, whenever I saw them like that, I wondered if maybe they were sleeping together.

There were times, too, he showed up without Kimberly. He'd

come in my room and ask questions. Honestly, how did I get along with Danny? Was there rivalry? Who did my parents prefer?

"Prefer?" I said. "Parents don't prefer anyone," though even as I said it, I pictured the way my dad and Danny glad-handed each other, all the tussling-type hugs that involved grabbing each other's necks and shoulders and wrestling around until they were panting and laughing, cheek to cheek. I thought of my mother at the washing machine, pulling Danny's dirty shirts out of his basket and holding them in front of her, admiring the stains as if they were art, every once in a while pressing them to her nose.

I worried that my cheeks were reddening, that Denis could somehow detect the warmth rising through my throat. It's not that the answer was particularly difficult to formulate. Or even revelatory. It had just been so long unspoken, whether out of politeness or denial or sheer obviousness (who needs to confess something that everyone already knows?), that it felt suddenly shameful to say, "Danny."

Denis smiled his sly, me-and-you-against-the-world smile. "Likability is overrated," he said simply and then shrugged, as if parents loving one kid more than another were no big deal. Win some, lose some. It was a generous gesture, one I appreciated, even if I knew neither of us fully believed it.

Sometimes he would run his fingers along the spines of my books. He picked up my copy of *The Sun Also Rises.* "Misogynist or truth-teller?" he said.

"Both, I guess," I said, surprised by the question.

"I read somewhere that Hemingway modeled his writing after Turgenev, of all people. You read much Turgenev?"

"Um . . ." I said, stumbling a bit. Did private investigators even go to college? I assumed they were the sort of people who couldn't hack it in the police academy, a rung or two above bounty hunters.

I must've betrayed something in my expression, because Denis said, "Yep, chimps can read."

"No, no," I said stupidly. "Haven't read much Turgenev." In fact I'd read nothing at all.

"Try *A Sportsman's Sketches.* It is pretty uncanny, the similarity. Same cadence. Same knack for understatement. It's not like you immediately think Turgenev when you're reading *The Old Man and the Sea*, but you'd be surprised."

I nodded. "That sounds neat." I hated myself for saying *neat.* Already Denis had a way about having conversations, a way most adults didn't, that made you feel important, as if what you said might actually matter. This could be daunting. "I mean, cool," I said, which was no better. I tried to think of something smart to say. I tried to think of other Russian writers. "Do you like Chekhov?"

"Sure," he said. "Who doesn't like Chekhov?" He slapped my book casually into his open palm. It made a soft, splutting noise against his skin.

I tried to think of something smart. "*The Seagull,*" I said. "*Three Sisters.*" As he nodded, waiting for me to continue, suddenly I was unsure how people made conversation, how anyone strung coherent sentences together. "Those are good ones," I finally said, and his nodding turned quick and charitable, like we were both agreeing to pretend that I had just said something clever.

I told Lola Pepper about him. How his eyes were dark enough to be pupilless, the deep brown blending into his irises and lending him a brooding quality, even when he was making a joke. How he had an aggressive, nearly hieroglyphic system of note-taking, full of deep slashes and jagged peaks. How he put his hand on the small of Kimberly's back as they walked down our front steps together. How his old sedan burped smoke out of the exhaust as it pulled away. Lola was always attentive in her Lola way, nodding at me from my bed where she lay with various combinations of rescue beagles, chewing loudly on her cherry or sour apple gum and paging through a *Seventeen* magazine instead of doing her homework. But she never seemed particularly interested. She never asked follow-up questions.

One day he popped his head into my room while she was there.

"Oh," he said when he saw I was not alone. "Sorry to interrupt."

"No problem," Lola said. "You're the private investigator." She untangled herself from Olivia, sat up on the bed, dusted the dog hair off her, and reached out a hand. "Lola Pepper," she said, grinning. "Nice to meet you finally." I felt a by-now familiar, though admittedly more potent, wave of animus for the bubbly, ingratiating way she had of presenting herself to all guys without even appearing to try.

Denis shook her hand and flipped through his notepad, repeating her name. "I've got you on my list somewhere," he said. Then, muttering to himself, "Friends with him, a cheerleader."

"Flag girl," Lola said, in a tone that indicated she was long sick of making that correction.

He found the notebook page he was looking for. "Lola Pepper—right. Do you have a couple minutes? I'd like to chat with you."

"Sure," Lola said.

"Maybe next door." He nodded toward Danny's room. "A little privacy." I felt stung. Lola bounced off the bed, Olivia yipping at her. Lola picked up the dog and slung her over her shoulder like a potato sack. Olivia licked Lola's ear. The rescue beagles loved Lola.

Denis nodded quickly to me as he closed the door behind them. "Kiddo," he said.

I listened to the murmur of their voices through the wall. It was impossible to make out the words, though I could hear Denis's baritone and the rise and fall of Lola's chirpy sentences. *Kiddo*, I thought, looking down at the T-shirt that hung limply over the barely visible bumps of my chest. I had grown over time immune to Danny's insults—*flat as a board* and *pancake*—if only for their repetition and predictability. But now, looking down at myself, scrawny as a child, I felt an unusually venomous heat, almost a sizzle beneath my skin, so deep and sudden was my self-hatred.

They were in there for a long time.

I paged through Lola's geometry notebook, looking at the vines doodled in the margins, the *i*'s dotted with circles, the half-played tic-tac-toe games, all in the same pen, Lola against herself. My watch made a soft but insistent ticking. *Pih-pih-pih-pih-pih*. I wanted her to come back and report what had happened. I wanted to hear Denis described in the easy, unashamed way Lola had of describing boys. But when it finally quieted next door and she opened my door, her eyes looked glazed and unfocused. She was silent when she sat back on the bed. Olivia was no longer with her.

"What?" I said. "What's wrong?"

"He's an *asshole*," she said. She whispered the last word. Lola wasn't one to call people assholes. "So. Rude."

"Why?" I said. "What happened?"

"Just his questions," she said. "He's like some FBI interrogator. And it doesn't even seem like he *likes* Danny. He doesn't even *know* Danny. How's he supposed to find him, acting like that?"

Lola was really upset, her voice insistent, her cheeks speckled.

"He's supposed to be excellent," I said. "He knows what he's doing." I tried to keep my own voice even, to betray nothing.

Lola looked at me like I was crazy, and I felt even more than usual the expanse between us buckling and straining. I was reminded of the old black-and-white filmstrip Mr. Fosback had shown us in AP physics of the Tacoma Narrows Bridge collapse, its concrete twisting and swaying as the winds of the Puget Sound blew. A lone man scrambled from his car to safety just before the cables snapped and the roadway wrenched apart and a whole span of the bridge, surreal as a nightmare, fell into the choppy waters below.

Denis began showing up at school. He stood in the hallway before first bell talking to Coach Kinsborough outside Coach's social studies classroom. He staked out the parking lot during lunch, catching Tip or Kent Newman or Gregory Baron or Dale Myerson before they left or as they returned to campus. There was a rumor going around that Principal Garver had given him permission to pull people out of classes, and another that Denis had made Dawnelle Ryan describe all of the sexual positions Danny used to like. "He separated me and Gregory," Tip said to a huddle of people gathered around his locker, repeating a story I'd heard him tell twice already. "Dragged each of us to different sections of the parking lot to question us. The guy's watched one too many episodes of *Matlock*." Min Mathers complained that Denis stood *this close*—she held her thumb and index finger centimeters apart—and that his breath smelled like a gutter.

People weren't so much upset by Denis as they were annoyed by his presence. No one acted like a painful wound was being reopened. There were no tears or sorrowful reminiscences. In fact, there was little talk of Danny at all. Instead, everyone seemed fixated on the idea of Denis as an irritant, like the guy who kept repeating a worn-out joke or who eagerly showed up in an outfit everyone knew had gone out of style several seasons earlier. His biggest offense appeared to be that of inconvenience. Min had been pulled out of a student council meeting. Tip had missed half of lunch. "Me and Gregory," he reported indignantly, "had to eat in the caf." No one seemed particularly heartened that the investigation was getting a fresh infusion of energy. Missing football players, apparently, were so 1995.

There was something both liberating and chilling in this. It gave me an unfettered feeling, an almost dizzying sense of freedom, like I could do anything: take flight, disappear, breathe fire. At the same time, it stranded me. I was alone—probably no more so than I'd ever been, but I felt it more acutely—as I walked down long hallways or sat at crowded lunch tables between Lola and the rest of the flag team, whose names I knew now (the familiar Bayard, plus Penny and Rochelle and Beth and Alexis and Diana), or listened to Ms. Villara recite the varied uses of *detrás* and *atrás*. The normalcy that had returned to Franklin High was at times smothering. There were moments I was convinced I was choking, in the middle of class or as we cleared away our lunch trays or as I marched to sixth period, when my heart beat loudly against my rib cage and my breath shortened and I was sure the color was draining from my face and my lips were turning blue. But no one paid particular attention, and by looking at the faces around me, the easy smiles or facile expressions, it appeared that everything was fine, just fine.

Some lunches I still spent outside. The ground was often slick with ice. Snow had been plowed to the edges of the parking lot, and it stood now as a heaping, chest-high, gray perimeter wall.

"Howdy, pardner," David Nelson said one day as I leaned against the building, eating my sandwich with mittens on. I started a little. I'd been watching Denis in the far end of the lot, talking to one of the guys I'd played euchre with at that first party. Martin, I thought his name might be. Or Marvin. Martin/Marvin was a tall, wiry kid, but he stood now with his chin down, his hands shoved deep in the pockets of his letter jacket, tilting far back, as if avoiding a right hook to the chin.

"Hey," I said to David. "No game?" He spent most lunch hours now in empty classrooms huddled around a ten-sided die with Adam Deselets and Adam Deselets's minions.

"Taking a break," he said and rolled his eyes, which made me feel momentarily hopeful. The innards of his egg salad sandwich resembled spackle.

"Cold," I said.

"Yessy indeedy," he said in a high-pitched British accent that I assumed was an imitation of something, though I wasn't sure what. Then he did a strange sort of bow at the waist. "Quite cold indeed," he said as he straightened, still in the same accented voice.

I smiled, but my cheeks felt stiff. David Nelson had always tried hard; now it was just more apparent. I pressed my feet against the packed snow. In the distance, clouds of words came out of Denis's mouth. Marvin/Martin didn't appear to be saying much, nodding some, shrugging a couple of times.

"You think Yeltsin's digging himself too deep a hole?" David said. He was a little like the soap operas my mother had taken to lately—whenever you tuned in, you could count on hearing the same patterns of dialogue about the Quartermaine's newest business scandal or the breakup and eventual reunion of Bo and Hope. It held a lulling, predictable appeal.

"With Chechnya?" I asked. I'd been following the news, but only barely lately. More and more, it'd grown hard to concentrate. A blanket of grogginess seemed to come over me as I scanned a paper or listened to the well-modulated voices of public radio.

David Nelson talked about the protests in Grozny and how Prime Minister Zavgaev had lost all popular support. "Yeltsin needs to get his head out of his butt," he said. "Or this occupation is going to turn into his own personal West Bank."

"Sure," I said, "sure, sure," trying to think of something else. David was wearing the same down jacket he'd had for the past two winters, mustard yellow and marshmallowy. It swallowed him up, making his head look tiny peeking out of the collar. "It wasn't a good move for Russian troops to fire into crowds of protesters," I said. There was of course something nice about standing out here with David. I wanted at least to try.

Out of my peripheral vision, I saw movement. Martin/Marvin marched toward his car as Denis made a straight line right to us. My heartbeat rose to my throat. I ate my sandwich intently, trying to think of conversation to be deeply involved in with David Nelson.

"The troops," I sputtered, mouth full of sandwich. "Why did they fire? I mean, who do you think ordered it?"

"Zavgaev," he said, "but Zavgaev is in Yeltsin's pocket, so it's just semantics. Any way you cut it, it's all Yeltsin." By that point, he too saw Denis striding toward us. "That's your PI?"

The idea that David Nelson knew who Denis was surprised me. Were even the most peripheral students of Franklin High—the gamers, the band geeks, the burnouts smoking in the courtyard—alerted to him? "We don't call him that," I said, and I could hear the slight edge to my voice.

"What do you call him?"

"Denis," I said. Saying his name made me feel childish and exposed.

"Oh, sorry. *Den-is*," David said with loud, dramatic emphasis. "I have not been so intimately acquainted with *Den-is*. I have not had that *pleas-ure*." He was trying to be funny.

"Stop it," I said too sharply, but Denis was almost upon us and I didn't want this to be the conversation he stumbled upon. I tore into my sandwich, the horseradish on my corned beef clearing out my nasal passages.

"You out here keeping tabs on me, Lydia?" Denis said in a loud, joking voice. Hearing my name from his mouth gave me the same childish, exposed feeling. "Supervising my work?"

My mouth was full. I tried to swallow, chewing and chewing; I feared I had horseradish on my face. Denis and David Nelson stood staring at each other. Denis was wearing the kind of hat you might see on a hunting trip, one lined with sheepskin and with long dangling earflaps. It was preposterous but endearing, a bold choice.

"Denis Jimenez," Denis finally said, reaching out a gloved hand to David.

David introduced himself, then said, "Your name has a distinct meter to it. A very clean rhyme."

"Thank you," Denis said, looking unsurprised, as if that were the sort of thing he heard all the time.

"Hi," I finally said after swallowing. "What's going on?"

He waved his notepad at us. "You know, just background information. You never know what information can spark a lead. You want to get a real fleshed-out picture of your subject before you go running off on wild goose chases."

I nodded. "Background's good."

"Sure is," he said. "Tell your folks I'm planning to come sometime next week to give them an update. Not that there's any big news. This kind of thing works inch by inch." The hat boxed his face in, framing his features in not the most flattering way. His nose looked wide, all nostril. His stubble was better groomed than usual, only a light sprinkling along his cheeks, but a red rash of razor bumps festered beneath. There was a patch of longer hair he'd missed in the dimple of his chin. Denis was a mess, but his eyes had their usual smolder, and I imagined him arriving at our home several days later. I thought of his voice rising from the kitchen and filtering through the rest of the house. I thought of him knocking on my closed door, asking if he could come in.

"I started *A Sportsman's Notebook*," I told him now, my words chalky in the cold air.

He looked at me blankly.

"Turgenev," I said. "You know, Hemingway?"

"Sure, sure," Denis said, nodding. "You like it?"

"It's good," I said. "There's a lot of wandering around and describing things, not really a plot. It's a little disjointed."

"Sure," Denis said. "He's more oblique than a straight-ahead narrator."

"Oblique," I said. "I like that. He conveys the anonymous days of Russians very well," I said, cribbing one of the ideas I'd read in the introduction. "It gives the work a real timelessness." I added, "Paradoxically." That's how it'd been discussed in the intro, as a paradox.

Denis smiled at me, openmouthed. "Smart cookie."

I smiled back. I couldn't help it.

David Nelson stared hard at me; I could feel it on the side of my face. "So, what, you're a professional PI and an amateur member of the literati?" he said. His voice bristled, but I wondered if Denis even noticed. For someone who didn't know David, it could've just sounded like the normal croaking of a pubescent boy.

"I wouldn't go that far," Denis said, chuckling. "Reading's probably just the least damaging of the available distractions."

David appeared to be in need of a comeback. Air clouded out of his mouth, but soundlessly. I felt bad for him, in the same low-level guilty way I would for years after high school, whenever I stumbled upon a memory of him. I did not, in the waning months of our friendship, do justice to our history. There was just too much else going on. When he looked at me during that lunch, though, there was something pleading in his eyes, some desperate imperative that I pretended not to see, that I hoped Denis was not picking up on.

"Listen," Denis said. "Can you ask your mom to dig out all of the letters from that file cabinet? Not just the nutters. All the correspondence she's saved, no matter how inconsequential-seeming. I want to take a look at everything she's got, see if I missed anything."

"I can get the letters in order for you." I tried to sound more dutiful than obsequious, though even I could hear the strain of eager puppy dog in my voice. "Is there any particular order you want?" David made a small, glottal sound, something between a hiccup and a cough, though with more incredulity than either of those.

"Great," Denis said. "Any order's great. I'm sure I can wade through." He slapped his notebook into his palm, a motion that was coming to seem like his trademark, a punctuation mark of sorts, often directly preceding his exit. "Good to meet you," he said to David, holding the notebook to his forehead in a quick salute.

Alone together again, the air crackled around David and me. Cars began making their way back into the lot, a few fishtailing on the slippery pavement, their wheels making dramatic grinding noises. I found myself wishing for a collision, just for the venting relief of such drama. But everyone navigated safely into spaces, without so much as a car door dinging the vehicle parked next to it. We spent the rest of lunch like that, neither of us saying much of anything, both pretending to be occupied by the mundane details; for David, something at his feet and, later, a muffler-heavy car in the street; for me, the slushy trails of boot prints and, finally, the leaden sky overhead.

13.

I had to make stealth work of the letters, given my mother's procliv-ity for hovering near the kitchen file cabinet. She spent her days at the breakfast table, an arm's length away, or pacing the small nook with a cigarette in hand, or opening and closing the three drawers as they squealed on their long hinges. The cabinet was her sole, un-contested domain. I did not want her to get wind of what I was do-ing, to mistake this for a collaborative venture. I could just imagine her fetishistic stroking of each envelope, her fresh recital of words read countless times, her shoulder-to-shoulder, breathy cama-raderie.

I timed things precisely so I could delve inside when she was out of eyeshot and earshot—during her brief trips to the bathroom or while she was taking naps or walking the dogs around the block. This one element of subterfuge quickly tinged the venture with an illicit little thrill. *A spy*, I hummed to myself as I fingered through the manila folders, listening for the sound of her footsteps. *A DEE-tec-tive.*

It was easy to get lost inside the drawers. There were rough markers of an organizational structure, sections labeled *History* and *News* and *Evidence*, though those had been long abandoned. Now fat folder after fat folder was crammed tightly into hanging files, where you'd find a tenth-grade math test (basic algebra, marked liberally with red *X*es, a *D+* at the top) alongside a recent clipping from the *Free Press* alongside a silvery certificate from the state swim meet alongside a photocopy of an early police report. Nothing was too inconsequential to keep—there was an old gum wrapper in one folder, a mucky used Band-Aid in another, the adhesive covered in dog hair and dirt, browned blood still spotting the bandage. Where had this once been? His elbow? Chin? And how had she come to find it and store it away?

The contents of the drawers were compelling and unsettling in the way crazy was compelling and unsettling. They were the shut-in who stacked years of newspapers into towers until his apartment became a narrow, moldering gauntlet. They were the paranoiac who jury-rigged a home security system from crisscrossing strands of dental floss and mousetraps. My first job, then, became one of simply rooting out the letters and secreting small stacks up in my room.

I'd never read any of them before; they'd struck me as invasive, one more way our life had become boundaryless and up for grabs, the community slithering in daily through our mail slot. I'd felt indignant at the Love stamps and the unnecessary *c* often added to our name, turning us into The Pasternacks, a family I came to imagine as existing in a parallel universe, their evenings spent around a fireplace, their coffee table littered with Renaissance art books and international newspapers, jazz music playing in the background.

Now, though, as I spread the letters across my desk and studied the inky cursive on monogrammed stationery or a typed missive on letterhead or a child's blocky print, they held new fascination.

Maybe it was the low-level but constant narration that accompanied the task, narration that would only grow in the coming weeks, capable of enlivening even the most ordinary or solitary of pursuits, characterized simply as *What I Will Tell Denis About This* ("Denis, seven out of every eight writers seem to be female." "Denis, did you see that three separate letters came from Georgia?"). Or maybe it was the challenge of the venture, the familiar appeal of trying to master something new: the puzzling together of many random bits of information into a sensible whole. Or maybe it was simply the appeal of having something to do.

Certainly I had school and homework and Lola and listening to the radio and feeding the dogs and making my lunches and going to Chuck, but all of that, no matter how pointed, had an overarching cast of aimlessness. The letters brought a satisfaction before I'd even started in on the work. How unwittingly desperate I had become for just such a sharpening of my attention, for the distillation of my long, shapeless days into a bite-sized, concrete problem set.

I read and sorted after school, before bed, in lieu of breakfast, and a categorizing system naturally emerged. There were, most voluminously, the Nice letters. These were the ones devoid of substance, filled instead with snippets about prayer and sympathy and love, the ones most likely to be written on store-bought cards featuring doves or flowers. Most Nice letters were simple and brief, a mention of seeing us on the news, heart going out, etc. A subset of them, though, invoked the shameless sentimentality reserved for grade-school love notes, *i*'s dotted with hearts, smiley faces attached as addenda to signatures. For all of the Nice letters, I penciled a small *N* on the back flap of the envelope.

Then there were the Crazy ones. These all existed in the same swirling universe as Melissa Anne's. They contained detailed theories (one promised that all the clues to Danny's whereabouts could be found in the movie *Seven* and implored us to pay careful attention to *GLUTTONY* and *VANITY* and *Kevin SPACEY*) or a garbled list of nonsense (one repeated *Hercules* and *life-force*, nineteen and twenty-three times respectively, in a single paragraph). After wading through so much illegible scrawl and garbled syntax, I came to almost admire the plainspoken, straightforward awfulness of Melissa Anne's work. She was, at least, good at what she did. I did to the Crazies what I did to the Nices: marked a *C* on the envelope flap.

Wrong letters were the simplest to discern. *I saw Daniel at an I-90 rest stop outside of Minnesota on July 29th.* This, four days before he disappeared. Or another: *As I have already told the police, I treated a boy who resembled your son on September 6th at St. Mary's Emergency Room in Saginaw. He had a broken arm. He reported a peanut allergy and had a large port-wine stain spanning his left shoulder.* No allergy, no stain. All, marked with a *W.*

As I completed each small pile of Nice, Crazy, and Wrong, I made new reconnaissance trips to the cabinet, refiling the completed letters and grabbing new ones from fresh folders.

There was a final category that I didn't return to the cabinet, stashing them instead in the top drawer of my desk. These were the Viables. Viables sounded more right than wrong, offered no good reason to be dismissed. These were the shopkeeper who thought Danny purchased a winter coat in Sault St. Marie, the cabdriver who allegedly gave him a ride through Akron, the social worker who swore she admitted him to a homeless shelter in Flint for two nights in October. The Viables were the most threadbare of all the letters, the most heavily scented with my mother's cigarette smoke, most pulpy from her repeated handling. She too had recognized these were different. These were the letters of her familiar tableau: hunched at the table, cigarette in hand, pages spread before her.

Yet.

For all her scrutiny and obsession, she had done nothing more than file them haphazardly away. She had never begun to make even the most rudimentary sense of them. A growing incredulity rose in me as I amassed Viables (there were nearly two hundred of them, out of over seven hundred letters total) and began matching them to each other. Three claimed to have seen a rusting brown sedan near Larkgrove Elementary the night Danny disappeared. Two contained reports of Danny hitching a ride along I-94, one near Chicago in late summer, another outside Minneapolis later in the fall.

How could my mother, I wondered, not have thought to seek out similarities? To group like themes? To look for the most basic of clues? For all her months of notes and index cards and manila folders, she was a terrible detective, simply the worst, rendered wholly ineffective by—what? Sentiment? Stupidity? I spent long stints of *What I Will Tell Denis About This* imagining how we would laugh at her rank amateurishness, her incompetence that bordered on negligence.

On my fifth day with the letters, I got out of bed to work on them. The middle of the night, I discovered, was the ideal time for such work, my parents well asleep, my mind naturally teeming. Soon I was matching the pair of sightings from across the border in Canada: a prep cook in Windsor who'd recognized Danny as a brief diner regular from mid- to late October, and a lady who insisted he passed through neighboring Essex in December. Three letters came from Indiana, a zigzag through the state from Valparaiso to Muncie to Terre Haute. Two letters placed him respectively driving over the Mackinac Bridge to the U.P. and spending November in subzero Marquette.

It was well past four when I finally finished. In all, nearly sixty Viables had been matched with at least one other. Letter after letter sat stacked along my desk in piles according to their relation to each other, an intricate cross-hatching. I imagined how I would sweep my hand in the air, telling Denis, *Look. At. This.*

I was buzzing with the adrenaline of a job well done. And with sleeplessness too. My eyes were starting to blur. *Danny here, Danny there, Danny everywhere,* I thought singsongily, almost as an afterthought. The task had been so much about figuring it out and getting it right; it hadn't been particularly (or at all) heart-wrenching. Now, as my brain began to loosen itself from the hours of hyperfocus, he swam in. I pictured him in Canada, on interstates, in rusty brown sedans. In the moments before sleep, I felt all-powerful, as if I had, just by the act of reading of him, repopulated the world with possible Dannys, sprinkling the map with an army of my brothers who might at that very second be sticking his thumb into an Indiana roadway or sleeping soundly in a faraway neighborhood or maybe even, I thought with a jittery nervousness, marching determinedly toward home.

Denis came over early the next week, Kimberly in tow. I was on the phone with Lola when they arrived. "Is that the Menace?" Lola said when she heard all the noise in the background, everyone saying hello to everyone, finding chairs around the table. My mom had prepared an hors d'oeuvre plate of sorts, unwrapping cheese slices and opening a jar of green olives with pimientos.

Lola said, "I don't have anything against Mexicans, but that guy is slimy. I'm not saying that to be prejudiced."

I told her I had to go. Denis was already sticking his hand into the olive jar, popping three in his mouth at once. Kimberly held up her hand as my mom held the plate in front of her. The cheese slices varied between white and yellow, though they were uniformly shiny and limp, except for a stray beagle hair sticking to a yellow one. "No thanks," she said smilingly. She was sitting up very straight.

"Tip says Jerold Terry thinks you're nice," Lola said quickly, as if she'd been saving this for the end as a way to keep me a bit longer. Jerold Terry was a sophomore wrestler. We'd sat next to each other at a basketball game the week before. He'd breathed heavily out of his mouth and made a cawing noise any time Franklin made a basket. I couldn't remember saying anything to him.

"So?" I said, trying to sound nonchalant.

"He's cute," she said unconvincingly. We both knew Jerold Terry wasn't cute. He had a receding chin and a huge gap between his front teeth. His braces looked as if they were shredding the insides of his mouth. Though no Franklin boy, aside from David Nelson, had ever thought anything of me. There was, despite myself, something stirring about this news. Denis and Kimberly already had their notepads in front of them, pens poised and ready, moving, as usual, in unspoken synchronicity.

"I gotta go," I repeated.

"Later, dater," Lola said—one of her many catchphrases meant to impart familiarity between us, though it often had the opposite effect.

I hovered just beyond the table—nobody offered me a seat—and listened as Denis summarized for my parents all the information he'd gathered so far: talks with the police and the neighbors near the basketball court and the men who'd been playing on the next court over, the friends and teachers and coaches at school. Anticipation thrummed through me, as if I were made of taut violin strings instead of muscle and tendon, and they were being soundlessly plucked and plucked. Denis covered familiar ground—Danny was a loyal, charismatic figure at school, well liked but also with well-known aggressive tendencies. He'd been benched from practice twice for getting too rough during scrimmages.

"That's what he was supposed to be doing during scrimmages," my dad said. "It's a rough game."

Denis nodded and didn't protest. He seemed to be growing inured to the defensive twang that accompanied nearly anything my father said to him.

My mother drummed her fingers on the tabletop. "What's this got to do with where he is?"

"You can't build a house without a solid foundation," Denis said.

My parents looked unimpressed by the metaphor. Denis talked about how there'd been no eyewitness reports of any sort of abduction, though there were a few reports of an unfamiliar brown sedan in Larkgrove that night.

"Rusty," I said. Denis turned to me, as if just realizing I was in the room. "A rusty brown sedan," I repeated, louder than I would've liked. My mother turned in her seat to get a look at me, squinting, her cigarette smoke ribboning thinly in my direction.

Denis nodded. "No plates, not even a partial. The police tried to follow up, but nothing panned out. We're staying on it, though." He talked of Danny sightings as far away as Florida, as near as western Michigan.

"Do you know about the one in Quebec?" I said. "That might count as farther than Florida."

My mother's squint deepened. My father blinked slowly at me, both of them looking like they were trying to remember where they knew me from. I imagined these to be something like the looks they'd had when I spoke my first sentence (I began talking in sentences, the story goes, having skipped single words entirely, leapfrogging from *gah* and *oooh* and *eek* to *Mommy, close the door*), though hopefully, back then, without the vague suspicion that seemed to color their faces now.

Denis shook his head, a Mona Lisa smile on his face.

"I did the letters," I announced, though only Denis knew what I was talking about.

"Ahh," Denis said slowly, then, "Right," as if just remembering his request.

"Excuse me," I told my mother, who sat in her usual chair next to the cabinet. I scooted behind her, opened drawers, and pulled out folders. She made a reflexive *Don't* noise, a corrective sort of hoot that suggested *Put those down*, though I began slapping folders on the table anyway. I explained about the Nices and Crazies and Wrongs, pulling letters from folders and pointing out the penciled notations on the flaps.

"I've kept everything," my mother said, and, when no one responded, "Saved everything." As Denis and Kimberly began rifling through letters, she flapped her hands in a strange, airy gesture, as if she were trying to take flight. "Careful," she said quietly, "no need to scrabble everything." I assumed she meant *scramble*. She looked—typically—on the verge of tears. But instead of feeling sadness or even pity for her, I had an urge to squash her, to rub her nose in this, to *burn* her, as Danny would have said.

"Hang on," I said, a bit of game-show hostess to my voice. "There's more." I ran upstairs to get the Viables, all paper-clipped and sorted into their own fat folder now. When I came back down, the kitchen was quiet except for the sound of rustling papers. Already Denis and Kimberly had pools of letters in front of them. I watched as Denis flipped to the back of several envelopes to look at my penciled notation. His smile had flowered into something broader now, though it was still hard to read. Bemusement? Admiration? My father watched with arms crossed over his chest, as if waiting for Denis to flub a magic trick. My mother was red-faced, the color starting at her neck and then splattering her jawline before finally dotting her cheeks in an uneven pattern reminiscent of Lola's freckles. Her expression, a mix of bewilderment and injury, suggested that instead of having helped in the investigation of her missing son, I had removed a vital organ in her sleep.

I held up the folder and announced, "These are the Viables." I detailed my system and gave examples—the I-95 grouping, the handful that had reported him hanging out on campus in East Lansing, the pair that insisted he was working behind the counter of an ice cream shop in Traverse City. When I dropped the folder in the middle of the table, it made an important-sounding *splat.* Envelopes spilled out the sides. The gesture was dramatic and a little silly; I was getting a bit carried away.

Denis nodded. "Good girl. Very, very nice. Above and beyond." The last statement he made to Kimberly, and she made a cooing, affirmative noise. I grinned. For a while the two of them looked through the Viables, murmuring to each other while the rest of us watched. I tried not to be bothered by the particular way they had of quietly conferring that left the rest of us feeling like we were eavesdropping. I interjected when I could. "That stack," I told them, "all came from Indiana," as if they were incapable of discerning the postmark, and "Those couple of anonymous ones came from River Rouge," again as if they'd grown suddenly illiterate.

My father remained stony, but my mother grew more and more fidgety, picking up stray envelopes, stacking them into piles, taking some of the pages out and eyeing them closely, as if making sure I had not defaced anything. "When on earth—?" she finally said, by now smiling strangely, trying to affect a tone of gratitude or admiration. But the strain in her voice, the particular pitch and tremble, betrayed enough to make Denis and Kimberly stop what they were doing to stare.

"Just when I had time," I said in a fake, breezy tone. "After school and stuff."

She took a long drag from her cigarette.

"You know, we've been talking of going to River Rouge," Denis said, holding the letters in his fist. I'd never been to River Rouge—the forty-five minutes separating Fairfield from Detroit might as well have been a continent, given the rarity with which we neared the city limits—but I knew what downriver towns were like: scabby homes, faded local businesses, factories decades past their prime. "There were sightings in the early weeks," Denis said. "Seems as good a starting point as any, in terms of canvassing beyond Fairfield."

Everyone murmured assent. Even my father nodded. "Reasonable," he said.

"Can I go?" I said, the words out of my mouth before I was even fully conscious of them, and with a breathy eagerness that left in its wake nakedness—me, a child begging for a new kitten or a trip to the ice cream store.

"Why on earth?" my mother said. The smile was gone.

My breathing came out loud. I feared the color of my cheeks.

"Uh . . ." Denis looked at me and then at Kimberly. "We should be fine on our own. But thank you."

"I don't really think we should be interfering," my mother said.

"I'm not trying to interfere," I said. "Maybe I can help." I waved my hand over the table, though already I could feel the initial surge of power fading.

"You have school," my father said.

"I can miss one day of school," I said. "One day. I haven't missed all year. My brother is missing." My voice caught when I said that. I wondered if I had ever actually said that sentence aloud. I had a panicky feeling, though I didn't think it particularly had to do with Danny, but rather with the forcefulness of wanting something and being utterly powerless to get it. My want felt suddenly like the monster I'd once seen in a late-night movie who'd burst, bloody and uncoiling, from a victim's writhing belly. Danny had laughed through that scene. I'd been sick with can't-look, can't-look-away terror, sitting next to him, burying my screams in his arm while he told me half seriously to quit it, to shut the fuck up already.

"Please," I said, and everyone was quiet. For months I'd been trapped in this house with the obsessers and mopers and blank-starers. It seemed suddenly clear to me: I was taking a stand, trying to align myself with the doers.

"I don't think so," Denis said, and then, quickly patting the nearest envelope, "This is really good work, Lydia. Quite impressive."

"Um . . ." I couldn't think of anything else to say.

"She could help me with the notes," Kimberly said. "It's sometimes good to have two sets of notes to compare." There was something undeniably pitying in her voice, but I didn't care; I loved her for it.

I pleaded wordlessly with my parents. *Don't,* I was trying to tell them with my eyes, *pick this as the time to suddenly be interested in my well-being.* Denis studied me in the way that I imagined he looked at a fresh crime scene, as if trying to unearth an elusive clue. I held his gaze.

"All right," he said, though his voice was unsure. "If no one else objects . . ." He glanced at my mother, who looked as if she needed very badly to shout or kick something. In a matter of days, she would come into my room and squeeze my arm and tell me how I'd done such a nice job for the detective. That's what she called Denis, *the detective.* But now my violation of her sanctum was too fresh, its evisceration still littering the table. Finally, though, she nodded, and I felt as if I could leap across the room and kiss her.

"You're there purely as an observer," Denis said quickly. "I don't want you muddying things up by getting directly involved in questioning. Though it could work to have the sister there, could soften some people up who may be reluctant to talk. But I don't want you running back here and spreading information we find around to all of your friends. Do you understand?" I could hear him talking himself into the idea, fighting against his better judgment.

I thought of telling him how I no longer really had friends. Instead I said, "I promise. Not a word. Scout's honor," and held up my hand in the Scout salute. It was a guess; I'd never been a Girl Scout.

Denis shrugged. Now that he'd made his decision, his face was impassive again, devoid of emotion. Kimberly, though, smiled at me in the way I imagined a big sister would, in a way that said both *Good for you* and *Poor little thing.*

14.

The inside of Denis's car had the salty, coagulated smell of fast food. Crumpled bags from Wendy's and Burger King, several bright red-and-yellow french fry containers, a whole host of waxy cups and plastic lids lay littered along the floor of the backseat. Denis and Kimberly sat quietly on the bench seat up front, Denis driving with one hand on the steering wheel, the other draped along the seat back. Kimberly stared out the window or occasionally flipped down her visor to check her lipstick in the mirror, all with the quiet calm reserved for girls with manageable hair and necks that resembled (at least from the back) a swan's.

I held a pad open in my lap, having gone to the drugstore and searched for the same one they always used, hard-backed and narrow enough to be held in the span of one hand, college-ruled, a thin spiral across the top. I couldn't find an exact match. Mine had a pearly pink cover, as if for a girl to list her favorite songs or practice her signature with the last name of the boy she liked. I'd flipped it open already to hide that part. Now I tested my pen, writing:

Gray morning

Pretty hair

before crossing both out for sheer stupidity. Slowly I tried to rip the offending paper from the top of the pad soundlessly, crumple it in my hand, and let it drop to the floor with the rest of the garbage.

The only noise came from the radio, an insistent, nasal-voiced man talking about Castro shooting down two planes over the northern coast of Cuba. I poked one of the fast-food bags with the tip of my shoe. An ossified, half-eaten hamburger bun slipped out, green with mold. I fiddled with the switches on my door until my window lowered a crack, letting in a loud rush of freezing air. Kimberly turned quickly around; Denis eyed me in the rearview mirror. I hurried to get it back up.

In the days leading up to this, I'd been sure he'd call and cancel or my parents would insist that I go to school instead. Just below the surface had burbled an edgy, anticipatory disappointment. Now that the moment was here, the feeling had not entirely left. I was having a hard time sitting still. I wrote on my pad, *Settle down, stupid*, though instantly regretted it, scratching it out, until I was left with an inky black block at the top of the page, also regrettable.

The radio host called Clinton a "no-good patsy." If Reagan were still in office, he shouted, Castro would be blasted to Haiti by now. Every once in a while Denis commented (*Nothing like adding some ad hominem attacks to your polemic*) and Kimberly said *Um-hmmm* or just nodded.

"Radio Martí," I said from the backseat, "was a good Reagan-era policy."

"Yeah?" Denis said, in a voice that wasn't unfriendly but wasn't particularly curious either. I told them about the U.S. radio station that broadcast anti-Communist propaganda from Florida into Cuba. It was a TV station now. He nodded. He had three moles along the back of his neck, just above the thick woolen collar of his coat. They looked soft, like the cloth buttons sewn down the front of one of my long-ago dolls.

"Glad Reagan got something right," he said into the rearview mirror and winked at me. The wink was a relief, as if I could let out my first breath since getting into his car.

I tried to ease into the seat, to relax and let my spine settle into the cushion. I wanted Kimberly to tell me stories of what college was like (I was assuming she'd been; she had the air of someone who'd been). I wanted Denis to turn around, to dip his hand into the backseat, to squeeze my knee and tell me thanks for coming. I wanted him to run the rough skin of his fingertip along the fabric of my jeans to see if it drew the staticky sparks of winter contact.

River Rouge was just as I imagined—bleak and sooty, reminding me of the dull black-and-white drawings in my history textbook. Long rows of factories lined the river, smoke wheezing out of anemic-looking smokestacks, often clustered in groups of three. The river had not even a hint of red, colored instead a brackish and forbidding gray-green.

We parked near the downtown commercial strip, one spotty street dotted with liquor and tobacco shops, vacuum service centers and men's wear stores displaying suits in chocolaty colors with bright stitching and broad collars easily two decades out of style. When we got out of the car, though, I was filled with something close to wonder. We might as well have been at the foot of Mount Kilimanjaro or at the doors of the eighteenth-century Bastille.

"So how do we find the people who wrote those letters?" I said. "They both mentioned Sonny's Groceries. It seemed to me like they could have been written by the same person, except one was on a computer and one was handwritten, right? But so many details were similar. Right?"

"Lydia," Denis said, fishing his bag out of the trunk, "you are here purely as an observer. You're the one who wanted to come along." I looked for signs of his usual congeniality—the curled corner of his lip, the mischievous glint to his eyes—but there was nothing. Maybe he saw something in my face, some crestfallen quiver, because he followed with a slightly kinder "Yes, we'll start at the grocery store."

Kimberly fell in step beside me as we walked to Sonny's. The air was bracing, the cold the sort that snatched the breath from your mouth. She said in a low tone, "Don't worry. He gets like this when he's preparing for canvass. It takes a lot of focus." Kimberly had the uncanny ability to make me feel both warmed and pathetic, like I was the mutt she was constantly rescuing from the pound. She offered a quick lesson in note-taking: "You write down everything that's unusual. Or notable. Or interesting. You try to capture the general gist of what they're saying, and especially capture any specifics. But you never know what will turn out to be relevant later. Try to capture everything."

They were terrible directions, really, the kind a substitute teacher who's never actually studied chemistry or English literature would give (*Class, now read chapters one through five and look for themes*). But I thanked her anyway and tried to keep up with her long strides. Already the cold had given her face a healthy pinkish glow.

I could feel my nose beginning to run, imagined the indecorous redness of my own face.

Sonny's turned out to be a wide-aisled, dusty store with large displays of stewed tomatoes and generic orange soda. Faded cardboard signs in the windows advertised sales on Winstons and Smoked Honey Ham. There were few customers inside, one rolling a squealing cart through the frozen foods, another buying lottery tickets. Neither of the cashiers or the bag boy recognized the picture of Danny. All three huddled around one cash register as Denis spread both letters on the rubbery conveyor belt. "He was seen here the second week of August. Do any of you recognize this writing?" They squinted closely, one by one shaking their heads.

I stood poised with pen to pad, scribbling whenever Kimberly scribbled, which was often, nearly nonstop, though I was still unsure what to write. I noted the bag boy's zitty chin, the light purple, almost white lipstick worn by one of the checkers. *Didn't see Danny*, I wrote simply. I jotted about the low buzz of the fluorescents and the tabloid magazines hanging next to the checkout, one with an unflattering picture of Chelsea Clinton, another with the blond girl from *Friends* supposedly doing cocaine. I wondered, with a slightly sick feeling, if I was going to have to turn this in.

After Sonny's we canvassed the rest of Jefferson Ave., with its dry cleaners and auto parts stores and mothy-smelling hat shop. We went to the cramped Coney Island hot dog restaurant and the sparsely stocked drugstore, a machinery parts shop and a concrete company. Electric signs were intermittently burned out (*P rty Sup ies,* one liquor store proclaimed), and reader boards didn't fare much better (*Sp k pl g heck*, announced one, *Wheel of Fortune*–like, in front of a mechanic's). Several stores were closed for the day—or the duration—with heavy metal gates barricading the façades. Even the ones that were open had a cooped-up, slightly stale feel, like the back rooms of vacation homes that had sat dormant all winter.

Everywhere it was the same. Denis flashed a picture of Danny at people, asking if they had any memories of seeing him or anyone who looked like him five or six months ago. The photo was Danny's junior yearbook picture. He was smiling strangely in it, his teeth clenched, as if he'd been forced to hold his pose a few beats too long. His hair was longer than usual, grown out enough that you could see the start of the cowlick that always split his front hairline into two defiant sprouts. He wore a navy oxford shirt; Coach Kinsborough always made the football players dress up for school pictures. The stiffness of the pose, the fake smile, the nice shirt, the blank blue backdrop—it all gave Danny the appearance of a benign stranger. This was the same picture the papers had run for weeks. It was starting to not even look like Danny, like a word you repeated over and over again until it lost its meaning. *Ocean. Ocean. Ocean. Ocean.*

For the long hours of the morning, we were in and out of businesses, talking to old ladies with sunken faces, men behind store counters who addressed Denis with a slightly surly *sir*, teenagers on the sidewalks whose hair was slickly Jheri-curled and who, like me, should've been in school.

I waited for Denis to thaw and warm, to turn to me and smile in recognition: *Good to have you here, Lydia.* I mentally prepared smart-sounding answers to his unasked questions (Denis: *Where are the likeliest places your brother would have gone in this town?* Me: *Do they have a gym? Is there a pool hall?* Denis: *What would stand out in people's minds about your brother?* Me: *He's got a big Adam's apple. And he says* man *at the end of lots of his sentences. And his legs are really, really hairy*). But he was all work. When he looked at me, it was with the same blank appraisal he trained on strangers. And when he did speak, it was to Kimberly, in their clipped, codelike way, about front-end questioning and secondary contacts. A gray feeling of disappointment threatened to well up in me, though I kept it mostly at bay with a combination of smiling a lot, squeezing my toes tightly in my shoes, and refusing to wear my hat outside, so that my ears rang with a distracting freeze.

And the task itself continued to be laced with a sense of intrigue. Holding the notepad in hand, standing next to Kimberly, scribbling in time to her scribblings, I saw how people responded to us, the way they snapped to attention and stopped what they were doing to listen. Many eyed us suspiciously, glancing sideways at the picture, as if we were a collection agency presenting an overdue bill. Others leaned in eagerly, their voices quickening, their eyes growing wide, seemingly grateful for the way we'd just made their day noteworthy, given them a good story to tell later. Either way, heads turned as Denis slapped Danny's picture down on countertops, as he unfolded the letters and asked people to take a look. It was hard not to feel, just standing several steps behind him, like part of something that might matter. Or even if it didn't, still, at least part of something.

And I found myself growing more deft at note-taking. By late morning I'd developed a system similar to the one I used during Hollingham's swirling tangents about martyrdom in the Middle Ages and the assault of Jerusalem during the First Crusade, in which I became the instinctive stenographer, recording scattershot details, not necessarily every word, but rather anything that struck an indefinable chord, anything important-seeming, even if I did not know why. (*The virgin martyrs,* Hollingham would shout excitedly, *weren't as demure as you might think.*) In a machine repair shop, I noted the scaly rash on the back of the manager's hand. Ibrahim was his name, and he hadn't seen Danny, but I noted the way he punctuated each sentence with an odd *yup.* "Boy doesn't look familiar, yup." "Wish I could be more help, yup." I noted that the long, deep wooden trunk behind the counter resembled a sarcophagus.

"I read about this," one of the ladies in Zephyr's Lunch told us. Zephyr's was a packed little diner, a late-morning crowd filling most of the booths and dotting the tall stools of the counter. The kitchen sizzled with grease. "He was kidnapped off a playground, right?" the lady said, glancing quickly at the picture. "I thought he was younger." Denis told her there was no evidence of kidnapping, but the woman continued as if she hadn't even heard. "That's why I don't let my kids go with people they don't know. They want to stay at a friend's house, I'm going to ask to meet the parents first. I'm going to want to see the fire escape out the second story. I understand those parents who keep their kids on leashes in the mall. You look away for one second and—" She snapped her fingers. "They're gone." She spoke so forcefully, spit sprayed from her mouth and landed on the table. When she handed the photo back to us, I saw flecks on it too.

I recorded her story about the fire escape, noted the remnants of french fries and BLT on her plate, the half-smoked cigarette, the quiet boothmate who had a splotchy birthmark on his left cheek. I noted that she dropped the *r*'s regularly from the ends of her words. *Togethah, mothah, whatevah.*

When I stole a glance like a plagiarist at Kimberly's pad, she had things like the time, the name of the restaurant, lots of quotes. Her penmanship was crisp, the lines and curves of her *e*'s, her *k*'s, her *p*'s precise even when she was writing at such a fast clip. Mine more resembled the fevered scrawling of a lunatic, some of the words unreadable even to me moments after I'd written them. But my notes were poetic to her efficient, the flourish to her robotic precision. Yes, Kimberly noted that it was 11:42 a.m. and that the woman appeared to be approximately five-foot-five and 125 pounds. But I had *smell of sugary ketchup*. And I'd written *broken nose*; Kimberly hadn't caught that.

"She had a broken nose," I announced when we were back out on the street.

"Interesting," Kimberly said, though without her usual coo. She was still busy scribbling.

"Good eye," Denis said, the first nice words out of his mouth.

"She had the hump right here." I pointed to the bridge of my nose. "You know, that jagged kind of hump?"

"Sure," Denis said, and then repeated, "Good eye," which seemed the best I could hope for. I made myself stop talking, so as not to appear desperate.

As lunch neared, we drove to the factories lining the river. At the food cart across from the lime plant, men in heavy Carhartt jackets and even heavier workboots waited to buy sandwiches, passing the picture down the line like a bucket brigade passing water to a fire. As soon as it got to a man whose eyes were ringed with the red welts of recently removed goggles, he started nodding and said, "Tanda Moore. That's the kid Tanda got all worked up about last fall."

"Whoua," I said, barely a noise. Kimberly turned just slightly in my direction, not lifting her pen from her pad, one eye on me, the other on Denis and the man. It hadn't been loud enough for Denis to hear, for which I was grateful.

Tanda Moore used to work at Haber's dry cleaners with the man's wife, the man said. After she saw this boy on the news, she was sure she'd seen him in town. "I think it was this kid," the man said, giving the picture a second look. "It was some missing high school kid. How many can there be?" He laughed—not a belly laugh, more like a chuckle, his expression turning serious again when none of us joined in. Everyone else in line quieted, listening to our conversation with Sal. Short for Salazar, he told Denis, as I scribbled furiously.

"You should talk to her," Sal said. "She was real worked up about it for a few weeks." When Denis asked where we could find Haber's, Sal said she'd quit working there because of back problems. Far as he knew, she spent her days home now.

Denis thanked Sal and then made his way to the back of the line. He didn't say anything about what we'd just heard. Kimberly too was expressionless. I felt a blustery sort of buzz, an urge to make an *eep*-ing noise or a *yawyawyawyawyaw*. How automatically resigned I'd become—almost instantly, it seemed now, maybe before we'd even stepped out of the car—to the idea that we'd find nothing today.

But here we stood, notes in hand from Sal, short for Salazar. It was a sweet, sudden high, the unearthing of a clue. Nothing like the buzz from alcohol. Instead of lapsing into sluggish stupidity, everything seemed to come into clearer focus: the individual voices of the men in line, the damp air off the river, the sharp, oily smell from the factory. And when we got to the start of the line and Denis grinned at me and said, "What's your pleasure?" his normal affability was back in full bloom. I could see that he felt it now too: the world suddenly awake with possibility.

The three of us ate huddled together on the sidewalk, the cold less bothersome than it had been minutes before. Denis and Kimberly talked quickly about finding Tanda's address, about whether or not to show her the letters, about possible lines of questioning. We stood in a cloud of our own vapor.

"It's important," Denis said in between bites of his tuna, "not to get excited about this kind of information." Kimberly nodded earnestly. They were both looking at me. "It's good that we got a name. She's someone to talk to. But most leads turn to nothing. Okay?"

But their manner betrayed the words. They were unusually smiley. And as we finished eating, they bantered about people I didn't know, the most relaxed conversation I'd heard all day. Tom was coming into the office tomorrow. Denis had to remember to call the phone guy. Kimberly made some joke about the phones and Siberia.

"You're quite the natural," Denis said, turning to me and pointing to the notepad sticking out of my coat pocket. "Doing all sorts of writing, weren't you?"

"I like it," I said.

"Philip Marlowe, on the trail," he said. "What do you have? I mean, what's something good that you got?"

I paged through my pad and told them about sarcophagus. I was, truth be told, exceedingly proud of sarcophagus. Kimberly looked puzzled. Denis did too, for a minute, before he started laughing. It was a loud laugh. Some of the men in the food cart line turned to look. I could see deep inside Denis's mouth, the shiny gold fillings in his molars, the bits of unswallowed sandwich still on his tongue. I laughed beside him, though more quietly and with a niggling sense of blasphemy, but still, it was nice.

We drove through slushy streets and sat at poorly timed lights on the way to Ecorse, the city south of River Rouge where the white pages had listed Tanda's address. Her neighborhood turned out to be as hardscrabble as the one we'd just left. She lived on a block almost entirely stripped of trees, the houses uniformly boxy and squat, with faded aluminum siding or equally faded brick, crumbling cement porches, and plastic weatherstripping or wooden boards adorning select windows. The 3 in Tanda's address hung crookedly, tilting lazily to the left, having lost its bottom nail.

Tanda was, as you could see as soon as she opened the door, the sort of woman not used to people ringing her doorbell in the afternoon. She blinked slowly at us, as if we'd just woken her. The sound of the television blared in the background. Tanda was big, with a fleshy red face and the receding hair usually seen on much older women. She looked like maybe she was in her forties, though it was hard to tell. Her chin did not so much end as just slide loosely into her neck. Her T-shirt was twisted sloppily across her torso, the collar gaping on one side, one sleeve pouching forward, the other straining against her armpit. She needed to shake herself out.

"Can I help you?" she said with both a detectable annoyance and an unidentifiable drawl.

"We're looking for Daniel Pasternak," Denis said simply.

"Wrong house," she said.

Denis held Danny's picture up to the screen door. "This is Daniel Pasternak," he said. Tanda's mouth puckered into a little *o*. She ran one hand over it, a thumb and middle finger pulling at the corners of her lips.

"You the police?" she said. *Police* came out *POE-leese.* The drawl, if I had to guess, seemed to be a mix of Cajun and drunk.

"No, ma'am," Denis told her.

"I had police come here after I called about that boy. A long time after. And I never had a ruder bunch of men in my house. Treating me like *I'm* the criminal."

"We're not the police. I'm a private investigator, and this is my assistant, and this"—he waved his hand toward me—"is the boy's sister." He clasped his hand on my shoulder.

I smiled at the sudden contact, though with Tanda eyeing me, it felt instantly wrong. I bit my bottom lip. "Hi," I said quietly. I raised my hand to her.

"We'd appreciate if you could spare a couple minutes of your time," Denis said, his hand still on me. Tanda looked as if she were calculating a complicated math problem.

"Don't mind the mess," she finally said as she opened the door, and then, by way of explanation, "Slipped disk." The room was dark and cluttered. Baskets of laundry sat next to the couch, unwashed dishes littered the coffee table, weeks' worth of newspapers covered the chairs. Tanda held both hands to her lower back as she sat slowly in one corner of her couch, the cushion long sunken from use. Denis and Kimberly took the only two chairs, leaving me to share the couch. It had a dense, mossy feel. I tried not to touch anything. Tanda muted the television; a talk-show hostess ran soundlessly through the aisles of her audience, microphone extended.

"So," Denis said, "can you tell us what you know about the whereabouts of Daniel Pasternak?"

"Is there still a reward?" she said and picked up her drink, an amber liquid with ice cubes clinking noisily. Droplets of condensation lined the outside of the cup. Similar droplets lined Tanda's hairline. "You want anything?" she offered, an afterthought.

No, we all told her, we're fine. Yes, Denis told her, there was still a reward.

"I saw him a long time ago, before I quit Haber's." She took a long swig of her drink.

"Can you recall the date?"

"No, sir. But it wasn't yet September. September's when my back started to go."

"And where did you see him?"

"At Sonny's Groceries. I was on my way to work, buying cigarettes. I seen a boy and a man going through the aisles, loading up all sorts of stuff into their cart—bread and soda and chips and all kinds of junk. Real full cart."

"And why, if I may ask, did they stand out in your mind? I mean,

I see people at the grocery store all the time, but I wouldn't then recognize their faces on the evening news." His voice was distinctly light and affable, as if he were trying to keep a child's attention.

"Yeah, that's what the police said too, like I was making the whole thing up. They kept telling me my tip was *uncorroborated*. But I'll tell you something, River Rouge's not a big town. You see the same faces at Sonny's. The cashiers know my name. I go in there and they say, 'Tanda, how's your back?' or 'Tanda, you need help to your car?' Strangers might stop off from the highway, but those people are getting a bag of chips or a drink. You don't see them filling a whole cart."

Denis nodded. I could smell Tanda's homebound musk, her ineffective sheen of deodorant.

"Also, he was out of it." She looked at me. "Your brother was really out of it. Looked half asleep. He's a big kid, right, but he was shuffling through the aisles like Frankenstein, you know? Real heavy arms and legs. There was something wrong with him. Oh," she said more loudly, as if she was just remembering, "his leg was scraped up too. He was bleeding from one knee." She took another long drink. "I seen him on the news a few days later and I knew, that's the kid from Sonny's. I called the cops that night. News was still going. I called as soon as they flashed the number on the screen."

I listened to everything as if she were talking about someone I'd never met. My mind began doing loop-de-loops. What about the benign stranger from the picture—what if I was right about that, what if he really existed, not as Danny but as Danny's doppelgänger? What if that was who Tanda saw stumbling about and bleeding from the knee? That would make more sense, as I found it unlikely that my brother had ended up in that state in a dusty, wide-aisled River Rouge grocery store. I caught Denis looking at me, his expression strange, and I wanted to smile at him but knew not to. The smell of this place—the liquored sweat of Tanda's living room—was getting to me. The back of my head tingled.

Denis asked her what the man with Danny looked like. She described a medium-sized man with a gray mustache. He was white. He wore a John Deere cap. He was average height, a little taller than Danny. No, she did not know his eye color; no, she couldn't remember anything else he wore (*regular clothes*, she said); no, she didn't see his car. It starts to make you feel crazy, she said, when no one believes you.

"I'll tell you something," she said. "They didn't look like they fit together, the kid and the man. They could have been father and son, I guess, but there was something off, you know? Something wrong. Something not right. I'm trying to think of a better word for it, so you get it." She stared at me then as if it were up to me to think of the word. I looked away.

"You didn't mention any man with him in the letter," I said.

"The letter?" She twitched a bit. "What letter?"

Denis was looking my way, not happily, his brow furrowed, but I couldn't stop myself. I was filled with an urge to pick a fight with this woman.

"We read the letters you wrote to us. That's how we found you. But you didn't say anything about the man." There was a childish quake to my last words.

Tanda reached across the couch, her upper body lurching wobblingly toward me, and put a hand on my hand. She squeezed with a vicelike grip. It was a startling gesture in its sudden, unexpected aggressiveness. "I didn't want to upset you people," she said. "I needed you to know he was here, but the police already knew all the details. I just wanted you to know he was alive and that he'd been here. I'd want to know that if it was my boy."

She held on so tightly I could feel the tips of my fingers going numb. "Uhh," I said, my inchoate plea for her to let go. She, of course, did not understand. The roller-coaster emotion of the day, with all its anticipation, nervousness, excitement—I could feel it all coming to a head here, right in the middle of Tanda's couch, my breath burbling in my throat. It came out in a strange, wheezy sigh, like I'd been gut-punched. Everyone looked at me. Tanda let go of my hand. My fingers were bright red. I tried just to breathe like a normal person, in, out, in, out, but the longer Denis stared, the less I remembered how to do this. It smelled like something burnt in there.

"Is something burning?" I said. My voice was thin in my ears.

Denis and Kimberly exchanged looks. "Kim," he said, "why don't you go get some air with Lydia?"

"Sure, sure thing," Kimberly said, but it sounded an octave too high.

"Sorry, hon," Tanda said. "Didn't mean to upset you."

"No, no," I said. "It's fine. I'm fine," though my voice was still strained, laboring for breath.

Kimberly and I stood on the porch for a long time. She said nice, evenly modulated things like "Every piece of news can turn into something good," "You never know how something like this will turn out," "I'm always surprised where things lead." Two houses away, a kid stomped around in the snow of his yard. I wondered what his excuse was for hooky. The longer we were out there, the more ashamed I grew for having exiled us, the baby and the babysitter.

"I'm okay," I kept telling Kimberly, but she resisted my suggestions to go back inside.

"Let's let Denis do his job," she said, and I wondered if there was an accusation in there.

When Denis finally came out, he said. "You okay, kiddo?"

"Sure," I told him. "I'm cool. The smell—" I pointed inside.

"I think we'll call it a day," he said.

"I'm *fine*," I said, and he told me we'd tapped out this town for now. He'd come back. "You have to know when to fold 'em." He was smiling, but I felt a clear defeat, a feeling that would trail me for the rest of the day and well into the next few.

In the car Denis spoke in a low voice to Kimberly, apparently to signal that this was a private conversation, though I could hear every word. There was the list of reasons not to believe Tanda (drunk, lonely, wanting reward money, differing written and oral recollections) and to believe her (the timing was right, details were plausible without being overprepared). "It's easy," he said full-voice into the rearview, "to think the worst from whatever you hear. What she told us could mean a million things. A million and a half. Don't let your imagination carry you away to some dark place. It doesn't do anyone any good. Okay?" He kept repeating "Okay?" until I nodded.

The rest of the ride back was quiet, not even the radio now. I picked at the lambskin seat cover, tapped my finger against the car window, hatching a pattern of dots and dashes. Images ran through my head—Sal's goggle-rimmed eyes, the woman from Zephyr's spittle, Danny's knee busted open, a trickle of blood running down his leg, pooling at the mouth of his basketball shoe, turning the tongue and laces a dirty crimson as he limped through the aisles, his whole body shifting crookedly, one foot sliding lamely behind the other, his face strangely awry, his features lined up wrong, his mouth too slack, his eyes clouded and confused. The snow came down harder now. Denis's wipers made an insistent scraping sound, and his headlights cast two long, hollow domes into a glinting white nowhere.

• • •

It was dusk by the time we arrived back. All the lights on the first floor were on, and a shadowy figure moved behind the living room drapes. I was relieved that Denis and Kimberly were coming in. It helped me avoid talking to my parents. My mother greeted us, wild-eyed and expectant, clearly having done nothing but wait for this moment since the second we'd left nearly eight hours ago. With her unbrushed, bathrobed appearance, she resembled no one so much as Tanda.

I turned to say some final thing to Denis, something reassuring or grateful or insightful which would cause him to forget my faltering and to see me instead as capable, confident, unflappable, as if he'd found himself a second Kimberly. But the moment had passed; already he was focused on my parents, guiding them both into the kitchen. I was tempted to stay and listen to his version of our day, but I was spent in a way that was making my bones ache. I went to my room and lay in my bed and pretended to sleep. Their voices rose around me, the words blurring into an indistinguishable murmur, though I thought maybe I could hear my mother crying. It was possible it was just the sound of the dogs, whimpering excitedly about having strangers in the house. I couldn't be sure, and I didn't go downstairs later, after footsteps marched back to the front vestibule and Denis's loud car sputtered down our long street, to check.

15.

It was not difficult to keep my promise of staying tight-lipped about River Rouge. No one even knew I'd made the trip, my one-day absence rating barely a blip. I returned too to Lola's single-minded determination to get Jerold Terry and me in the same room. At lunch she insisted we go watch Jerold play four-square with three of his stubby-necked wrestler friends. "Say something," she whispered to me as he gruntingly shoved the ball into the square across from him. I didn't have anything to say. The ends of Jerold's hair were shiny with sweat at the back of his neck. "Pussy!" he yelled when one of the guys shoved the ball out of bounds.

"Hi, Jerold!" Lola called, and I could see her future clearly then, the passel of children she would mortify at the shopping mall by bossing her way into their fitting rooms and talking too loudly about which boys they liked. Jerold turned to look at us quickly and distractedly, his mouth shining with silver as he smiled.

In the coming days, it became clear I had turned into Lola's project. In my room after school, she would make me try on her different color lipsticks, using tissue to rub my lips clean in between, until the friction turned them a bright, tender red. She brought over a bunch of her old tank tops and V-neck shirts. "Yeah, you should definitely do tighter," she said after I slipped on a ribbed shirt that clung to my boobs. I looked boyish and skeletal, the sort of child who would appear in a brochure about giving to the needy. "Don't be ridiculous!" Lola said, with what seemed like genuine ardor. "Do you know how many girls on flag would die to be as skinny as you?" She clipped my hair with a bunch of little plastic barrettes shaped strangely like apples or dragonflies. I thought, *Kimberly would never wear these.* But I let Lola do it, even though it seemed stupid and silly and the result made me appear—I was almost certain, despite her protests—clownish. The truth was, as loath as I may have been to admit it, Lola Pepper held an undeniable and seductive power. Her world was always so finely focused on a single thing—usually a boy like my brother or Tip, or a flag-team routine, or in this case the imagined future between Jerold Terry and me—that all else appeared to just fall away. She elevated myopia to an art form; it was almost a relief to get sucked in, or at least attempt to be.

I found myself in endless discussions about the smallest minutiae related to Jerold. Did I see that girl he was talking to at lunch? Is she the junior who just transferred from Larchmont? Did I notice how he looked dressed up on Tuesday? Why was he wearing that button-down?

There was a sense of trying to build a fort from blades of grass, piling tiny bits upon tiny bits in the hopes it would make something of substance. Sometimes it worked. I found myself lying in bed thinking *Jerold Terry, Jerold Terry*, without even really realizing it. More than one afternoon of Mrs. Bardazian's English class passed with me trying to fix on a mental picture of his face, the tiny chin, the fleshy earlobes, the eyebrows that blurred a little into each other.

But my hold on him, or his on me, was tenuous at best. If I heard Denis's voice downstairs while Lola and I lay scheming on my bed, or if a random smell reminded me of the mossy odor of Tanda's house, notions of Jerold fell quickly away.

"Hey," he said to me one time as I was hurrying to get my books from my locker for Fontana's trig class. There was about to be a quiz on hyperbolic functions I'd barely studied for. When I turned around, there he stood, shoulders hunched slightly forward, a glossy expression like he had a slight cold. I felt the rippling heat of having been revealed along with almost simultaneous pangs of disappointment. His eyes were beady like a squirrel's, his lips woefully chapped.

"Hey," I said back, clasping my books to my chest.

"What's up?" he said, and I told him I was on my way to trig.

"Trig," he said and chuckled, though I wasn't sure what was funny. He stared past me at my locker. "I had a locker on this hall last year." He scanned the hall, as if trying to locate it.

"Cool," I told him.

"I got psych," he said.

"Psych's interesting," I said, lying. All the jocks took psych. In it they watched filmstrips of patients in mental hospitals with strange disorders, like the woman who tasted colors and the man who could not remember people twenty seconds after meeting them.

He nodded and continued to scan the hallway. The strap of his backpack kept slipping off his shoulder and he kept pushing it back up. There was a Playboy bunny patch sewn onto it. I couldn't help but wonder who had sewn it there. It seemed doubtful that Jerold knew how to sew, but I couldn't imagine his mother taking part unless she wrongly understood the image to indicate her son's interest in small game animals.

"Well, take care," I said after a while, though as soon as I did, I was embarrassed by how stilted the words sounded, as if I were never going to see him again.

"Goodbye, Lydia," he said, sounding equally stilted. I walked toward trig with a throbbing in my chest, the heat of failure upon me (of this upcoming quiz? of this unhatched thing between me and this strange boy?) while his name rang nonsensically through my head, *Jer-old Ter-ry, Jer-old Ter-ry*, the dull cadence of the words matching my footsteps.

At home things were mostly the same. I had imagined that after River Rouge there'd be police and search dogs and renewed fervor from what we'd learned. But everything moved at a glacial pace. Denis (and often Kimberly) came over once or twice a week, he and my mother filling the kitchen with smoke, my father looking half spaced out, half ready to spring from the table, his palms braced against the edge, fingers splayed, me hovering nearby at the counter or against the fridge, the whole time with an anxious, amped-up feeling like I was trying to make up for something, trying to catch up.

There were updates. Denis and Kimberly had canvassed a larger and larger circle around River Rouge, talking to people in Ecorse, Lincoln Park, and Melvindale. He reported that Tanda was getting more aggressive about reward money, adding that this "does not necessarily speak well of the veracity of her tale," though they'd had two follow-up visits to her and had even come up with a composite of the man she'd allegedly seen with Danny. Denis had run the composite unsuccessfully against a database of known sex offenders and child abusers.

He slid a copy of the sketch across the table. My parents and I leaned in. It was an odd picture, a hollow-cheeked man with a ratty mustache and a cap that sat high on his head. The rest of his features looked ghostly, as if the details Tanda hadn't been able to remember as clearly—his eyes, nose, shape of his lips—were sketched tentatively, in lighter pencil, leaving only the most glancing of impressions. He was expressionless to the point of being inert. My first thought was that this was vague and useless; could be one of a million blank-faced men. My father's face turned a sallow shade of white. My mother gripped the corner of the paper in a palsied, clawlike way, carelessly crumpling it. Denis gave a standard speech about how it was important not to get emotionally worked up with each new piece of information. There was little indication they were listening.

"I have something," I announced, bringing out one of my dad's AAA maps of southeastern Michigan, having highlighted it with the likeliest routes to and away from River Rouge. "So I was thinking," I said, "if they went to River Rouge right from Larkgrove, here's the straight shot." I pointed to the green line I'd traced along the Southfield freeway. "I mean, it's less than an hour away, and Tanda didn't see him until a week after he went missing. So where were they for a week? If they were in River Rouge, someone else would've seen them, don't you think?"

Denis nodded. My parents stared at me in the same way they did whenever I participated in these discussions, my father looking cloudy and confused, my mother's mouth drawn in a faint scowl. Her tenor during the Denis meetings had changed ever since we'd taken apart her cabinet. At first she'd grown even more frantic, filling out a stack of new index cards with stats on all of Danny's friends: age, address, parents' names, sports played, affiliation to Danny. She'd gone back through and highlighted odd sentences in all of the collected articles, then interrupted Denis to tell him reporters used the phrase "no evidence of wrongdoing" twenty-eight times, waving a stack in her fist, the pages bright with yellow. But a precipitous drop-off soon followed, where she grew oddly more subdued, seeming to watch him—and me—from a wary remove. She sat quietly, though I saw lingering jitters in the way she tapped the cigarette a little too hard on the lip of the ashtray, the way she smoothed her hair off her forehead a little too frequently.

I continued. "So they had to be somewhere big enough where it's easy not to be noticed. That leaves"—I tapped on the map—"a week in maybe Dearborn or Detroit before they slipped out of town when they finally ran out of supplies." Denis's face was unreadable. "Just a theory," I said, and then pointed to one of my yellow lines. "And then afterward, maybe they hopped on 75 and then 1 and went across the Ambassador Bridge and into Canada. There were those letters from Windsor. Or here." I pointed to a different yellow line. "What if they got on 75 South to Toledo? After that, it's a straight shot west on 80 to the Akron area." Only the very northern tip of the western end of Ohio was visible on the Michigan map. I pointed to the eastern spot on the tabletop, an imagined Akron. "Lots of letters from Akron."

"Interesting," Denis said, "though we're still at a purely speculative stage. There's no corroboration of Danny in River Rouge. And no corroboration of a *they.*"

"Right," I said quickly. "Of course. Just theories to think about." I folded the map back up, the creases softened and pulpy from years of use. "You can use this if you want," I said, handing it to Denis.

"Nice work as usual, Lydia," he said, slapping the map against his palm.

My mother asked quietly, "What about *Unsolved Mysteries?*"

"What about it?" Denis said.

"I've been thinking about writing them," my mom said now, with a quavering forcefulness, as if already anticipating resistance.

My father rubbed his eyes with closed fists. When Denis looked my way, I rolled my eyes, but he didn't so much as twitch. My mother had recently grown obsessed with *Unsolved Mysteries*, gathering up the dogs and huddling on the couch every Friday night, arms clasped around her stomach as if it ached while she listened to the throbbing synth music and the baritone-voiced, well-coiffed host, who I'd seen before in some movie I couldn't place. She watched, rapt, as he narrated tales of UFO sightings and double murders and people who "simply disappeared" (dramatic pause) "out of thin" (second dramatic pause) "air." The reenactments were hokey, the voiceovers oppressive, and the acting embarrassing, especially when the real people played themselves. But my mother watched until her eyes glistened, seeming mournful when it ended, the dogs scrambling into her lap and licking her face as she nodded to no one and stared at the far wall.

Denis's face remained taut and earnest as he spoke now. "Bernice, I'm the first to entertain every avenue of investigation, no matter how outlandish. And I've only seen that show a few times. But my sense is that they dabble in the slightly more sensationalistic of crimes, like the serial-killer, alien-abduction end of the spectrum. Your story might not be quite sexy enough."

"Sexy?" my father said, with his usual tone of annoyance. "I'd hardly want to call my son going missing as sexy."

"Poor choice of words." Denis held up both hands. "Your story may not be quite provocative enough for the general viewing public of America. You need a hook of some sort."

My mother chewed on her bottom lip, she and Denis sucking silently on their cigarettes for several beats until she said, "Our son is a sports star. A popular boy. All of a sudden he's vanished." She said the last word with a breathy hush. "They do stories like that."

Denis shrugged. "Listen, if you're hell-bent on the idea, then do it. But let's say on the off-chance they want to run it—that's sure to bring lots of phone calls and tips, but it's also sure to put you at risk for a whole new slew of nutballs and unwanted admirers. You hate those smudgy little poems."

The mention of Melissa Anne sent a flutter through me. Her letters still slithered regularly through our mail slot, now with my worry that there would be a mention of me. There never was, though. The creases in my mother's forehead deepened. Her cigarette trembled slightly in her hand. My father rested a hand on her forearm.

"It can't hurt," she said, as if she hadn't heard a word of what Denis had just said.

"You do what you need," my father said. The presence of Denis often turned them into a united front in a way that not even Kirk Donovan's hot TV cameras had been capable of. Denis seemed not all that much to care; now he simply smacked his lips and shrugged. He looked a little bored. I imagined the incisive comment he would make about us later to Kimberly.

"That show's stupid," I said. Everyone turned to me, but I was looking only at Denis.

"Lydia," my father said, in a send-you-to-your-room voice, not that he'd ever sent me to my room.

"Denis is right," I said. "It's all Bigfoot sightings and ghosts and light patterns in the sky over the Arizona desert." I added in a dramatic voice, "UFOs."

My mother blinked at me.

"It seems like there are better uses of our energy," I said, though honestly, I couldn't think of any and hoped no one would ask for examples.

"It's just a letter," my mother said.

"The show's bull," I said. "A bunch of those stories are completely made up."

My father said my name again. He told me, "Enough." I didn't care. My mother was teary yet again, though not actually crying; her eyes shone. I didn't even really believe what I was saying. Sure, the ghost sightings and Loch Ness monster tales were fake. But I had, in spite of myself, sat with her on more than one of those Friday nights. Interspersed throughout the reenactments were the real-life interviews, and I recognized the haunted, half-dazed way people talked of kidnap plots or unsolved murders, disappearances or sudden deaths. Those people would feel right at home here. They could easily pull up a chair at this smoky table. But I was not going to admit that now. I was instead propelled forward by the same desperation that had gripped me in the abandoned factory with Lola months before, that had been trailing me ever since—the strangling need for someone to be mine.

"Why don't you listen to Denis when he tells you it's a bad idea?" I said. "That's why you're paying him for." It came out wrong, a stupid sentence, but I waved my hands toward Denis anyway.

Quiet followed. My mother stubbed out her cigarette with a particular forcefulness. Everyone watched the stabbing, a naked and uncomfortable gesture, until the quiet unfolded into the sort that felt irrevocable. My father patted her arm. I moved my feet around the floor in a stumbling little dance, not sure what to do with myself.

Finally it was Denis who spoke, his voice calm. "Writing a letter is certainly not going to kill anybody," and then, "Bernice, I wish all of my clients displayed the same level of motivation." He smiled at her.

"Uhhh," I said, hoping for a clever comeback.

My mother told him "Thank you," and the two grinned affably at each other, as if happy to be done with their silly little lovers' quarrel.

My face heated. There was more talk between Denis and my parents, the three of them huddled together. I jammed my thumbnail, a moonlike knife, into the thin layer of skin beside my eye, pressing hard into my skull, until all focus seemed to pool to that one throbbing spot of headachy pain.

It was not until later, as Denis was about to leave and fishing his coat from the front closet, that he took my wrist. He didn't clasp it so much as rest his fingers atop it, the sort of gesture you might see between two old people as they crossed the street together, on the cusp of a *Walk* signal turning to *Don't Walk*, one trying to steer the other from danger.

"A valiant attempt," he said softly, his head tipped toward mine, looking as if he might laugh.

"Have you ever been married?" I said, a question without forethought and one that seemed to surprise us both. Denis's face rounded into a series of *o*'s, his wide eyes, his puckered mouth. He was not easy to rattle. I felt suddenly, briefly powerful.

"Why?" he said.

"This looks like it wore a ring," I said, touching his ring finger lightly.

He laughed then, a cackling burst of noise. And then, in a moment so odd and unexpected, he tipped his face toward me and lightly tapped his forehead against mine. It was a gesture—when I thought (and thought and thought) about it later—that I'd only seen parents make to very small babies or gorillas to each other in the zoo. He reeked of ashtray and coffee cup. I did not care.

When he pulled away, he said, "You got me, you cagey little bird." It sounded a bit like an insult, except for his smile. "Once, not so long ago. Made it out with my skin, but barely." Again, the laugh.

Before I could ask who, and why, and why not anymore, my mother came from the kitchen, paging through her checkbook, pen poised. "Sorry, sorry, we keep forgetting," she said. I felt a quick jolt of guilt, as if I'd just been caught at something, though that quickly morphed to pleasure. I *wanted* her to appraise us suspiciously. I wanted us to be radiating the sort of chemistry that raised a mother's hackles.

But instead she just created a shelf of her left hip, balanced the checkbook there, and filled out a check. Denis folded it in thirds and slipped it in a back pocket. "Keep up the good work," he announced jovially enough to me, and with that, slipped his arms into his thick down coat and left. I could feel the spot on my forehead where he'd just been. Hours later I was still keenly aware of it—so much so, I searched myself in the mirror, convinced there must be a visible trace, like a small hickey or a bruise or the strange mark the Christian kids came to school with at Easter, foreheads dirty with smudges of Jesus.

Days later I ended up helping my mother with the letter, a result of both the lingering guilt of having given her a hard time and the arrogant sort of generosity that came from my covert little alliance with Denis. Thinking of the quiet understanding that was unfolding between him and me, I would grow expansive and exceedingly proud. *Oh, these poor little people*, I was prone to thinking as I watched my parents skulk and mope.

My mother and I sat on the couch together, her reciting, me writing, Poppy licking her paws between us, Oliver nuzzling my arm with his wet nose. "Our son is a beacon of light," she had me write. "He is an icon in the community." I wrote about his state swim championship and his seven quarterback sacks in a single season. I wrote about the disappearance and the search. I wrote for three full pages, my mother showing no signs of tiring. It was not long before she rambled on about the paper boy who bore a striking resemblance to Danny (I knew the paper boy of whom she spoke and I did not agree, though I didn't say anything) in both the jawline and the haircut and sometimes when he stopped at our front walk to throw a paper on our porch she wanted to say to him, "Come in."

"Do you want me to write that?" I asked, and she looked at me like I was trying to start a fight. Of course she wanted me to.

There were times, she admitted, when she looked at the faces on the sides of milk cartons and judged the other missing children—impish, dirty, bad teeth, underfed—deeming none of them as worthy of return as her son. She made bargains, she said, so many bargains—her left arm (her writing hand, she told me) to have him back, both her legs, her tongue. The dogs, she said, while petting Poppy. Her husband, she said in a strange voice, and I could not tell if she was joking. I waited for her to say me, that she had bargained with me. The omission soon seemed glaring, seemed to point only to the truth of it.

None of this, of course, would go into the letter. I pretended to be taking down every word, drawing my pen across the page in intricate scribbles. The letter would be penned by me alone days later, a one-page plea, playing up both Danny's popularity and the mystery of his vanishing. I would use the word *mysterious* eight times in three paragraphs. I would end with a flourish: "You would do both your show and our family a service by airing this story of heartbreak and devastatingly unanswered questions."

Sitting next to my mother, I could feel the heat coming off her, the dense, sweaty spice of feverish skin as she went on about his appendicitis scare in sixth grade or the way he resisted his "big boy bed" after the crib. I hoped for my father to walk into the room, for the dogs to begin a bout of their unprovoked howling, for the phone to ring. My father was no more pleasant to live with—he'd grown nearly impenetrable—but still, he was easier. He was at least self-contained.

My mother now leaned her head against my shoulder, her hair clumped in greasy strands. She talked about the smell of boys, the unmistakable odor of dirt and testosterone and awkwardness, her voice wistful and wet. I kept the pen moving nonsensically, my eyes fixed to my imaginary task, putting all my energy into appearing earnest and determined—*I am here to save him too*—so I would not have to look her in the face or give answer to her words.

16.

The composite took up residence atop the file cabinet. Long the repository for Danny-related detritus not yet "filed" inside, the top of the cabinet always housed a messy pile of papers. Normally, any new addition was quickly buried beneath even newer additions, though the composite proved the exception. Newer press clippings or letters or scribbled index cards were stuffed beneath it, creating a swell. Like a flag after battle, the ghostly face remained at permanent apex.

Whenever I came into the kitchen, there he was. It was impossible to be in close proximity without feeling at least a tug on my peripheral vision. It was, after all, a clue, and one so much more tangible, so much more palpably cluelike, than all the letters combined. In that sense, what began as a simple pencil drawing soon became a thumping pulse in the middle of the room. I found myself stealing glances as I got a glass of milk before bed or toasted bread in the morning. The more I looked, the more clearly he came into focus. I discovered wrinkles sketched around the eyes and mouth, making him look older—fifties, maybe even early sixties—and the flurry of thick eyelashes that seemed so girlishly incongruent, I wondered if they were a product more of artistic license than of Tanda's recollection. The picture grew both absorbing and repellent, with a magnetic quality that drew me to it but then left me with a gritty, sullied feeling after I looked for too long, which I often did.

In time the face lingered without the aid of the sketch, flitting through my consciousness, disembodied, as I lay in bed, as I sat at my desk to study, as I dialed the phone. Several mornings I woke with the sense that I'd dreamed of him, the cap, the ratty whiskers, the old eyes; it was an insistent feeling as I lay tangled in my blankets, like if I just cleared away the sleepiness, I could piece something important together. Hard as I tried, I never remembered any specifics.

Roy, I decided one night as I heated soup in the microwave and eyed him from across the room. That was his name. He seemed like a Roy. Roi. The king. The king of what? I wondered. Of the castle? Of my brother? A few times my mother came in as I stood next to the cabinet peering at him. I did a strange, embarrassed dance as she stared, brushing nonexistent crumbs off the front of my shirt, jumping into the middle of a conversation we hadn't yet started: "The history report is almost done," or "I'll call Lola in a few minutes." I grew red-cheeked and stammery, feeling like she'd caught me hitting on her boyfriend. It was amazing how much this one additional piece of information tilted me off-kilter.

I made myself slightly queasy with the idea of what I would tell Denis about this. *Guess what? I have named him Roy.* It quickly became clear I needed a plan, though one didn't come to me until I lay awake in bed one night, watching the shadowy pockmarks in my ceiling. I realized I could take the sketch to the Larkgrove Police Department and look through the mug-shot books to see if Roy matched any local offenders. Perhaps Roy had been a neighborhood cat burglar or exhibitionist before ascending to snatching kids from basketball courts. Having a plan softened my spine into the mattress, quelled the rising simmer within me, setting me right in the same way that reading the first question of a dreaded exam or the first page of a new book set me right, those moments when wide-open uncertainty was, if not resolved, at least whittled into something more tangible and concrete.

There were only a couple of variables to work out. One, when to go. The following Saturday seemed logical, the whole day open until an evening basketball game I'd promised Lola I'd go to as part of her grand scheme. Jerold would be in attendance; ergo, I should be too.

Two, how to get to Larkgrove. While Danny could easily jog between there and home, I was not Danny, and it was wintertime. I needed a ride. My parents were not an option for obvious reasons. Illegally driving myself, particularly to a police station, was also not an option, for equally obvious reasons. I could not stomach the frothy, movie-of-the-week excitement Lola would bring to an investigation of anything to do with Danny. I pictured her packing an oversized magnifying glass and accessorizing herself with a Sherlockian cape coat and double-billed cap. This left me with one option. I called the next morning, as soon as I was out of bed, waking from a short, thick sleep I couldn't remember having fallen into.

"Hi, hi," David Nelson said quickly when he heard my voice, two hurried bursts of air, as if a call from me at 6:45 a.m. on a Thursday was just what he'd been expecting. Then, slightly more casually, "Konnichiwa."

"Konnichiwa," I said. It'd been months since we'd talked on the phone. "How's it going?"

"Oh, mostly southwesterly." I could hear rasps of sleep in his voice. If I asked, though, I knew he'd tell me that I hadn't woken him, that he'd been up, that it was fine.

"Really?" I said. "I thought it was more a nor'easter day."

"That's because you're thinking all upside-down, like some bloody Australian." He said the last part with a bad Australian accent. *BLUE-dee Awz*-STRAY-yin.

I made a noise like a laugh. It was a valiant attempt at silliness, if not actually funny.

"What are you doing on Saturday?" I said, feeling unexpectedly nervous. David Nelson's birthday had been in December (*the Ides of December*, he liked to call it), during our silent period. He was sixteen now. I'd seen him driving to school a few times in his mother's boxy white Chevrolet, bumper stickers on the back about wishing the military had to have bake sales and keep your laws off my ovaries.

"Going with Adam to the Cape." The Cape was Cape Comics, a cramped, atticlike store a few towns over that smelled of boy sweat and mildew.

"Okay, cool," I said. "That's cool. How are you guys? I mean, are you still gaming and stuff?"

"What's up with Saturday?" he said.

"Nothing," I said. "I mean, nothing. It's stupid. I'm doing some investigating stuff. I thought you might want to come."

He asked me what kind of investigating. I told him about Roy (though I didn't call him Roy) and a little about Tanda, though not enough to violate Denis's rule about not blabbing, and finally my idea about the Larkgrove police.

"Sure," he said as soon as I finished. "That could be fun. I mean, I don't mean fun. I mean like I could help. I could help you with it."

"What about the Cape?"

"Screw it," he said. "I can reschedule. Adam's never doing anything anyway. We can go Sunday."

A slither of satisfaction moved through me, a surprising flush of victory.

He showed up fifteen minutes early. I was still up in my room getting ready when I heard the screechy, dramatic greeting from my mother and the heavy footsteps of my father rising from his chair, his low "Long time, Dave," and the dense slaps to David's back. My father had never hugged David Nelson before. He was now play-acting, perhaps, the prodigal son returns, though David's narrow shoulders and permanent slouch must have disappointed. My parents thought we were going somewhere to study; they hadn't quibbled over details, though I'd prepared an elaborate story about research at the library.

When David came into my room, he hung back by the door, not even unbuttoning his coat. Part of me wanted to tell him to relax, make himself at home, though I didn't really want him sitting on the bed or coming in a whole lot closer to watch me doing my hair the way Lola had shown me, trying to spray out the sides just a tiny bit to give them some body. I was wearing one of her hand-me-downs, a scoop-neck T-shirt with a gold silkscreen of a hummingbird across the front. I liked the hummingbird; it was cute without being altogether cutesy, a rarity among her castoffs. But glancing behind me in the mirror, I saw how David stared from across the room with a slightly stern look, and I felt suddenly self-conscious and stupid about both the hummingbird and the hair.

"It's cool," I said, apropos of nothing.

He picked up a couple books from my nightstand—one on Nixon and the media, the other *Othello*—and riffled through the pages absently. Then he nudged my water glass with a couple of his knuckles and drummed his fingers on my headboard. He didn't know, it seemed, what to do with his hands. Finally, in a deep radio announcer voice, he said, "Returning. To the scene. Of the crime."

I wished he hadn't. He laughed a laugh that was too loud and too hearty by several degrees, suggesting to me that he too wished he hadn't.

Then in the car it was weird. I watched him rest one palm on the center of the steering wheel, raise and lower the blinker stem, take sips from the pop bottle nested in the cup holder beside him, and fiddle with the radio station dial, all with the mindless efficiency of someone long used to this. He was driving and talking to me and leaning forward to scratch a spot in the middle of his back all at the same time. It made David Nelson seem older and more advanced, and I was struck with an unexpected, warm-throated feeling of having been left behind. As he fiddled with the electronic controls that adjusted his side mirror, I had the urge to poke his leg or call out *Scotland Barge*, the malapropism a substitute teacher once said for *Scotland Yard*, which resulted in such gaping incredulity by the two of us—*Did he just say Scotland* Barge?—we repeated it for months.

"Quit it," I said instead with unnecessary harshness.

He looked at me, surprised.

"That's bugging me," I said, slightly more nicely. "All the messing with the mirror. That whirring noise."

"Uhhh," he said, looking at me the way I'd seen him looking at myriad morons and simpletons. "I need to see behind me."

I had a brief flash of regret for having invited him, the way we made things more difficult for each other now. But soon he started to talk about the runoff elections in Benin, which I hadn't really been following. Even so, it was nice listening to him go on about President Soglo and former president Kérékou. I said something about Kérékou being too much of an autocrat to beat Soglo, though with a brief flash of worry that I was mixing my guys up. David, though, nodded, adding, "Don't underestimate the learned helplessness of a fledgling democracy."

When we got to the Larkgrove police station, only a few parking spaces were filled and the majority of those with black-and-white police cruisers. The air was frigid as usual, but with a rare cloudless sky. The sun provided, in lieu of warmth, a bright glare off the windshields and the ossified mounds of snow, which at least made me feel more awake and alert than usual. Before we went in, I showed David the picture of Roy. It felt deeply personal. I fiddled with my coat zipper as he studied it. He held the paper in his gloved hands—his cheeks and the tip of his nose were already pinking from the cold—and finally said, "He looks like the Taskmaster."

"Who's the Taskmaster?"

"The Avengers. Skull-faced bad guy."

All the comics stuff was new; I tried not to be irritated by it. "Thanks," I said dumbly, taking the picture back.

Inside, the station opened to a narrow waiting area filled with mismatched chairs and brochures about how to prevent car theft and break-ins while on vacation. An officer stood behind a long counter, listening to a woman who was fishing money out of a snakeskin purse and arguing loudly that her meter hadn't expired. The officer was expressionless.

"You'd need to contest it in court if the ticket was in error," he said, though the woman was already slapping a twenty on the counter. She called it robbery. She called him a robber. He nodded, seeming to indicate path of least resistance rather than agreement.

"Hello," I said when David and I took the woman's place. "I'm Lydia Pasternak."

"How can I help you?" he said. He had a thick, dense face, though it was just beginning to sag in the jowls and beneath the eyes, losing the elasticity of youth. This could be Tip or Kent in ten years. This could be Danny.

I'd expected him to recognize my face or my name or both. "My brother went missing from here last summer." David leaned up against me, in his habit of standing right on top of me, his arm pressing into mine, the nylon fabrics of our coats making a low, rustling sound. It was both comforting and annoying. "Not *here* here," I said. "Larkgrove Elementary."

For the first time, the officer's face animated. His name badge said *Overton*. "The kid from the basketball courts?"

I nodded, wondering how many possible kids could go missing from Larkgrove, a town even smaller than Fairfield, with only an elementary school, a bunch of suburban homes, and a couple anemic strip malls filled with awkward businesses like medical supply stores and Christian bookshops.

"That's a terrible thing that happened," he said, though still with a bit of the same remove as when telling the woman how to take care of her ticket.

I slapped the picture of Roy on the counter. "My brother was allegedly seen with this guy. We were hoping we could look through some of your mug-shot books to find any matches."

Overton eyed the sketch. "Which detective gave you this?"

"It's from our private investigator."

"Well, you can't just come in with a sketch and look through a mug-shot book. It doesn't work like that." He had a hint of a smirk, the closest he'd come to displaying an emotion. "You need to be working through a detective on a specific case."

"This *is* a specific case."

"I understand that. But we don't let people just come in and match up pictures with mug shots. Are you a crime victim? An eye-witness?" I shook my head. "Right," he said, shrugging. "Then you don't get access to the mug-shot books." He paused, moving his jaw in such a way, I wondered if he was chewing a stealth piece of gum. "Detective Blanchard is the lead on your brother's case. But it's Saturday. He's not in."

I recognized the name as one of the pale, mustached men who had spent days and days in our living room last August.

"You're going to need to give him a call about this on Monday," Overton said. "Or I can leave this for him." He reached for Roy, but I grabbed the paper first, with a feeling of panicky disappointment. I didn't want to hand Roy over. And I did not want to talk to Detective Blanchard on Monday. *I* was the doer here, not him. After the searches ended, we'd barely heard from the Larkgrove police again. I imagined they'd moved on to more pressing matters, like a cat in a tree or a spate of vicious eggings on neighborhood homes.

I felt myself slouching against David Nelson, envisioning the drive back home, the afternoon stretching before us as we tried to salvage something of it, halfheartedly studying or making strange conversation. Perhaps sensing my defeat, David stiffened beside me. Soon he cleared his throat.

"Are you familiar at all, Officer Overton," he said in oral-report voice, all projection and enunciation, "with the Freedom of Information Act of 1963?" Overton did not answer, though he crossed his arms across his chest and blinked slowly. "I would imagine you're familiar with the clauses pertaining to police records. 'All general records pertaining to criminals or potential criminals at large in the community are available to the members of that community upon reasonable request.' This includes, obviously, mug shots." He paused here, eyeing Overton. David Nelson looked taller than usual. "Listen," he continued, his tone shifting, more chummy, "we just want to take a look. We won't even ask you for names of the guys. If we find photos that seem like potential matches, we'll leave that information for the detective, who can evaluate the situation on Monday." He held up his hands at his sides. "No harm done."

"What are you," Overton said, the look on his face now as if he were about to laugh or spit, "legal counsel?"

"No, but my dad's a lawyer." David Nelson's dad was in fact a midlevel sales manager for a heating and cooling company. "And unlike your detectives, he doesn't take Saturdays off. I can have him come down here on Ms. Pasternak's behalf if you'd let me use your phone." He leaned across the counter like he might just crawl over it to the shiny black phone sitting on the nearest desk. It was an impressive display. I tried to stifle a smile.

Overton stared at us. I felt a tickle rising from the back of my heels and up my legs. I pressed my arm against David's. "Fine," Overton finally said. "I'll give you a half-hour. You come, you look, you leave. That's it. No monkey business."

The panic turned quickly to barely suppressed giddiness. I squeezed David's wrist. He had the just-aced-an-exam, just-solved-a-nearly-impossible-differential-equation look, gloaty and Cheshire.

"I didn't know you knew that stuff," I whispered to him as Overton led us to a room as antiseptic and nondescript as the Fairfield police station, except this one had newer computers and a smell like someone had just made popcorn in the microwave.

"I don't," David whispered back. "Made it all up." His grin spread even wider, like his jaw might unhinge from his face. I hadn't thought David Nelson capable of such quick-thinking deception. I knocked my shoulder lightly into his as we walked. Both of us started giggling. When Overton turned to glare, we quieted, though the laugh lay just below the surface, like a ball we were secretly juggling, trying to keep aloft.

The mug books were thick, wide, heavy photo albums; you had to turn the pages carefully, since there was very little give along the overstuffed rings. It was like looking through the family album of the most downtrodden, unkempt, red-eyed family, all of whose members were alarmed by, bored with, or made tearful by the flash. Overton had sat us at a deeply nicked wooden worktable in side-by-side metal folding chairs. The picture of Roy sat between us as we paged in tandem through the albums. There were six books in all, each marked *Male* and dated from 1971 onward.

It was hard to match Roy with any of the men. In all the mug shots, they were too concrete, their faces too fixed, too all there. I had a sense that when I found the right fit, I would simply know. But no one even came close. Whenever anyone had the vaguest resemblance, sharing the squinty but heavily lashed eyes or the particular constellation of cheekbones and wrinkles, David would veto it.

"Nope," he said, tapping the sketch. "Look at the axis of mouth to nose here. The nose isn't centered. It's way off to the right. You have to look for that asymmetry." He pointed to Roy's eyes. "These are uneven—look, the left one's higher than the right. That's a telltale characteristic. That's not going to change. And this," pointing to his chin. "His chin is weak. Though he could be fatter in a mug shot, so maybe we'll see a double chin. And you can't rely on the cheekbones in that case either. His cheeks could've easily been rounder

under a few more pounds." All of this came out in a low rush, David pitched forward in his chair, his eyes beady and focused. No one would take this as seriously as quickly and as unquestioningly as he did. I felt only a hint of proprietary chafing, not wanting him to suddenly be the expert on Roy or investigative techniques or whatnot. Mostly I was appreciative.

Overton seemed to have forgotten about us. A half-hour passed, and then a full hour. Every so often we would hear his voice from the front desk with that same tone of mild aggravation, and David and I would look at each other and let out a little peep of laughter.

David kept up a constant hum of noise, whistling softly or muttering, "Okay, okay, okay" or "Umm-hmmm," or simply making a breathy "Ah." I found myself more than once on the cusp of telling him to knock it off, though there was something reassuring about all of his sounds, something deeply familiar, even if they were simultaneously inching their way under my skin and driving me half crazy. I took to jabbing him lightly with my elbow whenever he started doing his three-fingered drum solos against the table.

At one point a second officer—beer belly, buzz cut—came over and asked us, "You need anything, kids?" He had several red-and-white-wrapped mints cupped in his palm, and David and I looked at each other. It was unclear whether he was offering them to us or simply carrying them around. I told him we were fine. David grabbed one of the mints, told the man thank you, and proceeded to unwrap and suck on it loudly. I jabbed him again with my elbow. We looked and looked. What I would tell Denis about this was *We spent several hours searching for potential suspects. We thought a great deal about the asymmetry and axis of the features in the composite in order to narrow the field of potential matches and assure ourselves of greater accuracy.*

And slowly we amassed a smattering of possible Roys. I had a nagging sense that we were talking ourselves into the similarities, given that neither David nor I was the type to put forth all this effort with no work product to show for it. But there was, as David had predicted, a fattened-up version of Roy; a couple of smooth-faced younger versions from the 1980s books; and finally one recent shot, the one I felt the strongest about, all hollowed out and ghostly pale in just the way I imagined Roy to be.

We'd been there more than an hour and a half when Overton stalked back and announced, "Time's up, Nancy Drew and Sherlock Holmes. Let's go."

I handed him the four mug shots. I would, I imagined excitedly (I could feel my mouth actually watering, the saliva pooling beneath my tongue), call Denis and leave him a message to get in touch with Blanchard early next week for news on *some potential leads I spent the weekend finding.*

Back outside, David and I stood in the parking lot, coats open in the cold, already recounting the highlights of the day, energized from a job well done: the Freedom of Information Act, the mints, the matching pictures. This had always been one of our favorite activities, the nearly instant replay.

"That shirt's weird," he said after a while, pointing to the hummingbird. I laughed. It seemed funny now. "It looks good on you," he quickly countered. "But it's weird."

"It is," I said.

After a while, when both of us started bunching up dirty snowballs and throwing them against the sidewalk to watch them smash apart, it seemed we were just avoiding getting back in the car. I could feel my nose running. When I wiped it with the back of my glove, it left a long, glossy stream of snot along the fabric. David called me Little Miss Gross. He pretended to throw a snowball in my face but never released. We guessed which cruiser was Overton's and made empty threats about smashing snowballs on its windshield.

David built a pyramid of snow in one of the empty parking spaces, crouching on his haunches, the collar of his jacket riding up to his ears. He told me about the book he was reading on medieval Russian history and the Rurik dynasty. There were, he said, people who didn't even believe that the original Rurik really existed. I tried to think of something insightful to say, though I knew nothing about Rurik, so I offered a few interested *huhs*. He packed more snow onto his pyramid, smoothing the walls with the palms of his gloves. I told him about my book, how Nixon tried to rehabilitate his public image by publicly questioning Bush's policy toward Yeltsin in '92. I hoped David wouldn't ask too many questions. I'd only read the intro.

"Do you want to do something tonight?" he said, peering up from the pyramid. It was a nice day we were having, David and I. The way he squinted into the sun as he waited for my answer, his eyes nearly closed, ears bright red, bottom lip shiny with spit, he reminded me of a little kid, reminded me of us being us from a long time ago, maybe from before we'd ever even met.

"Sorry," I said, "I have plans." His face clouded a tiny bit.

"With Lola," he said, with a hint of the resignation and judgment you might hear from a mother pronouncing the name of her child's deadbeat boyfriend, or perhaps a husband of his wife's lover. It wasn't a question, but I told him yes anyway. I made a joke about kicking Overton's tires and David laughed, but I could tell something had already changed. I could see it in the stiff way he held his cheeks.

"Lola Pepper. Of course," he said. "Of. Course." He reached a fist into his pyramid, a Godzilla-like move that quickly gutted the thing. He packed a handful of the disemboweled snow hard in his hands, fashioning an ice ball. "Do you really like her?"

"She's nice," I said. "She's really nice," which was true. Part of me was tempted to say something terrible about her, to crouch next to him and make some sort of elaborate snow sculpture with him, our own Tower of London or Notre-Dame. We could do it. We could spend all afternoon doing it. I thought of how easily I had always forsaken all others for David Nelson. It had just come naturally. But something in me, though tempted, resisted now.

"I like her," I said, feeling both strong and regretful as the words came out.

"The flag girls," he said, in the high-pitched, screechy imitation we'd always reserved for those dumber or more popular than us, which had been nearly everyone. "What do you do with her? Cheer for teams together?" I got the feeling he'd been wanting to say this stuff for a while now.

"We do whatever," I said quietly. I could have made some uncharitable comment about Adam, but it seemed pointless.

He gestured again to the shirt, and I felt stupidly nervous about what he would say, though it turned out he said nothing. Instead he stood, dropped the ice ball at his feet, and headed to his car. We were cordial enough on the ride home, soon talking a bit about bombings in Tel Aviv and sanctions against Cuba. We hit a string of red lights, though, one after another after another, a few of them senselessly long, the cross streets empty of cars. I made a joke about "arbitrary and capricious traffic-calming devices," which David normally would've found at least nominally amusing. But he just grew increasingly frustrated, hitting the breaks harder at each stop, clapping his palm against the steering wheel. I told him, "Calm down," then "Sorry," then "Thanks," none of which seemed to help.

17.

It was hard, the first little while with Lola. Sitting perched on the edge of her bed while she got ready for the game, I felt infected by David Nelson. Just being in her room felt a bit unseemly. I had the urge to say mean things about the porcelain dolls arranged in a row along her dresser top or the oppressively cheery rainbow-themed comforter beneath me.

After I helped zip her into her uniform, she danced her routine in front of her full-length mirror, pantomiming the flag in two closed fists. She made unwavering eye contact with me. "Can I get an Apache cheer from the crowd?" she said, and I made a quiet whoop. She looked at me with mock disapproval, like *You can do better than that,* though I didn't give it a second try. When she finished with the dance, she stood with her hands braced on her hips, still facing the mirror, asking if I'd French-braid her hair. She'd taught me how to weeks earlier.

"I'd rather not," I said, and she tucked her chin to her neck, sucked in her bottom lip in a sulk. I added, "I'm not that good at it."

"You're fine. Come on." She plopped herself between my legs, her body still warm from the exertion. "Please," she said, waggling her hair on my legs, making it nearly impossible to say no. Her silky hair slid through my fingers as I tried to wind it over and through itself.

"Jerold's coming to the game with Gregory and Kent," she said. When I didn't respond, she went on. "This is what you do. You act like you really want to talk to Kent so you can sit by them, and then you just give a little bit of attention to Jerold, but not too much. Keep him guessing, you know?"

"What am I supposed to say to Kent?"

"Anything. Talk about the game or whatever." I could not imagine a conversation with Kent about the game. I could less imagine a conversation about whatever. Kent spent most of the time shouting uncreative insults to the opposing team (*Your momma should've used birth control*) and making fart noises with his hand in his armpit.

When I was done with the braid, I thought it looked funny, cockeyed atop her head, the pulled-back hair only drawing more attention to the lopsidedness of her freckles. But she told me *perfect* and gave an air kiss next to one of my cheeks.

"Let's do you up now," she said, clapping her hands softly together. She clamped my eyelashes in curler brushes and drew eyeliner across my lids, her breath warm on my face. It was hard to stay prickly in Lola's world, pliant and fluffy as it was. Pulling her head back from mine, she gently rubbed blush onto my cheeks. "Mmmm, mmmm," she said, like she could eat me up. I smiled at her. "Shut up," I said, but nicely. She was psyched about the shirt.

She kept rocking on her heels about it, clapping her hands together, telling me I was absolutely adorable.

At the game, I ended up a couple rows in front of Jerold and Kent and Gregory, Tip having cleared a spot for me between him and Michael Chemanski. Tip greeted me by chucking my shoulder lightly with his closed fist and passing me a nearly empty Pepsi bottle. The alcohol had sunk to the bottom and my sip was a blunt, bracing mouthful of rum, which jostled my stomach momentarily and then spread a quiet warmth through me, which I tried to hang on to far longer than it could rightly last.

Players dribbled the ball and shot baskets and stumbled over each other as referees called fouls. Michael Chemanski went off on a long, and I assumed drunken, tangent about how he bet I could spell any word he could think of. He started out with ones like *psychiatrist* and *bureaucracy* and I felt a little like a trained monkey. His big joke was saying, "I don't fucking know" once I'd given my answer, or "Sounds good to me." When he said, "Supercalifragilisticexpialidocious," I said, "You know that's not a real word. That's a Disney word." He wanted to argue then about whether Cinderella was a real word. "Or what about the Matterhorn?" he said. Michael Chemanski used to come over and wrestle with Danny in the basement. One time they kicked a dent into the wall next to the old bookshelves and had to take off all the books and drag the shelf over to cover it up. When I told him that the Matterhorn was actually a mountain in the Alps, he said, with an inexplicable hint of bitterness, "Figures," and shook his head.

I was aware of Jerold the whole time, driven more by curiosity than all-out interest. I found myself laughing too loudly and animating my face more than normal from the expectation of being watched. I found myself too turning to examine the banners that hung on the wall behind Jerold, the long feltlike panels that hailed our state championship in basketball in '83 and track and field in '79 and '91. Jerold's face blurred in the foreground—I was controlled enough not to stare right at him—but I could see his slightly open mouth as he watched the game, the swirl of hair that looked unbrushed at the top. Throughout the game, he and Kent Newman and Gregory Baron took part in playful roughhousing, shouldering each other in the sides and teetering in their seats.

During halftime, Rochelle, the flag girl with the thick thighs, loudly dropped her flag, and everyone cheered. She looked like she might cry. Tip said to me before the second half started, "Are you wearing makeup?" which embarrassed me deeply, and I stupidly told him no. Lola joined us near the end of the game, still flush-faced and dervishlike from the routine. She practically sat in Tip's lap and made unsubtle conversation about what I was doing sitting here. I answered obtusely. She asked if we had noticed Rochelle, and Michael called Rochelle a dumb heifer and Tip called her thunder thighs and Lola told them to shut up, but without much conviction.

"Let's drive after this," she announced near the end of the game. "I've got my car."

Driving was the default weekend activity when no parentless house was available. I'd never taken part before. It consisted of cramming as many people as possible into cars and circling the city in wide, repetitive loops, honking at other cars full of either Franklin students or unfamiliar faces from other schools in hopes that something, somewhere would materialize, like a keg of beer in an open field or a restaurant that would let students take up tables for hours even though they ordered only coffee or pie and tipped very little, if at all. Likelier, though, it meant simply spending an hour or two packed into the backseat of a smoky car.

Franklin lost in the final minutes. A junior named Callas missed a free throw and someone chucked a pop bottle at him from the bleachers. It missed. The game was stopped for a few minutes while the rent-a-cops unsuccessfully searched the bleachers for the offender. The whole thing—the pop bottle, the loss—turned the crowd antsy and downbeat. Kent and Gregory got into a shoving match in the parking lot before a couple guys stepped in, yelling, "Chill! Chill!" People complained loudly about being fucking cold. Girls stood in groups squealing about indeterminate topics. Everyone kept saying, "Okay, what are we doing?"

Lola managed admittance to her car with the aggressive precision of a maître d' at a swanky restaurant. She selected Penny and Diana from the flag team (Bayard she directed to a crammed station wagon across the lot, Rochelle to a Chevy Bronco that was already pulling away); she then selected Kent and, of course, Jerold. She shooed me away from the front seat when I tried to go shotgun. It ended up with four of us in the back—Penny, then Kent, then Jerold, then me. We sat crushed together—we had no choice—and there was discussion of staggering ourselves forward, back, forward, back to make more room.

Jerold put his hands around my waist and guided me forward, positioning me in this weird tilt until I was half on the seat, half on one of his legs. He gripped me tightly, and I felt thick-throated and warm. I wondered if he could feel my heartbeat in his hands. When he let go of my waist, he left one hand resting on my coat at the small of my back. Kent grabbed a beer can out of his bag and passed it around, froth foaming from the mouth of it. I took a long swig, and it was flat and rancid-tasting, but I didn't care. I passed it to Jerold, who said, "Thank you, Lydia," the first words spoken between us that night. I watched him drink, feeling the familiar prickle of disappointment. A few wiry hairs grew from his chin. A rash of zits clustered between his eyes.

We passed all the familiar sights of Fairfield—the Radio Shack, the impotently flashing neon sign for the darkened Delta Car Wash, the nearly full parking lot outside of the Denny's. I pressed my face against the glass, though my awareness was on the hand at my back. The two of us sat quietly while Kent talked about what a chump Gregory was and the girls grew shrill and fluttery in their reassurances, trying to calm him down.

Soon Jerold slipped his hand beneath the bottom of my coat and placed it over the waist of my pants. He rubbed me there in small circles, which didn't exactly feel good—the friction of my waistband against my tailbone was mostly irritating—but still seemed to send all of my blood to that one spot. A dull tingling began at my cheekbones and soon spread along my entire face. Lola yelled from the front seat, "How's everyone doing back there?" and I made a noise that came out strange, a phlegmy laugh. I drank more beer each time a new can came around. Jerold's hand inched up my spine. His hands were soft and slightly clammy. I tried to imagine how it would be if these were Denis's hands, rough fingertips abrading my skin.

Lola kept turning around to grin at me. I could see from my peripheral vision the way Kent watched us. Each time Diana giggled, which was quite a few times, I was sure it had something to do with me and Jerold. It was damp and more than a little claustrophobic in here. For a while I just closed my eyes and arched my back some, trying with what little space I had to inch away. I didn't want to think of what might come next, if he were to try to reach around to the front of my shirt, try to make a grab.

Suddenly, though, Lola was rolling down her window, blasting us with air. Jerold's hand dropped from my shirt. There was a similarly packed car driving next to us, its passenger window down. A girl called out "Croft's!" Croft's was a sprawling park spanning several blocks. In the summertime its picnic tables were overrun with family reunions and kids' birthday parties, not so much because of quality as because of lack of other nearby options. At one end, old wooden playground equipment sat bowed and cracked. At the other end, a maze of crisscrossing trails wound through an anemic "forest" of trees, leading essentially nowhere. In between, there were several dilapidated picnic gazebos, weeds growing through cracks in the cement floors. In the winter the park sat idly beneath snowdrifts and ice, deserted except for cross-country skiers or the occasional hardy vagrant.

People were meeting up there. The idea of spending a cold night at Croft's amid a marauding pack of teenagers held little appeal, except when weighed against the option of staying in this car indefinitely, crowded onto Jerold's warm lap.

When we arrived, it seemed as if half of Franklin had beaten us there. A few stragglers wandered by themselves or in pairs, but for the most part, large groups gathered at the gazebos and the jungle gym, beneath light posts or at picnic tables. A few self-appointed monitors, like Gregory, who seemed not yet to have cooled off from the parking lot shoving match, and the junior class vice president, Daisy Montaine, who sported a fuzzy blue beret and a general air of self-righteousness, went around trying to break up the groups, imploring them to scatter into the darker recesses of the park so as not to attract the attention of the cops. "Put that down!" they would whisper-shout at the kids holding open containers in the lamplight. "Do you want us all to get busted?" They pointed to the houses lining the streets across from the park: "You think they won't call 911?" This temporarily scattered a few of the most easily spooked. But mostly people stood their ground, this little dance with danger seeming to be part of the appeal of Croft's, this doggie paddle toward the wrong side of the law.

I drifted between amoebas of people, accepting more beer as it was offered, which turned out to be a fair amount. The novelty of my appearing at such events had not worn off; people still tended toward the generous when they saw me coming. Jerold was following me, but tentatively, some of the momentum from the car already dissipating. He eyed me from across groups, occasionally sidling up and putting a hand on my waist as if he were going to start ballroom dancing. "Hi there," he kept saying, as if we were just running into each other.

I waited for the alcohol to do its normal stupefying thing, though the bracing air seemed to keep me unpleasantly cogent and aware. I wandered to the duck pond, where a knot of boys were hurling icy snowballs at the frozen surface to see if they could crack it open.

"Lydia," one said, "you want to try?" He was offering me his packed snowball. These boys were sophomores. One of them was in trig with me. Still, I was surprised for them to know my name and to use it so easily.

"Sure," I told him and hurled it overhand. It made a dull thud, and the boys laughed.

I found Bayard and Rochelle at a picnic table, drinking beer, talking quietly about people I didn't know. They looked at me amiably enough—at least Rochelle did; it was unclear if Bayard even remembered who I was—but made no effort to include me in the conversation. I thought about telling her it was okay about dropping her flag. When she burped a loud burp, Bayard crinkled his brow and she made a big display of blowing her burp into the air. I couldn't think of anything to say. The night was off to a strange start.

I wanted for it to gain just the right kind of traction that made the silly and stupid morph into actual fun.

I stood gamely enough beside Jerold as he talked to some of his wrestling friends, even once nudging him with my hip, though he acted different now, a quick nod my way between stories of hemi engines and takedowns. When I whispered (why was I whispering?), "Hi there," his smile was mostly polite. I wasn't sure exactly how this was supposed to work, though I was pretty sure I was doing it almost entirely wrong.

I continued to wander. Enough people kept offering me slugs from their drinks that the night slowly grew more enjoyable, the standing around, the listening in on snippets of conversations. At one point Dale Myerson handed me his cold metal flask. My eyes teared as I drank, the first sip burning my sinuses. Someone let out a low whoop. When I asked Dale, trying not to cough, what this was, he told me whiskey. A great deal of fanfare accompanied my continued sips, all sorts of whooping and encouragement until Dale finally took it from me and Lyle Walker called me a bruiser and spun me around like a ballerina. The park still twirled a little after he stopped.

Eventually I made my way toward the far end of the park and the trails to nowhere. While a few dark outlines of people dotted the trees at the head of the trails, it was much quieter here. I chose a trail at random and for a long time just listened to the sound of my shoes crunching through the snow, which had not melted as much back beneath the canopy of branches. The day's cloudless sky had held, and the moon hung above, a fat sickle. Even well past the nearest lamppost, it lit up the snowy limbs overhead, casting weird humanoid shadows onto the trail—there a rubbery pair of grasping arms, there an elongated leg, midstride.

I walked and walked. The cold began to feel good as I grew clammy, almost sweating beneath my coat. I thought about taking my hat off, though it seemed like a lot of effort. Every once in a while I heard a shout or laugh from the partiers, but those sounded far-off and muffled now. The trails went, indeed, to nowhere. Repeatedly I passed the same benchmarks—a felled trunk with saplings growing out of the stump, a discarded two-liter bottle of Mountain Dew lying on its side, the remaining liquid a frozen, neon yellow block. But the forest seemed to be a forest in earnest, far less anemic than I'd remembered. Perhaps this was because I hadn't been to Croft's in years. Or perhaps the snow added girth to the trees.

The drifts of snow, the shadows, the cracking sounds of wind through icy branches all managed to give the place a bit of an uncharted, otherworldly quality. I was Lewis and Clark on my way along the Oregon Trail. I was Cook in the Antarctic. For a short time I felt unbound, drifting through this blank space, absorbed in meaningless tasks like patterning my footprints into zigzags through the snow, breaking icicles off lower branches and sucking on them. By now the heat of the alcohol simmered low and constant at my center. I took to whispering to myself, feeling an urge for solemn, Jacques Cousteau–like narration: "So low hang the branches," "Here, a mundane mountain of snow." I amused myself with needless alliteration: "Whistling white wind." I lay on my back to make a snow angel. I poked at icy clumps of foliage with a twig. Being the lost one, I thought for the first time with a certain envy, wouldn't be so bad.

At some point—it was easy to lose track of time back there—I thought I heard footsteps mimicking my own. But the snow and the trees made it dense and echoey, hard to tell where noises were coming from. The sound rose and faded without a clear pattern, until I convinced myself it was not there at all. Soon, though, the crunching persisted, and I whispered, "Crunching cracking cacophony," though it didn't seem as amusing now.

"Hello?" I called, spooked for the first time about being alone in the dark.

"Pasternak?" a voice called, and the footsteps grew more definite, louder and closer, and though he was shadowy and far away, the outline that appeared just before the farthest bend in the trail was so undeniably massive and He-Man like, it could be no one but Tip. I couldn't believe how happy I was to see him. Company seemed suddenly like a great idea, in the seamless way alcohol had of accommodating any new variables into the equation.

"Jesus Christ, Pasternak!" he called as I jogged toward him. "You want a fucking search party or what?" He looked like the Michelin Man in his puffy down jacket. "What are you doing out here? Your boyfriend's totally looking for you. That kid's freaking out."

"I was coming back," I said when I got to him. The jog made me breathe harder, the exertion bringing a little rush. I worried that I'd just made it sound like I was going back for Jerold. "He's not my boyfriend," I said. Then, "You're the Michelin Man," and "It's so beautiful back here." I swung my arms in a wide arc, as if introducing Tip to the forest.

"Jesus," he said again. "You're drunk." He was staring down at me hard. I was trying not to pant. "You know something about Pasternaks?" he said, his voice a mix of light and stern, question and statement. "They like the drink."

I laughed. "I'm not drunk," I said, though just having another body beside me made the loose, soggy center of my drunkenness feel more pronounced, as if it fed off the very idea of audience.

"What are you even doing out here?" he said.

"I don't know. Walking and stuff. I did a snow angel. I poked things." The last statement cracked me up. As I laughed, Tip watched me like he was still waiting for the joke. "What are you doing *out there*?" I said, pointing to the park.

Tip told me about how Kent and Gregory had almost gotten in another fight but how a bunch of juniors had broken it up. Some girl, too, had mashed a snowball in Cindy Kahlen's face and Cindy had almost started crying. "Was her makeup all messed up?" I asked, all this the sort of meaningless nothingness that made these events enjoyable.

He said, "We should go," and took my arm, not exactly roughly, but with a rough sort of confidence. His gloved hand fit almost all the way around my arm.

"I swear, officer, I'm innocent."

"That's what they always say." He was smiling. "Let's get you back before people think you're dead." He delivered this in the same stern-jokey tone he'd used since he found me, but as soon as the words were out, something of a low shudder went through him. I saw it: a strange twitch to his lip, a quiver in the thick cords of his neck. He stumbled all over himself, soon stammering. "Sorry. I was just talking crap. I didn't mean—I don't know. Fuck. Christ."

At first I didn't understand what he was upset about. But as his forehead creased and his mouth wilted into a frown, this was the Tip who had sat in our living room those endless August days, the one who cupped his face in his hands for endless stretches of time, who looked up only to reveal red, wet cheeks and wet eyes, who kept repeating the same useless snippets to my parents about offering Danny a ride, Danny saying he wanted to run home, it still being light out, everything seeming fine.

And then I got it, his stammering, his upset, but it seemed stupid and silly and I didn't want to be all serious with Tip. I found serious Tip alarming, akin to when teachers dressed up during Spirit Week, Mrs. Bardazian in a bright green leprechaun outfit, Mr. Fontana with a spongy red clown nose glommed to the middle of his face. It was the alarm of incongruity.

"It's fine," I said. "No big whoop." I grinned, to display the no-big-whoopness of the situation. He smiled a little, but it was forced, and still we did not move, both of us just standing there in the middle of the trail.

Finally I said, "Listen. He's not dead."

"No. I know he's not. He's not." He was still holding on to my arm. "He's not."

"I know," I said. "That's what I just said." I meant it to come out less harshly than it did. I told him small bits about Tanda and Roy and the afternoon's mug shots. I told him about Denis's other leads—the rusty sedan, Akron, Windsor—all in the most general and hopeful of terms. I painted a picture of us as efficient, focused, and making real progress. It felt good to be talking about the investigation, like I was conjuring Denis here in this snowy netherworld, his smoky smell, his wrinkled brow, the Dias to my Da Gama, the Armstrong to my Aldrin. As usual, it barely felt like I was even talking about my brother.

"Cool," Tip kept saying, "very cool," though his face hadn't entirely righted itself, something still off-kilter. Maybe his nose. Or the way one eye was opened slightly wider than the other. It struck me then for the first time that maybe he was drunk too.

A loud noise of cracking branches overhead made us both flinch. Quickly we laughed at ourselves for flinching.

"Avalanche," I said with fake alarm, relieved for the tone change.

"Dangerous terrain," he said.

"We should go," I was finally the one to say.

As we walked, Tip braced his arm around my shoulder, guiding me down the path as if I weren't capable myself. I let myself be moved along by the heft of him. Always, with Tip, there was that tree-trunk sensation. I thought of the deep-voiced tree in *Wizard of Oz.* That's what Tip was. I told him something to that effect, though when he asked what I was talking about, I was too lazy to repeat myself. "I don't want to make out with Jerold," I said instead, with uncharacteristic candor.

Tip laughed. "Who said you had to? The kid's kind of a tool."

I laughed too. "Totally a tool," though until that point I had only used that word to describe the likes of Danny and Tip.

He told a story about a shoving match Jerold had supposedly gotten into with Horace Lingham in the guys' shower after gym class last year. Horace insulted Jerold's older sister (I hadn't known Jerold had an older sister), and Jerold jammed Horace against a showerhead. "A fight," Tip said, full of scorn, "in the showers?" as if Jerold had broken a cardinal rule in the jock code of honor. Then he said, "You can do better."

The earnestness of his final statement surprised me. He said it like it was so obvious.

"Yeah, right," I said.

"Your problem, Pasternak, is that you're like this little grown-up already. Nobody fucking knows what to do with you. But like give it a few years. Give it college or something. I don't know, after college, when you have some job running the world and the rest of us are just your little employees, you're going to be like a total guy killer, with like a male secretary and shit."

Even though he was saying all this in the smirky tone of the fun uncle spinning a tale, still, it might have been the nicest thing he—or anyone else—had said to me in recent memory. I wondered if he thought these were the sorts of conversations Danny and I used to have behind closed doors.

"Thanks," I said, feeling stupid for the slight wobble in my voice.

"I'm serious," he said. "I'm fucking serious." He squeezed his arm even more tightly around me, in a way that verged on painful. "Look at me," he said, and when I did, he was searching my face as if he were suddenly looking for something.

"Thanks," I said again, just for the sake of saying something, because otherwise it was uncomfortable being looked at that way and I feared he was going to say something about needing to tame my eyebrows or consider a nose job if I wanted anyone good to ever really like me.

Instead, though, he leaned down, and honestly, for a second I thought it was for some sort of joke, like he was about to chew on my ear or leave a wet slurbert on the side of my face. But as his face hovered just above mine and his hoppy breath warmed my face and streaming clouds of air came from his nostrils, I realized what was about to happen. And that realization brought with it shock and then titillation and yet more shock about the titillation. I began to feel shivery and a little undone, all of this in one swirling second. And then his mouth was on mine. His tongue moved my lips apart and he made a low rumble of a growl, as if deciding between eating and kissing me. He squeezed me close, my neck bent at an awkward right angle, him being so much taller.

This was *Tip.* Tip *fucking* Reynolds. His mouth tasted like beer and something meaty, a taste mostly but not entirely unpleasant. He lapped at my tongue with his. I wondered what to do with mine. It felt fat and useless in my mouth. This was my first real kiss, and it was startling and discombobulating and unexpectedly pleasurable, the way I was wrapped up in Tip's hulking limbs. It was like being hugged by a building. A giggle rose in my throat. Tip *fucking* Reynolds. For a second time that night, I thought about what if these were Denis's hands on my back, though somehow this seemed closer—the broad sureness, the firmness of the grip, the way it seemed I could lean all the way backward in a deep, deep dip and still not lose my footing.

Tip moved one hand to my face, touching my cheek, moving my hair off my forehead. But he was still wearing his gloves, and they were thick and padded, the kind one would wear for skiing. There was something clodlike about it, and again the Michelin Man popped into my head and I started laughing, a quiet laugh, but a laugh nonetheless.

He moved his mouth from mine and stared at me. I stifled the sound to a giggle. I felt buzzed and hot and cold and happy. "Sorry," I said, an eek of a laugh escaping around the corner of the word.

"Whoa," he said, a low whisper, which I took to mean *Wow.* But then when he repeated it a little louder, there was an unmistakable judgment attached. *Whoa, Nelly.* "I'm more buzzed than I thought," he said, and blinked and blinked. For a second I thought that perhaps he had something in his eye.

"Me too," I said gamely, but already he was letting go and rubbing his gloves over his own face. When he looked at me again, his expression had flip-flopped once more, this time to a faraway, slightly puzzled look, as if he were trying to place me, an expression not all that different from my parents' usual gaze.

"Huh?" I said dumbly. Then: "Sorry for laughing." He looked at me like he wasn't sure what I was talking about, and I filled with that old, familiar feeling when it came to Tip, like I was the butt of his joke, an unwitting dupe to his pranks. Suddenly I felt not drunk at all. I imagined him saying *Gotcha* and pointing his finger triumphantly at me.

Instead he rubbed his face one more time and announced, "Brainiac," flashing me this huge, unfathomable smile.

"What?" I said, wondering if I had heard correctly.

"You're so fucking smart," he said. He wasn't looking at me, though, looking instead at the tips of his shoes as he kicked up little flurries of snow. A sharp pang of humiliation moved through me. I wondered what sort of compliments he gave other girls, about pretty face and hot body and nice breasts.

He reached for me again, running his monstrous glove up and down my sleeve and then pulling me to him, and for a moment I thought that we'd just had a brief pause and were about to start again. But instead he held me in a strange embrace, patting the side of my hat. I could hear the clap of the nylon against my ear. Then he pushed me gently away, bracing me by both shoulders. I was beginning to feel like a rag doll.

"We should get back," he said, his tone neither plaintive nor embarrassed. His voice sounded perfectly normal, as if we'd been spending our time back here building a snow fort. I wondered if this was the sort of thing they did, Danny and his friends—make out with people midway through conversations and then just stop.

Our walk back was mostly silent. He mentioned something about the game, about it being too bad about Callas and the free throw, and I gave some mumbled assent, not trusting myself to talk, as I could feel, with a dawning horror, a simpering, needy thing hatching within me, one that wanted to yowl or start clawing at him or make him at least hold my hand. *Drunk,* I kept telling myself by way of explanation. *Drunk, drunk, drunk.*

The more we walked, the more unbound from the situation I felt, with a sensation of floating away, of watching from a distance as Tip asked me how my classes were going. I hovered in the spot usually reserved for Danny, where I often imagined him lingering. But he was not here now. I was floating alone, wondering what he would make of this, Tip at my side, our feet crunching through the snow in noisy tandem, the ring of skin around our lips a bright, raw, matching red.

As we neared the trailhead and heard the first sounds of other people's voices, Tip leaned down and kissed the side of my head quickly, his mouth landing half on my temple, half on my eye, coming down hard, more of a shove than a peck, leaving a damp, cold spot when he pulled away. A quick, whiny noise escaped my throat, part surprise, part frustration, part unasked question. I coughed, pretending that's what it'd been all along. In a matter of seconds we would be back in the clearing, greeted by Lola and Jerold and a smattering of flag girls. Tip would hold up two fat gloved fingers in a peace sign before wandering off and getting reabsorbed into the party. I would drink and drink and tell rambling stories about nothing to whoever would listen and bounce violently on a teeter-totter with Lola and pretend not to see Tip out of my peripheral vision, even though he loomed large as a bear, an ox, a modestly formidable continent. My sense of a hazy, nearby Danny would linger. I would glance for him in the treetops as the night wound on and on and on (it seemed like we would never go home) and wonder what he made of this scene—my soggy pant cuffs, my late-night shrieking laugh, my numbed fingers gripping the neck of another bottle. I wondered if he would look upon me with a certain surprise, some strange pride, or a small, stuttering hiccup of shame.

18.

All day at school on Monday, I propelled myself mindlessly forward (Tip who? Lola who? Jerold who?) in anticipation of my conversation with Denis. I'd left him a detailed message on Sunday about Blanchard, the mug shots, Overton. When I got home, there was no message in return and I flapped around the house, occupying myself with unlikely tasks—alphabetizing the long-unused jars in the spice rack, cleaning up months of plastic grocery bags that had mushroomed in the cupboard beneath the sink, wiping away mold from the corners of windowsills. My mother came up behind me as I leaned into the living room's bay windows, the blackening spread both disgusting and fascinating. Up close, you could see pale fingerprints on the glass, streaky trails from the last time someone did a rush Windex job.

"You okay?" she asked.

Her voice startled me. I wasn't used to her sneaking up or inquiring as to my well-being.

"Sure," I said, a little too quick and loud. I held up the blackened rag. "Gross. Maybe we should think about a maid."

Her mouth puckered its usual hurt pucker. When I finished with the windows, I chiseled away the thick layers of frosty ice from the freezer.

"I don't think you're supposed to do it like that," my father said as he passed through the kitchen, pointing to the bread knife I held like a spear. Ice cube trays and bags of frozen peas perspired on the counter. I shrugged and he shrugged back and the freezer hummed a loud, strained hum.

The call didn't come until well past dusk, nearly seven. Denis told me, *Real good job.* He told me, *Nice legwork.* He told me he'd left a message for Blanchard and he hoped the guy would call him back ASAP. He pronounced it *Ay-sap.* He sounded different on the phone, like he was in the middle of nine things. I could hear him moving stuff around, and pictured the phone crooked between his ear and his shoulder, his hands shuffling through a stack of papers. I told him about Overton, about facial symmetry, about the six heavy books.

"You better watch it," he said. "You're going to run me out of business."

I laughed. It was a corny comment, but I was happy to play along. I told him there were four possible matches.

"Yep," he said. "I got your message. I'm on it, I promise." Another voice said something in the background; it sounded like a woman. A low, scratchy sound came from his end, him muffling the receiver. He said things I couldn't hear. I wondered if he was at the office or home. When he came back, he said, "You did great, Lydia." He had to go. He'd be in touch soon.

I hung up, even more restless than before. I'd expected to feel sated; instead, I imagined him scratching my name from the bottom of a messy to-do list and leaning toward Kimberly in his cramped, gumshoey office, conferring with her in the impenetrable way they had of conferring. Or perhaps he was at home, and the voice hadn't been Kimberly at all, a prospect that was even worse. I sat alone in my room, feeling particularly young and stupid, with a familiar feeling of the world rushing along without me, not even wise enough to know to miss me.

The next call was a little better—later in the week, after the first two mug shots had been ruled out. One was a born-again Christian in Frankfurt, Kentucky, who'd not set foot in Michigan in years; another had been verifiably away at a hunting cabin with three buddies for nearly all of August. "Chin up," Denis said, reminding me that nine out of ten leads come to nothing. "It's the tenth that matters."

I told him I'd been researching models of cars that might match the rusty sedan seen the night Danny went missing. I told him about the Chevy Caprice Classic and the Pontiac 6000 and the Mercury Marquis and the Ford Crown Vic.

"Thorough as usual," he said. But he said it weirdly. There was something about not seeing his face that made our communication a little sideways. I couldn't tell when he was smiling. I wanted him to be standing in front of me, tipping his forehead to mine.

The third call, I didn't even get to talk to him. When I got home from school, my mother called me into the kitchen, looking more frayed than usual. She'd missed a button on her shirt. Her pants had a quarter-sized stain on the left thigh. She was at the table, rifling through a pile of papers. On top, an old permission slip. Beneath, Roy's left ear poking out.

"I spoke to Denis Jimenez," she said. "He wanted you to know the final two men did not pan out. One's dead. The other has a parole officer who can account for his whereabouts." She delivered the news like she was tasting something foul on her tongue.

I told her thanks, asked if we had any juice in the fridge. I knew we didn't have any juice. We never had any juice.

"What's going on?" she said, her voice rising on the last word. And then, in answer to her own question, "He was surprised I had no idea what he was talking about. He told me about your trip to the police."

"Okay." I shrugged and gave her the vaguest sketch about Lark-grove, making it sound like a brief, spontaneous jaunt. "I wanted to help," I said. "I mean, you heard him. I found some new leads."

She looked unconvinced, perched between further interroga-tion and meltdown. "Why," she said, "all the secrecy?"

I shrugged again. "I didn't want to bug you."

She stared at me. "I have a lot of information here," she finally said quietly, waving a hand over her pile. It was a halfhearted wave.

"I know you do," I said, expecting to feel more satisfaction in this moment, in such easy victory. My mother—she had to know then how impotent and silly she was. But the moment turned out to be just smoky and empty and depressing, my standing there in her kitchen. A draft moved through the room. The windows were old. They needed replacing. I listened to them now, the low rattle against the wooden sills.

I told her I was hungry. That I was going to make a sandwich or some soup. That I would be happy to make her some too. She said no thank you. I couldn't remember the last time I had seen her eat an actual meal. I told her she should eat something and she ignored me. I heated soup and sat with her at the table. I couldn't remember, either, the last time the two of us had sat at this table alone together.

She pretended to read a report card, an eighth-grade graduation program, a dog-eared police report, her face taut, though I could see her eyes weren't scanning anything, were fixed in a stare.

"What's that you have there?" I asked.

Without looking at me, she handed me one of his long-ago full-class photos. Fourth grade. Mrs. Lathem. The kids stood on bleachers, all gap-toothed and goofy. Danny was near the end of the second row, his hair several shades lighter than the deep brown it would eventually become, his eyes heavy-lidded, just shy of a blink. I studied it, nodding, making low affirmative noises, pretending it meant something.

And then came a period of unprecedented silence. Denis's calls stopped. He and Kimberly didn't schedule their normal update meeting with my parents; one week passed without them coming by, and then another and even a third—an unprecedented hiatus for Denis and one that filled me with dread and foreboding. What if something had happened to him? What if he had decided he was sick of our hopeless case? What if he and Kimberly had run off to Vegas or some South American country for a quickie marriage? What if his ex-wife returned from whatever it was that had turned her into his ex-wife?

Without Denis and Kimberly's visits to break up our days, edginess and temper burbled up from below the surface. When my dad's most recent issue of *Car and Driver* went missing, he tore apart the living room, flinging area rugs, tossing cushions from the couches. When a sparrow flew blindly into the glass of our kitchen window, my mother went into a fit of tears even more gasping and prolonged than usual. She used her bright yellow garden gloves to retrieve the bird from our icy driveway and asked me to help dig a hole in the backyard. Dad came out as I struggled with the shovel and started yelling about the stupidity of sparrows for not flying south like the rest. I could barely chisel a dent in the frozen ground, so we ended up just wrapping the carcass in a blue plastic newspaper bag and stuffing it between the garbage bags in the can beside the garage.

And school didn't help—if anything, it was a worse fit than usual. When I passed Tip in the hall, he seemed overemotive and strange, starting in again with the whole Bluebird thing—"Morning, Bluebird!" "What up, Bluebird?"—and pretending to clock me in the chin with his fist. He spoke to me as if I were very young or very stupid, his eyes wide, his tone cheery as he explained to me that he'd just had Taco Bell for lunch or was about to boff a test in chem. He was apish and used words like *boff.* I felt embarrassed for myself and for him, Croft's already seeming implausible or imagined except for remnants of a terrible throbby feeling in my chest that I couldn't entirely quash as I stood next to him. Ridiculous ideas ran through my head, like touching his face or sniffing his shirt collar. I told him, "I'm busy," and "I gotta go now," which evoked nothing but his same toothy grin, as if he were continually poised on the cusp of patting me on the head.

As for Lola, she remained stuck on the notion of Jerold and me, which made my interactions with her even more contrived and shopworn than usual. I told her nothing about Tip. One, what was there to tell? Two, however little there was, I didn't think it could hold up to the microscopic scrutiny that was very much Lola's wont. Three, I didn't know if she'd be jealous. And I didn't know how to tell her I found Jerold slightly repulsive. So we remained in a holding pattern, one where she peppered me with questions about him (Had he tried to kiss me? Had he told me he liked me? Why wouldn't

I call him? Maybe she should give him my number?) and I feigned alertness.

Add to this that the trip to Larkgrove seemed to have reopened a vein of familiarity between me and David Nelson. He was newly emboldened, approaching me at lunch and whispering in an overly stealthy way, "Can I speak with you, Lydia?" Lola's face always took on a schoolmarmish disapproval when he was around. The already iffy social capital of a flag-girl lunch table was diminished considerably by David Nelson hovering nearby. He regarded her with similar disdain, wearing a deliberately bored, I-couldn't-care-less expression as he scanned the inhabitants of the table. If he wore glasses, he would be peering over the top of them, shaking his head.

Whenever I stood from the table, David Nelson took me by the elbow and led me to a less noisy corner of the cafeteria to whisper his newest ideas about Roy. "We should do a local door-to-door canvass," he said one day. Another: "If we can gain access to DMV photos, imagine the possibilities." He was pink-cheeked with earnestness. Spit gathered in the corners of his lips. I knew to be grateful—they weren't bad ideas—but I found myself irritated by his bent toward co-ownership. I was also distracted by the way the flag girls gaped and tittered from the table. I knew it was stupid to be embarrassed—what did I have to be embarrassed about? I was standing in the cafeteria with David Nelson, something I had done for years without the slightest thought. Now, though, it felt a little like holding up my underpants for all to see. I told him each time, "Good, good" and that I would call him to plan things out, knowing I probably wouldn't.

I left Denis trailing phone messages about nothing. "I was thinking too," I said after the beep, "about the Oldsmobile 88 or

Volvo 240 DL," or "I wondered if you guys had gone to Windsor yet." But day after day I came home to the light on our answering machine glowing a solid, unblinking red, the easy winner of a staredown.

"What's wrong with you?" Chuck said when I showed up for our session.

I imagined what other, better therapists said instead of this.

"What happened there?" He pointed to my arms, the series of long red welts running from wrist to elbow.

"I've been itchy," I told him, which was true. Along with the insomnia came a recent bout of itchiness. I had tried calamine lotion and ice cubes, to no avail. The itchiness rang below my skin, a further defense against sleep. Talking about it now awakened it—it didn't take much—and I raked my nails over my skin.

"I don't think that's good for you," Chuck said. He winced a little. "Maybe you should try to sit still." I felt sorry for Chuck. That was one of my prevailing feelings in here. "What's been going on?" he said, still looking at my arms.

"Nothing," I said. Chuck was the third least likely person I'd tell anything to, right after my parents. He didn't know about Denis, Roy, Larkgrove, Croft's, anything. I'd stopped telling him stuff in early winter.

"You look not so great," he said. This from the man who had recently replaced his wire-rimmed glasses with oddly thick-framed rectangular ones and grown his sideburns out till they were distractingly close to muttonchops. I imagined saying to him, "You're one to talk."

I scraped my forearms against the sharp corners of the chair arms, a momentary relief. "I've been thinking a lot about Danny," I said. It was so easy to figure out how to get just the right rise from him.

"You don't say? What about?"

"The bad stuff." Chuck loved the bad stuff. "He used to try to strangle me." I told a story of how I woke up one time and Danny had his hands around my neck. Like most of my stories in here, it was loosely based on something that had actually happened, Danny trying to wrestle me once, jamming an arm across my larynx, blocking my air for a few seconds, long enough for my lungs to go into spasm, for my vision to begin to spot. After I flailed and kicked wildly enough, he got off me and said *Sorry, sorry, sorry* as I coughed and spit and rubbed my neck and threatened to tell our parents. He said it was an accident, which it maybe, probably, at least partially was.

But I made it Technicolor for Chuck, made it me waking up in the middle of the night to a homicidal brother. Because sometimes I wanted someone just to feel sorry for me. Sometimes it was a relief to have a person look at me the way Chuck looked at me now, in the moment before the onslaught of predictable questions (*How did you feel when it happened? Why do you think he did that? Did you tell your parents? How did they respond?*). Chuck was pitched forward in his chair, lips moist and in the slightest of frowns, fingers braided tightly together, eyes bouncing from side to side as they scanned my face—the look of someone readying the plan for my imminent rescue.

At home I decided to redouble my investigatory efforts, going back through the piles of ruled-out letters, rereading all of the Nices and Crazies and Wrongs, quickly recognizing all the familiar quirks and idiosyncrasies: the kid who'd adorned the margins of his Nice letter with humpback whale stickers, the Crazy who believed Gore Vidal was somehow involved. There was a lulling comfort in combing back through. I culled a paltry few. One insisted a blond Danny was scooping ice cream at a Stucchi's in Ann Arbor, but the date was a week too early, though perhaps, I reasoned now, simply an error in memory. Another was unduly fixated on the transmission of vital information through fiber-optic cables but nonetheless reported a Danny sighting outside Trenton, a town not all that far from River Rouge.

I left Denis a long update message, trying to sound chirpy and informative, bright and needless. I had grown intimately familiar with the particulars of his answering machine: his unexpected use of *y'all* (*. . . and I'll get back to y'all at my soonest available opportunity*), the way the long beep warbled unevenly if several messages had already been left on the tape, the unforgiving tendency it had to cut you off if you spoke too softly or paused, resulting in most of my messages being half shouted in a long slur of unpunctuated sentences.

I rinsed dog dishes, checked the dial tone, picked lint from the dryer lint catcher, counted water stains on my ceiling, sorted the mail. *Sports Illustrated* sent an expiration notice. *Publisher's Clearing House* wanted Danny to know he may have already won a million dollars. Whenever the phone trilled, I ran for it. The sound of my dad's colleague asking me to remind him about the Friday food drive or of Lola Pepper wanting to make plans to shop for hair bands or handbags or blouses came to seem like the punch line of a bad joke. When David Nelson called with an idea he'd gotten from watching *Law & Order* about hiring an artist to go back to Tanda and carve a 3-D version of Roy's head, "to get a better sense of his overall dimensions," I felt impatience rising up in me like heartburn.

One night, refrigerator cleaned, cobwebs cleared from corners of ceilings, I heard my parents in the living room, my dad saying to my mom, "We're paying him enough. I'd expect more than a phone call."

"Who called?" I said.

My father was slouched in his chair. I saw his startle at my entrance—a slight stiffening, hands grasping into quick fists—as if he'd forgotten someone else lived here. He looked at me for a long while, as if weighing whether or not to answer. "Your good friend Denis Jimenez." My dad wasn't normally sarcastic.

"When did he call?" All the dread fantasies—him and Kimberly pretzeled languidly in a tropical hammock; him caught up in a dangerous government conspiracy case; him finally repelled by my parents' animus—were better than the fact of him simply not returning my calls. The fact that he'd called my parents galled me. I couldn't think of more useless people for him to call.

My father blinked from the chair. He'd begun to look more jaundiced lately with a permanently yellow cast to his skin. He couldn't remember exactly when Denis had called. Sometime in the last few days.

"What was the news?" I was trying to sound normal, though I felt like I could scream. I saw the way he and my mom both looked at me, as if I were a small animal behind glass. I tried to stop rolling back and forth on my heels.

There was no news, my dad said. Denis had nothing to report. They'd hit a dead end. My dad nearly spat the sentences.

"Did he leave any message for me?" I knew how I sounded, a little frayed, just shy of screechy, past the point of trying to appear reasonable or composed even though it was a pointless question. I knew the answer before my father responded, before he shook his head, before my mom cocked her chin at me (what was that, a challenge?), before they looked between them in some meaningful, coded exchange, and one said in an unfamiliar tone, both syrupy and grating, “Perhaps more of your focus should be on school, dear,” and the other quickly agreed, as if they’d grown momentarily confused, mistaking me for their remedial child, their halfwit prince.

19.

And then, after nearly a month of silence, Denis returned. It was late afternoon, a random Wednesday, one of my rare times home alone, my father still at work, my mother having ventured uncharacteristically into the world to buy tampons, dish soap, and dog food, a trifecta of scarcity that even she could not ignore. I was sprawled on the couch, drifting on the brink of a nap (how much easier sleep came in the daytime), reading about feudalism for Hollingham's class, soldiering slowly through textbook sections on Roman *patricinium* and German *mundium*, when I heard the familiar wheezing strain of Denis's car. By then I had invented the noise so many times, scrambling to the window only to find a neighbor's sedan creeping down the street or a snowblower being pushed a couple of driveways away, I no longer trusted my own ears. I didn't even run to the window to look, so convinced I was by then of my own folly.

But then came the loud knock against the front door. No one but our postman came to this door, and he rang the bell. Only Denis used the heavy brass knocker. I jumped off the couch, suddenly alert. "Okay. Okay okay okay," I whispered to myself. Making my way to the door, I worried about my face, whether it was patterned with the velvety imprints of the couch cushions, and my hair, a tangled mess on the side I'd been lying on. I patted it down with one hand, running my fingers through it while unlocking the deadbolt.

"Lydia," Denis said to me as I opened the door. The word came out warmly, and he was smiling at me as if it had been only a couple days since we had last spoken.

Instead of the rush of questions—"Where have you been?" and "Didn't you get my messages?" and "Why didn't you return my calls?"—I simply said, "My parents aren't home."

"Well, good," he said. "I was hoping to see you anyway."

I smiled then, a swollen, naked smile. The dogs skittered into the vestibule and circled wildly at Denis's feet. They jumped at his calves and nipped playfully at his hand as he leaned down to pat them. I told them to stop, but they didn't listen, and I apologized to Denis for it, to which he kept saying, "It's fine, it's fine." Poppy left a trail of drool on the tiles, she was so excited.

"How've you been?" he said.

"Good," I lied. "I've been good. How have you been?"

"Sorry I've been away so long. Real busy," he said. "Way too busy." He clapped a hand on my upper arm and smiled his broad smile. The mix of cigarette and slight perspiration that was Denis Jimenez wafted through the air. It was like he'd never been gone.

"Good to see you," he said. He was inches from me.

"Good to see you too," I said, imagining the color dotting my cheeks.

As I led him to the living room, it struck me as intimate and almost provocative to be moving away from the stiff chairs and hard tabletops of the kitchen, which had been, up to that point, Denis's sole domain. Now he eased into one of our overstuffed chairs, sinking down like someone with nowhere else to be. Poppy and Oliver snorfled at his feet, rubbing their heads on the carpet and making mournful baying sounds. Olivia circled my legs. I scratched her behind the ears, her fur oily and slightly gritty. The dogs needed bathing. I hoped Denis wouldn't touch them too closely.

When he saw my history book, he asked what I'd been reading. I told him about William the Bastard. He made some passing comments about feudalism. "Not a bad system if you were the top one percent. Not so different from today." He clasped his hands over his stomach, atop a shirt tucked sloppily into his waistband. His belt had small nicks all along the leather, as if he didn't keep his belts hung neatly on hooks inside his closet like my father, but rather in a tangled pile next to his bed. Maybe he stepped on them in the night, I thought, when he got up to pee. I loved the nicks. They seemed so Denis, so wizened and who gives a crap.

"What have you been up to?" I said, my voice upbeat and cheerfully curious. This, the closest I would come to interrogation.

"You know," he said, "quite a lot. We'd hit a bunch of dead ends in your case." I liked that it was *my* case, not my family's case or my brother's case. "So we decided to start over, go back and piece together everything we knew, look at it freshly, see what we may have missed."

"And?"

"We're cogitating." He rested his head against the back of the chair, as if to display what it looked like to cogitate. "So, listen, I thought you could help again. You've been so helpful in the past."

I nodded, told him yes, anything. If I had spent every day for a year with Chuck, if we had paid him thousands of dollars, I doubted we would ever have found even an iota of this natural rapport. Chuck, I thought with uncharacteristic tenderness, was a tragic failure. He was the stuff of Greek myths. He was Sisyphus, I the rock. I was filled with grandiosity, sitting across from Denis. I felt a little like shouting or jumping up and down.

"Tell me more about your brother," he said.

"What do you want to know?"

"I don't know. What was it like living with him?" Denis sat forward in his chair.

I talked about Danny's loud voice, some of the less humiliating teasing (hiding in the front bushes and trying to scare me when I got home from school; picking up the phone extension while I was talking to David Nelson and making sex noises). I described his girlfriends, like Hindy Newman and Dawnelle Ryan. Denis wasn't taking notes as he usually did. Instead he was just sitting and nodding, staring at me. I said how Danny would eat all the eggs and peanut butter and cookies and cereal as soon as my mom came back from grocery shopping, how a couple days after she'd filled up the fridge, it'd be cleared out, the rest of us having barely gotten anything.

"What a pain in the ass," Denis said. If there was a singular thing I loved about Denis, it was his steadfast indifference toward Danny. I had feared that even though he knew my brother only by lore, Denis would one day surrender to the tales of charisma and popularity and charm and be taken in like the rest of them. "Do you miss him?" he said.

I leaned forward on the couch and imagined describing this scene later to Lola, the way I would try to coax her from her feelings of derision toward Denis, explaining the hum of conspiracy that had finally returned between him and me.

"Miss him?" I said. "Sure. I mean, of course."

Denis nodded, stretching his neck in such a way it made a series of hollow popping sounds. "Old man bones," he said. Then: "Not sure if I'd miss him."

"I mean, of course I miss him, because it's sort of miserable here now." I waved my hand in the air, as if he needed help in figuring out what I meant by *here.* Olivia started barking, thinking I had a treat for her. I shushed her. Denis nodded at me slowly in his knowing way with the half-smile, and I recognized that he was giving me silent permission, giving me an out. And it was titillating, his tendency to tread where so few others dared. Who else, I thought, was so willing to concede that Danny might be hard to miss?

"He was difficult." I said. "I mean, he was intense."

He nodded. "Sure. He sounds like he can be a piece of work."

I talked quickly then—it came out in a rush—about the oppressive, nearly suffocating quiet of the house now, but at least we were free of the ever-present vigilance of the tracking and cataloguing of Danny Pasternak's every move. I described the countless evenings of waiting for him to get home from swim or football practice as the spaghetti sauce simmered on the stove and my parents busied themselves with tasks, my mother wiping down the dinner table, my father sorting through the mail, but really, all of us just waiting to see if he would come bursting through the door after a missed pass or a butterfly stroke that clocked nineteen seconds slower than usual, full of venom and glowering. Those were dinners spent gingerly passing the rolls, the three of us making polite conversation, trying to avoid the vitriol that could roll so easily off his tongue (*Why you have to chew like a cow, Lydia? Who overcooked this pasta? Do we have to eat* this *again?*) as my parents impotently chided him.

And then there were those days he came home after a winning scrimmage and he would swing me like a potato sack over his shoulder, or kiss my mom on the cheek, or ask my dad if he wanted to toss the ball around in the backyard, all with a buzzy air of courtship. Most of the time I thought he was too obtuse to really recognize his singular influence on the mood of the house. Other times, as he stalked into the vestibule, his brow knit in familiar anger, I just thought he was careless in his power.

Denis was making *Um-hmm* sounds as I described this. The amazing thing about his face was that he was able to look at you intently, though with an expression free of judgment. That's not to say he was expressionless; his lips were slightly pursed, his forehead creased in a look of almost devout interest. The stubble and untrimmed mustache made him seem rough and nearly sad-looking. He had a grizzled vulnerability. I resisted asking if he wanted to come sit on the couch with me. This, I thought, in a tranquil, bright moment of clarity, this was all I wanted. Right here. I didn't need to be greedy or voracious. This was enough.

"Give me a typical fight you two had," he said.

I remembered him asking me something similar months earlier. I tried to think of something good. I told him about the time when Danny jammed my bedroom door closed with his desk chair so I was trapped inside for hours until my parents got home from work. I told him about when Danny ripped my National Junior Honor Society certificate off the fridge and then denied it when my dad found it torn to bits in the garbage.

"Jesus," Denis said, shaking his head.

I told him then about the whole titless wonder thing, about Danny one time kicking me in the shin and leaving a flowery bruise, about splattering bleach on one of my favorite shirts. I was no longer worried about humiliating myself, instead feeling like this was my chance to shift things permanently, to ensure that Denis would never be lulled by the gravitational pull of all things Danny. The light filtered through the blinds with the grayish tinge of evening, and I talked faster, worried that my mom would come back and wilt in the doorway, bags in hand, trembling and tearful from the myriad offenses of the world, like the harsh fluorescent lights of the grocery store or the rush-hour traffic on Penfield Ave.

When I stopped, Denis just smiled at me. He was nodding a little, staring directly in my eyes. I tried holding his stare but felt a tickle rising in me and couldn't quite do it. For a while he didn't say anything, and I tried to think of small talk, something about "How's Kimberly?" or "What other cases are you working on?" but then he said, "So what got you interested in the investigation?"

"Muh—" I said, a quick sound before I could stop myself. Then I laughed a little. Denis shifted farther forward in his seat, tugging at his belt loops as if to adjust himself. The question unnerved me. So did the way he kept staring, as if he already knew the answer and was just waiting for me to say it. There was no way to tell him I got interested because I liked him. The very idea sent a queasy shiver through me. Finally I said, "I want him to come home." But my voice was loud and unconvincing, Miss America.

"I mean," Denis said, "did you even like him?"

I shrugged. "Sure," I said.

"Really?"

"I mean, more when we were younger." Again, I remembered having told Denis a lot of this before.

"But now?"

"Now, you know, now is now. He could be a piece of work, like you said."

"So why work so hard to get him back?" he said.

I wasn't sure what he wanted. "He's still my brother."

"But you were resentful of him?"

"Sometimes."

"Jealous?" There was a new way he was looking at me, the slightest of changes, almost imperceptible really, his eyes a bit more squinty, his smile slightly plastic, the sort a clown would flash at a birthday girl only because he was getting paid.

"Sure. A little. I mean, he's not that smart, but he gets a lot of stuff."

"Stuff like your parents' attention?"

"And friends and girlfriends and popularity."

"And you didn't like that?"

"I mean, I didn't really care," I said, the tenor of the interaction going I knew slightly cockeyed. The way he was asking questions, different now from just a minute ago. But I couldn't stop. I was driven by momentum, a need to explain myself till we got right side up again. "Except it seemed like he never had to earn anything. And it wasn't like I ever wanted to be popular. I'm more popular now and it's just kind of stupid."

"So you're popular now that he's gone?" Denis said, leaning so far forward in his chair now, he seemed balanced on the cushion by just the tip of his tailbone.

"It's not like that," I said.

"What's it like?"

I wasn't sure exactly what he was asking. "It's like nothing. I'm not really popular. I just know his friends now."

"And you like it better this way?"

"What way?" I said.

"With your brother gone?"

I worried about the chill moving through me, the way my nipples were hardening beneath my shirt. Would he see that? I was ashamed of not wearing a bra. I never wore a bra. What a horrible fact that now seemed.

"No," I said. I was trying to keep my voice even. "I wouldn't put it that simply."

"How would you put it?"

"I wouldn't put it."

He didn't say anything. I didn't say anything. Aside from Poppy pawing at the carpet, the room was quiet. Denis watched me, his face unreadable. I acted like I was fascinated by what Poppy was doing.

"You know," he finally said, another tone change, now back to folksy and conversational, "early in my career, I had a client whose wife of twenty years had left him. Disappeared without a trace one day. He was desperate, the poor fellow. He'd been a crappy husband, cheated on her, lost his job. But he was ready to turn it around. And when he came to me, he was going out of his mind with worry. He was probably the most helpful client I think I ever had." The half-smile was back, the head cocked to one side, though his eyes still searched mine, and his hands picked intently at the wrinkled pleats in his pants.

"The guy would dig up her old high school yearbooks for me or give me her journals—I mean, some of these were twenty years old. He'd track down the phone numbers of the guys she'd dated when she was nineteen. He was thorough. He was like my unpaid assistant. And I couldn't have been happier for his help. I mean, I was green back then. Real green. Had maybe closed a handful of cases."

He chuckled at this. I chuckled back.

"But it got to a point where he was feeding me so much information that led me in so many different directions. His old lady had a big grudge against her boss, and also she had a cousin who lived in

Oaxaca and she'd always talked of wanting to retire there, and also she'd spent a couple months in the locked mental ward of the state hospital in the late seventies. I just started going in circles. Chasing my proverbial tail. And at some point you have to ask, is the guy trying to be helpful or is he trying to obfuscate? Does *he* have something to hide?"

Denis had stopped picking at his pants. His elbows were perched now on his knees, hands clasped in front of him. He stared at me in a way I'd never seen before, almost predatory, the way he was not blinking, the way his mouth was sealed so tightly shut.

"What?" I said. And "Wait." I could feel the churn of my belly, the acidic rise of food, hours old, through my esophagus: milk and stale cornflakes, a too-brown banana. I thought I might be sick. I had read of Raskolnikov, of Perry Smith, of Claudius; I should have known what it was to be tested for a crime. I should have easily discerned it far earlier, as anyone surely could've, from his first grinning strides into my living room, from the eager way he had let the dogs lick his hands. But I was dumb; Denis had made me so. Dumb as dirt, dumb as a meaty-faced boy who got himself one day disappeared.

"Now I'm not saying . . ." He held up his hands, shaking his head. He let his voice trail off and his face softened a little, though he still stared at me, unblinking. I wondered if he'd staked out our house for hours or maybe days, waiting and waiting until I was the only one home.

"He used to be nice," I said, and "I liked him." Denis didn't so much as twitch. It was too late. So far past too late. The things I thought to shout now—about the two of us sharing an inflatable raft when we vacationed in Maine years before, paddling past the breaker waves to the spot where we rescued water bugs and tried to touch our toes to the seaweed below; building a fort during our final fall in Abernathy with all the branches that'd been knocked off our maple in a giant windstorm; dragging beanbag chairs or Easy-Bake ovens into the long line of toys for the bridge game—seemed like the last-minute pleadings of a convict, the ridiculous denials of a shoplifter caught already with the clothes in her purse. My brother was a complete asshole; I'd just willfully, enthusiastically annihilated everything else. I'd reveled in it.

Denis stared and stared. I thought I might scream or flail wildly about, anything to get him to stop. "Listen—" I said, though nothing followed. What was he to listen to? That he'd gotten it all wrong? That I'd only said what I'd said and done what I'd done to get him to like me? That I was an opportunistic and black-hearted girl? "What happened to the guy's wife?" I finally said. I was squeaking.

"You're a smart girl," he said, though he said it in a terrible way. It made me actually catch my breath, an audible intake of air. A long pause opened between us, the silence even more terrible than the noise. My eyes welled and I sank into the cushions behind me. The back of my throat grew slick and salty, and the sudden effort required in trying not to cry, gargantuan. I thought, with some disgust, of my mother. There I sat, like her, trembling and helpless. My chest heaved. I tried to steady my breath. I even tried, ridiculously, to smile. Anything.

Denis made a noise, a snort or a sigh. Something breathy and from the nose. Later I would wonder if it'd been a laugh. "No stone unturned," he told me, and once again his voice was different, softer, his face returned to nearly normal. The way he was looking at me, he was just looking; he wasn't boring in. But he still sat perched on the edge of the chair, and I was so tired from trying to keep up with him, I had no idea where we were now. He held his hands in the air, both palms turned up to the ceiling. He was, it seemed, shrugging, and I had no idea what he meant by it. *Sorry, Charley?*

Whoops? All in a day's work? "Gotta look at everything," he said, "no matter how . . ." But he didn't finish, and I wondered desperately, as I would for days, what the missing word was, if it offered apology or further accusation. No matter how outlandish? Hurtful? Horrific? Unlikely? Painful? Ugly? Stupid?

Soon enough my mother returned. Denis was by then reclining again in his chair, his hands resting affably on his belly, the questions between us having returned to a more benign, though no less surreal, volley. He was back on something about Danny's temper or his friends—it hardly mattered—when she stumbled into the living room. Her cheeks were flushed. The plastic bag handles strained against her freezing hands, her fingers red and chapped. She should have worn gloves, I thought, but without my usual derision. I watched, out of my peripheral vision, the careful way Denis watched her and me. I suddenly wanted her to pat my shoulder or run her fingers through my hair, like when I was little and flu-ish and she would huddle next to my bed, her palm to my forehead, her breath on my face, making me believe I would be okay.

20.

In the days that followed, everything took on the tinge of a sick joke—the few frayed yellow ribbons that had survived the season, heavy with ice now, frozen stubbornly to tree trunks and mailboxes; the pep rally for the varsity athletes, Jerold slump-shouldered at one end of the gymnasium floor, Tip all puffed up at the other; the shiny pegs of the Lite-Brite that Lola and I stabbed through the black paper on our way to making an unintentionally ghoulish clown face or monstrous flower garden.

One morning I woke with a burst blood vessel in my left eye, a shocking cloud of red in the white of my sclera. Even my parents were alarmed by the sight. My father put his hand to his mouth at the breakfast table, my mother asked what on earth had happened to me. But the night before had been no different from any other, fitful and unrelenting. All day, and for days after, people asked what had happened, and always I told them I didn't know, though I found it satisfying, in the sick-joke sort of way, that the violent unrest of my nights had finally left a mark.

I stopped seeing Chuck. My parents believed me when I told them the sessions weren't doing any good, and the insurance had maxed out after twenty-six anyway. I spent most evenings in front of the television with one or both of them. I'd never been a fan of TV but now came to understand its allure. There was something wholly consuming in its bright pictures and white noise.

We watched, of course, the alien abductions and haunted houses of *Unsolved Mysteries* and soon added *America's Most Wanted* to the lineup. My mother discovered *Cops* and made derisive noises from the couch as poorly shaved, shirtless men were thrown against the hoods of police cars. With my father I watched the college basketball tournament. My father tried to muster the enthusiasm of years past, when the NCAA tournaments had been a time of great celebration in our household. He and Danny would stock up on beer and soda pop and pretzels and chips, camp out for entire weekends, eating meals on TV trays, scribbling wildly onto the sixty-four-tiered brackets they'd printed out from the computer. Now my father sometimes pounded his fist on his chair arm if he was unhappy or let out a hiss of approval at a good play, but mostly he just sat. Often when I looked he wasn't even watching the television, focused instead on a dust clot dangling in the corner of the ceiling or Poppy's tail as it thwapped against the carpet. Every once in a while he would try explaining things: "They're just trying to run down the clock," or "They'll keep fouling him because he's terrible at the free-throw line." Late into one afternoon, as the TV glowed in the darkening family room, he even passed me the last few tepid sips of his beer. "Don't tell your mother," he warned. And "It's going to taste bitter," as if this were my first.

It was during one of the games—Princeton vs. Mississippi State, Princeton trailing by nearly 20, my father's expression unreadable (other than Michigan, it was unclear who he was rooting for)—that my mother came into the room more energized than usual, almost bouncing on her tiptoes, both hands cupped in front of her as if ready to receive an offering. But the offering had already come. A slim envelope rested in her hands, the return address a black circle filled with the bubbly white lowercase letters of *abc.* It had been nearly eight weeks. *Unsolved Mysteries* was answering us.

"You open it," she said to me, her voice insistent and suddenly girlish. "Mute it, mute it," she told my father. My father moved slowly for the remote. Halftime had just begun, a well-choreographed herd of marching band members and cheerleaders descending on the court. I thought of Lola. My mother held the envelope out to me.

Even before I took it, before I slit open the flap with the side of my index finger and unfolded the thin paper to look at its generic paragraphs—the letter not even an original, copied instead many times over, gaps in the ink appearing from an aging Xerox machine—I sensed (and it was a strong sense, like the smell of rotten eggs or the taste of ipecac) the disappointment I was about to bring. And I thought, very clearly, do I really need to be the bearer of any more disappointment?

"Dear Viewer," I began. "Thank you for your interest in *Unsolved Mysteries.* All of us at ABC are heartened by the success of this show and proud of the many viewer tips that have poured in in response to many of our segments. With your help we have been able to apprehend suspects in an untold number of cases, such as Robert Creeley of Huntsville, Alabama, currently awaiting trial for the murder of his girlfriend and her twin daughters, Hannah and Abigail." These were inelegant, clunky sentences, I thought, probably written by some unpaid intern. "Men like Mr. Creeley," I continued, "would not be found without your vigilant viewership and phone calls. We wish we had time to answer each inquiry personally, but we appreciate your interest and hope you will continue to join us in solving America's *Unsolved Mysteries.*"

There was a pause when I finished. My father studied his hands; my mother still looked at me, her eyes intent, her mouth opening a bit wider. She leaned toward the piece of paper, her whole body an unspoken *And? And?*

"That's it," I said.

My father was suddenly rapt over the muted pageantry of half-time, watching the marching band as it patterned itself into an M, an S, and a U along the court. Someone in a bulldog costume did a long series of back flips. My mother said, "That doesn't even say anything. They didn't even read what we sent them."

"I'm sure they read it," my father said, but without feeling and without looking at her. "They're busy." I wondered what it was like for him all day at work. Was this how he spoke to all of his colleagues? Or did he fake it so well for them, this was all he had left for us?

My mom grabbed the paper out of my hand and studied it, moving it near to and far from her face, even flipping it over to examine the back. She cried quietly. Tears fell; her cheeks shone.

"It's okay, Bernice," my father said, and I wanted him to rise from his chair and go to her, though I knew that to be something he was constitutionally incapable of at that point. He did seem to falter at the remote for a moment—I'll give him that—struggling with his decision to turn the volume back on, which he eventually did. The band bleated out its fight song, heavy, like all the fight songs we'd heard in the past weeks, on the downbeats and brass.

. . .

When Denis came over now—and he still did, with increasing frequency and always with Kimberly—I would not look at him. He rallied my parents around the kitchen table, and the ritualized nature of the talks—he gave updates, they asked questions, smoke swirled heavily between them—began to strike me as mostly artifice, Denis leading them down a path of half-clues and faint hopes in order to justify his continued fees. There had been a few more visits to Tanda, he told them. He presented a follow-up composite that looked as hazy and amorphous as the first Roy. There was a state prisoner named Elvin Tate who faced sentencing in an attempted murder case and was said to have information about Danny. Denis talked importantly about making the drive to Jackson to meet with the man, but I listened to such stories numbly, often perched on the stairs, a room and a half away.

The few times he and I ended up in the same room, he smiled or spoke my name, saying, "Well, hello there, Lydia," giving no indication of our afternoon in the living room. "You get in a fight?" he said when he saw my eye, a note of genuine concern in his voice. I sometimes felt crazy, as if maybe I had invented the whole thing, maybe I had entirely misinterpreted what had happened between us, coloring it with my own paranoid hues.

I would have urges to lurch toward him then, maybe press my face against the messy hairs of his cheek, maybe bury my nose in his neck. But then I thought I saw him narrowing his eyes at me, or smiling in a way that was not so much friendly as scheming, or licking his lips as if readying for a challenge, and I would wonder if Grandma was the wolf, and if I was the idiot with the death wish, wanting to still skip and skip along, swinging my basket of cookies at my side.

• • •

By the end of March, the weather turned erratic in the jarring way it always did near the end of winter. For a day temperatures would rocket into the sixties, the air smelling dewy, the remaining snow melting in dramatic fashion, sheets of water sluicing along the edges of the roads and pouring loudly into storm drains. By the next morning, though, the cold would return, the streets and sidewalks would be dangerously slick, and branches would snap from trees from the weight of new ice, making people even more downcast and irritable than usual, such weather now an affront. The cold, Lola said one day, was like a welshed bet. I was surprised at the cleverness of the sentiment, though I told her that expression was racist. She blinked at me blankly. When I explained about the inhabitants of Wales, she said, "Princess Diana?" and then put her hand to her mouth, like she couldn't believe she'd insulted the princess.

It was on one of those recidivist cold days that I turned sixteen, an event marked by almost no one. I had told Lola my birthday was in July (*Cancer*, she'd said skeptically. *Weird*) to avoid the brownie-and-Rice-Krispies-treat tower, the *You look like a monkey and you smell like one too* that was a birthday at Lola's lunch table. My dad had arranged to pick me up after school and take me to the DMV for my driver's test. As I walked toward the line of waiting cars—strange to see my father's silver Taurus there—loud footsteps approached from behind. It was the heavy noise of running, and when I turned around, David Nelson was almost upon me, skidding to a stop.

"I wanted to catch you," he said, panting a little. "I looked for you at your locker. What are you doing out here?" By *here*, he meant the school's west entrance, the domain of underclassmen with parents willing to play chauffeur or at the very least arrange carpools. I imagined these also to be the parents who peopled the PTA and volunteered to pass out the juice cups at the blood drives. Normally I left through the front entrance to a waiting bus.

I pointed to my dad's car across the street, half a block down. David waved, though we were far enough away, I couldn't see if my dad was waving back through the windshield or even looking in our direction.

David said, "I would be cool with going with you to look at the Fairfield police mug books sometime. I think that makes sense to do too. Covering all the bases." He'd left me a message saying as much a few days earlier. He'd left an earlier one about a book he'd started reading on forensics, how elements of crime scenes can be inadvertently preserved for years, especially when cold is involved.

"Listen," I said. "I'm done with that."

"Done with what?"

"The investigation. It's fucking stupid."

He looked a little like I'd slapped him. "The investigation to find your brother is *stupid*?"

I didn't know how to explain. Not to him. "Listen, I gotta go." I waved in the direction of my dad's car.

David's mouth hung a tiny bit open. A bustle of people filed past us on the sidewalk. Kids opened passenger doors. Parents started up cars, trying to ease backward and forward out of their tight spots. It was a bleak day, the sun shrouded behind clouds, the sky looking small and forbidding, as if it ended just above the treetops. David's nostrils flared, his eyes widening. He looked unsatisfied, in need of something more. Him being in need of something more made me hate him a little. I shrugged, for lack of a better response. He busied himself rummaging through his backpack and I told him again that I had to go.

"Wait!" he said with unusual force. When he was finished rummaging, he handed me a card, not even looking at me anymore. *Bering*, it said along the envelope in his small, precise handwriting, a nickname from my straits period. It surprised me and made me feel like a heel; a small, tight, blockish thing traveled up through my chest. David Nelson had always made me handmade birthday cards on his computer, with inappropriate quotes (one year, the front read: *"Hastiness and superficiality are the psychic disease of the 20th century."* —Alexander Solzhenitzyn) or with pictures of fractals or nebulae.

"Thanks," I told him, training my voice to sound nicer. I thought of other things to say, about being sorry or taking things back or was there anything I needed to look out for on the driving test, but I didn't want to keep my dad waiting, and I didn't want David to watch me read the card. He was squinting at me now, his face a question. I squeezed his shoulder. It felt weird squeezing his bony shoulder through his coat, felt a little like I could snap him apart right there, like he might let me. I thanked him again and called things over my shoulder as I ran to my dad, about later, about good, about bye.

The woman who took me out for my road test snapped her gum and drummed the end of her pen against her clipboard. She gave out every direction as if my presence were an imposition: *Come to a full stop. Make a left turn. Merge with the center lane of traffic.* I scraped the back wheel against the curb while parallel parking, gunned the motor once when accelerating from a red light, turned on the brights when I'd meant just to use the left turn signal. I'd barely driven since being pulled over, and now the slick roads made me go slowly; my dad had warned ominously of black ice on the way over. But shortly into the test, some sort of autopilot seemed to kick in, a calmer, more competent part of me that knew how to steer the car within a lane, how to scan the traffic around me, how to check my blind spot without even really having to think about it. I did not cross a yellow line. I did not exceed 25 on residential streets. I stopped at the pedestrian crosswalk.

The end came without flourish. Instead of congratulations, the woman handed me a pale yellow slip of paper to take to the counter, then ushered me back into the lobby, where I waited for my number to be called and my father paged through the Spanish-language version of the driver's manual (he didn't speak Spanish). We waited a long time. I watched the flashing red numbers of the NEXT sign. I watched a woman breastfeed a squawky baby. Eventually I pulled David's card from my bag.

It turned out to be store-bought, with a pastel drawing on the front of deer in a field. Inside was a printed poem following a basic meter and simple rhyme scheme (*The seasons are turning*, one line read; *which means you are growing and learning*, read the next). At the bottom David had written simply *Happy Birthday* and signed his name. I was a little surprised. Had he meant it, I wondered, as a bit of a dig? Did he think me now the sort of person we'd always made fun of, the kind who liked this Hallmarky sort of bad poetry?

I ran my fingers over the picture of the deer, the grass embossed with a scaly pattern. The card seemed a concession of sorts, a signal of some newfound resignation from David Nelson, as if at least some of the fight was going out of him. And for that I felt both a little sad and cautiously relieved.

Finally the man who worked the camera called my name and posed me against the white backdrop. "Smile, beautiful," he said, the same thing I'd heard him say to the humpbacked old lady before me. The red still lingered in my left eye, making me look tearful in the picture, or possibly drunk.

In the parking lot, my father tossed me the keys, the gesture so uncharacteristically playful ("Heads up," he said), I didn't protest, even though I felt suddenly like I wanted to retain my status as simply passenger. The act of getting my license hadn't brought the heady buzz of accomplishment I'd imagined, but instead a slightly achy and uncertain feeling as I stepped blindly into . . . what? I couldn't see what. That was the problem. When I told my dad "Thanks," and walked to the driver's side door, my voice came out dense and gummy, a sound that would've embarrassed me if I'd thought he noticed.

By now the sky was fading in earnest into night, the sun casting its last sliver of light just above the horizon. It was after five and the swell of rush hour was crowding the road, an exponential increase in traffic since my test. My headlights cast faint pools of pale light, and it was hard to tell the difference between wet spots and ice. My dad grew quickly tense in the passenger seat, gripping the door handle and starting forward whenever I tapped the brakes.

"Signal," he told me in a clipped voice as I veered into a left turn lane. "Slow down," he told me half a block before a stop sign. He shared, it seemed, my almost instantaneous regret at this shift in power.

I tried to remember how much I'd enjoyed driving the previous summer, the soothing way it had forced me to focus my attention, filtering out everything but the most essential bits of information. I tried to look only at the taillights of the car in front of me or the dotted yellow line in the road, but I had a hard time letting my gaze focus on any one thing, sure I was about to miss something elsewhere. My breathing was audible, shallow and reedy, my awareness of it bringing quick shame. When I looked at my father, he was steeling himself the way roller-coaster riders did as they crept up the rails before the first descent.

"Sorry," I said, about nothing, everything, trying to regain the calm autopilot of my road test.

The lights of the car behind me shone blindingly into my mirror.

"Are that guy's brights on?" I asked.

"He's just high up," my dad said, giving me directions on how to adjust my rearview mirror to dull the shine. I pressed on the tab the way he told me, but it only seemed to flash the lights even more directly into my eyes. Nearby a car honked, and I jumped in my seat.

"It's not working," I said as I continued to fight with the mirror.

My dad grabbed the mirror and yanked it around in an unhelpful way. When he was done, it seemed to be focused on the cushions of the backseat.

The back of my neck ached from the strain of sudden concentration. Stimuli flooded me: the taillights brightening ahead of me, the endless signs (MERGE, CURVE AHEAD, LEFT LANE ENDS), the loud, wet noise of cars passing on either side. As I tried to ease into the seat, tried to breathe from my diaphragm, we hit a patch of ice, and suddenly, without warning, the car was possessed, jerking violently in a long, sharp series of stutters. The steering wheel pulled quickly through my fingers. The front of the car swung wildly into the left lane.

I screamed. The noise was so piercing, so entirely without thought, it shocked even me. Car horns screamed back.

My father yelled, a stream of surprising *shits* and *goddamnits*, and in what seemed like slow motion—I was sure we were going to jump the curb and fly into the grassy island between us and the oncoming traffic—he grabbed the wheel and steered us fully into the left lane, to more angry sounds of screeching brakes and car horns.

With one of his hands still on the wheel, my dad kept yelling,

"Gas, you need to give it more gas! Look in front of you! Pay attention!" It was not until he said, in a voice straining against anger and fighting for calm, "We're okay. Stop crying," that I realized I was, that I felt the coolness on my cheeks and tasted the salt on my lip.

"Pull over," he said. "Pull over onto the shoulder."

Slowly—putting the blinker on, checking over my shoulder again and again—I merged into the center lane, then the right one, finally pulling the car onto the gravel and bringing it to a stop. My fingertips burned. My ears buzzed. I couldn't stop shaking.

It was there, in that car—and in later cars, as I imagined my doom at the hands of drivers who could careen blindly out of alleyways or run a red light or veer across the double line into my lane—that fear caught up with me. Starting in that moment and continuing into the years that followed, it would not be while walking alone in the dark or sitting in doctors' offices awaiting biopsy results or on blind dates with aggressive, grabby men that I would feel the deep, sickening fear of a world without parameters, a world where all bets were off. It would occur, inexplicably and potently, while I drove a car. Whenever I was granted respite from the knowledge that my brother had one day gone missing—such welcome moments of forgetting—it would never be while behind the wheel. When I drove, I saw the world in its undeniable state, as a place that protected no one, that held nothing sacred, that pitted all of us against each other.

"Let me drive," my father was saying, his voice still firm but nearly his own again. He unclicked first his seatbelt and then mine, opened his door, came around to mine, told me I could go sit in the passenger seat. "Come on," he said, placing a hand gently on my head, smoothing my hair. "It's okay," he said, more softly now, the last hints of impatience gone. For a second he touched my shoulder, ever so lightly kneading the muscles with his fingers. "Come on," he repeated, guiding me out the door, and for the first time in a long time, I remembered a little bit that he loved me, so I loved him a little bit back.

21.

It was not long after, during the first tentative days of April, when the daylight stretched just past 6 p.m. and the sun stayed visible for brief handfuls of days in a row, that Lola cajoled me into going with her to the Pep Recognition Dinner and Awards Ceremony. The PRDAC, as she called it, or *Predac.* The lunch table had been a-twitter about the Predac for weeks. What were people going to wear? Who was taking whom? It was a big deal for them, complete with dresses and invitations and statuettes. Months of fundraising car washes and bake sales served as a run-up to this one night: a rented room in the back of an Italian restaurant, a portable microphone and dais, recognition of the best of the flag team, dance team, and pep squad. I tried to feign polite attention through the endless conversations, though even that proved a challenge; they ran the topic into the ground with even more gusto than their typical fare (boys, purses, diets).

The biggest upside to Predac, as I could see it, was that it trained Lola's attention away from matchmaking and onto something that had nothing to do with me. I was going only because Lola had handed me an invitation with unexpected solemnity and said, "Please come. You're my best friend." I felt sorry for her then. What a cruddy lot that seemed for someone as bright-eyed as she.

The restaurant was the kind with red velvet curtains draped over the windows and gold-painted candelabra overhead, flame-shaped light bulbs flickering their synchronized flicker. The servers held white napkins over their forearms and the busboys wore bowties. The place, appropriately, tried too hard while still missing the mark. The breadsticks in the basket were slightly stale, the air smelled pungently meaty and insufficiently ventilated; the flowerpots on the way to the restroom were filled with obvious fakes.

But the night turned out to be not terrible, offering the same cordial, benign escapism as events like basketball games and parties. Lola was full of her usual good cheer, though for once I didn't feel cowed by it. It was a bit like watching an animal in her natural habitat. All night, girls from the pep squad and the dance team came up to compliment her on how great the flag team was doing this year, how much they liked her new choreography. I hadn't realized Lola did the choreography, hadn't realized either that she was particularly respected among her peers. I had come to assume she was well enough liked though naturally seen as something of a joke.

During dinner, Bayard amused the table with his imitations of an American accent: "Eye *aynt* gaht noe tayme fur yer *crap.*" The lasagna wasn't bad. I couldn't remember the last time I'd been to a restaurant, the last time I'd used a salad fork. People made fun of Diana for the dollop of honey mustard dressing on her chin, though not meanly. We weren't allowed to order alcohol, though thick-thighed Rochelle started a trend of Shirley Temples, which were sweet enough to at least bring a quick, sugary rush, especially when drunk very fast.

For the awards, the teams' parent sponsors and faculty advisers handed out certificates and plaques and trophies for everything from most improved dancer to best song choice. When Ms. Lefton, family and consumer science teacher and flag team adviser, called out Lola's name for the Brenda K. Jenkins Leadership and Team Spirit Award, I assumed that, given the lateness of the evening and the length of the award name and the loudness of the cheers (Beth and Penny were up from their seats, hands over their heads), and the deep, deep red spreading up Lola's neck and cheeks, this was a very big deal. She hugged Ms. Lefton for a long time. When she stood at the dais, she held the microphone too close to her mouth as she talked of honor and hard work and pride in her team. The words came out loud and squelchy, and I kept waiting for Ms. Lefton to adjust the mike. But instead she just stood beside Lola, a huge grin on her face. Other people were enthralled. Diana murmured assents and Rochelle clasped her hands together at her neck, like she might break out in song. Lola's voice cracked with emotion near the end, and she kept sputtering *Thank you, really, thank you, thank you.* People clapped and hooted as she finished; I whooped a low whoop.

When she came back to the table, I hugged her. She was warm with excitement. I could feel her shaking a tiny bit. I whispered in her ear, "Great job. Great job," and held on longer than usual, thinking to myself that a life could be made of such moments, bearing witness to other people in their small, silly happinesses. It wouldn't be so bad.

. . .

When I got home, Denis's car was parked out front, the driveway blocked by a police cruiser. It was as if the still sugary taste in my mouth and the lingering remnants of the night's unexpected goodwill made me temporarily dense, because I barreled inside, half curious, half uncaring, half wanting to tell a loud, braggy, partially true story about the good time I had had with my friends at Predac, because what mattered to me most still was proving something to Denis. It seemed as if nothing would ever matter more.

There was a tableau in the living room: Denis and two officers lined up before the mantel, performing a show, Denis's arms slicing through the air while he spoke, the officers nodding along, their hats in their hands, Kimberly standing a few steps away, staring at the floor, her fingers worrying the hem of her blouse (I had never seen Kimberly fidget before), my father tilted forward in his chair, his face a strange color, a green-gray, the joking shade of a cartoon character who pinches his lips together as his cheeks fill with vomit, my mother contorted, both arms wrapped fully around her head, her head dipping into her lap, her whole body hiccuping in a series of tiny convulsions. For a moment they stayed fixed like that, before the dogs barked at my entrance, and in that blink of time I thought of the stiff napkin that had just been in my lap, the heavy crystal water glass, the pink stir stick of my Shirley Temple. I told myself, even as Olivia bounded over, followed quickly by Oliver and Poppy, all three yapping loudly, the point at which everyone turned their heads and looked, their faces so pallid and drawn they might have been staring at me from the gallows, that I had already made it through the aftermath. I had already arrived, bruised but intact, at the other side. I was, I told myself (the voice in my head calm, modulated, like the narrator from the filmstrips in social studies about the Yanomami Indians or the rainforests in Costa Rica), already done.

I heard Denis tell me simply, *Oh*, like the wind was being knocked out of him, and then the officer with the mustache tell me something *found* and something *gone*. It was Kimberly, of all people, who extended a hand in my direction, though I did not go toward it. The dogs yipped loudly at my ankles, one of them scratching at my pant leg. Everyone's mouths kept moving, my mother emitting moans, my father maybe saying my name, Kimberly cooing something, the other officer talking a quick, slurring stream of *clothing remains northeast jail search*. I thought of breadsticks and tablecloths. I thought of salad forks.

The words from my living room, they were a cacophony of discordant sound, washing over me rather than penetrating, the meaning elusive, a puzzle that would be pieced slowly together in the days to come. "What?" I remember saying, the sole word I spoke. "What? What?" My breath was so sweet from the grenadine. I could taste it on my lips.

People answered me—I saw my father's mouth moving, maybe Denis's too—but it was just more noise. Had a linguist stood beside me in the front hallway, I was convinced he'd have discovered a new language that night, a guttural, frayed derivative of English, a tongue just barely comprehensible, inflected as heavily as it was by paroxysms of bewilderment and grief.

Gar

22.

Elvin Tate killed my brother.
Elvin Tate. Killed my brother.
Elvin. Tate. Killed. My. Brother.

If ever there was a sentence more quickly imprinted in my consciousness, more oft repeated, one that stood as more of an arbiter against which to judge all else (*I do not understand inverse functions; Elvin Tate killed my brother. I am unloved; Elvin Tate killed my brother*), I do not know it. In the beginning, the repetition was the numb sort, the words impenetrable. Only occasionally did they have the power to stop me midstep as I walked upstairs. Or seize my stomach as I ate. Or clear my head as I attempted to speak. *And . . . and . . .*

and . . . I heard myself saying over and over again, knowing no cogent thought waited at the end of my stammer. *And* was just a delay tactic, and not a very sophisticated one at that, a noise to make until I figured out a way to remove myself from whatever conversation I'd found myself trapped in.

Mostly, though, the sentence served as staticky background noise, ever-present, fading in and out of meaning, the stubborn line of a forgotten poem. As the mob of mourners descended and our phone shrieked with continual noise and flowers piled on our doorstep, I shaped my mouth silently around the seven syllables, fixated on the sound of them: the oddly aristocratic tinge to *Elvin Tate*, the aspirated start of *killed*, the light, feathery sound at the end of *my brother.*

People tried to talk to me. My mom's sister, Aunt Pat, asked how I was holding up and I was distracted by her yellow teeth; they looked almost fluorescent. It'd been years since I'd seen Aunt Pat. The teeth seemed like something I'd remember.

I told her, "Like an ill-fitting sweater." She got tiny creases between her eyes. I smiled to try to make her feel better. Her creases deepened.

When Denis called to check on us, I didn't know what to tell him. He called me his usual *kiddo*, which made me want to scream, though the impulse came from some remote place, like a director sitting far offstage whispering, *Lydia, think now about screaming.* The conversation turned to mad cow. I'd been reading about it, I told him. It seemed like people were being hysterical. There was a pause. He asked if I'd considered any kind of medication. "For mad cow?" I asked, giggling, that sound too coming from the same remote place. The director was giggling.

For shock, he told me.

I didn't feel like I was in shock. I felt like I hadn't slept in eight months. I felt like my brother was dead. I wasn't sure what that was supposed to feel like, though I was pretty well convinced that the muddle of exhaustion, incredulity, and confusion was a fair approximation. Days swam by. How, I wondered, did people manage to differentiate a Tuesday from a Wednesday? News arrived jigsaw puzzle-like, strange bits next to incongruent pieces. I had an insatiable need to know details, though details were scarce. The police told us some, Denis more. We read about ourselves in the newspaper.

This much we knew: Elvin Tate had been in jail awaiting trial for bashing in his girlfriend's skull with the face of an iron, leaving her alive but brain-damaged. During his pretrial period, he unsuccessfully attempted to implicate his cellmate in Danny's death. He'd been trying to gain leverage with the DA, but within days his story fell apart. His cellmate had an alibi, and Elvin knew far too many details not released to the press—the birthmark on Danny's lower back, the card he carried as a joke in his wallet with a hammer and sickle, his membership in the Communist Party.

Eventually Elvin confessed to picking up Danny blocks from the basketball courts on the night of August 2nd. He'd been driving a 1990 Dodge Dynasty. They'd taken a meandering route up north and east for three and a half days. On the fourth day he strangled my brother and buried the body in the woods beyond a cherry farm just below the Upper Peninsula. Again: He strangled my brother. And buried him in the woods. Behind a cherry farm.

I thought a lot about the cherry farmers. Who in the world became northern Michigan cherry farmers? I pictured them as an old, grizzled couple, skin permanently rough and dried out from the harsh winters. I imagined them tight-lipped, hardy, and not prone to displays of emotion. Certainly they'd endured dry seasons and poor crops. They had to be intimately familiar with heartache, acclimated to the vagaries of nature and fate. But I wondered what this did to them, the unearthing of this boy from their ground. I wondered if the familiar creaks of their old house now felt ominous and forbidding. Or the spring wind a wolf huffing and puffing. I wondered if they spoke quietly to each other about their terrible luck, each privately cataloguing past transgressions that would account for such a thing happening to them. I wondered if they found themselves achy and tender at the end of the day, rolling toward each other before sleep for the first time in years, trying to quell their growing sense of smallness, a sense they hadn't had since they were very young, since before they ever met, when their current life was some far-off dream, or maybe not even a far-off dream yet.

Elvin's mug shot was flashed continually on the local news—that and an old, oft-repeated grainy photo of him standing on a browning front lawn in a sleeveless T-shirt and cut-off shorts. He was slight, with a narrow chest and knobby elbows, the cowering posture of someone who'd been punched one too many times in the gut. How could someone like that, I wanted to know, have overpowered an eighteen-year-old defensive end? How had he managed to lure Danny into his car? Why would Danny ever agree to go with him anywhere? Why had no one seen them? And what exactly had happened for those three and a half days?

The police revealed additional details only sparsely. When a paunchy officer came to the door one day—this one familiar, though the names never stuck; he the one who looped his thumbs through his belt loops in an Old West sheriff stance—he wore the grim, familiar expression of bad news. As we all gathered in the kitchen, waiting, he said to my parents, "Your daughter?" He wouldn't even look at me. Quickly my mother nodded. "Lydia," she said, "why don't you wait in the other room?"

I filled with a heady sort of rage that pressed against the insides of my eardrums and made my cheekbones quiver. Now would not be the time for them to turn protective. I was not leaving this room. My father must have sensed something, because he simply put a hand to my arm and squeezed my elbow lightly. The officer looked between my father and me, and it seemed that he'd continue to object. But then he began speaking with exquisite tenderness, his apparent attempt to diffuse the potency of the words, though it achieved just the opposite effect. There was something particularly horrific about this man kindly whispering to us the stuff of nightmares.

The body—how instantaneously it had gone from *Danny* to *the body*—was decomposed after all these months, he told us. However, there were detectable signs of postmortem sexual abuse. Eight of the fingers were broken, telltale signs of defensive wounds. The face—not *his* face, the *body's* face—had been beaten; that, combined with corpse degradation, meant he'd had to be identified through dental records. My father was swaying; he reached for the back of a kitchen chair. My mother slumped against the wall. The details, rather than bringing the situation into clearer relief, just made it so outrageous, so exaggerated and disproportionate, the whole thing slipped easily into the realm of joke or tall tale.

"Do you know the farmers?" I asked.

Everyone looked at me. The officer said, "What farmers?"

"The cherry farmers," I said. "Where they found him. I was thinking of writing them a letter." My voice had a weird sound to it, a queer lightness. I sounded like a quiz-show contestant.

The police officer looked at my parents. My dad pressed a hand to my elbow again, this time squeezing harder. My mom was biting determinedly at her lips, searching my face. No one answered. The police officer talked more to us, about *medical examiner* and *autopsy* and *skull fractures.*

It turned out Tanda had been a liar or a drunk. Or both. There was no Roy. Elvin looked nothing like the composite—he had buck-teeth and eyes that bulged from their sockets. His chin jutted forward like a hook. And the route he'd taken had passed nowhere even close to River Rouge. His Dodge Dynasty, though, had been brown, the front panel indeed rusted above both wheel wells. This one piece of information brought me outsized solace. *Something*, at least, had borne out from the investigation, though when I tore back through my notes, I'd not listed the Dynasty among the cars for Denis to look into. The omission gutted me; I felt like I had to lie down. As soon as I did, though, I had to get right back up. It was hard to be stationary. Lying in my bed now as I had for all those months—it seemed sometimes like the only thing I'd done was lie prone on my mattress from the day he left to the day we found out—brought a vertiginous sort of nausea, a dizzying stomachache.

I took small comfort in the fact that Melissa Anne had been wrong too. Yes, he'd been buried, but not inches below the surface as she'd prophesied. The grave had not been shallow. There'd been, it turned out, nearly four feet of dirt to dig through before Danny's remains had been unearthed. He was almost at the clayey subsoil.

The funeral had to be moved from B'nai Israel to a Masonic hall due to anticipated attendance. More than nine hundred showed up, according to the TV news, which flashed pictures of the overflow crowd swelling into the street, all listening through auxiliary speakers set up just for this occasion. At the time I didn't once turn around from the front row, feeling like the pulsing, hungry throngs could pull me apart limb by limb. I just stared at the plain pine box, wondering what was inside. Only my father had seen the remains. I had asked him what he'd seen when he came back from the medical examiner's, I'd asked him what it looked like, I wanted to know, but he made only a noise, something like *Gar.*

The rabbi spoke senseless, droning Hebrew, which filled me with fury. I wanted, at least, to understand what he was saying. I watched him up on the stage, the shawl wrapped around his shoulders, the beanie perched high on his head, and sang the sentence to myself—*Elvin Tate killed my brother*—the words having morphed into the most ghoulish of nursery rhymes, like singsong tales of Humpty Dumpty's broken body or Old Mother Hubbard's starving children.

An infestation of people arrived for shiva, the aunts pinning torn pieces of black fabric to our shirts, relatives I barely knew asking strange questions about school and if I was still playing the clarinet. I hadn't played clarinet since fifth grade. People touched my face, cupping my chin in their palm or brushing the backs of fingers to my cheek. They served me plate after plate of gummy food like egg salad and noodle kugel.

Outside, TV vans parked up and down the street and camera crews tromped across our lawn, forcing us to close all the blinds, lending a siegelike feel to the whole venture. My father had taped a handwritten note to the front door, an inelegant Sharpie missive about leaving us to our family and friends, thank you very much. I watched through the slats of the blinds as cameramen came up our steps and filmed closeups of the note. Kirk Donovan and the lady from Channel 4 staked out competing territory on the sidewalk, both fiddling with their microphones and their hair. The lady from Channel 4 looked smaller and more deflated in person, as if the hand had been removed from her sock puppet. Min Mathers stopped and cried for her on the way in, the camera brightening her face.

Inside, each side of the family quickly self-segregated, the loud, dark Pasternaks taking over the living room, eating constantly and telling unembarrassed stories of rheumatoid arthritis and hemorrhoidal sitz baths. The Davidsons scattered themselves throughout the kitchen and den, balancing plates awkwardly on their knees and looking bewildered, as if waiting for someone to please tell them what to do. My mother sat at the kitchen table or in the corner of the couch, a cloud of well-meaning cousins trailing her, bringing her plates of food, kneading her thigh, holding her hand and cooing words I did not get close enough to hear. My father, having sat for all those months and months, now paced, stopping to speak with people if they spoke to him first. Harry, his family called him. I wasn't used to people calling him Harry. My mother called him Harris or nothing at all. Harry reminded me of the dog in one of my long-ago children's books.

Lola Pepper's mom brought an elaborate cold cut tray, carrots and radishes carved into roses, rolls of meat speared with ribboned toothpicks, sawtoothed slices of pickles decorating the edges. She told me it was kosher and I thanked her without informing her we'd never kept kosher. Lola gurgled and wailed in a way that made me want to punch her in the face.

David Nelson showed up in the same tie I'd seen him wear for the National Junior Honor Society dinner, green with gold polka dots. I wondered if it was his only tie. It looked like it was choking him. He said things like what a good funeral it'd been and how Danny had been a good guy. He kept repeating *good.* I told him you don't have to wear a tie to shiva. It wasn't, I told him, a job interview.

Tip Reynolds shared the couch with an uncle and assorted cousins. At one point Dawnelle Ryan went and sat next to him and I watched the way their thighs pressed together. One of my uncles stared obviously at Dawnelle's huge boobs; they were packed tightly into her fuzzy black sweater. For a while she rested a hand on Tip's forearm, twiddling very softly his thick arm hair. I saw him touch the back of her neck. I tried not to keep looking. I told myself, *Dead brother dead brother dead brother.*

But I was a terrible mourner. I tried to make myself cry, going into the half bath and pinching the tender skin on the inside of my arm until a clot of tears built up in my throat, but performance anxiety always stifled me, even behind a closed door, perched alone and fully dressed on the edge of the toilet seat. One night, when the rabbi asked me to help set up rows of folding chairs in the living room for his interminable nightly service, I burst into sudden laughter. I recognized the look he gave me then, the prurient curiosity, part gaping, part pitying. It was the same way I looked at the special ed kids as they were wheeled through the halls with their palsied limbs and protective helmets. I was a remedial griever.

When shiva finally ended and the house cleared of relatives and neighbors and classmates, the three of us got really sick—vomiting, swollen glands, cheekbones sensitive to the touch. It was not a fleeting illness; it was entrenched and lingering. The moment it seemed one of us might be getting better, the symptoms morphed into something new. For three days my throat burned so hotly I couldn't swallow and had to carry a spit cup for my yellow-green phlegm. My father got long rows of blisters in his armpits. My mother's tongue grew white and almost furry. We were deeply, undeniably miserable, though being sick was almost a relief for me, the way it finally made me properly wet-faced, broken down, funereal.

We spent the following days listless on the couch, wrapped in blankets, full of sweaty chills even though the cold outside had finally broken and the spring thaw had set in in earnest. Melted snow collected in wide puddles across our patchy lawn, turning quickly to mud from the footprints of the most stubborn of camera crews and lingering reporters. We ignored the knocks on our door, the phone calls from newspapers or television stations or members of the state senate who talked about crime bill sponsorship. We ignored Denis, who wondered how we were holding up. We ignored the strangers, some who talked about heaven, others about vengeance, a few whose cries into the answering machine sounded like loud, angry squirrels.

Mostly we just sat, wordless, foodless, in and out of a dissatisfying half-sleep. It was easy to get confused about day versus night, about other stuff too. After a particularly violent burst of nausea or in the midst of a headache that made me see purplish red starbursts inside my eyelids, I found myself wondering:

Elvin Tate killed my brother?

Elvin Tate?

My brother?

I might lie curled in the dark, my feet pressed gingerly against my mother's leg as she huddled at the other end of the couch, my mind hiccuping, then sputtering until I eventually came to think of the recent turn of events as nonsensical and unreal. Of course Elvin Tate had not killed my brother. Don't be silly. I grew convinced that all we were doing here was waiting, still waiting. I could feel it on a cellular level, the wide-open freefall of possibility still before us. I tried, in those moments, to tell my parents something reassuring, mumbling about Denis or Roy or Melissa Anne, my father maybe mumbling back at me, my mother pressing her leg weakly into my foot.

But there were too many concrete items, too much morbid memorabilia now littering our house. Whenever I was well enough to venture from the living room, I found things like the Ziploc bag that sat in the freezer, of all places, containing his few belongings returned by the police, covered with flaky, graying mud and crystallized now with frost—his slim nylon wallet, the braided string cut from his wrist, the four poker chips plucked from his pocket: three blue, one red.

In the vestibule sat a stack of unread newspapers, many with Elvin Tate's bug-eyed face peering from above the fold.

Atop the file cabinet was the lone crime scene photo. I would spend coming weeks digging through drawers, searching for others—surely there were more—to no avail. This seemed the only one in our possession: a forest floor covered in a crusty layer of snow, shoeprint trails, yellow tape strung around four tree trunks in a flimsy, diamond-shaped barricade, a deep hole in the center, tall piles of dirt lining the lip, the hole itself an empty mouth, nothing but black, either before they got to him or after he was already gone. I wondered how he had been placed down there, whether Elvin Tate had rested him gently at the bottom in a fetal position or pushed him unceremoniously over the side, limbs sprawled, his face jammed into the dirt. I thought of the dissected pig from eighth-grade bio class, the tiny snapping sounds of its legs as they were pulled unforgivingly back from its body, the bones not even sounding like bones, sounding like something else entirely. Tinker Toys. Pick-up sticks. My mouth tasted of bile as I studied the picture. My mouth had tasted of bile for days. Maybe weeks. I thought, *Gar.*

This circuit of the house usually ended at the kitchen table and the stack of extra funeral programs, the photo on the cover a rare unfamiliar one, its potency not yet drained from overuse on posters or in newspaper articles. In it, Danny was sitting on the hood of someone's car, his feet on the front bumper, his elbow on his knee, chin resting in an upturned hand, a bastardized *Thinker*, though the picture did not look staged. His hair fluttered in the wind and he was looking off to the side. The uncharacteristic softness of his features—his mouth open just a bit, a slight tinge of a smile, his eyes looking almost wistful and without a hint of his usual swagger—made it seem like he'd had no idea the picture was being taken.

It was a really good picture. He looked gentle and almost girlish in his beauty. I sat for long daytime hours in a kitchen chair staring at it, as the soles of my feet and the small of my back ached. I tried to think of times he'd looked like this in real life, so placidly thoughtful. It was there that I would eventually cry, from the exhaustion of a body rigid with constant, thrumming pain and from the guilt that lay beneath my sick. How little I had missed him, and how wrongly (the first dread inklings already beginning to stir) I had envisioned the place we now inhabited. I'd thought we'd be fine here—swift and gutting pain, yes, but with a wound, at least, to seal—in the dark, fleeting, and many moments I had dared to hope for this.

23.

It was nearly a month before I returned to school, to the last six weeks of my sophomore year and the classes I'd lost track of and the mountain of assignments I'd missed and the shrieking noise of classmates who came at me collectively and without apology under the auspices of sympathy, though sympathy seemed far too soft a word, like *heather* or *tissue.* People grabbed me by the arm or followed me into the girls' room to ask, "Are you okay? Really? Are you?" through the closed stall door. They tried to ingratiate themselves with me through the use of urgent irrelevancies: "I used to sit next to him in chem." "I almost rear-ended him one time on Coolidge." It all felt violent as an avalanche, the force with which the whole student body, it seemed, exerted its attentions upon me.

Mrs. Bardazian announced loudly "You've been missed" as I found my seat, and a strange smattering of applause followed. David

Nelson was one of the applauders, which felt like betrayal. Mrs. Bardazian stood at her desk and read Donne's "Death Be Not Proud": "And soonest our best men with thee doe goe/Rest of their bones, and soules deliverie." Kids turned in their seats to look at my face, which I tried to hold as still as possible, though I could feel a faint flutter at the corner of my right eye, the start of a tremble in my clenched jaw.

My locker was wrapped in much the same way football players' lockers were wrapped on game days, the front covered with butcher paper, the perimeter decorated with construction paper daisies, giving it a disturbingly festive feel. Classmates had written crowded notes, drawn frowny faces with cartoon tears, and scribbled countless *Sorrys*. I wondered at the etiquette of this, the number of days that had to pass before I was allowed to tear it down.

Danny's shrine too had been reborn. It was more sprawling this time, a longer stretch of wall filled with notes, team photos, a football jersey, swim goggles, newspaper coverage of the funeral. Old bouquets sat piled against the wall, their green cellophane wrappers still intact though the flowers had shriveled. Had they been dying in this hallway for close to a month now?

After a few days back in Fontana's trig class, David passed me a note about not knowing how to talk to me anymore and being sad about that and being sorry for everything that had happened to me. It was in more careful handwriting than normal, and I wondered how long he'd spent on it. It went on for several paragraphs, and I couldn't bring myself to finish. I felt him watching me from across the room, so I sat with the piece of paper open in front of me for a long time, affecting a posture of concentration and then avoiding him when the bell rang.

In the middle of my first week back, Tip offered to smuggle me off-campus for lunch. "Who's going to stop *you*?" he said at my locker after second period. He'd come up behind me and wrapped both his arms around my neck. He wore a black armband around his biceps. All the jocks had started wearing them. He was talking to me while draped like that, his mouth right up to my ear. Since I'd been back, he had taken to touching me a lot: resting a hand on my shoulder, even once tucking a strand of hair behind my ear. Shivers moved through me when he did things like that, and I contemplated, semiseriously, letting my legs turn to jelly and falling entirely into him as he held me from behind. It seemed he would catch me.

"Let's," he said into my ear, "meet up in the parking lot and take off." I told him yes. I wondered what the inside of his truck would be like. I wondered what we would talk about for an hour.

But when I got to the parking lot, it turned out to be him and Dawnelle Ryan waiting. They were holding hands. It was a relaxed hold, their fingers twiddling loosely together as if they'd been doing things like holding hands for such a long time now, they barely had to think about it. My feet felt like bricks as I walked toward them, my arms pendulous at my sides. They both had funny smiles, the *awww, how cute* sort.

"You can sit in the middle, puss," Dawnelle said to me as we got into the truck. I remembered her habit of using improbable pet names from when she'd dated my brother. Punky, she'd called him, and Giggles. She made no effort to brace herself in the truck cab and let her body loll heavily against mine as we rounded corners. She took one of my hands in both of hers and kneaded my fingers. "How terrible terrible must be," she said nonsensically but with feeling. She smelled rosy with perfume, and as we idled at each red light, I thought of all the steps required for escape: leaping over her lap and jimmying open the passenger door and flinging myself out onto the street.

At the Arby's, they sat across from me in the booth. They shared french fries. Tip talked of wanting to kill that cocksucking faggot monster Elvin Tate. Dawnelle patted his arm. She called him Bear. I watched her hand as it moved up and down his arm, her long fingers, the clear polish on her nails. A ringing began in my ears, a common precursor to the headaches that still lingered. I excused myself to go to the bathroom. When I looked in the mirror, I was surprised by how pale my skin had become. Blue veins were visible along my cheeks and the sides of my nose, and the circles beneath my eyes were dark enough to look like bruises. My hands shook with a slight tremor and I gripped the lip of the sink to try to still it. A girl came out from one of the stalls. She was from Franklin too—this Arby's was sick with Franklin kids at lunchtime—and she gaped at me in the mirror as she washed her hands, staring so hard she missed the soap as it came out the dispenser. It landed in a pearly pink blob on the floor.

"Your soap fell," I told her in a way that I hoped sounded insulting.

I sat in a stall until Dawnelle came looking and then told her a half lie about food and my stomach. On the ride back I let them sit next to each other and pressed my head to the cool of the passenger window, telling them *okay, okay, okay* each time they asked how I was.

And then at the end of that first week, we had Friday afternoon assembly. I'd never liked assembly for the buzzing, hivelike way the various groups arranged themselves in the bleachers—the jocks in the back rows, the gum-cracking student council girls filling a wide swath in the middle, the Goths and burnouts huddled in the corners, the smart kids sprinkled where we could find seats. Assemblies always seemed like powder kegs, just one tense misstep away from some sort of violence, the way everyone was forced into unnaturally close proximity.

This one, though, without the normal loud excitement, was even worse. There was a collective hush as class after class filed in quietly and found their seats. Lola sat with her arm draped heavily around my shoulder, upset that we were not in the first row (I'd pressed us back to the fifth). She was already proactively sniffling, with a ready supply of tissues wadded in her fist. Everyone looked at me as they settled in. Some stared openmouthed and without expression, as if I couldn't see them. Others offered smiles or earnest frowns, to which I imagined the caption *Boo-hoo-hoo.* More than once during the week Lola had reported that the student council and the administration had unanimously agreed to delay this until my return.

Soon after everyone arrived, the lights went down. Music swelled from the speakers, a pop song about *I believe that love will find a way*, and a slide show began. *Memorial*, the first slide said, *for Danny Pasternak.* Then there he was, grinning from a cafeteria table, carrying Cindy Kahlen piggyback around the baseball diamond, wearing a hula skirt and lei with his cheeks rouged red at some dance. Next his team picture, down on one knee, smiling in his uniform, the same one we used on the old Missing posters. Someone shouted, "Pasternak!" You could hear the crying. It went on like this for a long time.

When the lights came up, girls' faces were wet and pink, some guys' too. Principal Garver was at the microphone making pronouncements about strength and perseverance and the legacy of life left behind by Danny. It was full of all the fiery emptiness of a campaign stump speech. Then came Mrs. Douglas, the grief counselor for hire, who'd set up temporary shop in the guidance offices. She talked of the rarity of a student like Danny who comes along every so often and unites the school. *Do you mean now or when he was alive?* I wondered.

The crowd vibrated around me. I could feel it. There was a smell in the air, a feral, sweaty funk, a mix of deodorant, BO, and hot breath, but something else too. If there was a pheromone excreted for barely suppressed hysteria, this was it, this cloud of spicy, bitter tang. Years later, when I watched horrific news from halfway around the world of gunmen trapping hundreds of hostages in an elementary school gym, I remembered that smell, tasting it in the back of my throat, acrid as crushed aspirin or swallowed perfume.

I grew sweaty and easily claustrophobic in the bleachers. The wooden bench was unforgiving beneath me, and all of the nearby bodies—not just Lola leaning all of her weight into me—swelled into a crush. The person behind me sniffled loudly from what sounded like just behind my left ear; the guy in the row ahead leaned so far back his shoulder blades nearly rested on my knees. I could not get my breathing to normalize—the steady in, out, in, out had quickened to a pant, which Lola apparently mistook for crying from the way she pressed her head against mine and ran her hand up and down my back in hot circles. Her own crying was a gurgle in my ear, and I felt more clearly than ever (and I had always felt it, but on a low, murmuring level) the imminent end to our friendship.

Coach Kinsborough was up next, wearing his incongruous baseball cap and suit. Danny, he said, was a champion, a brave soldier, a warrior. The crowd murmured assent. I made a noise like a cough, a strange, gurgling yelp. The boy in front of me turned to look, and I wished I were Medusa.

This grandiose treatment, the stuff of only the most ambitious and hopeful of suicide ideations, only elevated the situation to the realm of surreal. My brother had already been snatched off the street one night well before dark, killed, raped, beaten, and buried in a deep, wormy hole. The situation wasn't in need of any more surrealism.

I searched the crowd for disaffected faces. Two Goth girls with blue mohawks a row in front of me who rolled their eyes at each other. A boy several rows back who was reading a book in his lap. And Bayard, of all people, down the row from us, past Rochelle and a half-dozen other flag girls, an ear cocked toward the counselor, his expression one of complete bafflement. I wondered how much was the language barrier and how much general incredulity. Either way, I found such bewilderment a relief.

Next came Min Mathers and Mike Chemanski, representatives of the student council and the football team. Min wore a short black shirt and a bodice-hugging gray tank top. Her hair was pulled sternly into a bun, though her makeup was bright. She looked like what a mourner would look like in a music video. Mike Chemanski said he imagined that Pasternak fought like an Apache until the end. He pumped his fist into the air, his armband tight around his muscles. A pressure pulsed at my temples and the bridge of my nose, bringing with it the ripples of warm heat that often signaled a bout of nausea. I rubbed the palms of my hands into my eyes until gray snowflakes appeared behind my lids.

The final speaker was the head of the PTA. She talked of the memorial they'd already raised $3000 for (people hooted), which would be displayed either in front of the school or along the sidelines of the football field (more hooting). She held up a plaque. "A small token," she announced, "for the Pasternak family to hang on to until the project is completed." When she called my name, I did not move. It was not until Lola shook my arm that it occurred to me that this was indeed happening and inescapably so.

People clapped as I maneuvered between the four rows of bodies. Someone shouted my name. My shoes squeaked against the gym floor. The PTA woman grinned, holding the plaque in one hand, her other arm outstretched. It became clear only after it was too late to do anything about it that she intended to hug me. As she did, the applause from the bleachers seemed to rise into a roar.

She smelled strongly of hairspray and talc. I was caught in her grip, my arms pinned at my sides. The heat of the gym and the noise of the crowd swirled around us. I swallowed hard, trying to keep my bearings, but my face broke out in a sweat and I felt myself stumbling. I attempted to say *Let go*, though it came out funny and she seemed to grip only more tightly. My vision went spotty. The last thing I remembered was the roar from the bleachers turning to a messy, broken noise, no less loud but disordered now—many voices speaking all at once.

Only later, in the nurse's room, as a cool washcloth lay across my forehead and a pale-faced nurse whispered to my unkempt mother about loss of consciousness and stress and *Keep an eye on her*, did I begin to imagine the way my body must have buckled, falling into the PTA lady as if I were a Shakespearean lover. And I thought too of how the whole spectacle must have delighted the crowd—such a pitch-perfect closing act to assembly, such fuel for their insatiable, morbid glee.

Denis made a final visit to us, returning pictures he still had, handing us the fat stacks of notes he'd compiled over the months. "People sometimes find these useful," he told my parents, "just for further information. And to see work product."

"Thank you," my father said, with unusual softness. We were all standing in the front hall. No one made any move to invite Denis farther inside. "Thanks for your efforts."

"We included a final report," Denis said, tapping a manila folder on the top of the notes. His eyes were red, his cheeks especially ruddy. The stubble trailed farther down his neck than usual. "We managed a couple of visits to Elvin Tate this month, got some information from him that you might find useful . . . for closure." He shrugged as he said this, as if he were apologizing. "It's gratis," he added. "The report. Not part of the fee. Just something we wanted to do."

My father nodded. My mother did nothing to signal she was listening. There was something crusted—dry skin? food?—at the corner of her mouth.

"Kimberly and I," Denis said, and with such ease and intimacy, it struck me for the millionth time that they were probably doing it, though I found I did not really care, "are really, really sorry. We wish we could've done more. You never want to see an end like this."

"Nothing more you could've done," my father said. He sounded mainly tired. I wished for some of his old vitriol, for one final riot act read to Denis.

Denis turned to me. "You're a remarkable girl. So smart. Interested in everything. I haven't met a lot of kids like you. Okay?"

"Um," I said. While there was a small flutter of surprise from the direct address, when I tried to elicit any of my old feeling for him, there was nothing but a low pulsing in the tips of my fingers. I felt like baring my teeth and growling, like saying something wildly inappropriate. I understood why girls made up terrible stories that brought police to innocent men's homes.

But I just stood there. Denis seemed like an artifact now, an evocation of a lost, naive era. He looked like a grungy old guy. In the days after the news of Elvin Tate, I had waited almost breathlessly for apology, vindication, turnabout. But nothing came, and soon, as everything else unfurled around us with head-spinning grisliness, something inside closed up and sealed over, that part of me full of girlish hope. "Okay," I said now, and then, "Good luck."

It seemed remarkable how quickly and easily the goodbyes came. First Denis to my parents, then my parents to him. Then him to me. Me to him. Devoid of sentiment. Or tragedy. Or particular meaning. They were just words. I was becoming, it seemed, expert at them. Sayonara, as David Nelson used to say.

We all stood in the front hall.

Goodbye.

Goodbye.

Goodbye.

Goodbye.

24.

I grew, in the following weeks, easily obsessed with Elvin Tate. I pored over the slim folder Denis had left, reading over and over the few notes he'd typed in neat bullet points. Elvin had stopped to ask Danny where he could find a tire shop, giving him some story about thinking he might have driven over a nail, and then lured Danny into the car with pot. Danny had seen a roach in Elvin's ashtray and Elvin asked if he wanted a hit, saying (Denis quoted him directly here), "I got more. I can hook you up." It happened as simply and stupidly as that, Danny getting in the car to smoke a joint. Elvin had been in possession of a taser gun, which he used to subdue Danny while they wound through the back roads of central and northern Michigan. When asked what his plan had been, Elvin said, "You know, go on a little trip." When asked what they did those four days, Elvin said: "You know, had a good time," reporting that they just talked and drove and drank a lot of beer like they were college buddies on a fraternity road trip. He said Danny had tried to run only once, at a gas station in Howell, and that's when Elvin had had to bash his left eye in. When pressed about why he had killed Danny, Elvin balked. "Things got bad. Dark. Real dark," was all he would say. Denis wrote: *Subject refuses to elaborate, even when repeatedly pressed.*

I watched one night as Kirk Donovan conducted a jailhouse interview on the eleven o'clock news. Elvin hunched forward in his pea green jumpsuit and spoke with a slight lisp (his *th*'s had the slightest, most awful sibilance), saying he didn't know what had happened. With his overbite, his front teeth sat lazily over his bottom lip. It was almost laughable, the bad teeth and the lisp. His lawyer sat to his side, a pinched man in a cheap-looking suit who kept touching Elvin's arm when Elvin began to say too much.

Elvin said that he had "black spirits" he sometimes couldn't control (the lawyer's hand came into the frame) and that "I didn't mean nothing bad" (lawyer's hand), and then he repeated what would become his insane mantra: "We had some real good times together" (no hand). The camera flashed to Kirk Donovan, who sat nodding, his face pancaked with his familiar expression of sympathy. He spoke in the same low, consoling voice he'd used each time he'd come over here and sat in this very room with us. For a brief, blistering moment, it was Kirk Donovan's offense that cut more deeply.

I had thought it would bring some relief, knowing details. Instead, the information—taser gun, good times, the smashing of an eye—scooped out something essential from the center of me, leaving only a wide, whooshing hole instead.

. . .

And then, without warning, time resumed its normal march forward. Just as it had during the previous winter, the tone of frenzy proved unsustainable at school. My classmates returned to talk of finals and college and Senior Skip Day. Lola was going to prom with Lyle Walker. David Nelson had a summer internship at a software firm in California; he would live with his aunt outside Sacramento and learn about Perl programming and JavaScript. Tip received a football scholarship to Utah State University. He was going to be an Aggie, and he took to wearing a slick navy-and-white jersey nearly every day. Hollingham lectured about Constantinople, Principal Garver made announcements about graduation tickets, and all the while something crawled beneath my skin.

Scabies, I thought. Mites.

I spent class time scraping at my skin, first with fingernails, then with the lead tip of my pencil, even occasionally with the needle-sharp point of a protractor. I kept taking the wrong books with me—my fat chem book to history, Dickens to trig. I became easily, entirely distracted by Devorah Birnbaum's tapping foot two desks over from me or the three robins in the treetop out the window. I stopped doing homework.

I ate in the cafeteria less and less. The noise in there, the constant scrambling bodies, the bright fluorescent lights—too much. As the flag girls went on about upcoming stretch limos and afterparties, I scratched at my thighs and the side of my neck and had thoughts of taking my dull cafeteria knife and, rather than using it to saw through my meatloaf, stabbing it through the leg of the nearest flag girl.

I found some comfort in watching Bayard down at the other end of the table, the brooding way he ate his turkey loaf or sloppy joe, chewing slowly, eyeing the burger with slit-eyed suspicion. Ever since assembly I'd taken greater notice of him—the way he tiptoed alone through the halls in his strange, chunk-heeled shoes or sat stiffly at his chem table near the front of the classroom, legs crossed at the ankles, hands in his lap, as if he were at a tea party rather than in front of a Bunsen burner. I found something appealing in the alien air he gave off. Often he eyed the rest of the lunch table the same way he eyed his sandwiches, with a pinched expression just short of a scowl, as the girls chittered about Diana trying out for cheerleading or Penny being too much of a chicken to ask Marty Grindell to prom. "Bok-bok-bok," Rochelle said to Penny, her fists cupped in her armpits, her elbows flapping. Bayard got up then, the remains of his cheeseburger piled on his tray. I felt the blood rush to my face, with a clear sense of being stranded, and I was up and nearly running across the cafeteria before I even had time to think about it, trying to catch up with him as he set his tray on the conveyor belt.

"You get tired of them?" I called. The question came out screechy. When he turned, he squinted at me in the same suspicious way he squinted, it was becoming clear, at everything.

"Is strange," was all he said. I remembered him saying exactly the same thing the day of the search. *Eez strinj.* Apt then, still apt now.

"I'll show you something," I said, inexplicably emboldened. I couldn't remember the last time I'd started a conversation with someone. "Do you want me to show you something?"

I'd recently found a quiet hallway by the cavernous family and consumer science classrooms. There were no lockers there, only long murals of multicolored children holding hands in a circle or of farms with two of every animal. This cut down on almost all lunchtime foot traffic. I could spend the hour alone there, sitting or pacing, mostly pacing.

We walked in silence. Bayard's shoes clicked against the floor. I couldn't think of anything to say, and he didn't seem one for conversation. When we arrived at the home ec hall, I slid down the wall, a pair of alpacas at my back, and sat on the floor.

"This is it?" he said. *Zees ees eet?*

"Yeah," I said, embarrassed. I remembered how little I'd liked Bayard in the factory with his glib, impassive attitude about everything.

"It looks like a nursery school." He flapped his arms at the murals. *Nur-zree skull.*

"I know," I said quickly. "But there are no *people* here." *Get it?* I wanted to say to him. *Get it?* I felt a desperate need for him to, though I realized the odds were against me, given that he was a costume-wearing, foot-stomping, hip-shaking member of the flag team.

"Americans," he said, "are tiring."

I wasn't sure if he was including me in this characterization, but I didn't much care. Soon he was sliding himself down the wall and sitting on the floor across from me.

"I am sorry about your brother," he said, picking at the skin around one of his fingernails.

"Are you *zorry*?" I said, but when he looked at me, I realized the imitation wasn't funny, so I said, "Thanks." Strange, I thought, how his time here had been marked by the events of my family. Was this what he reported about in letters home? Were his parents worried that he too would be snatched by a stranger in America? It would not be until much later—years, really—that I considered that other people may have found the events of my life incidental to their own, unworthy of particular note, that perhaps someone like Bayard filled his letters home with greater preoccupations, such as the joys of cable television or the glut of available McDonald's.

"Are you homesick?" I said.

His finger had started to bleed, a bright sliver of red next to his nail. "Sure," he told me. "Of course." He had a way of talking, his accent and his tone, that made it seem as if he could add *stupid* to the end of every sentence. *Sure, stupid. Of course, stupid.*

"Me too," I said, and he nodded at me, unsurprised.

25.

I sought out Bayard more and more, finding him in the cafeteria and sitting nearby, poking at my fish stick with a fork or chewing on the inside of my cheek until I could bear the tablemates or the sweetish smell of the tartar sauce no longer. I implored him to walk with me through the halls.

"How do you say," I would ask, "radius? Hotpad? Leapfrog?" This was, I found, the easiest conversation to make, a distracting buzz of noise with endless possibilities.

"Rayon," he told me. *"Dessous-de-plat, saute-mouton."*

I began trailing him to his host family's house after school. "What are you doing today?" I would ask and would take his shrug or his *Nuzzing* as invitation. Bayard's host family, the McAllisters, had a house dotted with the sort of ornamental bric-a-brac—a small wooden cow on a windowsill, a pair of woolly sheep on an end table, a ceramic milkmaid in pointy hat and apron on the back of the stove—that made it seem like nothing bad had ever happened to them.

"Put that down," Bayard often told me, of the tiny gold-painted teacup or the glass horse I carried around. Sometimes I listened, often not. I was obsessed with the chore chart that hung on the fridge, fashioned out of two paper plates, a pinwheel fastener in the middle, and meticulous drawings for each slice of the pie: a broom for floors, Oscar the Grouch for garbage. "Don't," he told me as I spun the inner plate, the one with the names on it. *Dunt.* "You're screwing it up." I couldn't stop touching things. More than once I pressed the polished surface of a purple geode to the tip of my tongue.

Two elementary-school-aged children ran screaming around the McAllisters'. Bayard referred to them as Fick and Fack. The nicknames were interchangeable, uttered out of frustration more than affection (*Sit down now, Fick. Fack, stop screaming in my ear*), though the children, a boy and a girl, appeared delighted by any attention from Bayard, dissolving into giggles even when he chastised them, which was often. They easily put their hands on me, sticky and grabby, asking the first time I met them if I would play Go Fish, if I knew how to jump rope.

Bayard's host parents were both doughy and round, with ruddy faces and overly friendly manners to match their children's. They said, "It's a terrible thing, what's happened to your family," and "We've prayed for you," both sentiments less creepy than usual since their expressions were so plain and open, devoid of the hungry, searching look most people had when they met me. They smiled through even the highest-pitched shrieks from their children. They offered up baked goods and card tricks with ease, seeming like just the sort of people who would open their home to a foreigner for a year, and just the sort not to seem disappointed when it turned out to be one as remote and odd as Bayard. Being around them brought a heady mix of comfort, indignation, relief, and injustice. Why had Bayard lucked out in such a way? Or Fick and Fack, for that matter?

It was so weird in their home, so simultaneously restful and disorienting. I tried to relax into it but often found myself twitchy with disbelief or wonder. The first time Mrs. McAllister invited me to stay for dinner—something she would come to regularly do—I was stirred with such simultaneous excitement and inconsolability, I called out, "Zah!" She didn't even pause, smiling and nodding as if I'd said the *Yes* I'd intended. I managed a reasonable enough "Thank you" in return while fingering the painted wooden egg I'd secreted into my pocket hours before.

As for Bayard and me, we took walks through his neighborhood similar to the ones we took through the school hallways (*chat tigré*, he told me for tabby cat, *prise d'eau* for fire hydrant). We sat in his room, me frequently asking, "What do you want to do now?" as I paged through anything with pages: a French-English dictionary, his fat stack of car magazines. I rocked back and forth at the edge of his bed or tapped my feet or asked barrages of questions: "Why don't you take more of an interest in politics?" or "Why did you come to the United States?" or "What's your family like?" He often seemed to find me either crazy or unintelligible, leaving my questions unanswered, blinking at me or staring at the brown shag of his rug as if I hadn't even spoken. I would think, *Does he hear me? Am I making myself clear?*

I suffered indignities from Bayard I would have suffered from no one else, mostly because I found solace in his displaced otherness, the low-level, constant hum of alienation coming off him. He still didn't know how to conjugate verbs; he still couldn't comprehend seventeen-theater multiplexes, bulk-food aisles, or SUVs.

What at first had appeared to be his cool detachment upon closer inspection looked more like an ongoing effort to tamp down his oft-rising befuddlement.

One night we sat on the creaky plastic swings of the McAllisters' swing set after dinner. I pumped my legs in the air, grateful for the continual motion offered by a swing. The shaky metal frame made ominous buckling noises.

"Careful," Bayard warned. He was hardly moving in his, dragging the tips of his shoes in the grass. It was the time of year when the days had grown noticeably longer. The extra hours of daylight felt illicit, ill-gotten.

"Fucking spring," I said. Talking didn't really help. Not talking didn't either.

"I hate summer," Bayard said.

"Me too," I said, but this was a lie. I had always enjoyed summers, spending past ones teaching myself the tenets of Buddhism, learning conversational Italian, reading the Brontë sisters. It was impossible, though, to imagine the coming summer. It felt like trying to imagine a solar system beyond ours or what it was like to have Down syndrome. The idea that summer was coming, then fall, then winter, then spring, then summer again brought forth that same sick, illicit feeling.

"So much sweat," Bayard said. This, his explanation.

I kicked harder, my swing groaning loudly, jerking through the air. The whole swing set felt like it could come down around us. Rust from the chains turned my fingers orange and gritty.

"You love swing sets," Bayard said, with a derisiveness so typical of him, it just became white noise after a while. I kept pumping, sweat beginning to sprout beneath my shirt. A TV blared from the house next door. A German shepherd nosed at his food dish on the other side of a Cyclone fence. The mundane details of other people's lives, in turn, reassured me and filled me with the impulse to let go of the swing and flail wildly through the air.

"Are you excited to see your family?" I shouted. My questions to Bayard were often the obvious sort you'd find on the back of a postcard.

"Sure," he said. *Sure, stupid.*

"Tell me something funny about them."

He stayed quiet for so long it seemed it would be one of my unanswered queries. I tried to propel myself higher, tried to calculate exactly the point in the downward arc to begin kicking for maximum momentum. Finally he said, "My brother, Lucien, has a limp. He was borned with one leg too short than the other."

"That's not funny," I said.

He shrugged. "It was what I could think of."

"Danny once convinced me he'd had six toes on each foot," I said, flying past Bayard, starting to breathe harder from the exertion, "and that my parents had made him amputate the extra ones."

"That's a joke?"

"Kind of," I said, though I remembered having been uneasily obsessed for days. I'd been seven or eight and had made Danny take off his socks over and over again to show me the bony red spots at the outside edges of his pinkie toes, until finally I asked my parents about it. I had an urge to share all this with Bayard, then an equally strong urge not to. Of everyone in Fairfield, he was the one person with absolutely no dogs in this fight. Best, I thought, to keep it that way. How I liked his apathy; it was possibly what I liked most about him, preferring it to the chafing closeness of my friendship with David Nelson, or the fake jollity with Lola, or especially the ugly, unrequited mess of Denis and me. This suited me best, the final bowl of porridge for my finicky Goldilocks. I was capable of this much: another beating heart beside me, relievedly free of any curious poking.

I swung and I swung, ignoring Bayard's sideways glances, his low, irritated calls for me to slow down, to stop. I liked the sting of night air on my cheeks, the steady pounding in my chest. At some point Fick and Fack came running through the sliding back door, a last burst of energy before bed. "You want to play Museum?" Fack yelled to us, his nostrils stuffed with dried boogers.

"We're busy," Bayard said.

"You going to do an around-the-world?" Fack yelled to me.

"I don't know. Maybe," I called. It didn't seem like a bad idea, propelling myself over the top bar. I wondered if it would bring weightlessness or a blinding rush of blood to the head.

Bayard told them to shoo. Fack grabbed at one chain of Bayard's swing and shook it hard. Fick grabbed at the back of Bayard's shirt, trying to unseat him, looking like she just might succeed.

"I'll play," I announced. I'd never said yes before, falling easily in line with Bayard's rebuffs. But as I watched Fick and Fack squirming and giggling and bouncing around, their restless energy seemed so familiar, so naturally akin to mine. Of course I would play with them. I jumped off my swing and they squealed, grabbing my fingers and my jeans, leading me across the lawn and telling me the rules to Museum, an overly complicated cackle of commands that revealed the simple, nonsensical game. They would be frozen statues. I would be the museum owner who had to leave at the end of the day, turning off the light and closing the door, which unfroze them for the night.

They ran quickly into place—it was clear they'd played many times before—contorting themselves into strange positions. Fack twisted his arms around his torso and wobbled on one foot; Fick tried to maintain a backbend with her ankles crossed. I could hear Bayard creaking slowly on his swing. I turned off the pretend light and walked out the pretend door.

Instantly the kids went wild, dancing, shouting, flailing about. They made such loud howling noises, I called, "Shh, shh," but they paid me no attention, clapping their hands and stomping their feet and shaking their whole bodies in rhythm to some unheard music. Fack grasped both of Fick's hands in his and they twirled and twirled in a circle, leaning far back from each other, screaming and laughing. I remembered—or was I just imagining?—doing the same thing, the centrifugal force pulling us as we went round and round, the willful, happy dizziness, the feeling that I would go flying backward if he let go. Even then, so simply and naturally at his mercy.

Fick and Fack fell to the ground, giggling and squirming in the grass, not yet vented of their endless energy. Their limbs, erratic, spastic, flailing, hardly seemed like their own. They looked possessed. I watched them with some of that flying-backward feeling; I always seemed to have some of that feeling now. Their legs tangled sloppily together, her foot poking his thigh, and their arms flopped about. At one point one of his hands sat wedged in the crook of her neck. They hardly seemed to notice, laughing and laughing, calling my name, wanting to start over again.

At home, during the few waking hours I spent there, I watched my mother's frenetic energy reawaken, this time by the computer. She discovered the Internet and its support groups for grieving parents, and the long squeal of a modem quickly became the birdsong of our household. She had barely used a computer before but with single-minded determination rooted out Internet Relay Chat rooms and usenet groups. Soon she'd migrated from the kitchen chair next to her cabinet to the household's only unused computer, conveniently located in Danny's room. She became friends with people named Sheela_Bird and DoctorREYREY and would talk about them frothily.

"Sheela Bird's daughter was killed by a thresher," she said, trapping me in my bedroom or at the kitchen table. "I didn't even know that kind of thing happened anymore. It sounds so 1850s. Death by thresher. She went to a friend's farm after school one day and got caught up in the arms of it, or whatever it is a thresher has, and bled out right there in her friend's field. Never even made it to the hospital."

I never knew what to say to these stories. It was usually just the two of us in the house, since my dad was working later and later. Whenever he finally arrived, he was sweaty and bedraggled, as if he'd ridden home in a sauna. His hair had turned a bright and sudden white in patches near his temples, giving him a distinctly Bride of Frankenstein appearance.

"How was your day?" he would sometimes ask me, a banality so rare I would stumble for words, trying to think of something that set this day apart from others. "We had a quiz in trig," I told him, and "The French word for mud puddle is *flaque de boue*," and "I saw a deer on the way home," a lie born of my panic for material.

Our only family outings were trips to the cemetery. In the beginning all three of us went every Saturday morning, but soon the schedule grew loose. The trips splintered to just me and my mom or me and my dad, a pattern I would look back on as an obvious sign of things to come. One of them would stick his or her head into my room on a Tuesday evening or a Sunday at five and ask if I wanted to go. I hated the cemetery and chafed at the idea of the long trip there and back, but I was seduced by the inclusion, surprised each time that they thought to ask me along. It was unusual for them, the inclination toward doing something consistently and together, and I found an unexpected pleasure in being asked, a little like being picked not-last for softball.

I had no idea what to do with myself there. I found myself wishing we were Catholic so I could at least have a rosary to move meaningfully through my hands. My parents each had their own ritual, my father's to do with pacing and a low, indistinct mutter, though occasionally I could catch a terrible few words. *Dearheart*, I could've sworn he'd said once, *baby* another time. My mother knelt in the dirt, crying and unafraid of dirtying her pants or pantyhose.

I gnawed on hangnails, dug my heels into the soft ground, slapped my thighs. If I closed my eyes and forced a vision—the pine box eroded beneath us with worm holes, Danny's eight broken fingers, the crushed phalanges, the ripped flexor and extensor muscles, the cracked fingernails—I could sometimes build a heat in my throat or get a slick feeling behind my eyelids. But mostly I went blank. Grief on demand, the sort expected at my brother's fresh, grassless grave, required a flattening of all complication of which I was not capable.

"Girl. Tragically. Loses. Brother," I could hear the narrator from *Unsolved Mysteries* saying, and it made me incapable of standing still. I marched around to other gravestones. Annabelle Grier died when she was twenty-four, in 1976. I imagined her feathered hair, her knobby knees and spindly arms. Lamont Eyers when he was forty-three. He was the son of Lucille, the father of Laura and Leonard, the alliteration both admirable and annoying.

"Ready?" my dad said one time when he found me at Griselda Jenkins's gravestone, and I heard the note of consternation in his voice. I made an apologetic noise, a swallowed murmur.

"Her name's Griselda," I said by way of explanation. My hand flew from my side, pointing. He looked at the gravestone, then at me, his face pale to the point of being spectral, his eyes bleary and swollen. When he shook his head, it barely moved, and I felt a regret so deep it seemed to swim up from my toes.

"You like your job?" I asked him in the car, a couple minutes from the cemetery, Fairfield still nearly a half-hour away. My voice was crazy-sounding, unmodulated and loud. I had already pressed all of the preset buttons on his radio but found only country or classical. The look he'd given me told me to stop fiddling.

"You like it?" I repeated. It had been nearly two months since the funeral, and I could count the total words spoken between my father and me on my fingers and toes.

He looked at me, made a long *Uhhhh* sound, and then, "Sure," and then, "Most days."

"What do you do exactly?" I said, because I'd never really understood. Or cared.

"Manage the mortgage lending," he said, though in a thin, tired voice.

"Is it hard?" I wished I could stop shouting. I tried to remember how normal people talked.

"Some days," he said.

"I wonder what I'll be," I said. I wanted us to have a real conversation. The thought of our house, miles away but growing closer by the minute, made me want to bash my head against the passenger window.

"President," he said, and the word came out strangely, as if he were accusing me of something.

"No, really," I said.

"You can be anything you want," he said, though he was looking blankly at the windshield and his voice lacked conviction. It sounded like a line out of a parenting manual or a Dr. Seuss book. I watched the yellow lines in the road, the empty words on the passing signs. Two-for-one sale on preowned videos at the Blockbuster. HAPPY ANNIVERSARY RITA AND MARTY at the Holiday Inn.

"Hhhh," I said, a noisy stream. He didn't ask what in the world. He didn't ask anything. My chest tightened, disappointment welling up. Through everything, it seemed, I still harbored visions of a reconstituted family. Some part of me remained stubbornly convinced there had to *something* beyond this precarious place, someplace we three would find together, and in it a smaller table, low conversations, newfound rhythms. There—what?—my mother and I would stand hip to hip in front of the stove, she beating a whisk against a metal stirring bowl, I fingering the rows of spice jars? And my father would take me on the day trips he used to take Danny on: fishing on Lake Erie, snowshoeing outside Saline?

But as I watched his drooping profile beside me now (what had happened to his chin? When had it shrunk so fully into his neck?), it was clear what a child I was. And not a child as in mirthful innocent or even as in precocious cherub, but rather as in someone who, in the face of all contrary evidence, was still full of witless hope. What we were doing now was not a forward march together. It was something else entirely: biding our time, counting the days, silently gnashing and moaning beside each other.

Soon we would be home and my father would absent himself to the television. My mother would say hello from the computer, maybe turning her head to look, maybe not, the last lingering smell of dirty teenage boy replaced with the oniony odor of a grown woman who'd long forsaken bathing. That we had come fully apart was abundantly clear, though I grew more and more doubtful that we'd ever been anything but. Maybe all Danny had done was mask our very basic incapabilities as a family. He had always been the loudest, meanest, strongest, funniest, dumbest one in the room. How easy it had been to fix our collective gaze on him, how reflexive and lazy and natural. So how effortless—inevitable, really—to just keep forgetting and forgetting each other without him.

26.

School ended without my failing any classes, primarily a result of my teachers' collective sympathy. Papers had been left undone and more than one final exam flunked, but still, my final report card read all *A*'s except for Ms. Villara's still generous *B+*. Looking at the grades left me with an uneasy feeling of erasure, as if the past however many months had simply not occurred.

Lola had a barbecue in her backyard the weekend after school was out. It was an end-of-year party, an event that I didn't have the wherewithal to refuse, especially since her overtures had increased in frequency and urgency as I'd begun to drift. She called several times a week. Did I want to go get some frozen yogurt? Did I want to shop for purses with her? I always told her no, though even as I tried to dodge her calls, I found something admirable about her dogged persistence in the face of constant rejection.

"You're coming on Saturday?" she'd said every day during the final week of school, as if by sheer stubbornness she could bend my will. And it felt, in the end, like the least I could do.

Bayard and I went together and shared one of the green plastic Adirondack chairs, him in the seat, me perched uncomfortably on one of the wide arms. Paper plates of hot dogs and chips sat balanced on our laps. I watched the scene from a distance. Lola's dad manned the grill, her mother brought out trays of bright blue virgin cocktails, the flag team huddled around a picnic table, the JV quarterback, a wiry guy named Lucas something, stood beside one of the house's downspouts and looked bored. There weren't very many people and no graduated seniors since it was daytime, without alcohol and with parents. Lola bounded nervously around, scanning the sparse crowd and whispering furious-looking orders to her parents, who then did needless things like bring out more chips or drag the kitchen garbage can onto the patio. "You can throw out your stuff here," Lola announced, waving her arms officiously.

"Can we go yet?" I'd whispered to Bayard minutes after we'd arrived, initially a joke, though I kept repeating it at regular intervals. He kept shushing me.

Lola circled most closely around Lucas the quarterback, touching his arm a lot. She was telling him a story, a loud one about a really funny commercial she'd seen on TV with a dog driving a sports car. "It was a *dalmatian*," she said, the apparent punch line, and Lucas flashed a thin smile. When he dipped inside—an escape to the bathroom?—she came our way.

"You guys having fun?" she asked loudly. Lola had been asking this or a variation on this every twenty minutes or so. Tension belied her usual cheerfulness. She bit the corner of her lip and checked her watch with a ticlike frequency. It was four. The party was supposed to have started at two-thirty.

"Fun, fun," Bayard said in typical Bayard fashion, the line between sincere and sarcastic indiscernible. "It's good," I said, a pronoun intentionally without a referent. Having steeled myself for a flurry of unwanted attentions and sympathies, I had expected the party to be different. But aside from Mrs. Pepper having asked about my parents as I came in and one of the flag girls squeezing my hand too hard and asking a meaningful "How are you doing?" there had been nothing. People ate their potato salad with quiet determination. Flag girls stuck their blue tongues out at each other. This tepid barbeque brought that same feeling of erasure.

I had no idea what I was doing here. How had I ended up as someone who came to Lola Pepper's end-of-year party with the French exchange student? Narration ran continually through my head, as if I were trying to convince myself that what was happening was in fact happening: *Here we are eating our hot dogs and pickles. Here we are listening to a story about the camp for kids with cancer where Lola will soon be a counselor.*

"So what have you two been up to?" Lola said, attempting to sound breezy, though she eyed me and Bayard in much the same way she'd come to in recent weeks, with a probing, what-exactly-is-going-on-here? look.

"Nothing much," Bayard said. *Nuzzin match.*

"Flag won't be the same without you next year," Lola said, pressing a palm against his shoulder.

"No, it will not," he said, not one for false modesty.

"When will you go back to France?" she said.

He explained how his parents were vacationing at the beach through July. Bayard did not like the beach. Too much sun, too many people. He would stay here till August, then return to Chateaurenaud when his parents were home.

"You'll like it?" she said, glancing at the sliding door for signs of Lucas.

"Will I like Chateaurenaud?" he said.

Lola looked at him like he was being silly. She checked her watch. "What?"

"Will I like what?" Bayard said.

"What?" she said again, her brow knitting with confusion, her eyes clouding for a second. Something dark passed over her face. A flush of red deepened her cheeks. She looked suddenly angry—about this failed party? I wondered. About the shifting configuration of the three of us? It was one of the few times I wondered if I might have underestimated Lola Pepper. But as quickly as it appeared, it disappeared, replaced by her toothy smile and her fervent voice. "I'm so glad you came," she said, quavering with sentiment.

"Of course," I said, because I felt for her. She was made up of only two things, good intentions and need. If I had been a sweeter and more forgiving girl, less prone to judgment and scorn, I would have stayed friends with her. Even as I sat in her backyard, desperate for this to be the last time, already envisioning how the summer would grow long between us, her phone calls finally petering out without my even noticing, I looked at her speckled skin and bright eyes and almost convinced myself that maybe I was wrong, maybe we'd forge on together. "Thanks for inviting us," I said.

She gave me a quick, unexpected hug, squashing my plate between us. "Careful," I said, meaning the ketchup and her dress, though it came out more stern and she let go quickly and I didn't explain.

"I thought there'd be more people," she said, her shoulders drooping just a bit. When Lucas came back out, she did not see him. I watched as he grabbed his windbreaker from a patio chair and disappeared quickly back into the house. Bayard watched too, and neither of us told her that he'd gone.

. . .

I spent the summer at the McAllisters', escaping my house most mornings before my mother was awake. The nightmares had begun in earnest by then—ones that would continue for years—of Danny, broken-faced and gurgling bloody words, or Elvin Tate slithering beneath my blankets into my bed, or my mouth filled with loamy earth. So my sleeplessness, if possible, was even more pitched and intense than usual. Mornings, then, became the time to coax myself back into normalcy, to talk myself into the coming day.

Usually I arrived well before Bayard was out of bed, when Mr. and Mrs. McAllister were still scurrying around getting ready for work, Fick and Fack bleary-eyed before day camp. I helped tie Fick's shoes. I offered to clean the dishes. I asked if they had any errands needing done. Mrs. McAllister always told me not to be silly. She told me to sit and offered cooling scraps of bacon. Sometimes she kissed me on the top of my head before she left, just the same way she did to Fick and Fack. It often made me want to cry.

After everyone was gone, I fingered ceramic ducks and Russian nesting dolls. I scanned up and back, up and back through the several hundred TV stations. I flipped randomly through the paper, reading headlines aloud. "Sales tax will go up a quarter cent in September," I announced to no one. "Fourteen people died in Gaza." I spun the chore chart. I slammed kitchen cabinets and turned up the volume of the TV to wake Bayard.

"What do you want to do?" I would say as soon as he appeared. He usually just rubbed his eyes and blinked at me, his hair nappy on his head. It took Bayard a long time to fully wake, to shower, to start his day with me, when we would walk around the neighborhood or flip through TV channels or just sit. Bayard was often trying to convince me to just sit. I hated the just sitting. "Come on," I was always telling him.

When Fick and Fack returned each afternoon from day camp, I would watch the princess cartoons and Power Rangers shows with them for a little while before trying to bribe them into going outside. I would help them make a lemonade stand, I said. I would find them a big anthill. I liked the way they ran themselves ragged in the yard. I liked their blur of motion, their "What next? What next?," their go and go and go.

"I'll draw you a hopscotch course," I said. "I'll turn on the hose." The hose was one of their favorites, me spreading my thumb over the spout, creating a wide, feathery arc for them to leap in and out of. They'd scream beneath the freezing water, their hair plastered to their heads, the outlines of their ribs visible along their scrawny chests. Sometimes they grabbed me with their wet hands and I worried they could feel something red-hot in return, some unstable electricity beneath my skin, but they never gave any indication, never stopped their jumping around and yelping.

I showed them how to whistle through fat blades of grass, how to weave crowns of dandelions. I told them rambling stories of Miggleman, the imaginary man Danny had made up when we were little. Miggleman lived under beds of sleeping kids and came out at night to eat cookies and play with dogs.

"Don't scare them," Bayard called to me from the front porch. *Dun skeer zem.*

"Miggleman isn't scary," I said, feeling stupid for the defensiveness in my voice. Danny used to whisper to me about Miggleman when our parents thought we were both asleep, the window of time after we were put to bed when they were socked away in some downstairs room. Danny would sneak over from his room and crouch at the end of my bed. In the dark, I could see only his glinting teeth or the flash of fingernail as he moved his hand excitedly through the air, whispering wildly. I loved Miggleman stories, the way it seemed like the entire upstairs was ours and we could stay like that all night.

I taught Fick and Fack an outdoor version of the bridge game, lining up deck chairs and Big Wheels and an emptied kiddie pool in a long trail across the front lawn. They threw themselves into the game with the same abandon they threw themselves into everything. Fack stomped across his belongings and made a big display of balancing on one foot on the seat of his Big Wheels while it wobbled beneath him. Fick dragged over a plastic home plate and a bevy of beach pails. It was only occasionally that I had to walk away to sit briefly in the shade of their maple tree, ignoring the way the kids called my name, reminding myself to breathe and breathe and breathe.

We were in the middle of the latest round, Bayard lying prone in his usual spot on the porch, Fick crying to Fack about him having dragged out her Barbie nail salon, a prized possession she didn't want to use for the game, when a woman rode by on her bike, wearing an incongruous outfit of a ripped flannel shirt and old gym shorts. She hauled a small, rusty, two-wheeled trailer of empty beer bottles and pop cans behind her. Sweat dripped down her face; I could smell the BO from where I stood. A drizzle of rancid, hoppy liquid leaked from her trailer, that stink potent in the heat too.

I was on my way over to the kids about to intervene in their fight when the woman glanced at the four of us, eyes beady in her round head. Though her stringy hair was gray rather than bluish black, the sight of her made my legs quiver.

It was Melissa Anne. I was sure of it.

My throat grew both gluey and dry. "Yaa," I said, something between *You?* and *Yo!*

Fack held a thumb and finger over his nose. "Pee-yew," he said from atop his tom-tom.

Melissa Anne was concentrating hard on propelling herself forward, her whole body leaning into each pedal, her ass high off the seat, but she paused to look toward Fack, an unreadable expression on her face. Was that a smile? A wince? Her eyes were doing the same thing they'd done months before on my porch, skittering around in their sockets. Bayard called out some admonishment. I wasn't sure to whom. Fack? Melissa Anne? My body was frozen, caught between the impulse to flee and the impulse to scream her name.

"What you got?" Fick yelled to her. This, the way they were with strangers, running to ones walking big dogs or riding past on skateboards. Everyone, a benign fascination.

Melissa Anne's face broke open even wider. She was, it appeared, baring her teeth. She'd stopped pedaling now, and the bike was coasting, the wheels of the trailer letting out a low squeal. It seemed like she could leap right off, could bound easily onto the McAllisters' lawn and toward these children.

Something unraveled in me as I watched the scene. The actual physical sensation of unloosing was so strong I could have sworn that my bladder had opened, that piss ran down my leg and puddled on the grass. Fack stepped down from his drum and walked toward the sidewalk. Before any thought, there was movement: me running toward him, yelling, "Get!" and flapping my hands in the air. "Get!" I kept yelling, so loud that both kids whipped their heads around, staring at me openmouthed. Melissa Anne, as if noticing me there for the first time, stared too, or as close as she could come: her eyes skipped across my face and flitted to something behind me. I waited for whatever terrible thing was sure to follow, whatever bile might spew from her mouth.

But quick as that she sat back in her seat, focused again on the sidewalk in front of her, and resumed her pedaling. She regained momentum and swiftly moved several feet past us, beyond the next house and the next.

It was over in a matter of seconds. I watched as she neared the end of the block, thinking she would turn and look at me again, thinking she would come back. But she didn't. She rounded the corner without even a glance, leaving only the drizzly, splattered trail in her wake. The street returned to its normal noises—far-off cars, a radio in someone else's backyard—and I just stood there, an ache in my belly like I'd just been punched. If it was a relief for her to be disappeared again, the lack of recognition was unexpectedly crushing. It made me feel invisible. Like nothing.

The kids had already started back to their game. I heard Fick saying something about her Barbie nail salon, and I was galled at the speed of their reset. In an instant I went after both of them, grabbing their wrists, lassoing them to me, shouting about strangers, about danger, about *you never know.* Fick let out a little yelp. Bayard called my name. I shouted about *you can't just la-dee-dah around* and *you need to stay on the lawn, do you understand what I'm telling you because I'm serious.* Soon Bayard was on me, pulling at my arms, telling me to let go. I could not remember Bayard ever touching me before. The kids' faces were red and quivery, and they looked far more scared of me than they'd just been of Melissa Anne.

I let go. I sputtered that I was sorry, though I didn't know if I was. Fick and Fack rubbed their wrists. I wanted really badly to hug them or slap them. I felt like I might do something terrible, like I might already be in the midst of it. "I got to go," I said, because suddenly I did. For several steps it seemed I was going to give chase, follow Melissa Anne's trail of stink. But at the corner I turned left to her right, feet slapping on sidewalk, my body on autopilot. A car honked at me. I stopped, flailing my arm around my head, my heart thwapping in my chest. The driver yelled at me about *head in the clouds* and I yelled back about *watch where you're going.* I did not care that he was a man, I a girl. Then I took off past him.

I was going home.

I never went home in the daytime. But now I was hurtling myself, the long blocks past the McAllisters' seeming endless. Sweat dotted my shirt. "Gah," I heard myself saying. "Bah. Ha." The noise was propulsive.

In the last block and a half I broke into a sprint, the humidity like gulping a warm blanket. I had not sprinted in years, since the days of the fifty-yard dash, and even then halfheartedly. Quarter-heartedly. Eighth-heartedly. By the time I scaled the steps of my porch, I felt like I was going to vomit.

Inside, the air conditioning stung my skin. I pressed my back against one wall of the vestibule. Waiting. And then, nothing. Nothing.

The house stewed in its usual quiet. If I listened carefully, I could hear my mother upstairs, clacking, one of the dogs barking in the backyard. But aside from that, it was just like always. Of course. What had I expected? I ran between rooms looking for something familiar, something even vaguely reassuring that might calm me down. I opened kitchen cabinets and junk drawers, upended couch cushions and ottomans. Surely my mother heard my noise, my heavy footsteps, the commotion of my breath still trying to catch up with itself.

In the living room I went for the stereo, which had sat so long untouched. Danny, insisting on his constant din, was the only one who'd ever used it. I wheeled the dial to what I guessed to be one of his stations—thumping bass, arrhythmic syncopation, voices shouting—and turned the volume up and up and up, till it would turn no more. The walls shook and the speakers let out an alarming, rasping crackle. My head pounded. My ears seemed as if they might burst. The noise. Ah, the noise.

My mother finally appeared, bounding down the steps, her familiar bathrobe fluttering behind her like a cape, her face a mess, her hair a mess, her a mess.

"What in the world?" she shrieked at me. "What in the world?" though the music drowned her out and I could only read her lips and I pretended the alarm on her face was rapture, the words from her mouth:

"What a good girl. What a good girl."

27.

When I returned to the McAllisters' the next day, everyone regarded me more warily. Bayard, never one to start conversations, attempted tentative ones about "You like the gymnast girls in the Olympics?" and "What kind of car you want one day?" He didn't mention anything about the day before. Neither did the kids. They played on the lawn and looked embarrassed when I tried talking to them about needing to be more careful, quickly squirming away and going back to their games without inviting me to join.

It was no matter, though. I had a plan. I would stake out a spot near the sidewalk and wait for Melissa Anne's return. I would, I'd decided the previous night, make sure she never got close again. I'd be on the lookout for her bike, her creaky little trailer, her oozing bottles and cans, and the next time I would ward her off sooner and more threateningly, make myself huge and whoop and growl like you were supposed to with mountain lions. Maybe clang something. I took Fack's tom-tom and one of his toy mallets and rooted myself at the front of the lawn, my attention focused on either corner, listening for the far-off squeals of her trailer wheels, watching and waiting.

But the McAllisters' street remained as quiet and uneventful as usual, people driving to work and back home, teenagers passing by on scooters and skateboards, an occasional ice cream truck sending kids into frenzy. I watched the mailman doing his paces up one side of the block, back the other. One afternoon a leashless, ownerless dog ran along the street. The next, a new refrigerator was delivered to the house across the road. Soon enough Fick and Fack were back to entreating me to set up the Slip 'N Slide for them, to play teacher to their pretend schoolchildren, nurse to their pretend ailments. But I couldn't ease back into things. By the time it was clear she wasn't returning, the days of anticipation and waiting had already done their damage. I couldn't stop thinking about the round face, the stringy hair, the smell. She became the itchy thing beneath my skin. Just as I had once culled and culled through the details of Roy (oh, how indulgent those days seemed now, how *Mr. Mustard in the study with the candlestick*), now it was Melissa Anne. I thought of all the months she'd done this same thing to my parents, wormed her way so easily in.

I went eventually in pursuit, telling myself it was just our normal walks, mine and Bayard's, though now I was always on guard, scanning for signs of her wet, drizzling trail, her clanking noise, her skittering eyes. I made us walk in longer and wider circles around the neighborhood, never letting on what I was doing. I couldn't have explained myself to Bayard even if I'd wanted to. Something to do with warning her away, with scaring her. Something. Blisters started to form on the backs of my heels. My nose and cheeks grew pink and tender and sunburned.

Bayard complained that we were going too fast, too far, that this was no fun, that he was getting moist. I did not know anyone else who would use the word *moist* so easily and I tried to be amused, tried to let him serve as the distraction he had so easily, so recently become, though already I could feel that slipping away. I could barely catch my breath beside him. I could not stop looking: down driveways, up alleys, around corners.

He insisted regularly that we stop, that he needed to rest. I wanted to punch him or just to leave him there when he did such things—we needed to go, to keep going; that much I clearly knew—but I had little sense of what I would do by myself. Already the long, hot hours were interminable with someone beside me. It was impossible to imagine them solo. So I found myself circling and circling in the street as he lounged beneath a leafy oak or a dying birch.

"Come on," I told him. "Come on."

"No, no," he said. "Two more minutes."

I groaned. I pulled at the peeling bark of the birch, which was shedding itself in fat curls, but all the while I was watchful, as if she might come moseying out the front door of a nearby home or be found kicking her feet on the wooden swing two porches down.

"I am going to fly apart into a trillion pieces," I said, half shouting. Bayard tapped his feet on the street and looked at me the same way he always looked at me: blankly neutral or neutrally blank. He was so unmoved by me. And there was something in his dull, forgetful stare, something in his unseeing eyes, that made it seem, if only for one quick moment, like all the terrible things that had come to pass, all the blights on my home, all the bodies dug up and reburied, all the bloody, broken grotesquerie, amounted to nothing at all. And for that I loved him. I loved him, briefly and deeply and inexorably, as much as I had ever loved anybody.

I stumbled to him, my limbs uncooperative. When I tried to lean, I fell instead into his lap. It was not pretty or graceful, the way I was upon him, pressing my lips to his, the way I grabbed at his shoulders, trying to steady myself. But I did not care—I was so far past the point of caring. His lips were rough and chapped, and even though I felt his immediate recoil, his undeniable hiccup backward, I did not stop, so convinced I was of a promise of oblivion.

He made a noise, a closed-mouth cluck, and still I didn't stop but pulled at his arms and tried to bring him to me. He began moving his face, making it seem like he would at least give this a try, maybe open his lips, slip his tongue in my mouth, until I realized that all he was doing was shaking his head back and forth: *no.* Still I kept going. I kissed until I couldn't any longer. Until it became inescapable, the sick, sober state of things.

When I pulled back, his face was wide-eyed and pale, his lips moving now but wordlessly, his expression one of surprise and something else—a curdle, maybe disgust—not so dissimilar, I imagined, from what David Nelson had seen so many months before.

"Merde," he was saying. *"Putain,"* and I was on my knees, kneeling before him, saying, "Stop, stop, stop. It's fine." It was hard to look at him, his face so nakedly emotive now, hardly even his own. I wanted to explain that it was nothing, I had gotten carried away. I thought of shouting that I had never really stopped thinking he was gay. But he was up already, brushing off his shorts and his shirt as if I had splattered him with something.

He must go, he told me. *Muz goo.*

And I told him no, even though I knew it was useless. "Stop!" I called, blood rushing into my face, my ears ringing. He did no such thing, prancing down the sidewalk in his sandals the same way he had always pranced in those high-heeled shoes. I had never asked him about those high-heeled shoes. "Why," I shouted, "did you wear those shoes?" but he did not turn around. If anything, he sped up, as if fearful I was gaining on him, though I still had not moved, was kneeling in the same spot, teeming with the knowledge that I had just destroyed the last of the good and okay things offered to me that year. "Those shoes!" I called, my voice shredding. A sound: a laugh like a cry. Was I making that sound?

I had no place to spend my days. Home, not an option; the McAllisters', of course not. I walked. I drank rusty water from sprinklers. I poked at my blisters with my fingernails. I kneaded my calves as they ached. A stitch began in my left side, radiating from my abdomen, growing so insistent I pressed the heel of my palm to it and said to no one, "Ow. Owowow," Squirrels stared at me. I stared back.

I thought of trying to bargain with Bayard, trying to work out joint custody of the McAllister house: he could have Monday/Wednesday/Friday, I'd get the rest. Sometimes I walked as far as the corner of their block and peered at the lawn, watching the kids play, looking for Bayard on the porch. I didn't go any closer.

And so. The search. It became everything, even when I no longer remembered why I'd begun. I marched and marched, on constant alert. I had no idea what I would do if I found her. There was no plan. No half-plan. There was only compulsion, one far deeper than with the letters or the straits. This from some gaping, growling chasm where nearly a year of sleeplessness stirred, where Danny said to me things like *Rydia* and *Burn on you* and *Jesus Mary Jehosephat.* Some days I was so certain of his voice I would turn around to see who was messing with me. It was easy to mistake the smell of my own sweat for his, that dewy spice of continual motion. I could not stop.

For so long there was nothing, just trees and homes and cars speeding by. I began to wonder if it'd really been she who passed by, and even if it had been, if that suggested a regular route in this area. There were days I contemplated stopping. Thought about sitting down. But one afternoon I found her stinking drizzle along a whole strip of sidewalk. It was already starting to dry, baking away, though still with the lingering ferment coming off it. And too a remnant of her dense sweat. She had to be close, the way she still clotted the air, and I ran around nearby blocks, panting, once even shouting her strange name. But she was nowhere. Again, nowhere. Though I hardly cared, buzzing from having come so close. This. Close.

I lost count of days, though I was hazily aware of Bayard's departure date, hazily aware of August. Aw-gust, I thought as I stared at a calendar page in a gas station where I stopped for water. What a strange and weird and screwed-up idea. Aw-gust.

It turned out to be an afternoon like all the other afternoons (humid, unforgiving, a dense hum of crickets) on a block like all the other blocks (stout houses, deep lawns, leafy trees) when I finally saw her bike blocking the sidewalk, tipping drunkenly on its kickstand at nearly a forty-five-degree angle to the ground, the rusty little trailer still hooked behind it. At first it shocked me, the same way it had shocked me when we'd found Tanda Moore, the same way it had shocked me when Denis, Kimberly, and the police had converged in our living room. How quickly the search became the thing itself. A nervous shiver rose in me, though it was more violent than a shiver. I thought I might spit, might yelp. My pulse rang painfully in my throat.

Melissa Anne was nowhere in sight. I examined the ripped bike seat and dirty yellow stuffing poking through, the nearly empty trailer. The cans were gone, replaced by a crumpled blanket and a moldering pile of newspaper. I tore through the paper, with no idea what I was looking for. The pages were smeared and stuck together, that same fermented stink rising off them, along with a thick, dense mold. I gagged. It was a loud, nasty noise, the noise itself making me gag again. Things crawled around the blanket, raced across my hand, up my arm.

I shook myself out, dancing wildly on the sidewalk, wondering if this was all I'd find, if she'd abandoned the bike and taken off for parts unknown, a thought that both terrified and relieved me. But then I heard loud, clattering noises up a driveway past the nearest house, beyond where I could see. It sounded like she was messing through garbage cans, and soon she emerged, grasping in her arms like a baby three beer bottles, a crumpled windbreaker spotted with what appeared to be coffee grounds, and a half-moldy orange. She gripped a broken mug in one hand.

Her face—it was that same terrible face: toothy and round, sweaty wisps of the gray hair sticking to her temples and cheeks, her skin scabrous-looking, mottled red and brown.

I had no idea what I was doing here. I had the thought to run.

"Get!" she screamed as soon as she saw me at the bike. "You get!" just as I'd last screamed at her. She wore the same gym shorts, but her shirt was a sleeveless smock, exposing her shoulders and back, sunburned and peeling in spots, dotted with moles in others. It made me a little sick, looking at so much of Melissa Anne.

What was I to say now? *Leave me alone? Leave Fick and Fack alone?* None of that, of course, made any sense. It was a ridiculous feeling: here, finally arrived, and to nothing. To only myself, standing stupidly before her, wordless. She was coming fast toward the bike, toward me, her eyes bouncing from lawn to sidewalk to something in the sky, her face pinched in a growl. She clutched her new possessions so tightly her muscles grew taut and ropy along her arms. They looked like strong arms. I thought again of running.

"I'm Lydia Pasternak!" I shouted. "My brother was Danny Pasternak!" This was the last time I would ever speak that sentence. No need. For years, I would be still surrounded by people who already knew, and then by people who didn't, and the relief of that change, so strong, so strong.

But Melissa Anne heard me. She stopped a few feet away, her gaze briefly settling on my shoulder or my chin. I watched her swallow deeply. I watched her grasp the windbreaker more closely to her chest. She straightened, her chin lifting, an unmistakable swell to her chest. And then the smile: huge, crooked teeth, wolflike and carnivorous.

She was beaming, Melissa Anne, beaming at the mention of my brother's name, and I felt the spit pool in my mouth and heat creep up the back of my throat. She was staking a claim on him, the same way countless people—Min Mathers, Kirk Donovan, Tip Reynolds, Principal Garver, and on and on—had laid claim to him, as if he were so simply, so uncontestedly theirs. The muscles from my head to my neck, from my neck to my shoulders, from my shoulders to my ass, from my ass to my thighs, clenched as if ready to seize or spring. I thought a million thoughts, of holes and sedans and bridges and cherries and posters and dark, but none more clearly than how much misery this woman had heaped upon my family.

"Danny," she said, and it was so infuriating, his name from her mouth. I kicked at her rusty trailer. She made a little yelp, the smile fading. I liked the sound of the yelp. I liked it very much.

"Yeah!" I called, kicking the trailer harder. It buckled some, pulling the bike with it, both seeming like they would fall over. "You don't like that, do you?"

Her smile was entirely gone now, her face crunching into a little fist. I kicked at the bike, the rubber of the wheel, the rusty frame, the spokes, slicing one of my toes as I went. The blood came quickly and without pain, my toe not even seeming like my toe. I kept kicking and the bike toppled with the most satisfying of rackets, a jangling noise of metal and cement. Melissa Anne let out a series of shrieking whoops; a wonder that no one came running from their home. How easily—had I ever truly realized?—someone could meet their terrible fate in these quiet streets.

There was something coursing through me now—adrenaline? bravery? rage?—that brought everything into such bright relief. The startling blue of the sky. The wavy air off the hot street. The alarming stink of this woman: abscess and outhouse and rot, all so warm and festering, it made me want to do horrible things. I let out a loud, throaty growl and ran at her, prepared for a chase. But she did not run, instead cowering in her spot. The mug shook in her fist, and the sound she was making was a whine. I was so close, right on top of her. I tried not to breathe.

"Look at me," I yelled. My toe began to throb, a pulsing, nearly comforting feeling. Here I was. "Fucking look at me," I said. How great it suddenly was to swear. How had I not always done it? How had I gotten by? "Fuck you," I said. "Fuck." I could see she was trying to focus, her eyes skittering across my face and back, looking to my neck, to my chest as it heaved. I grabbed her wrist, her skin loose and thick beneath my fingers, with a texture like half-healed scabs. It was so gross to touch her, but I did not let go. Her whimpers rose and she tried to pull away, but I only squeezed tighter. "Fucking. Look. At. Me," I said.

I needed her to focus. I needed her to look into my eyes and tell me what she saw now. I needed to know if anything had changed.

"Come on," I said. I took the heel of my sandal and ground it into one of her crumbling, laceless tennis shoes, feeling her foot under mine, muscles and tendon, bone. But she offered nothing, her face turning crimson, her eyes alternately squeezing shut and blinking quickly, filling with tears. I clamped down as hard as I could on her arm, twisting her rough skin in my hand (*Indian burn*, Danny said in my ear). She dropped the mug and it shattered easily. An errant piece sliced my leg. From the noise she made, one sliced hers too. Still I did not let go, my hand beginning to cramp from gripping for so long, my arm starting to shake.

"Did you," I whispered, my voice suddenly hot and hoarse, "really see him?" She said nothing, the only noise her breathing. This, all at once, was why I had come. Why I had marched and marched and marched.

And then she looked, she finally looked. Her eyes on mine. One clear, unwavering moment. "Yes," she said, and even though her gaze so quickly fluttered away—to the ground, the house behind us, my left ear—I had seen it. And for the first time, with unexpected clarity and vigor, I believed her. She had. She had she had she had.

My body grew so loud: my pulse thumping, my breath coming in a wheeze, the sound in my head a screeching squeal. Like my skull was going to split open. Like I might burst at my seams. Quickly I was upon her, pulling her to me. The smell was woozy-making so close, but I pressed myself into the windbreaker anyway, let the necks of the bottles stab my ribs. I put my mouth to her ear.

"What," I whispered, "was it like for him?" She did not answer, but the questions flew from me anyway, a hot rush of words. "How much did he suffer? Did he know what was happening? Had he prayed? Had he called out for us?"

She was crying against me. I could feel it, the quake of her body, so small-seeming all of a sudden. She felt like a child, a dirty, pungent, rotten child. "Had he," I hissed in her ear, "thought we were coming for him?"

She buried her face against me, her forehead grinding roughly into my shoulder. I thought she would bite, but she didn't. I could hear only a muffled panting. Her muscles were slack now, past the point of resisting; it was like holding a puddle. "Please," I said. I could not imagine a time when we would not be clasped together like this on the sidewalk. I could not imagine what would follow from here. I could not imagine that anything would. "Please," I repeated, though I knew nothing would come.

"I did everything I could," I told her, which was a lie, but she did not know that. She had no fucking idea. It seemed like it meant something, at least, to have a need to confess.

I waited for Danny to say something more, to tell me to crush her or beat her down or wrestle her to the ground. But there was no voice. Of course there was no voice. My brother was dead. I was a smart girl. I knew that dead people did not really whisper in my ear. I knew they did not linger in nearby treetops. I tried to remember the last time I'd imagined him up there, floating in the branches, smirking down at us. Months before, when everything was still fantastic and far away, none of this anything more than a story. Now it was just the air up there, hot and fetid, damp. Nobody was watching. We were alone. At once a dreadful thought and a relief, a startling relief.

When I let go, Melissa Anne would not look at me, only at her feet and the sidewalk between us. I was covered in coffee grounds, dark swaths smeared across my shirt, along one arm. Blood ran down one leg, the other foot. Melissa Anne's right ankle was scraped, bleeding freely. Even her blood looked dirty, a browning pool on the cement. Her crying was quiet, surprisingly contained. You would not have even known except for the quivering crown of her head, where thinning hair revealed an alarming amount of bright red scalp. I wondered for the first time what sort of life turned a person into Melissa Anne, what terrible blight she must have endured. I did not even let myself imagine. Already I was left to too much imagining.

"Okay," I said, zapped of all energy. Even the word was effortful to say: "Okay, okay, okay." I was wrung dry, bloodless, baking in the sun.

I cleared the pieces of the mug from the sidewalk, the shards large enough to cup in my hands without injury. When I handed them to her, she just shrugged without reaching for them. She did not want them. Why would she possibly want them? "Okay," I told her, and "Sorry." I felt bad about the mug. I felt bad about nearly everything.

"You should," I said of her ankle, "get that cleaned up." I went next to the bike. "Come on," I called when she did not follow. "Just come on." I had bent one of the wheels and tried briefly and unsuccessfully to bend it back. "And," I said preposterously, "you should get this fixed." She was still staring at the ground, but nearer to me and nodding, likely afraid of what I would do if she did not simply agree.

After coaxing from her the windbreaker and the bottles and the orange, which had split open and begun drooling a bitter citrus drool, I placed them all in the trailer and dragged the bike to her, offering it by the handlebars. "Take it," I said, and she did, still without looking up. She pulled it slowly, roughly down the sidewalk. Even after I stopped watching, I could still hear the terrible noise of it, a squealing, grinding, broken sound.

I took the mug home with me and lined the pieces along my windowsill. That night, when I couldn't sleep, I stood at the window, running my fingers along the shards, watching our dark street, the low pools of lamplight, the leafy canopies, figuring out where the smooth grooves of ceramic gave way to the sharper breaks so I could take my hand away in time. Sometimes I pressed down for the small bite of pain instead. It came as a surprise, a reassurance, reminding me of my skin, of my blood coursing beneath, so stubborn and insistent, the way it pumped through me, filling my heart and releasing, filling my heart and releasing, over and over again.

One of my parents shifted in their bed. One of the dogs lapped at its water bowl. The house hummed its usual hum—refrigerator, fan, dripping faucet. For once, none of it felt ominous or empty or fraught with particular meaning; it was just a house, just the noises of a house in the nighttime. I pressed and pressed into the cut of the mug, until the pain turned to something else: a loosening of muscles, a slowing of breath. But I didn't move from the window. Even as my legs started to ache and the base of my neck grew sore with tiredness, I wouldn't let myself be fooled into thinking sleep was coming. I had been fooled so many times, far more than I could count. The darkness was not even dense yet, just the thin gray of midnight. I was not the kind of girl who fell asleep at midnight anymore. I would easily be up for hours still. Getting back into bed, I knew all I was doing was readying for the next round of battle, now just from a prone position. Even as I crawled beneath the covers, I knew. Even as I closed my eyes. I knew and I knew. Except for this—next came brightness and the noise of birds, like a magician pulling the dove from his hat in a fluttery blink. Morning.

A Different Sort of Alchemy

28.

I went back to Fairfield for my ten-year reunion. This was not a common occurrence, me returning for any reason. For years I happily spent orphan Thanksgivings with friends who passed platters of marshmallowy sweet potatoes and shared in jokes with their aging parents about the time Aunt Fern pulled her dentures out on the pork roast. Colleagues welcomed me to their feminist seders, where ladies in earnestly batiked blouses set out a cup for Miriam next to the one for Elijah.

The longer I stayed away, the more the very idea of home felt otherworldly, like a place I'd made up in a fit of fantasy (*and there'd been three dogs and also a boy . . .*). Only my mom remained in Fairfield. She and my father had quietly separated and then divorced while I was at Brown, my father relocating, strangely, to Atlanta and, even more strangely, making a second family with a woman named Dolly and their twin girls. Save the irregular phone calls from one of them—my mother reporting on the latest missing, found, or dead child in the tri-state area, my dad ineffectively shushing his squealing girls—it was so easy to let memories of Fairfield recede. Home became only that which was right here in front of me: my apartment, with my overstuffed bookshelves, my claw-foot tub, my exposed dark wood beams spanning the length of the ceilings. Oh, how I loved those dark wood beams, loved my whole neighborhood, in fact. It had become fashionable of late to dislike my area of D.C. for its touristy gentrification, its well-trodden restaurant row, its traffic congestion, its overpriced, brightly painted row houses, but I remained unbendingly enamored—the defensive, reactionary loyalty of the refugee.

Months before the reunion, the onslaught of Lola Pepper calls had begun. She'd waged a similar campaign before the five-year reunion, my phone ringing at odd hours, her chirpy voice on the other end jarring and anachronistic, wanting to play "remember when" about events I could barely recall and conversations I suspected she may have had with other people. *Remember when we tried to dye your hair red? Remember that time the Ouija board said I'd have six kids?* That we hadn't once spoken in the intervening years was never mentioned. That we hadn't left Franklin High as friends or even acquaintances also remained unsaid. Lola's capacity for only the good and the light was still unfailing. She issued a simple, plaintive "Aren't you coming back for the reunion?" at the end of each call. It had been easy to beg off then. I was lingering in Providence after graduation, living in a rickety Victorian with six roommates. I was broke, I told her. I was in the middle of trying to find a job. There was no way I was coming home.

But there was something more disarming in the recent bout of calls, a new chord of exhaustion tingeing Lola's voice. I listened as she held her hand over the receiver to speak in a singsong voice to a small child. She had a two-year-old, she told me, making jokes about wanting to nip Lacey's bottle with whiskey at bedtime. I recognized the desperate rasp of sleeplessness. "Don't you want to see everyone?" she asked, and "Aren't you the slightest bit curious?" I told her, honestly, "No" and "Not really."

I felt bad about the pauses that followed, though Lola, even with the vague wistfulness she evoked, had little staying power. Thoughts of her quickly faded after I hung up, easily replaced by the wheezing sounds of the Metro bus on the street below or the yeasty late-afternoon smell of the Ethiopian restaurant down the block.

But there was also the matter of Gene, the man I had been dating for nearly two years, who unfailingly rubbed the achy balls of my feet before bed, who was as consumed with his obscure job as a Smithsonian nineteenth-century archivist as I was with my obscure job analyzing data about sediment transport in estuarine systems, who quietly collected early daguerreotype portraits and hung them above his bed, his dining room table, in the nook beside his coat closet, who had an acute sensitivity to gluten that eliminated pizza, cereal, pasta, bread, soy sauce, and pastries from his diet, turning restaurants and grocery stores into gauntlets, but which I grudgingly appreciated for the singular way it revealed him to be high-maintenance, the one tear in his otherwise unflappable veneer.

Gene loved me and, as was the general consensus among our friends, wanted to marry me. He'd been talking for months now about me letting my lease lapse at the end of the year and moving in with him to his three-bedroom place in Dupont Circle. There were no ultimatums or even direct entreaties—those weren't Gene's style—but rather a low-level, ongoing conversation about the L-shaped desk he'd seen online that we could share in the study and how nice it would be not to have to schlep a change of clothes and toothbrush across town on the Metro anymore. Sometimes it was fun to talk about the king-sized bed we would get or where on his countertop I would put my Kitchenaid mixer.

Except I hadn't agreed yet, because other times the thought of each day waking and eating my granola and changing out of my pajamas and taking my birth control pill beneath the gaze of the dead-eyed, high-collared families of the 1800s made the blood rush from my face and throb at the base of my neck. There were nights when I sat at Gene's dining room table, enjoying a perfectly nice glass of wine after another of his meticulously cooked meals (lamb with mint yogurt sauce, a side of honeyed green beans), and I would grow keenly aware of all the eyes upon me. It made me prickly and petulant, awakening in me terrible urges like the one to take my closed fist and smash the nearest piece of dinnerware.

I liked my life with Gene. At times I liked it very much. In the evenings we read on my couch or his, our toes touching on the footrest. We kept a running list of words we found compelling tacked up on his refrigerator. *Étouffée*, he'd recently added after a Cajun diner. *Ague*, I added after listening to a friend's tales of his Peace Corps years. We told funny stories at parties—there was the one about us getting lost on our road trip in Vermont, the one about the yappy stray terrier we rescued for a week.

But this was how I'd always been, whether with Martin, the willowy philosophy major who I'd dated most of my junior year at Brown, or Stan, the architect and casual pot dealer who made my toes curl just from touching my wrist during my first six months in D.C.—finite in my capacity for tolerating simple day-to-day contact. I could handle it just fine, all the way up to the point that I couldn't anymore, as if I existed on a tether, and not a particularly long one, finding myself able to wander only so far into the territory of another human being before snapping back into myself.

Gene overheard several of the calls with Lola, at least my end of cagey evasions, and was perplexed as to why I wouldn't want to go home, why I wouldn't want to take him home. This, to him, was how things worked. You fell in love, you met each other's families, you moved in together, you . . .

We'd already weekended with his parents a handful of times, in a beach house in Virginia, in New York City, where we visited MoMA and the Trade Center site and Chelsea galleries. All of it was fine and exhausting and hard the way other people's families always were, especially in their small, easy intimacies: Gene holding his mom by the elbow, steering her along the crowded Fifth Avenue sidewalks; his dad patting Gene's belly, making a quick joke of *You working on a paunch there, son?*

Gene knew about my family, about Danny, but only in the most general and newspaper-headline of ways. I had a brother who'd been killed, just like our friend Lisbeth had a father who was gay, just like our other friend Jonathan had survived a teenage bout of leukemia. Gene had learned early on not to probe, the same way I learned that wine made him snore and the soles of his feet were painfully ticklish.

But the topic of the reunion drizzled into our conversations regularly enough that I knew it had come to matter to him, to mean something. "I bet you're the only one in your class who can say she saw the head of the Senate Appropriations Committee at happy hour," he said over Cheerios, his hair still tousled from bed. He sent e-mails about it in the middle of work with links to the African American History Museum in Detroit, writing simply, "This looks interesting." I recognized here the need for concession. I was the limiting factor of the relationship. I was the *no*. And I was not an idiot. Even the most patient and imperturbable of people, which Gene could easily lay claim to being, had only so much capacity for evasion and sulk. He was a good man, and Fairfield, in that it was time-limited and at the very least a known entity, was the easiest—the only—yes of which I was capable.

My mother was still in the old house. Over the years it'd taken on a greenhouse scent of dirt and incubation from her constant presence. She gave a "tour" when we arrived. "Here's the living room," she told Gene facilely, cracking her gum as we walked. She always chewed gum at the start of visits, a show of trying to quit smoking, though the years of smoke still perfumed the air, especially when a curtain was riffled or a door swung quickly open. I could see that she had just cleaned; vacuum trails divided the carpet into fresh rows. She was dressed in a skirt and blouse, and her hair was parted neatly and combed flatly across her head. But there was a cabbagey wrinkle to her shirt collar, and her outsized dress loafers slid easily off her heels like flip-flops.

Gene's mother wore pressed pants and cropped silk jackets; at the beach, a sarong in complementary color to her swimsuit. If Gene now noticed my mother's unshaved legs or the dry-skin flakes in her laugh lines, he gave no indication. He smiled his usual affable smile, even though I knew he was feeling peaked from the flight. He'd been excited about the trip, and in a rare unguarded moment ate a few stray pretzels from the airline's snack mix. Even though he'd stopped almost immediately, sheepishly handing me the small foil bag, I could see it now in his pale face and the tiny beads of sweat over his top lip.

I fished out the pewter paperweight from my bag, a replica of the Washington Monument, purchased last-minute at the airport gift shop along with my bottled water and the *New York Times*.

"Ooh," my mother said, weighing it in one hand, almost doing a series of mini-curls.

"It's a paperweight," I said dumbly, embarrassed by it now.

"I'm surprised they let you on the plane with this," she said, holding it like a spear, lurching playfully toward Gene as if she were going to stab him. He acted fearful in return, arms up. She went on about how much she loved the paperweight, and her effusiveness only increased my embarrassment. She went on too about how she'd always loved *Smithsonian* magazine as a child. It was the first place, she told Gene, she'd seen photographs of a woman's breasts. She laughed at her own confession, a strange, birdlike noise. Gene laughed too, correcting her gently: he worked at the museum, not the magazine.

"Oh, oh," she said, bringing her hand to her chest and giggling. She was nervous, I could tell. I'd never brought a man home before. I hadn't seen her in close to three years. Her face was rounder now, with traces of an emerging double chin. Weight gain was a side effect of all her meds, the cocktail of sedatives and antidepressants and antianxieties she'd been on for years.

"And how's your job?" she asked me, shepherding us into the kitchen. Condensation dotted the stove and countertop from a recent wipe-down. The air smelled of the bracing remnants of cleanser.

"Good," I said. "It's going really well." I loved my job. I loved being a research analyst. I loved puzzling through data and looking for patterns. I loved making sense of what appeared to be a mess of random numbers. I loved it that I had known absolutely nothing about sediment distribution or erosion and accretion or hydrodynamic models when I'd begun at my environmental consulting firm, but I'd soldiered through to figure out what the heck was going on and was able to talk shop now with colleagues who'd been in the field for years. It was hard to explain any of it to laypeople, though, especially to my mother. She had a particular way of twiddling her fingers and nodding before I even spoke, smiling at Gene and playing with the rattan on the back of the kitchen chair, that suggested the combination of eagerness and absence of which she seemed uniquely capable. It made the tips of my ears burn.

"I'm still on mud," I said. This my standard line about sediment transport models.

"Mud is good," she said. My mother and I smiled at each other.

Moments unfolded, followed by more unfolding moments. Gene put a hand on the small of my back. Eventually she announced, "Let's eat." She'd carefully cubed pineapples and watermelon and bananas, having called three times in the previous week trying to figure out what Gene could eat.

At the table she talked about her most recent volunteer work, the girl who'd gone missing from Western Michigan University while walking home from the library. My mother was helping the family set up a listserv to coordinate search efforts and helping with a Web site, findjacqueline.com. I scanned the fruit plate for dog hair. Oliver and Poppy were both dead. Only an arthritic Olivia was left, following us stiffly through the house. Gene kept leaning from the table to scratch her beneath the collar.

My mother said that Jacqueline's boyfriend had received a nonsensical text message from an unknown number at 4 a.m., eight hours after she was last seen. Cryptologists had been analyzing it for any sort of code.

"You mean cryptographers," I said, and she smiled uncomprehendingly. I knew she thought we'd said the same word. I had a particular dislike for these conversations, not just because they were ghoulish and rubbernecky—I understood the appeal of ghoulish and rubbernecky, was still drawn to coverage of school shootings or tsunamis or terrorist attacks—but rather because she didn't know to be embarrassed by her excitement.

Gene asked about search-and-rescue operations and her HTML background. They could've been talking about migratory patterns of midwestern birds or the benefits of regular lubrication for car engines, from the mild set to his face. Same when she dragged out the dreaded scrapbooks, all the clippings and letters and police reports, the file cabinet distilled into book form. When I tried to object, both shushed me, Gene while smiling. He was always smiling at me.

My mother narrated as she turned the pages. "This is the first local story after he went missing." "This is the article from *Newsweek*. *Newsweek*! Can you imagine?"

"I can't," Gene said simply. I found myself watching his expression, waiting for something more. I had worried in the days leading up to the trip about his reaction to this place: shock? repulsion? Now, though, there was only his normal placidity. How thrilled I usually was about this very quality—his incapacity for needless drama. It seemed so clear-eyed and revelatory, even. But as he sat beside my mother, nodding and nodding, I had the urge to kick him in the calf, to leave a welting charley horse.

"This is about the arraignment." My mother soldiered on, pointing to articles. "This is the groundbreaking for the memorial." When she finally finished, he placed a hand on the back of hers. "I'm so sorry, Mrs. Pasternak." She told him to call her Bernice. I had the urge to give her a charley horse too.

After a few minutes, Gene asked if there was someplace he could lie down and my mother sputtered quickly about being sorry for upsetting him and he reassured her, no, no, it wasn't that, and explained about the pretzels and she patted him on the arm and said good, good, and that I'd show him upstairs.

• • •

My old room had a skeletal feel to it, with the bare bookshelves and desktop, the nearly blank walls. All of my old furniture was still here, but any mementos, any indication that someone had inhabited this place for eighteen years, were gone. There was something comforting in the austerity. Aside from my framed diploma hanging in one corner, we could have been anywhere.

Quickly Gene was down to his boxers and under the comforter. He looked huge in my bed, his feet trailing off the end. "Do you want to lie down with me?" he said, but we both knew the answer. I hadn't had insomnia in years, but I still treated bedrooms with a ritualistic reverence, replete with eye pillows, blackout shades, and white noise machines. I'd never turned into the kind of person who could laze around casually in a bed, willfully awake.

"That is tremendously sad about your brother," he said. I nodded and kissed his eyelids. He liked to be kissed on his eyelids. "You okay?" he said. I nodded again, though I wasn't sure if he meant in this moment or in life. It was clear from his expression that he expected something more, a conversation, and suddenly he looked so sad, his whole face drawn. Here was the opening I had moments before hoped for—*Yeah, it is sad, isn't it?*—though now I found myself empty in the face of it, with nothing to say. I was terrible at this topic.

I asked about his stomach, and he studied me below a knit brow that gave way to a half-smile, his familiar expression of being confounded but deciding not to push it. He said it was okay. I told him he still looked pale. We talked for a bit about little nothings, if he'd left enough food for his cat, what time we needed to leave for the reunion. I studied his face, his slightly stubbled chin, the tiny scar that bisected his left eyebrow. He looked funny here, out of context, bordering suddenly on stranger. *Gene, Gene, Gene,* I told myself, touching the tip of his nose. I kissed him, the familiar taste of his waxy lip balm, his breath slightly sour from a morning of travel and a stomachache. But he didn't taste bad, really, just like a person, another person. When I pulled away, he smiled, his eyes already closed.

I found my mother in Danny's room, at the computer—such a familiar pose, though the computer was new, with a large, flat monitor. Danny's room had become a strange amalgamation of preservation and reinvention, my mother having entirely taken over the desk area. Next to the new computer sat a wiry, stacking file organizer with a cascading column of manila folders: *Maynard; Smith, T.; D'Agostino.* Already the Washington Monument sat atop a pile of yearbook stills and newspaper articles. The old file cabinet had been moved from the kitchen, joined by a pair of newer ones. A giant bulletin board hung overhead, crowded with photos of her small army of missing kids. Some had Post-it notes attached, indicating *Found*, others with dates: 12/30/87–3/9/01.

But all of Danny's old things were still here too: the bed, the dresser, the wall-spanning single bookshelf lined with trophies and old, yellowing comic books. A lone, improbable beer poster still hung above his bed, the corners curled from age, a rip snaking through the scantily clad, big-haired woman. Inside his closet, I suspected, his clothes still hung.

The room unsettled me, making it seem like my mother spent her days in a tomb. Though, admittedly, it wasn't all that much worse than my father's bright, antiseptic house, with its matching leather furniture and Berber rugs that pulled easily and often, leaving Dolly on her hands and knees with cuticle scissors, clipping the errant threads. There you'd find well-placed photos of me and Danny on a back table in the den or on one end of a mantel filled mostly with more recent shots of Dolly, Dad, and their towheaded girls. There was something creepy about the pictures of me and Danny, something eerily undifferentiated. It didn't matter that one of us was dead and the other alive; we were both just the kids he used to have.

My mother clacked away at the keyboard.

"Hey," I said.

She spun in her chair. "Oh," she said, a hand to her chest. "You startled me." A cigarette smoldered in the ashtray next to the keyboard.

"Still smoking," I said. It came out sharply.

She looked at me and then into her lap. She shrugged. Gone, all the girlish excitement she'd had around Gene. I tried to think of something nicer. "Working?" I said.

She told me yes, her hand moving automatically toward her cigarette, then stopping.

"It's fine," I said. "I don't care." I'd meant that, at least, to sound nicer. "You're working on the Western Michigan girl stuff?"

"Oh, no, no," she said. "I have about four other kids right now. I'm e-mailing a father in Wisconsin. His ex-wife, looks like, ran off with their son during a custody weekend." She paged through the folders in the wire rack. "Here," she said, pulling out a picture from one of the files. The boy was little, six or seven, with wheaty hair, his lips a shiny, shiny red.

"Evan," she said, with feeling. "His name is Evan." She was insatiable when it came to this stuff.

"Evan," I repeated, trying to affect a little bit of the airy countenance Gene seemed to come by so naturally.

She smoked. I picked at my torn cuticles. Eventually she said, "I like Gene."

"I like Gene too." If you listened carefully, you could hear the low, slurring noise of his breathing from the next room. He would sleep for hours. He could nap like an infant, Gene.

My mother stared at me, as if waiting for my next thought. I didn't have a next thought, except maybe that the new roundness of her face made her look soft, almost babyish, which made eye contact difficult, and I found myself glancing instead at her shoulder or the bright tip of her cigarette. Or that the bulletin board was even worse than the daguerreotypes.

"Don't let me stop you from what you're doing," I said. She looked at me strangely. I tried to smile. If I were of sound mind, I would have simply gone downstairs and sat by myself on the couch and patted Olivia in relative peace. But something rooted me in the doorway, the same occasional impulse that guided me through record stores, looking for the old serpent-tongue-and-red-rose-dotted Chili Peppers album that had been Danny's favorite, or sent me on an Internet search of Elvin Tate (pages and pages of results, unsettlingly), the impulse toward prurient surrender, the want to look. Leaning against the doorjamb and peering at the geometric sheets of his childhood bed, the figurines on the trophies, worn now of their gold paint, revealing a pale plastic beneath, the framed photo—that once ubiquitous yearbook shot of the blue background and the cowlick—I felt an unmistakable if infinitesimal slackening, something approximating an exhalation. This, perhaps, was the singular distinction between home and everyplace else. The reason I stayed away. The reason I came back. Here I could do this, look and look.

My mother asked if I wanted to help. She had some pamphlets that needed to be prepped for mailing. I said no. She said something else about Gene and nice. I didn't have a response. I just wanted to stand there, left alone if possible.

When it became clear I was neither coming nor going, she said an uncertain "Okay" and went back to what she was doing, finishing her e-mail and printing something out, stuffing, stamping, and sealing an envelope. Occasionally she turned to look at me, and I continued to try smiling. "Honey—" she said once, but did not finish.

Her phone rang a couple times. The first call was from a man named Douglas. She asked him if he'd gotten in touch with the Duluth police yet. She read aloud through a list of drop-in centers and homeless shelters she'd found in northeast Minnesota, all with a note of calm efficiency I wasn't used to. Our own calls were more of a collective stammer.

The second call was from a woman, Franny. Even from where I stood, I could hear the sobbing, a sound that never failed to make me want to rip my ears from my head. My mother appeared unfazed. She slowly repeated Franny's name, then said, "Listen to me. We are going to get through this. I am here." And then for a very long time she simply sat and listened to the woman's howls, nodding slowly as if Franny could see her. As the crying faded, my mother began with low questions: "What's happened today? Any new news?" She took notes as Franny talked. *Six mo anniv,* she wrote. *Frank @ hotel.* I found myself wondering who Frank was and why he was at a hotel.

"This," my mother told her, "would be a good time for more media. When was the last time you were on the news?" Again with the same low tone of authority, shades of, amazingly, Denis Jimenez. It had never occurred to me that she might have grown good at this by now. I shifted my weight against the doorframe, suddenly feeling like a voyeur, telling myself to stop lurking, to go read the data from work I'd brought with me, to go curl up next to Gene.

My mom and Franny made plans to check in the next day. Afterward, my mom did an Internet search for Columbus television and radio stations. She printed some pages. She scribbled long notes into a file. She kept telling me how it would just be a few more minutes, soon we would visit.

"It's okay," I told her. I didn't particularly want to visit, and I could see it wouldn't be just a few more minutes. There was something I recognized in the piecing together, the sorting and arranging, the absorption in the task at hand. I stared at the oldest of the file cabinets, where large orange starbursts of rust were corroding the paint. I wondered what the inside looked like now. I thought of saying something to her, something about having never lost the investigatory impulse either—my job, a daily mining of meaning from chaos—about me too still making up for how wrong we'd gotten it the first time. I watched the back of her head, smoke unfurling around her. My mom was getting old. Her hair was thinning, a dime-sized bald spot now revealed at the crown of her head. I'd never seen that before.

"You're doing good," I said, and when she turned to me, the furrow to her brow, the deep crinkle at the bridge of her nose, made me think she'd misheard me. For a moment she stared at me with such a familiar expression of disorientation—(*And* who *exactly are* you?)—I thought I might shake her by the shoulders and scream. But then her mouth quivered slightly and she gave the most sheepish of smiles, as if it had bloomed in spite of itself. Her eyes glistened with a sheen of the wetness that used to be ever-present, used to spill so easily down her face.

But she wasn't crying now. She was nodding at me, smiling, and there was something shameful in realizing how little it took to make her happy. My mother, the original rescue beagle. I could not recall the last time I had paid her a compliment, genuine or otherwise.

The last time I had said a kind word to her. For years I'd thought of it as me waiting for her, me the one who had given up on the waiting. What, I wondered, if I had gotten it backward?

"It's good work," I said again, and I meant it. It made some sense, her choice to spend her days in this room, to remake a life from exactly the point where our previous one had imploded. What else had we—me, my dad too—offered?

"I like it," she said. "I really do. It makes me feel like I'm doing something." She sounded girlish, hopeful and excited. She patted the foot of the bed. "You can help."

It'd been years since I'd stepped across the threshold of this doorway. There had always been something repellent about it. When I paused, my mother added quickly, "Only if you want. You don't have to," and already the familiar sound of defeat had returned. What must it have been like for her, I wondered, to have been left with me, only me, the child who'd had so little feeling for her, so little propensity toward consolation or sympathy? Two blights on her house, my poor mother.

I went in.

The mattress sagged easily beneath me. I was imagining it, I knew, the way I thought I might be able to detect a whiff of him beneath the smoke and the oily musk of my mother. A hint of sweat or dirt or Tonka Truck or baseball glove. It was a complete impossibility, particulate-wise. I was aware of that.

"I can smell him," I said. It wasn't more than a whisper.

Again her look of surprise. Again her smile.

"I know," she said, searching and searching my face. I worried that this would turn into something big, something grasping and tearful and too much. But she just handed me the flat stack of pamphlets that needed folding. *What to Do in the First Days*, it said on top of the far right column, and I was grateful for the task. It was good to have something to do with my hands. She gave me directions—I didn't need them, but I let her tell me anyway, her chair scooted close, her knees pressed into mine. I creased the pages carefully, one fold, then the next, lining up the corners exactly, piling neat stacks next to me on the bed until just before they toppled. When I handed her fistfuls, she said, "Very good" and "Excellent," and even though I knew it was work anyone could do—a small child, a trained monkey—I didn't protest. I let her say nice things, imagining us to be the kind of women who were always like this, ones who sat in quiet tandem, murmuring sweetly.

29.

Lola Pepper had hips now. Her red hair had lost some of its shine, looking almost brown, and her skin tone, if possible, had deepened since adolescence, blending more with the myriad freckles, which no longer seemed such a distraction. David Nelson had a pregnant wife, a plain-faced woman with long, unstyled hair hanging down to her tailbone. They lived in Ames, Iowa, where he was a first-year assistant professor in poli sci at Iowa State. Jerold Terry had grown a gut and managed a paint store in Livonia. He talked with interest about things like semiglosses and the need to use a primer even if you're going darker.

We were all squeezed into a staticky, windowless hotel ballroom, a makeshift bar spanning one wall, a DJ sequestered at the far edge of a dance floor. People talked loudly, laughing in dramatic guffaws. Already several women (were they the girls from the tennis team? student council?) danced in a tight, shoeless circle to an old song about *Rock your body*, their brightly polished toenails straining against their nylons.

Gene stood at my side, a hand loosely gripping my elbow, drinking a plain tonic to my gin and tonic. The nap had helped him a little, but he still had the greenish cast and glassy eyes that often preceded a bout of full-blown sickness. A stream of people were upon us, eager to spout opinions about the election once they found out where we lived. D.C. was always helpful that way, as a conversation starter, since everyone had a stake. People nodded attentively as I tried to explain my work, or as Gene talked about the letters he was archiving about Mandan Indian trade routes. People smiled and smiled and smiled. I lost count of the number of compliments about my thinness, my short haircut, how I barely looked over twenty-one.

The afternoon in Danny's room had already lent a spacy, which-side-up quality to the day, a feeling that only increased among this crowd of half-remembered people, their breathy enthusiasms, their tendency toward standing nearly on top of us and touching their hands to our arms, laughing at everything. If one thing distinguished today from a decade ago, it was that everyone was nice, really nice, almost cloyingly so. I easily lost track of what people were saying, distracted by trying to place them. Thick-thighed Rochelle had only grown thicker, her broad shoulders straining against her blouse. Adam Deselets was almost unrecognizable from his Dungeon Master days, with his full beard and a ponytail past his shoulder blades. Before long, stories of Peace Corps or real estate investments or childbirth or weddings all blurred together.

I steered us regularly back to the bar. Gene asked in the line, "Are you having a good time?" He'd been asking me that since we arrived. I told him yes, which was true; this was more or less pleasant, mostly benign. But his repeated question made me antsy. Wasn't I acting like I was having a good time? I thought of adding some glib comment, like *If empty chitchat is your idea of a good time*, but such gibes made Gene uncomfortable. Misanthropy offended his sensibilities.

As we snaked forward in the line, I tried to think of conversation, a funny story or some small intimacy that would elicit that delicious us-versus-the-rest-of-them feeling, which seemed, at times like this, the best reason to have a date. But I couldn't think of anything good. He was, I could tell, eavesdropping on the conversation behind us, a man talking loudly about his IRA investments. I knocked my shoulder playfully against his. He knocked back.

We'd been there nearly an hour before anyone mentioned Danny, and then it was a virtual stranger, some woman who veered from talk of the renovation on her Hamtramck house to "I think about what happened to your family all the time," as if this were a natural progression. The lilting concern in her voice suggested a history between us more intimate than anything I could remember. When she'd first approached, I'd recognized her tight blond curls coiled like springs: we'd had a few English classes together.

"It seemed really like a nightmare," she said, "like so nuts," and a low tingling moved through the back of my head, the particular alertness that came from being on display in just this way, a state I'd managed to selectively forget in the intervening years.

"It was pretty horrible," I said, trying to sound appropriate. Gene placed a hand on my waist. I couldn't remember the last time this topic had passed as small talk. All through college I had successfully maintained a vow never to speak Danny's name, my only reminder being a small cut-out picture in my wallet behind my coffee punch card and video store membership. In D.C., I mentioned him only rarely and often inappropriately, when it seemed I was losing my footing or needing to impress, shouting out what had happened to him like a joke or a confession, never getting the response I hoped for, though in truth never having developed into the sort of person who knew exactly what I hoped for anyway.

"I mean, especially now that I'm thinking of having a baby," the woman said.

"Mmm," I said. She watched me with an intense stare, an unspoken question lingering between us. There was something daunting in her expression. How I remembered that hungry look, the one that suggested I *owed* something to these people based on this thing we'd all gone through together, or at least that they thought we'd gone through together.

"Your kid'll be good," I said. She looked a little confused. I'd meant it to be reassuring, and I didn't know what else to say. I didn't know this woman. That's what these people had always seemed to forget—I'd barely known any of them. When Gene stepped in to ask how she had found her contractor and was the housing market starting to rebound in Michigan?, I felt an upwelling of love for him. He was so good at asking questions—a champion, really.

Lola intermittently found us in the crowd. Aspects of her were incontrovertibly older-seeming: the grayish circles beneath her eyes, the efficient, layered cut of her hair, the lower center of gravity. She seemed to carry herself from her midsection, emphasizing her more substantial hips and butt. But she was still Lola, still talking in an excited blur, still emphatic and slightly bouncy. I would not have been surprised if she'd whipped out an UNO deck from her pocket and insisted that we play a round right there on the floor.

She and Gene chatted easily, even though he was still greenish, sweating by now. He kept pushing his damp hair from his forehead. She laughed at a joke he made about two-year-olds being excellent blueprints for despotic leaders. Lola's husband was dancing with their daughter, cupping the girl beneath her arms and twirling her around. When they returned from the dance floor, the girl let out a piercing scream and Gene said, "Take note, Stalin." Lola laughed some more.

I held up my empty glass, asked if anyone else needed a refill. Gene said no thanks. I ignored his appraising glance between my glass and me. I rarely drank this much. We were more the wine-with-dinner types. But there was something about the warming web of alcohol that felt essential to this act of reuniting. I had never stood around and socialized en masse with this particular crowd without it.

Lola's husband asked for a beer. On the way to the bar, I passed David Nelson in a small huddle with his wife, Adam Deselets, and Adam's wife. David and Adam were tipped close together, talking intently, elbow to elbow, shoulder to shoulder. The women too were on top of each other, Adam's wife fingering David's wife's earlobe, admiring her earring. David's wife looked like she'd just stepped out of a Wyeth portrait, clean-scrubbed with sturdy cheekbones. Her pregnancy had not yet spread to her face but was fully contained in the swell of her loose beige blouse. As I neared, she placed her hand gently on the other woman's forearm. They were talking softly, closely, without the loud catch-up of the surrounding clusters, who shouted about army reserves or summers spent backpacking through Europe. This clearly was not the first time they had all met.

I smiled at David as I passed. We'd spoken for a few minutes just after Gene and I had arrived, everyone shaking everyone's hand, exchanging names, basic stats. He didn't look so small anymore, the curled slouch and the slim hands passing somehow as professorial. Absorbed in the talking, he didn't see me now. I felt silly, marching by with my empty glass, grinning, and soon I stared into the farthest corner of the room, as if I hadn't noticed them either, though as I overheard the tail end of Adam's joke—something about Bush in a blender—then David's laughter and the women's tittering, I felt a sizzle of self-consciousness. For the second time that day, I was filled with the warm wash of the interloper.

Gene found me at the bar. He was feeling crappier and crappier, he told me, trying to make a good show of it, though he didn't think he could hold out much longer. He was having a really nice time, he said, looking genuinely crushed. I told him it was fine. He told me he'd take a cab. I told him not to be silly; I'd go back with him.

"No, no," he told me. "Don't let me ruin this."

"You're not ruining anything," I said.

The bartender set down the two drinks, the foamy head of the beer dribbling over the side of the pint glass. Gene kept repeating the plan of him taking a cab, me staying. I kept telling him no. He wouldn't stop, though, and something about this insistent sort of deference—so typically Gene-like, so high road—increasingly irrtated me. Soon the appeal of making an early, easy escape was replaced by the appeal of disentangling myself from these negotiations. Gene, if he was so determined, could be the one to go back to the house first, the one to make late-night chitchat with my mom.

"Fine," I said, though in a way that made him ask whether I was mad. I breathed deeply, trying to get beneath the loose grip of the gin, which, a few drinks in, could easily make me careless or full of unnecessary candor. I stroked his damp hair and told him no, of course I wasn't angry, I was sorry he was sick. I told him to take care of himself and get some sleep. I got on my tiptoes and kissed his sweaty forehead. "I'll miss you," I said, though already the thought of being able to drift through the ballroom more quietly and alone, without the pressure to perform, made me lighter. I squeezed his hand and insisted, at least, on my being the one to take the cab. He eyed my drink and relented, though not without making a show of stuffing far too much money in my purse, a clot of tens and twenties. I made an unfunny joke about that being plenty for a cab ride directly back to D.C.

I lingered for a while on the periphery, trying just to watch everybody. People drank. People danced. Two former student council members made out in a corner. Everyone gawked openly at the girl who used to be drum major, nose to nose on the dance floor with her wide-hipped, short-haired girlfriend. They wore matching Doc Martens.

When anyone approached—a boy who had been in Hollingham's class, the cat-eared flag-team girl—I told the same amusing stories that I'd been telling for years: the final I'd slept through at Brown, my shoebox-sized first apartment in D.C. with its Murphy bed and hot plates in lieu of a stove. Lots of people were satisfied by this and volleyed their own stories back: bar exam foibles or the ongoing struggle to find halfway decent maternity clothes. There remained, though, a stubborn knot who were just waiting for me to pause so they could interject something about the tell-all book Elvin Tate was supposedly going to write, or ask if I'd seen the memorial recently, or reminisce about the time my brother and Kent Newman had turned all the tables upside-down in Fosback's physics classroom, as if all that other stuff was good and well but could we just get down to the meat of it? The quiet that had settled over us in the last two years of high school—the topic of Danny had naturally faded out by then—was clearly destroyed by the decade-long gap. This again was what people wanted to talk about.

But somewhere into the night the impulse began to seem less predatory than when we were teenagers. This sort of curious prodding, it seemed less to do with me in particular and more to do with the very nature of a reunion. Everyone was doing it to everyone. And really, what else did these people have to talk to me about?

"Remember his sack at the end of that Stafford game?" a paunchy man asked. His name tag said *Ben.* He used to wrestle with Jerold, I was pretty sure.

I did not. I had no recollection of the Stafford game, or any football game for that matter. But something stopped me from saying so, from making the biting, incisive remark about brutality and sport I'd have made ten years earlier. Maybe it was the gin. Maybe it was Ben's earnestly ruddy cheeks or his silly tie, cartoon bear after cartoon bear lying in hammocks. He had that same expectant expression, that same hungry, searching stare, but for once it didn't feel oppressive or daunting. I had forgotten what it was like to be regarded this way, to be regarded with my brother in mind. It was, at least for a moment, unexpectedly expansive, a phantom limb returned, filling newly with blood. A phantom phantom limb—I'm not even sure I'd known it to be missing.

"It was a good one," I said of the Stafford game, and it didn't feel like a lie. Ben smiled. He clinked his glass against mine. He looked so happy. These people, the way they didn't know me—it was at least something, something more than the way everyone since didn't know me either.

Ben rushed the dance floor when the song changed, him and a whole bunch of other people, all whooping and doing a step dance full of hand claps, turns, sliding feet. I didn't know it but swayed a little where I stood, my fingers and toes feeling pleasurably airy and far removed.

"Lydia Nikolayevich Pasternak," David Nelson said, coming at me from the side, saluting me. It was an old joke, Boris Yeltsin's middle name.

"David Nikolayevich Nelson," I said, saluting back, quitting the swaying.

"It's good to see you," he said, though quickly he stopped looking at me and instead watched the crowd.

"Same here," I said, watching the crowd too. I scanned it for his wife and the Deseletses, though I didn't see them.

"Pretty crazy," he said, nodding toward everyone.

"Indeed."

He told me a story about a woman named Lydia who'd been in his grad program at Michigan and how he'd always expected that she'd be cooler and smarter than she was. But she asked inane questions in seminars about material they'd already covered and had an annoying tendency to talk about herself in the third person. "She disappointed constantly," he said. "Couldn't live up to her namesake."

It was a nice thing to say, though a wisp of melancholy moved through me. Standing next to David Nelson felt both deeply familiar and deeply foreign. We talked of our jobs, Iowa, D.C. He told me about snowdrifts that came up to his neck. I told him the Appropriations-chair-at-happy-hour story. He told me he'd Googled me before the trip—I was impressed by his frankness—then asked questions about wastewater treatment and habitat conservation. The song changed from the step dance to the terrible, warbling theme from *Titanic.* Couples draped arms around each other and moved in slow rotations, spinning on their own axes. I kept waiting for David to have to go, but we talked about Gene and Amy (that was his wife's name, and I was disappointed for a second by how pedestrian it sounded; I'd expected a more substantive Georgette or Bernadine) and the coming baby.

"Fatherhood," I said. "Fa-ther-hood." I was making my voice low and dramatic. "Wow."

"I know," he told me. "Sometimes I wonder what I'll do if he turns out to be utterly regressive, you know? I mean, what if he wants to toss the baseball around? Or vote Republican?" He laughed. His laugh had changed, deeper now, more of a wry chuckle.

"It's a boy?"

It was. They'd found out at the latest sonogram. Something about this news sent another low wave through me.

"That's so great," I said, though my voice sounded affected and Lola Pepper–esque.

Eventually the dancing devolved into a ragged bunny hop, the dancers snaking through far tables and letting out all sorts of whoops and cheers.

"How are you doing?" David finally said. "Are you well? Happy?" The sraightforward tone, the simple interest, absent the night's undertone of voyeurism and *I'll show you mine if you show me yours* competition, caught me off-guard and made me not know the answer. Gone was the old bristling feeling I used to have with him. I couldn't remember now, even as I strained to, why such attentive-ness, such familiarity, had once seemed so repellent. The whole side of me that faced him grew warm. Not from embarrassment. It was something else. I was struck then by a bodily memory of having been like this with him, side by side for all those years, that runup of time before everything that happened happened, a period that slipped so easily from memory, that seemed almost sickeningly precious or just plain unreal in the face of everything that came after, when he and I lolled together on our carpets or beds, thinking nothing of using each other's backs as pillows, of wearing each other's sweatshirts and woolly socks when we got cold.

I told him I was. Well. Happy. I asked him the same. He was, he was. As he told me about meeting Amy while they'd both volunteered at a Thanksgiving soup kitchen and about the addition they were currently building for the baby and about his research in mass political behavior, I had a flash of what it had so long ago been like to find him, the certain sense of no longer being alone. It was, it seemed to me now, the last time such a thing had happened.

For a stretch of time I sat at an empty table near the bar, dropping all pretense and simply drinking. There was something so appealingly juvenile and wrongheaded about this. I reveled for a while in the heat of the liquor just beneath my skin. There was an echoing sensation in my ears, and I felt entirely absorbed in and removed from the dwindling crowd. At one point the DJ shouted, "You've been great, class of '98!" and started packing his equipment. The room seemed briefly cavernous and white-noisy without him.

A woman sat down on the other side of the table. Name tag, *Jenine.* Her face, shiny at the nose and the chin, the foundation rubbed off, yielded no recognition, like so many other faces of the night. We talked the talk—what you do, where you live, what you have or don't: house, husband, kids, pets.

"How's your family?" she said. "Your parents?"

"You know, I barely ever even think of him," I said, and her face did the slightest of twitches. "Like," I said, "maybe when I see someone with his Adam's apple. Or meet some Danny. They're all mostly Dans or Daniels once you're grown up, you know?" I laughed at the idea of us being grown-ups. "Or there was this one receptionist I had, she always said *irregardless* and *supposably.* But other than that, I don't really think about him."

Jenine was nodding, squinting a little. "Okay," she said, though she said it slowly: "Ohhh-kay."

I tried to explain to this woman—didn't I have Bardazian with her? I asked, though I didn't wait for an answer—that it was not that Danny had disappeared entirely from me. It was that he had both receded and embedded himself. He was the watery, oval vaccination mark on my left bicep, the chicken pox scar on my lower back, the penchant for cataloguing world leaders, the fear of wide-open roadways and of dark middle-of-the-nights. All of these, the remnants of childhood that, rather than transforming themselves—as I had long imagined would happen through some nameless yet magical process—into a divergent, distinct adulthood, simply became who I was.

I didn't say it like that, though. I said it in blips and blaps. Jenine played with the snap on her pocketbook, fiddled some with her watch. I had the sense that I should probably stop, but also the sense that I maybe couldn't. I went on about all these men in this ballroom with their slumped shoulders and wire-rimmed glasses and mustaches and how you had to at least wonder how he would've fit in, if he would've mellowed or plumped or thinned or grown slouched. Would he have grown lines on his face or a slight shuffle to his step? Would he have had to become more careful or more kind? Or would he have simply turned into one of those brash adults who chucked you on the shoulder as he said nasty things?

"You know?" I said.

"Sure," Jenine said. Her mouth was drawn, and there were little creases at the bridge of her nose. "I always thought that you were a sweetheart." It seemed like such a strange thing for her to say, so apropos of nothing.

"Really?" I asked, and she nodded. We looked for a while at each other. I wasn't sure what had gotten me started. "What did you ask?" I said, but before she answered, a goateed man, tie unloosened, faint sweat rings at his armpits, came up behind her and put a hand on her shoulder. She stood quickly and introduced us, but in a way that I knew meant goodbye.

"Listen," she said. "Do you have a ride home?"

I told her about the cab. I told her about Gene and the money. She came over to my side of the table and squeezed my shoulder the way her husband had just squeezed hers. Her nail polish was impeccable, a deep, flawless red. I told her so and said I always chipped my manicures. She smiled and told me again I was a sweetheart. I told her she was too. I still wasn't sure who she was. She told me it had been really good to see me. Her husband said it was nice to meet me, even though I hadn't said a word to him.

"Hang on," I said as they were leaving, because I hadn't finished my point, though when they turned around, I knew from their expressions to shut up. I waved goodbye and the man slung his arm easily around Jenine's waist and I didn't call out to them that the real question was not who Danny would be now. The real question was who he and I would have become to each other. I didn't say that truly, the single most horrific thing about his death—far more than the grisly circumstances—was that he and I had never been able to right ourselves, had never been able to be okay in the simple way we had once been okay.

Jenine and her husband were gone. I got up from the table, knowing it was time for me to go too, probably well past.

. . .

At the coat rack, Lola was upon me, her eyes bright and wet, saying how they were heading out—Lacey was ridiculously tired and up way past her bedtime—but she didn't want to leave without at least telling me how for a long time she didn't believe in God because of what had happened to Danny but now, now since Lacey, she knew there was a God because otherwise how could things like giving birth happen, if there was no God, where did these innocent little creatures come from, so if there is a God, which she knows 100 percent there is now, then Danny has to be someplace good and safe, she knew that for sure, now, 100 percent sure, and she was so happy to finally see me again because she'd wanted for a long time to tell me this but it didn't feel right in a letter or over the phone. She was grasping my hands in hers, all the words a breathless rush, classic Lola.

I did not believe her. But as she leaned over to kiss me, I also did not hate her. When I was in high school with all of these people, I hated them for the way their collective anguish seemed to distill grief into an even more potent form. They had made an unbearable situation that much more unbearable. Now, though, as I stood in this room full of people who had known my brother, who still, ten years later, knew me almost exclusively as the girl who had lost him, I was capable of a different sort of alchemy. Grief shared was grief diffused. It was nice now to hold hands and look plainly in the face of a girl who loved him too.

I stood in the parking lot waiting for the cab, dampness sprouting in the hollow of my collarbone and beneath my arms after only minutes in the humidity. I leaned against the bumper of a car, watching as others left the lot. A silver car passed but stopped a few feet ahead of me, the driver's window rolling down.

"Lydia?" It was David Nelson, craning his head out his window. "Do you need a ride?"

"No, no," I said, waving my arms, my hands feeling slightly mitteny. "I got a cab. Coming."

"I'm happy to drive you. You staying at your parents'?"

"My mom's," I corrected. He, of course, had no idea my parents had divorced. How strange that he had no idea. "My dad," I said, "has twins. Fucking twins. In Georgia." I laughed a little. "Hot-lanta."

David Nelson reversed the car until he was flush with me. He was the only one inside. When I approached his window, the cool of his AC streamed onto my face. I think I made a noise, an *Mmmm* sound.

"Lydia?" he said.

"Where are your people?" I asked.

"My people?" He was looking at me strangely. "They all went back already. Amy gets tired now," he said, putting a hand to his belly. "Listen, we're staying at the Deselets'. You're on the way." He named the northern suburb that Adam lived in, sprawling homes with circular drives and multiacre lawns. I was a little incredulous that Adam Deselets had ended up in such a place.

"The cab." I pointed to my phone. "It's coming."

He shrugged. "Who cares?" This surprised me. David Nelson had never been one to flout convention so easily. I was briefly disarmed, unable to think of a reason to keep resisting.

The car was plush and almost unfathomably leathery inside. It was easy to sink into the seat. There was a bright pine smell, and the interior was pristine.

"I never imagined you'd have a car like this," I said.

He told me it was a rental. He said I had to clip my seatbelt. "That's why it's making that noise." He pointed to the dashboard's bleating alarm. This struck me as very funny. I laughed and told him he'd make a good dad. He looked hard at my face. It was maybe the first time all night he had looked at me so straightforwardly.

"What?" I said.

He shook his head. "I've never seen you drunk before."

"I'm not drunk," I said, and when I saw his expression, "I'm not."

We drove through bright intersections, and I asked him as soberly as possible about the straw poll, the only thing I knew about Ames. And that easily, we were here in this car together, him going on and on about the odd ritual of it, the live bands and food booths and pointless vote counts, the uniquely American pull toward intentionally injecting artifice into the electoral process, and it could've been a day as easily as ten years. I imagined him delivering these words to a lecture hall full of students. I imagined them calling him Professor Nelson.

I thought of saying that I was proud of him or that I was sorry or that it was so strange sitting in his passenger seat. Wasn't it strange? I wanted to ask him. Wasn't this weird? If only for how unweird it was? I studied his profile, the thin sideburns, the tiniest hints of age lines beside his eyes, the spot where the wrinkles would set in in earnest a few years from now. All the rigid self-consciousness of adolescence was gone. Now his jaw was relaxed. One hand rested on top of the steering wheel; he navigated turns with only the fleshy heel of his palm. I wondered how much I would remember of him ten years from now, at our next reunion, likely the next time I would see him. The thought made being an adult seem like such a Swiss-cheesy proposition, full of so many holes.

"What's marriage like?" I asked, not sure I wanted to know. He talked about what a good mom Amy would be. He talked about her research in the history of women's suffrage in Asian nations. He wasn't really answering the question. I listened for a note of uncertainty, any hint of ambivalence.

For a while we were quiet. I kept sneaking looks at him; he seemed so well rested, half smiling and kicked back in his seat. I wondered, is this what it looks like to have no regrets? To have been mostly kind and goodhearted? A pressure different from the heat of the alcohol built behind my rib cage and through the base of my neck. I cleared my throat. I bit down hard, grinding my molars. This was, I realized, longing. How strange to feel it for David Nelson. He'd always just been mine, until the day I hadn't wanted him to be anymore. Longing had never entered into the equation.

Part of me wished we could just drive in wide circles so I could confess to him about Gene, though I wasn't sure exactly what I would confess: something about the initial allure of the easy, companionable, half-empty man but then the slow slide into stupor. I was not going to give up my lease come December. I knew that. Maybe even Gene knew that. And I was never going to marry him. I had no idea why he would even want to ask me, to be honest. I was, I would confess, terrible at loving people.

But David Nelson knew this already, he, of course, my first victim.

"Do you remember," he said, grinning, "the talented-and-gifted trip?" It took me a minute to realize we were back on D.C. He was talking eighth grade, a weekend in the capital for gifted thirteen-year-olds and their chaperones. "I remember looking for whale penises at the Natural History Museum," he said. "Someone had told me all the scale models were anatomically correct. I kept searching."

He chuckled. I laughed, perhaps a bit too loud. I entertained the idea of touching his hand, recognizing even then how far away and foolish this might seem the following afternoon as I rolled my bag to the skycap, stood in line for a boarding pass, wound my way down a narrow aisle to my window seat, clamped the teeth of the seatbelt closed in my lap. But I didn't care. This, the person who'd known me when my nights were dreamless, when *bad things* still referred to unfair grades and ignoramus classmates, when the world was still and simply whole.

I listened to his self-deprecating stories of the first year of teaching: the meticulous lecture slides eaten by his computer, the office hours spent arguing with students about grades. He described the terrible writing of his undergrads. He said he'd woken one day this winter to the realization that he'd consigned himself to a life among the dim bulbs. "It's like," he said, staring at me, not the road, "being perpetually stuck at Franklin High."

We laughed knowingly, righteously. The laugh lasted longer than the joke, briefly contagious between us. Countless, the number of times we'd laughed like that. The noise petered out slowly. He nudged a hand to my arm, somewhere between a slap and a pat. He was grinning at me. I wondered what he meant by it. I held his stare. Quickly—a little too quickly?—he turned back to the road, looking purposefully at the windshield. It seemed as if he were breathing slightly more heavily, that a bit of the pinch was returning to his jaw.

If he turned to me again, I would touch his hand.

Life seemed briefly whittled down to the inside of this car, the blinker tinking loudly at each turn, the vents swirling a raspy whisper of air. Everything else—Gene, my mother's house, even my beloved D.C.—felt far off and imaginary. I could taste my heartbeat. There was a part of me that had long curled in on itself and atrophied, perhaps beginning the day Danny slipped unremarkably out the front door, perhaps long before that. I could feel it unfurling now, churning through my watery belly and rising up my throat, coming out my nostrils and my mouth, dragon breath singeing my earlobes and making my face sweat even in the breeze of the AC. I wanted to use his back as a pillow. I wanted to wear his socks. I wanted it to be easy to know someone again.

David talked beside me of baby names. Joshua, he said. And Carsen with an *e* and Bryan with a *y*. I waited for him to stop and look at me the way he used to look at me.

When he veered into the wooded streets of Fairfield, I thought at first he'd made a wrong turn. The houses looked unfamiliar, lawns deeper, streets more winding than I remembered. An occasional home—its white shutters, its swath of yellow siding—stirred loose some memory and I would briefly know where we were, able to anticipate the coming YIELD sign or forked road, able to calculate how far we were from my mother's house: just minutes away. But in another turn or two I would again lose my bearings from the sameness of house after house and tree after tree. Soon that's what I was trying for, the feeling of being lost and not unpleasantly so.

And it struck me then that maybe this was how it had been for Danny, after the first few hits off Elvin Tate's joint, as the two of them drove through similar nearby streets. Maybe he too had sat in the passenger seat and given himself over to such willful disorientation. Maybe this was why he'd not screamed for help or elbowed Elvin in the jaw or jumped out at a light during those first nearby miles, when it became clear that there would be no tire store, clear that the route had already grown strangely meandering. Maybe he had allowed himself some heady excitement for the way his day had taken an unexpected turn. Maybe he'd invented a quick mythology, a host of fantastic stories about the man beside him. Maybe he'd watched, bemused at the ease with which his life—and a good, happy life it was—simply receded behind him. Maybe such a thing felt surprisingly nice, being freed, without even realizing he needed to be, from all his mistakes and small cruelties. Maybe, as a strange world whirred past his window, he sat right here, jangling with possibility and promise, his future wide open.

Acknowledgments

The debt of gratitude owed for a first book is not only to those who helped with its writing and publication but also to the many who came before its opening words were ever penned during the long process of learning how to write.

For their help in that process, I owe thanks to: everyone at the University of Oregon Program in Creative Writing, though no one more so than Ehud Havazelet; all of the amazingly generous and supportive folks at the Wisconsin Institute for Creative Writing; Tom Spanbauer; the careful readers of my early work, including Connie, Jessica, Sarah K., and the ever-encouraging Teeny B., who belongs in a category all her own.

For their help with bringing this book to life, thank you to: Emily Forland, whose unflagging belief in my work makes her not only a great agent but also a backbone to my writing life. And Emma Patterson, who set so much in motion when she first pulled my stories from a pile and decided she liked them. Caroline Goyette for her always thoughtful reading and feedback on an early draft. Jamie Passaro for her ideas, input, and incomparable championing of the manuscript from its earliest form; believe me when I say not one breath of your cheerleading was wasted. Literary Arts for their financial support. And everyone at Spiegel & Grau, especially Mike Mezzo, whose passion for Lydia and her story often—and to my delight—appeared to rival my own.

Finally, there is no way to forge the strange, uncertain, joyful roller coaster of an existence that is a writer's life without an unwavering community of family and friends. Thanks seems such a puny and inadequate word for: Cole Coshow, who set the bar so high on writing and on friendship, I continue to aspire. Liz Larson, whose treehouse is waiting. My father, who has been joyfully prognosticating this for years. My mother, who knows the difference between *bear* and *bare* and can explain such mysteries. The Gerblack family—Rebecca, Tim, Eliza, and Nora—who have sent more love, care, and support my way than one person rightfully deserves. And lastly, Jordan, who did what for so long seemed impossible: made a home where this restless gal could finally sit her butt down, stop worrying about what might come next, and simply write.

A Note About the Author

Miriam Gershow graduated from the Program in Creative Writing at the University of Oregon and was a Fiction Fellow at the Wisconsin Institute for Creative Writing. Her stories have appeared in the *Georgia Review*, *Black Warrior Review*, and *Quarterly West*, among other literary journals. This is her first novel. She lives in Eugene, Oregon.